Praise for *Never Knowing*

"Stevens's unnerving stand-alone thriller about a woman's search for her birth parents matches the intensity of her impressive debut, *Still Missing*." 　　—*Publishers Weekly*

"Finely calculated in its escalating suspense . . ."
　　　　　　　　　　　　　　　　　　—*Kirkus Reviews*

"A knockout, starting strong and finishing even stronger."
　　　　　　　　　　　　　　　　　—*RT Book Reviews*

"A riveting read . . ." 　　　　　　—*Chatelaine* magazine

"Block off the weekend, grab a comfy seat, and prepare for the rocket ride of your life! *Never Knowing* will consume you with the desire to read every page, gasp at every twist, and know every last secret between one woman and her serial killer father."
　　　　　　　　—Lisa Gardener, #1 *New York Times*
　　　　　　　　bestselling author of *Love You More*

"A terrifying, chilling scenario that unfolds into a nightmare and had me keeping the light on at night."
　　　　　—Rosamund Lupton, bestselling author of *Sister*

"*Never Knowing* is a chilling thriller with enough twists and turns so every time I thought I knew where it was going I was taken somewhere else. I have a feeling that Chevy Stevens is an author who is going to keep getting better and better with each book! I hope I'm still around for the next six—at which point she'll probably give me a heart attack. But what a great way to go out!"
　　　—Lois Duncan, author of *I Know What You Did Last Summer*

Praise for *Still Missing*

"Crackling with suspense . . . [*Still Missing*] will have you glued to the page." —*People* magazine

"This is not a book to read alone in bed at night." —*O: The Oprah Magazine*

"*Still Missing* runs deeper than the chills it delivers, the surprises it holds, and the resilience of its main character." —*The New York Times*

"Praise of this highly touted debut includes comparisons to Karin Slaughter and Lisa Gardner, and those authors' fans will like this thriller . . . the 'what would I do' aspect of the reading experience may make this a match for some Jodi Picoult readers as well. Highly recommended." —*Library Journal* (starred review)

"Stevens's blistering debut follows a kidnap victim from her abduction to her escape—and the even more horrifying nightmare that follows. . . . A grueling, gripping demonstration of melodrama's darker side." —*Kirkus Reviews* (starred review)

"Stevens's impressive debut, a thriller set on Vancouver Island, pulsates with suspense that gets a power boost from the jaw-dropping but credible closing twist." —*Publishers Weekly* (starred review)

"It's a knockout, a psychological thriller that pulls no punches . . . relentless and disturbing, Stevens's dark, mesmerizing character study follows a twisted path from victimhood toward self-empowerment. Sure to leave readers looking over their shoulders for a smiling stranger." —*Booklist* (starred review)

NEVER KNOWING

CHEVY STEVENS

St. Martin's Griffin
New York

NEVER KNOWING. Copyright © 2011 by René Unischewski. All rights reserved. Printed in the United States of America. For information, address St. Martin's Press, 175 Fifth Avenue, New York, N.Y. 10010.

www.stmartins.com

The Library of Congress has cataloged the hardcover edition as follows:

Stevens, Chevy.
    Never knowing / Chevy Stevens. — 1st ed.
        p. cm.
    ISBN 978-0-312-59568-5
    1. Adoptees—Fiction. 2. Women—Identity—Fiction. 3. Fathers and daughters—Fiction. 4. Serial murderers—Fiction. 5. British Columbia—Fiction. 6. Psychological fiction. I. Title.
    PR9199.4.S739N48 2011
    813'.6—dc22

                                                              2011006370

ISBN 978-1-250-00931-9

10 9 8 7 6 5 4 3 2

For Connel

NEVER
KNOWING

SESSION ONE

I thought I could handle it, Nadine. After all those years of seeing you, all those times I talked about whether I should look for my birth mother, I finally did it. I took that step. You were a part of it—I wanted to show you what an impact you had on my life, how much I've grown, how stable I am now, how balanced. That's what you always told me, "Balance is the key." But I forgot the other thing you used to say: "Slowly, Sara."

I've missed this, being here. Remember how uncomfortable I was when I first started seeing you? Especially when I told you why I needed help. But you were down-to-earth and funny—not at all how I imagined a psychiatrist would be. This office was so bright and pretty that, no matter what I was worried about, as soon as I walked in here felt better. Some days, especially in the beginning, I didn't want to leave.

You told me once that when you didn't hear from me you knew things were going well, that when I stopped coming altogether you'd know you did your job. And you did. The last couple of years have been the happiest of my life. That's why I thought it was the right time. I thought I could withstand anything that came my way. I was solid, grounded. *Nothing* could send me back to the nervous wreck I was when I first met you.

Then she lied to me—my birth mother—when I finally forced her to talk to me. She lied about my real father. It felt like when Ally used to kick my ribs when I was pregnant with her—a sudden blow from the inside that left me breathless. But it was my birth mother's fear that got me the most. She was *afraid* of me. I'm sure of it. What I don't know is why.

It started about six weeks ago, around the end of December, with an online article. I was up stupidly early this one Sunday—no need for a rooster when you have a six-year-old—and while I inhaled my first coffee I answered e-mails. I get requests to restore furniture from all over the island now. That morning I was trying to research a desk from the 1920s, when I wasn't laughing at Ally. She was supposed to be watching cartoons downstairs, but I could hear her scolding Moose, our brindle French bulldog, for molesting her stuffed rabbit. Suffice it to say, Moose has a weaning issue. No tail's safe.

Then somehow or another I got this pop-up advertising Viagra, which I finally got closed, only to accidentally click on this other link and find myself staring at a headline:

Adoption: The Other Side of the Story

I scrolled through letters people had sent in response to a *Globe and Mail* piece, read stories of birth parents who've been trying to find their children for years, birth parents who didn't want to be found. Adopted children growing up feeling they never belonged. Tragic tales of doors slammed in faces. Joyful stories of mothers and daughters, brothers and sisters reuniting and living happily ever after.

My head started to pound. What if I found my mother? Would we instantly connect? What if she wanted nothing to do with me? What if I found out she was dead? What if I had siblings who never knew about me?

I didn't realize Evan was up until he kissed the back of my neck and made a grunting noise—a sound we picked up from Moose and now use to signal everything from *I'm pissed off* to *You're hot!*

I closed down the screen and spun my chair around. Evan raised his eyebrows and smiled.

"Talking to your online boyfriend again?"

I smiled back. "Which one?"

Evan clutched at his chest, collapsed into his office chair, and sighed.

"Sure hope he has lots of clothes."

I laughed. I was forever raiding Evan's shirts, especially if he had to stay with a group at his wilderness lodge in Tofino—three hours from our house in Nanaimo and right smack on the west coast of Vancouver Island. Those weeks I often wore his shirts around the clock. I'd get caught up working on a new piece of furniture, and by the time he was home the shirt would be covered in stains and I'd be exchanging all sorts of favors for his forgiveness.

"Sorry to break it to you, honey, but you're the only man for me—no one else would put up with my craziness." I rested my foot on his lap. With his sable hair spiked in all directions and his usual outfit of cargo pants and polo shirt, he looked like a college student. A lot of people don't realize Evan actually owns the lodge.

He smiled. "Oh, I'm sure there's a doctor somewhere with a straitjacket who'd think you're cute."

I pretended to kick at him, then said, "I was reading an article," as I started to massage the throbbing pain on the left side of my head.

"Getting a migraine, baby?"

I dropped my hand down to my lap. "Just a little one, it'll go away."

He gave me a look.

"Okay, I forgot my pill yesterday." After years of trying various medications I was now on beta blockers and my migraines were finally under control. The trick was remembering to take them.

He shook his head. "So what was the article about?"

"Ontario's opening up their adoption records, and . . ." I groaned as Evan worked a pressure point on my foot. "There were all these letters from people who were adopted or who gave up their children." Downstairs, Ally's giggle rang out.

"Thinking about finding your birth mother?"

"Not exactly, it was just interesting." But I *was* thinking about finding her. I just wasn't sure if I was ready. I've always known I was adopted, but I didn't realize that meant I was different until Mom sat me down and told me they were having a baby. I was four at the time. As Mom grew bigger and Dad prouder, I started worrying they were going to give me back. I didn't know just how different I was until I saw the way my father looked at Lauren when they brought her home, then the way he looked at me when I asked to hold her. They had Melanie two years later. He didn't let me hold her either.

Evan, willing to drop things long before me, nodded.

"What time do you want to leave for brunch?"

"A quarter past never." I sighed. "Thank God Lauren and Greg are coming, because Melanie's bringing *Kyle*."

"Brave of her." As much as my father loves Evan—they'd probably spend the entire brunch planning their next fishing trip—he despises Kyle. I can't say I blame him. Kyle's a wannabe rock star, but as far as I'm concerned the only thing he's playing is my sister. Dad always hated our boyfriends, though. I'm still shocked he likes Evan. All it took was one trip to the lodge and he was talking about him like he was the son he never had. He's still bragging about the salmon they caught.

"It's like she thinks if they're around each other more Dad will see all his good qualities." I snorted.

"Be nice, Melanie loves him."

I gave a mock shudder. "Last week she told me I better start working on my tan if I didn't want to be the same color as my dress. Our wedding's nine months away!"

"She's just jealous—you can't take it personally."

"It sure feels personal."

Ally came barreling into the room with Moose in fast pursuit and threw herself into my arms.

"Mommy, Moose ate all my cereal!"

"Did you leave the bowl on the floor again, silly?"

She giggled against my neck and I inhaled her fresh scent as her hair tickled my nose. With her dark coloring and compact body, Ally looks more like Evan than me even though he's not her biological father, but she has my green eyes—cat's eyes, Evan calls them. And she got my curls, though at thirty-three mine have relaxed while Ally's are still tight ringlets.

Evan stood up and clapped his hands.

"Okay, family, time to get dressed."

A week later, just after New Year's, Evan headed back to his lodge for a few days. I'd read a few more adoption stories online, and the night before he left I told him I was considering looking for my birth mother while he was gone.

"Are you sure it's a good idea right now? You have so much going on with the wedding."

"But that's part of it—we're getting married and for all I know I was dropped here from outer space."

"You know, that might explain a few things. . . ."

"Ha, ha, very funny."

He smiled, then said, "Seriously, Sara, how are you going

to feel if you can't find her? Or if she doesn't want to see you?"

How was I going to feel? I pushed the thought to the side and shrugged.

"I'll just have to accept it. Things don't get to me like they used to. But I really feel like I need to do this—especially if we're going to have kids." The entire time I was pregnant with Ally I was afraid of what I might be passing on to her. Thankfully she's healthy, but whenever Evan and I talk about having a child the fear starts up again.

I said, "I'm more worried about upsetting Mom and Dad."

"You don't have to tell them—it's your life. But I still don't think it's the best timing."

Maybe he was right. It was stressful enough trying to take care of Ally and run my business, let alone plan a wedding.

"I'll think about putting it off, okay?"

Evan smiled. "Riiight. I know you, baby—once your mind is made up you're full speed ahead."

I laughed. "I promise."

I did think about waiting, especially when I imagined my mom's face if she found out. Mom used to say being adopted meant I was special because they chose me. When I was twelve Melanie gave me her version. She said our parents adopted me because Mom couldn't have babies, but they didn't need me now. Mom found me in my room packing my clothes. When I told her I was going to find my "real" parents she started crying, then she said, "Your birth parents couldn't take care of you properly, but they wanted you to have the best home possible. So now we take care of you and we love you very much." I never forgot the hurt in her eyes, or how thin her body felt as she hugged me.

The next time I seriously thought about looking for my birth parents was when I graduated, then when I found out I was pregnant, and then seven months later when I held Ally for the first time. But I'd put myself in Mom's shoes and imagine what it would feel like if my child wanted to find her birth mother, how hurt and scared I'd be, and I could never go through with it. I might not have this time either, if Dad hadn't phoned to ask Evan to go fishing.

"Sorry, Dad, he just left yesterday. Maybe you can take Greg?"

"Greg talks too much." I felt bad for Lauren's husband. Where Dad despised Kyle, he had no use for Greg. I'd seen him walk away when Greg was in midsentence.

"Are you guys going to be home for a while? I was just going to get Ally from school and come by for a visit."

"Not today. Your mom's trying to rest."

"Is her Crohn's flaring up again?"

"She's just tired."

"Okay, no problem. If you need help with anything, let me know."

Throughout our lives Mom's health had been up and down. For weeks she'd be doing fine, painting our rooms, sewing curtains, baking up a storm. Even Dad was almost happy during those times. I remember him lifting me onto his shoulders once, the view as heady as the rare attention. But Mom would always end up doing too much and within days she was sick again. She'd fade before our eyes as her body refused to hang on to any nutrients, even baby food sending her rushing for the bathroom.

When she was going through a bad spell Dad would come home and ask what I'd been doing all day, like he was trying to find something, or someone, to be pissed at. When I was nine he found me in front of the TV while Mom was sleeping. He dragged me to the kitchen by my wrist and pointed to the stack of dishes, calling me a lazy, ungrateful child. The next day it was the pile of laundry that set him off, and the next, Melanie's toys in the driveway. His big workingman's body would loom over me and his voice would vibrate with anger, but he never yelled, never did anything Mom could see or hear. He'd take me out to the garage and list my shortcomings while I stared at his feet, terrified he was going to say he didn't want me anymore. Then he'd barely speak to me for a week.

I started doing the household chores before Mom could get to them, staying home when my sisters were out with friends, cooking dinners that never got my father's approval but at least didn't earn his silence. I would do anything to avoid silence, anything to keep Mom from getting sick again. If she was healthy, I was safe.

When I phoned Lauren that night she told me she and the boys had just gotten home from dinner with our parents. Dad had invited them.

"So it was just my kid who wasn't allowed over."

"I'm sure it wasn't like that. Ally just has so much energy, and—"

"What does *that* mean?"

"It doesn't mean anything, she's adorable. But Dad probably thought three kids were too much." I knew Lauren was just trying to make me feel better before I went on a rant against Dad, which she hates, but it drives me nuts that she can never see how differently Dad treats me, or at least never acknowledges it. After we hung up I almost called Mom to check on her, but then I thought about Dad telling me to stay home, like a stray dog who's only allowed to sleep on the porch because she might mess in the house. I put the phone back on the charger.

The next day I filled out the form at Vital Statistics, paid my $50, and started waiting. I'd like to say patiently, but I practically tackled the mailman after the first week. A month later my Original Birth Registration, or OBR, as the woman at Vital Statistics called it, arrived in the mail. I stared at the envelope and realized my hand was shaking. Evan was at his lodge again and I wished he could be there when I opened it, but that was another *week*. Ally was at school and the house was quiet. I took a deep breath and ripped open the envelope.

My real mother's name was Julia Laroche and I was born in Victoria, BC. My father was listed as unknown. I read the OBR and the adoption certificate over and over, looking for answers, but I just kept hearing one question: *Why did you give me away?*

The next morning I woke early and went online while Ally was still sleeping. The first thing I checked was the Adoption Reunion Registry, but when I realized it could take another month to get an answer, I decided to look on my own first. After searching Web sites for twenty minutes, I found three Julia Laroches in Quebec and four down in the States who seemed around the right age. Only two lived on the island, but when I saw they were both in Victoria my stomach flipped. Could she still be there after all this time? I quickly clicked on the first link, and let my breath out when I realized she was too young, judging by her article on a new mom's forum. The second link took me to a Web site for a real estate agent in Victoria. She had auburn hair like me and looked about the right age. I studied her face with a mixture of excitement and fear. Had I found my birth mother?

After I drove Ally to school, I sat at my desk and circled the phone number I'd jotted on a piece of paper. *I'll call in one minute. After another cup of coffee. After I read the paper. After I paint every toenail a different color.* Finally I forced myself to pick up the phone.

Brrring.

It might not even be her.

Brrring.

I should just hang up. This was a bad way to—

"Julia Laroche speaking."

I opened my mouth, but nothing came out.

"Hello?" she said.

"Hi, I'm calling . . . I'm calling because . . ." *Because I stupidly thought if I said something brilliant, you'd instantly regret giving me up, but now I can't even remember my own name.*

Her voice was impatient. "Are you looking to buy or sell a home?"

"No, I'm—" I took a deep breath and said it in a rush. "I might be your daughter."

"Is this some kind of joke? Who are you?"

"My name is Sara Gallagher. I was born in Victoria and given up for adoption. You have auburn hair and you're about the right age, so I thought—"

"Honey, there's no way you're my daughter. I can't have children."

My face burned. "God, I'm sorry. I just thought . . . well, I hoped."

The voice softened. "It's okay. Good luck with your search." I was about to hang up when she said, "There's a Julia Laroche who works at the university. I get calls for her sometimes."

"Thanks, I appreciate that."

My face was still hot as I dropped the phone onto my desk and headed out to my shop. I got most of my paintbrushes cleaned, then sat and stared at the wall, thinking about what the real estate woman had said. A few minutes later I was back at my computer. After a quick search the other Julia's name came up under a list of professors at the University of Victoria. She taught art history—was that where I got my love of all things old? I shook my head. Why was I letting myself get excited? It was just a name. I took a deep breath and called the university, surprised when they put me straight through to Julia Laroche's extension.

She answered, and this time I had my speech ready. "Hi, my name is Sara Gallagher and I'm trying to find my birth mother. Did you give a child up for adoption thirty-three years ago?"

A sharp intake of breath. Then silence.

"Hello?"

"Don't call here again." She hung up.

I cried. For hours. Which kicked off a migraine so bad Lauren had to take Ally and Moose for me. Thankfully, Lauren's two boys are around Ally's age and Ally loves going over there. I hated being away from my daughter for even one night, but all I could do was lie in a dark room with a cold compress on my head and wait for it to pass. Evan phoned and I told him what had happened, speaking slowly because of the pain. By the next afternoon I'd stopped seeing auras around everything, so Ally and Moose came home. Evan phoned again that night.

"Feeling better, baby?"

"The migraine's gone—it's my own stupid fault for forgetting to take my pill again. Now I'm behind on that desk and I wanted to call some photographers this week and—"

"Sara, you don't have to do everything right away. Leave the photographers for when I get back."

"It's fine, I'll take care of it." I admired Evan's laid-back personality in many ways, but in the two years we've been together I've learned "we can do it later" usually translates into me rushing around like a crazy woman to get something done at the last minute.

I said, "I've been thinking about what happened with my birth mother. . . ."

"Yeah?"

"I was wondering about writing her a letter. Her address is unlisted, but I can just leave it at the university."

Evan was silent for a moment. "Sara . . . I'm not sure that's a good idea."

"So she doesn't want to get to know me, fine, but I think the least she could do is give me my medical history. What about Ally? Doesn't she have a right to know? There could be health issues, like . . . like high blood pressure, or diabetes, or *cancer*—"

"Baby." Evan's voice was calm but firm. "Take it easy. Why are you letting her get to you like this?"

"I'm not like you, okay? I can't just brush things off."

"Listen, cranky-pants, I'm on your side here."

I was silent, my eyes closed, trying to breathe, reminding myself it wasn't Evan I was angry at.

"Sara, do what you have to do. You know I'll support you no matter what. But I think you should just leave it alone."

As I made the hour-and-a-half trip down-island the next day I felt calm and centered, confident I was doing the right thing. There's something about the Island Highway that always soothes me: the quaint towns and valleys, the farmland, the glimpses of ocean and coastal mountain ranges. When I got closer to Victoria and drove through the old-growth forest at Goldstream Park, I thought about the time Dad had taken us there to watch the salmon spawning in the river. Lauren was terrified of all the seagulls feasting on the dead salmon. I hated the scent of death in the air, how it clung to your clothes and nostrils. Hated how Dad explained everything to my sisters but ignored my questions—ignored me.

Evan and I talked about opening a second whale-watching business in Victoria one day—Ally loves the museum and the street performers in the inner harbor, I love all the old buildings. But for now Nanaimo suits us. Even though it's the second largest city on the island, it still has that small-town feel. You can be walking on the seawall in the harbor, shopping in the old city quarter, or hiking up a mountain with an amazing view of the Gulf Islands all on the same day. Whenever we want to get away, we just take the ferry to the mainland or drive down to Victoria to do some shopping. But if things didn't go well in Victoria this trip, it was going to be a long drive home.

My plan was to drop off the letter requesting information at Julia's office. But when the woman at the front desk told me Professor Laroche was teaching a class in the next building, I had to see what she looked like. She wouldn't even know I was there. Then I'd leave the letter at the front desk.

I slowly opened the door to the auditorium-style classroom and crept in with my face turned away from the podium. I found a seat in the back, scrunched down—feeling like a stalker—and took a look at my mother.

"As you can see, architecture of the Islamic world varied . . ."

In my daydreams she was always an older version of me, but where my hair is auburn, falling in unruly waves down my back, her black hair was cut in a sleek bob. I couldn't see her eye color, but her face was round, with delicate bone structure. My cheekbones are high and my features Nordic. The lines of her black wrap dress revealed a slight boyish frame and small wrists. My build is athletic. She was probably a couple of inches over five feet and I'm almost five nine. The way she pointed out images on the projector's screen was elegant and unhurried. I talk with my hands so much I'm always knocking something over. If her reaction on the phone wasn't still haunting me, I'd think I had the wrong woman.

As I half listened to her lecture, I fantasized about what my childhood might've been like with her as my mother.

We'd have discussed art at dinner, which we'd eat off beautiful plates and sometimes light the candles in silver candlesticks. On summer holidays we'd have explored museums in foreign countries and had deep intellectual talks over cappuccinos in Italian cafés. On weekends we'd have browsed bookstores together—

A wave of guilt swamped me. *I have a mother.* I thought of the sweet woman who raised me, the woman who made cabbage-leaf compresses for my headaches even when she wasn't feeling well herself, the woman who didn't know I'd found my birth mother.

After the class ended I walked down to the stairs toward the side door. As I passed near Julia she smiled, but with a questioning look, like she was trying to place me. When a student stopped to ask her something, I bolted for the door. At the last second, I glanced over my shoulder. Her eyes were brown.

I went straight back to my car. I was still sitting there, my heart going nuts inside my chest, when I saw her leave the building. She walked toward the faculty parking lot. I inched my car in that direction and watched her get into a white classic Jaguar. When she pulled out, I followed.

Stop. Think about what you're doing. Pull over.

Like that was going to happen.

As we drove down Dallas Road, one of the more upscale areas in Victoria along the waterfront, I kept back. After about ten minutes Julia turned into the circular driveway of a large Tudor house on the ocean. I pulled over and got out a map. She parked in front of the marble steps, followed a path around the corner of the house, then disappeared through a side door.

She didn't knock. She lived there.

So what did I do now? Drive off and forget about the whole thing? Drop the letter in her mailbox at the end of the driveway and risk someone else finding it? Give it to her in person?

But once I reached the big mahogany front door I stood there like an idiot, frozen, torn between tucking the letter into the door and just sprinting back down the driveway. I didn't knock, I didn't ring the doorbell, but the door *opened*. I was face-to-face with my mother. And she didn't look happy to see me.

"Hello?"

My face was burning.

"Hi . . . I . . . I saw your class."

Her eyes narrowed. She looked at the envelope clutched in my hand.

"I wrote you a letter." My voice sounded breathless. "I wanted to ask you some things—we talked the other day. . . ."

She stared at me.

"I'm your daughter."

Her eyes widened. "You have to leave." She moved to shut the door. I put my foot on the jamb.

"*Wait*. I don't want to upset you—I just have some questions, it's for my daughter." I dug into my wallet and pulled out a photo. "Her name's Ally—she's only six."

Julia wouldn't look at the photo. When she spoke her voice was high, strained.

"It's not a good time. I can't—I just *can't.*"

"Five minutes. That's all I need, then I'll leave you alone."
She looked over her shoulder at a phone on a hall table.

"Please. I promise I won't come back."

She led me into a side room with a mahogany desk and floor-to-ceiling bookshelves. Moved a cat off an antique, brown leather high-backed chair.

I sat down and tried to smile. "Himalayans are beautiful." She didn't smile back. She perched on the edge of her seat. Hands gripping each other in her lap, knuckles white.

I said, "This chair is gorgeous—I refinish furniture for a living, but this is pristine. I love antiques. Anything vintage, really, cars, clothes . . ." My hand brushed the fitted black velvet jacket I'd paired with jeans.

She stared at the floor. Her hands started to shake.

I took a deep breath and went for it.

"I just want to know why you gave me away. I'm not angry, I have a good life. I just . . . I just want to know. I *need* to know."

"I was young." Now her voice was reedy, flat. "It was an accident. I didn't want children."

"Why did you have me, then?"

"I was Catholic." Was?

"What about your family, are they—"

"My parents died in an accident—*after* you were born." The last part came out in a rush. I waited for her to say more. The cat brushed against her legs, she didn't touch it. I noticed a pulse beating fast at the base of her throat.

"I'm very sorry. Was the accident on the island?"

"We—they—lived in Williams Lake." Her face flushed.

"Your name, Laroche. What does that mean? It's French, right? Do you know from what part of—"

"I've never looked it up."

"My father?"

"It was at a party and I don't remember anything. I don't know where he is now."

I stared at this elegant woman. Not one thing about her fit with a drunken one-night stand. She was lying. I was sure of it. I willed her to meet my eyes. She stared at the cat. I had an insane urge to pick it up and throw it at her.

"Was he tall? Do I look like him, or—"

She stood up. "I told you I don't remember. I think you'd better go."

"But—" A door slammed at the back of the house.

Julia's hand flew up to cover her mouth. An older woman with curly blond hair and a pink scarf draped around her thin shoulders came around the corner.

"Julia! I'm glad you're home, we should—" She stopped when she saw me and her face broke into a smile. "Oh, hello, I didn't realize Julia had a student over."

I stood up and held out a hand. "I'm Sara. Professor Laroche was kind enough to go over my paper with me, but I should be off."

She took my hand. "Katharine. I'm Julia's . . ." Her voice trailed off as she searched Julia's face.

I jumped into the awkward silence. "It was nice to meet you." I turned to Julia. "Thanks again for your help." She managed a smile and a nod.

At my car I glanced over my shoulder. They were still standing in the open doorway. Katharine smiled and waved, but Julia just stared at me.

So you understand why I had to talk to you. I feel like I'm standing on ice and it's cracking all around me, but I don't know which way to move. Do I try to find out why my birth mother lied or heed Evan's advice to just leave it alone? I know you're going to tell me I'm the only one who can make that decision, but I need your help.

I keep thinking about Moose. When he was a puppy we left him in the laundry room one cold Saturday when we went out, because he wasn't housebroken—little guy piddled so much Ally tried to put her doll's diapers on him. We had this beautiful, bright-colored rope rug we'd brought back from a trip to Saltspring Island, and he must've started nibbling one corner, then just kept pulling and pulling. By the time we got home the rug was destroyed. My life is like that beautiful colored rug—it took *years* to sew it together. Now I'm afraid if I keep pulling on this one corner it's all going to unravel.

But I'm not sure I can stop.

SESSION TWO

I thought about everything you told me: how I didn't have to decide right away, how I needed to be sure of my expectations and reasons for wanting to know more about my past. I even made a chart of all the pros and cons like we used to do together. This time I put everything in neat little columns, but I still didn't have an answer, so I stomped out to my workshop, cranked Sarah McLachlan, and sobbed my heart out while I attacked an oak armoire. With each layer of paint I stripped off, I felt calmer. It didn't matter whether she lied or where I came from. What was important was my life now.

I'd called Evan the minute I fled my reunion with my birth mother, so when he came home that weekend he brought me chocolates and red wine, an early Valentine's surprise—that man's no dummy. But smartest of all, he didn't lecture, just gave me a hug and let me rant and rave until I ran out of steam. And I did—run out of steam. But then the depression kicked in. It had been so long since I'd had one I almost didn't recognize it at first, like an ex-boyfriend you bump into and you can't remember what it was about him that made you feel so awful, so angry at everything. It wasn't until a couple of weeks later that I almost started feeling back to normal. I should've stopped there.

Evan had headed back to his lodge, and Lauren's husband, Greg, who works for our dad's logging company, had just left for camp, so Ally and I hightailed it over to Lauren's for dinner. I do all right in the kitchen department if I'm not obsessed by my latest project, but Lauren's roast beef and Yorkshire puddings put my stir-fries to shame.

While Lauren's two boys—towheaded, with big blue eyes, just like her—chased Ally and Moose around the backyard, Lauren and I took our coffees and dessert to the living room. I'm glad we're having a mild winter this year, although it never really gets cold on the island, but it was nice to curl up in front of her fireplace and catch up on our kids' latest events. Her two have usually just broken something, while mine is generally in trouble at school for bossing the other kids around or talking when she's not supposed to. Evan just laughs and says, "I wonder where she got that from," whenever I complain.

When we'd scraped the last trace of chocolate from our plates, Lauren said, "How are the plans coming for the wedding?"

"God, don't get me started. My file is *huge*."

Lauren laughed, tilting her head back and revealing a

scar on her chin from when she fell off her bike all those years ago. Of course, Dad gave me hell for not watching her properly, but nothing could spoil her natural beauty. She rarely wears makeup, but with her heart-shaped face, honey-gold skin, and lightly freckled nose she doesn't need to. And Lauren is one of those rare people who are as nice as they look—the kind of person who remembers what brand of shampoo you like and saves the coupon for you.

She said, "I told you weddings are more work than you think. And you thought it was going to be so easy."

"This from the woman who wasn't stressed about hers at all."

She shrugged. "I was twenty. I was just happy to be married. Mom and Dad's backyard was all we needed. But it will be beautiful at the lodge."

"Yeah, it will. But there's something I have to tell you. . . ."

Lauren glanced at me. "You're not getting cold feet?"

"What? Of course not."

She let out her breath. "Thank God. Evan's so good for you."

"Why does everyone say that?"

She smiled. "Because it's true." She had me there. I'd met Evan at a garage while we were waiting for our vehicles— his was in for a tune-up, mine was on its last legs. I was worried they weren't going to be able to fix my car and had no idea how I was going to pick up Ally, but Evan assured me everything would be fine. I still remember how he put the cardboard sleeve around my hot cup before he handed it to me, how relaxed and steady his movements were. How calm I felt around him.

Lauren said, "So what do you want to tell me?"

"Remember when I used to talk about finding my birth family?"

"Of course, you were obsessed when we were kids. Remember that summer you were convinced you were an Indian princess and tried to build a canoe in the backyard?" She started to laugh, then looked at my face and said, "Wait, have you been searching for real?"

"I found my birth mother a couple of weeks ago."

"Wow. That's . . . huge." Lauren's expression changed from surprise to confusion to hurt. "Why didn't you tell me?" It was a good question and one I couldn't answer. Lauren married her high school boyfriend and had the same friends she'd had in elementary school. She had no idea what it felt like to be rejected, to be alone. But the other reason was her husband. It was impossible to talk when Greg was around.

"I needed to process everything first," I said. "It didn't go very well."

"No? What happened? Does she live on the island?"

I filled Lauren in on the whole mess.

She made a face. "That must've been awful. Are you okay?"

"I'm disappointed. Especially that she didn't tell me anything about my biological father—she was my only chance of finding him." Most of my daydreams growing up were of my birth father whisking me away to his mansion, where he'd introduce me to everyone as his long-lost daughter, his hand warm on my back.

"You haven't told Mom and Dad, have you?"

I shook my head.

Lauren looked relieved and I stared at my plate, the chocolate now sour in my mouth. I hate the wave of guilt and fear that comes whenever I worry about Mom and Dad finding out, hate myself for resenting it.

I said, "Don't tell Melanie or Greg, okay?"

"Of course." I searched her face, wondering what she was thinking. After a moment she said, "Maybe your father was married and she's scared of it coming out after all these years?"

"Maybe. . . . But I think she even lied about her name."

"Are you going to talk to her again?"

"Hell, no! Pretty sure she'd call the cops on me. I'm just going to drop it."

"It's probably for the best." Again she looked relieved. I wanted to ask who she thought it was "best" for, but she was already picking up our plates and moving toward the kitchen, leaving me alone and cold in front of the fire.

As soon as we got home Ally and Moose tumbled into bed and I tidied up the house—I have a tendency to let things get a little out of hand when Evan isn't around. After my chores were done I wasn't in the mood to hit my workshop like I usually do when I'm wired on coffee and chocolate, so

I turned on my computer. I'd planned on just checking my e-mail, but then I remembered Julia's words.

My parents died in an accident.

Had Julia told me the truth about anything? Maybe I could at least find her parents' names online. First I Googled "car accidents, Williams Lake, BC." A few results popped up, but only one fatality involved a couple, and they'd died recently—wrong name too. I expanded my search to all of Canada but still didn't find any accidents with my birth mother's last name. If they'd died years ago the article probably wouldn't even be online, but, not ready to give up yet, I Googled "Laroche." Odd hits, random mentions here and there, but other than the university directory I'd found before, nothing connected to Julia.

Before I packed it in for the night, I decided to look up Williams Lake. I'd never been there, but knew it was in the heart of the Cariboo—the Central Interior of BC. Julia hadn't struck me as a small-town girl and I wondered if she'd escaped as soon as she graduated. I stared at the screen. I wanted to know more about her, but *how*? I didn't have any contacts at the university or with any government agencies, and Evan didn't either. I needed someone with connections.

When I Googled private investigators in Nanaimo, I was surprised to see there were a few companies. I browsed their Web sites, growing more confident when I realized they were usually retired police officers. When Evan called later I ran the idea by him.

He said, "How much do they cost?"

"I don't know yet. I was going to make some calls tomorrow."

"It seems pretty extreme. You don't know for sure she was lying."

"She was definitely hiding something—it's driving me nuts."

"And if it's something you don't want to know? She might have a good reason for not telling you."

"I'd rather deal with that than spend the rest of my life wondering. And they might find my birth father. What if he doesn't know I exist?"

"If you feel like it's something you need to do, then go for it. But check them out first. Don't just hire anyone out of the phone book."

"I'll be careful."

The next day I called the private investigator with the slickest Web site, but as soon as he told me his fees I knew how he paid for it. Two numbers led straight to an answering machine. The fourth, TBD Investigations, had a barebones Web site, but the man's wife was friendly when she answered, telling me "Tom" would call me right back. And he did, an hour later. When I asked about his background, he said he was a retired cop and did this to keep himself in golfing money and his wife off his back. I liked him.

He told me he charged by the hour, with a five-hundred-dollar retainer up-front, and we agreed to meet that afternoon. Although I felt like a cliché as I pulled alongside Tom's sedan in the public parking lot, I was more comfortable after we talked for a few minutes and he told me anything he discovered would be confidential. I filled out his forms and drove away with mixed emotions: guilt about invading Julia's privacy and giving out her address, hope I might find my real father, and fear he wouldn't want to meet me either.

Tom had told me I might not hear anything right away, but he called a couple of days later when I was cleaning up after dinner.

"I have that information you were looking for." The friendly grandfather tone was gone, replaced by serious cop.

"Do I want to know?" I laughed. He didn't.

"You were right, Julia Laroche isn't her real name—it's Karen Christianson."

"*That's* interesting. Do you know why she changed it?"

"You don't recognize the name?"

"Should I?"

"Karen Christianson was the only survivor of the Campsite Killer."

I sucked in my breath. I'd read about the Campsite Killer— I've always been interested in serial killers and their crimes. Evan says I'm morbid, but when *Dateline* or A&E features a famous murder case I'm glued to the TV. They all had lurid names, like the Zodiac Killer, the Vampire Rapist, the Green River Killer, but I couldn't remember much about the Campsite Killer—just that he'd murdered people in the Interior of BC.

Tom was still talking. "I wanted to be sure, so I drove down to Victoria and took some shots of Julia at the university, then compared them to online photos of Karen Christianson. It looks like the same woman."

"God, no wonder she changed her name. So she must've met my father after she moved to the island. How long ago was she attacked?"

"Thirty-five years ago," Tom said. "She moved to the island a couple of months later and changed her name. . . ."

Something cold and dark was unfurling in my stomach. I said, "What month was she attacked?"

"July."

My mind raced to calculate dates and times. "I'm turning thirty-four this April. You don't think . . ."

He was silent.

I stepped backward and collapsed into a chair, trying to grasp what he'd just told me. But my thoughts were all over the place, fragmented pieces I couldn't pick up. Then I remembered Julia's pale face, her shaking hands.

The Campsite Killer is my father.

"I . . . I just—are you *sure*?" I wanted him to contradict me, to tell me I heard wrong, made a mistake, something.

"Karen's the only person who can confirm it, but the dates match up." He paused, waiting for me to say something, but I was staring at our calendar on the fridge. Ally's best friend, Meghan, had a birthday party on the weekend. I couldn't remember if I'd bought a present for it yet.

Tom's voice sounded far away. "If you have any more

questions, you have my number. I'll e-mail the photos I took of Karen with your receipt."

I sat in my kitchen for a few minutes, still staring at the calendar. Upstairs I heard a cupboard door slam and remembered that Ally was in the bath. I'd have to deal with this later. I forced myself off the chair. Ally was already out of the bathroom, leaving a trail of raspberry bubble scent and damp towels behind her.

Normally I love bedtime with her. When we're snuggled up she tells me about her day, part little girl as she mispronounces words, part little woman as she describes what the other girls are wearing. Back in my single days I let her sleep in my bed all the time. I loved the closeness, loved feeling her breathing next to me. Even when I was pregnant and Jason was out partying, I could only fall asleep with my hand on my stomach. He usually didn't come back until the wee hours of the morning. When I flipped—and I always did—he'd push me out of the room and lock it. I'd scream at him through the door until I was hoarse. I finally left him when I was five months pregnant, and he never got to see his daughter—he wrapped his truck around a tree a month before she was born.

I've stayed in touch with his parents and they're great with Ally, telling her stories about Jason and saving his things for when she's older. She spends the night at their house sometimes. The first time, I worried that she'd wake up crying, but she was fine. I was the one who couldn't sleep. Same with her first day of school—Ally sailed through it, but I missed her every minute, missed the noise in the house, missed her giggles. Now I crave this little window into her life outside our home, want to know how she felt in each moment: "Did it make you laugh?" "Did you like learning about that?" But that night Tom's words kept flashing in my mind: *the dates match up.* It didn't feel real, couldn't be real.

After Ally drifted off, I kissed her warm forehead and left Moose with her. In my office I turned my computer on and Googled the Campsite Killer. The first link was a Web site dedicated to his victims. While the site played haunting music, I scrolled through photos of all his victims, with their names and dates of death below each picture. Most of the attacks were staggered every few years from the early seventies on, but sometimes he'd hit two summers in a row, then go years without surfacing again.

I clicked on a link that took me to a PDF map that had a little cross marking every location where he murdered someone. He'd moved all over the Interior and northern BC, never killing in the same park twice. If the girls were camping with their parents or a boyfriend, he murdered them first. But it was clear the women were his real target. I counted fifteen women—healthy, smiling young women. All told, they believe he's responsible for at least thirty murders—one of the worst serial killers in Canadian history.

The Web site also mentioned the only woman who ever

got away: his third victim, Karen Christianson. The photo was grainy, her head turned away from the camera. I went back to the Google home page and typed in "Karen Christianson." This time numerous articles popped up. Karen and her parents were camping at Tweedsmuir Provincial Park in the West-Central region of BC one summer thirty-five years ago. The parents were shot in the head while they slept in their tent, but he hunted Karen in the park for hours until he caught and raped her. Before he was able to kill her she managed to hit him in the head with a rock and escape. She'd been lost in the woods for two days when she stumbled out of the mountain and flagged down a passing motor home.

In most of the photos she was hiding her face, but some industrious journalist found her senior year picture from the high school yearbook, taken just months before that fateful summer. I studied the photo of the pretty dark-haired girl with the brown eyes. She did look a lot like Julia.

The phone rang, making me jump. It was Evan.

"Hi, baby. Is Ally already in bed?"

"Yeah, she was tired tonight."

"How did your day go, any word from the PI?"

Normally I tell Evan everything—the good, the bad, and the ugly—the second he walks in the door or answers the phone, but this time the words caught in my throat. I needed some time to think, to sort through it all.

"Hello?"

"He's still looking into it."

That night I lay on my bed and stared at the ceiling, trying to get the horror out of my mind, trying not to think about Julia's face turned away from the cameras, turned away from me. Hours later I woke from a dream, the back of my neck soaked with sweat. I felt hungover, my mouth dry. Snippets of the dream came to me—a girl running through dark woods in bare feet, a bloody tent, black body bags.

Then I remembered.

I turned and looked at the clock. Five-thirty a.m. No chance of falling back to sleep after that nightmare. Like metal to magnet I was sitting at my computer again. I studied the photos of the victims, every article I could find on the Campsite Killer, my body filled with fear and disgust. I read every newspaper article on Julia, every scrap of information in every magazine, examined every photo. The reporters had hunted her for weeks, staked out her house, and followed her everywhere. The media frenzy was mostly in Canada, but some American papers had picked up the story, comparing her to one of Ted Bundy's victims who had also escaped. When Karen disappeared the articles changed to speculation about where she was, then gradually the coverage disappeared.

That morning I also got the e-mail from Tom with Julia's photos at the university, walking to her car, outside her home with Katharine. I compared hers to online photos of Karen Christianson. It was definitely the same woman. In one shot Julia was touching a student's arm, smiling encouragingly. I wondered if she touched me after she gave birth, or just told them to take me away.

This week I went through the motions, but I felt flat, disconnected—angry. I didn't know what to do with this new reality, the horror of my conception. I wanted to bury it in the backyard, far away from anyone's eyes. My skin crawled with knowledge, with the evil that I'd looked into, that had created me. I took long showers. Nothing helped. The dirt was on the inside.

When I was a kid I used to think my birth parents would come back if I was just good enough. If I got in trouble, I worried they'd find out. Every good grade in school was so they'd know I was smart. When Dad looked at me like he was trying to figure out who let me into his house, I told myself they were coming. When I watched him play piggyback with Melanie and Lauren after telling me he was too tired, I told myself they were coming. When he took the girls to the pool and left me to mow the lawn, I told myself they were coming. They never did.

Now I just wanted to forget they existed. But no matter what I did or the million ways I tried to distract myself, I couldn't get rid of the dark, heavy feeling pressing down on my chest, grabbing at my legs. Evan had been out of cell range for most of the week with a group. When he was finally able to phone I tried to listen about the lodge, tried to make the appropriate responses, tried to share about Ally's day, then I ended the call after a while, claiming fatigue. I was going to tell him, I just needed more time. But the next morning he picked up on it right away.

"Okay, what's going on? Don't want to marry me anymore?" He laughed, but his voice was worried.

"You might not want to marry *me* after you hear this." I took a deep breath. "I found out why Julia lied." I looked at the door, knowing Ally would be up soon.

"Julia? I don't know who—"

"My birth mother, remember? I heard from the PI last week. He told me her real name's Karen Christianson."

"Why didn't you tell me you found her?" He sounded confused.

"Because I also found out my real father is the Campsite Killer."

Silence.

Evan finally said, "Come on. You don't actually mean—"

"I mean my real father's a *murderer*, Evan. I mean he *raped* my mother. I mean—" I couldn't say what else has been driving my nightmares: my father's still out there.

"Sara, slow down. I'm trying to take this all in." When I didn't say anything, he said, "Sara?"

I nodded, even though he couldn't see me. "I don't . . . I don't know what to do."

"Just start at the top and tell me what's going on." I leaned against my pillow, clinging to the strength in Evan's voice. Once I was done explaining everything, he said, "So you don't know for sure Julia is this Karen person?"

"I looked at her photos online myself. It's her."

"But there's no proof the Campsite Killer is your father. It's all just speculation. She could've hooked up with a guy after."

"Rape victims don't usually just 'hook up' with someone right away. And there was a woman at her house—I think she might be gay."

"She might be now, but you don't know what she was into back then. For all you know she was pregnant at the time of the attack. This private investigator could be scamming you."

"He used to be a cop."

"So he says. I bet he calls and tells you he can find out more for a price."

"He wasn't like that." But was Evan right? Had I jumped to conclusions? Then I remembered the look on Julia's face. "No, she was seriously freaked out."

"You showed up on her doorstep and demanded she talk to you. That would scare anybody."

"It was more than that. I can feel it—in my gut."

Evan paused for a moment, then said, "E-mail me the links—and the photos that guy sent you, his Web site too. I have some time this morning, I'll read over everything and call you at lunch. We'll talk about it, okay?"

"Maybe I should call Julia—"

"That's a really bad idea. Don't do *anything*."

I didn't answer.

"Sara." His voice was firm.

"Yeah."

"*Don't.*"

"Okay, okay."

Ally was now talking to Moose in her room, so Evan and I said our good-byes. I tried to be cheerful for Ally as we made toad-in-a-holes with ketchup smiley faces. But every time I looked into her innocent eyes I wanted to cry. *What will I say when she's old enough to start asking about my family?*

After I drove Ally to school I took Moose for a hike, thinking the fresh air might help. But I knew it was a mistake as soon as I stepped into the woods. Normally I love the scent of fir needles in the air, of earth rich and fragrant after a rain the night before. All the different woods: red cedar, Douglas fir, Sitka spruce. But now moss-covered trees loomed over me and blocked out any light. The air seemed thick and quiet, my footsteps loud. Every dark corner of the forest caught my eye. A gnarled stump with one branch reaching out, a dead tree with ferns growing from it, the gap behind it blanketed by rotting leaves. *Did he rape her in a spot like that?* Moose, running ahead, startled a deer and it bounded off, its brown eyes wild with fear. I imagined Julia fleeing through the woods, her body cut and bleeding, her breath frantic, hunted down like an animal.

I came home and tore apart my workshop. The plan was to organize my supplies and clean my tools, then hang them back up in some semblance of order, but when I saw the mess I'd made—chisels, rubber mallet, clamps, orbital sander, brushes, rags, and paper towels piled up all over my workbench—I couldn't think straight enough to hang a ruler. I picked up a broom and started sweeping up shavings.

Evan phoned at lunch as promised, but his cell kept cutting out.

"I'll call when . . . off . . . water. . . . Following . . . pod . . . humpbacks."

Back in my shop I concentrated on sanding a mahogany Chippendale-style chest. As I smoothed away years of scratches and grooves, I reveled in the fresh wood scent, the rasp of sandpaper. With each stroke my muscles relaxed and my mind began to calm. But then the mahogany wood made me think of Julia's office. No wonder she didn't want to talk to me—she was still traumatized by what had happened, and seeing me brought everything back. But she didn't have to be scared of me. Maybe she was just afraid I might expose her secret? I stopped sanding. If I reassured her I wouldn't tell anyone . . .

The phone was on my desk. Julia's number at the university was still on a Post-it stuck to the base of my computer.

After four rings I got a computer recording: "You've reached the mailbox for Professor Laroche in the Art History Department. Please leave a message."

"Hi, it's Sara Gallagher. I don't want to upset you again, I just . . ."

The silence stretched out. I started to panic. What if I said something wrong? *Stop, calm down.* I took a deep breath and said, "I wanted to tell you I'm sorry I came to your house like that, but I understand now why you were so upset. I just need to know my medical history. I was hoping we could talk?" I rattled off my number, twice, and my e-mail. "I know you've been through a lot, but I'm a nice person and I have a family and I don't know what to tell my daughter and—" To my horror my voice broke and I started to cry. I hung up.

I just about had to break my hand to keep myself from dialing back and leaving another message apologizing for the first, then another filled with all the things I'd wanted to say but didn't. For the next hour I went over the call in my mind, my embarrassment greater each time. When Evan finally called last night, I felt so bad for going against his advice, I couldn't even tell him. He'd checked out the links and agreed that Julia Laroche did look a lot like Karen Christianson, but he still wasn't convinced the Campsite Killer was my father.

I said, "So what should I do?"

"Only two things you can do—tell the cops and they'll look into it, or just let it ride."

"If I tell the police they'll probably do a DNA test and I'm sure it would come back positive. What if the results got out? He could find me. I don't want anyone to know about this." I took a deep breath. "Does it change how you feel about me, knowing who my real father is?" I hated myself for asking, hated how weak it made me feel.

"Depends. Are you going to get him to knock me off?"

"Evan!"

His voice was serious when he said, "Of course it doesn't change anything. If he is your father, then it's scary he's still out there, but we'll get through it."

I let out my breath, pulling his words over me like a soothing blanket.

Evan said, "But if you're not going to talk to the police, then you have to just accept it, forget it, and move on."

If only it was that easy.

Evan also doesn't think I should tell anyone other than you—he's just as afraid as I am that it will get out and all hell will break loose. I thought about telling Lauren, but she likes things light and fluffy—she doesn't even watch the news. How can I tell her about this? I'm scared to read anything more about him myself.

When I first started seeing you after I pushed Derek—the first man I allowed myself to care about after Jason died—down those stairs, I was afraid I might have some horrible genetic predisposition, but you suggested I might be looking for something or someone to blame, so I didn't have to take responsibility for my own actions. It made sense at the time. I wasn't proud of what I did, even if the cheating bastard wasn't really hurt. But it scared me.

I can still hear the words coming out of Derek's mouth, still feel the pain of them: "You knew I wasn't over her when we met." And he was right. I did know, but it didn't stop me from going after him. Did I tell you how we met? It was at a party when Ally was a few months old—I hated leaving her, but Lauren forced me to go. Derek was smart and funny, but that's not what attracted me. The minute he said, "I'm not ready for anything serious right now. I

just broke up with a girl," I was hooked. That was my cat-
nip in every relationship: unavailable with a high chance
of breaking my heart. It wasn't until the brutal ending of
that one that I finally realized I owed it to myself—and
my daughter—to get some help.

I wish I could say it ended there, but as you know, I
bounced from bad relationship to bad relationship for the
next few years. I guess that's why I gave Evan such a hard
time when we first started dating. You probably don't remember the story because I stopped seeing you not long
after I met him, but he sent me a message through Facebook. Thinking a man as good-looking as he is who also
owned a fishing lodge had to be a player, I brushed him off.
But he kept sending little *How was your day?* notes, asking
about my work and my daughter, commenting on my status
updates. Because I wasn't viewing him as a potential boyfriend, I'd tell him about my problems, my fears, my jaded
view of men and relationships, anything that was on my
mind.

One night we talked on MSN until three in the morning, drinking wine, getting half blitzed in our own homes.
The next day he sent me a link to his favorite love song—
Colin James's "These Arms of Mine"—which I must have
played ten times in a row.

After a month of talking online I finally agreed to go on
a date, walking in the park with Moose. Hours sped by
without one anxious moment, just laughter and the wonder-
ful feeling of being safe while totally being myself. When
he met Ally a couple of months later, they adored each other

instantly. Even moving in with each other was easy: if one of us was missing a household item, the other had it. But in those early days I still caused arguments, trying to push him away, testing his loyalty. I was just so scared of being hurt again, so scared of losing myself like I had with Derek—of what might happen if I did.

When I was a kid I felt angry a lot, but I kept it bottled inside, which is probably why I was depressed so much as a teenager. It wasn't until I began dating that I started losing my temper. But I always managed to stop myself at a certain point—until that moment with Derek on the stairs. When he told me he'd spent the night with his ex-girlfriend all I could feel was shame. All I could think was how everyone was going to know I wasn't good enough. Then my hands were reaching out and he was falling.

Afterward I was shocked and horrified by what I'd done, even more by how powerful I'd felt. It terrified me—this sense that there was something dark inside me, something I couldn't control. And I wanted to believe what you said, that it was the same trigger it always was: abandonment issues, intimacy issues, low self-esteem, all of the above. But now we know one of my parents is violent, *beyond* violent. It's looking like maybe I was right to be scared.

This morning I was in my shop sanding that mahogany chest, trying to forget everything, and it worked for a couple of hours. Then I nicked my finger. As blood welled up I thought, *I have a killer's blood in me.*

SESSION THREE

I'm angry and confused, all right. I'm so stressed out I want to take a baseball bat and smash the crap out of something. I can't believe it's been over a month since I was here. I worked all that weekend on that mental exercise you taught me. Imagining how life would be if I wasn't worried about my family or genetics, what I would be doing with my time. I tried to envision myself feeling light and happy as I looked at wedding decorations and invitations. But I still couldn't stop thinking about the Campsite Killer—where he was, who he was. I even went back to the site and looked at the photos of all his victims again. My thoughts always turned to Julia. Did she get my message? Did she hate me? On Monday I got my answer.

I was out in my workshop, scrubbing varnish off my hands while Stevie Nicks belted out *"Sometimes it's a bitch . . . ,"* when I heard the phone. I scrambled through the pile of tools and equipment on my bench to a mound of rags, under which was the cordless. The number was private.

"Hello?"

"May I speak to Sara, please?"

I recognized the cultured voice. My pulse sped up.

"Is this Julia?"

"Are you alone?" Her voice sounded tight.

"I'm in my workshop, Ally's at school. I was just getting ready to go inside for some lunch—I skipped breakfast this morning. . . ." I was babbling.

"You shouldn't have called again."

"I'm sorry. I'd just found out who you really are and I wasn't thinking—"

"Obviously." It hurt, and I caught my breath.

"Don't call here again." And she hung up.

I handled it with my usual grace and aplomb—chucked the phone clear across my workshop, which knocked the battery out of the back and sent it spinning under a shelf. Then stormed into the house and ate a bunch of Ally's Oreo snack packs and Ritz Bits cheese sandwiches, cursing with every mouthful. She'd spoken to me like I was something she'd stepped in, something she wanted to scrape off her shoe. My face burned and tears stung my eyes when I thought what I always thought after an ex-boyfriend dumped me or stood me up, or when Dad didn't hold my hand when I reached for his: *What's wrong with me?*

An hour later I was still too upset to focus on any work.

And wedding stuff? Forget about it. I considered calling Evan, but then I'd have to explain what I'd done in the first place. I grabbed my car keys.

Lauren and Greg still live in the first house they bought after they were married—Mom and Dad helped with the down payment, which meant Dad told them what to buy. It's just a basic 1970s-style four-bedroom box, but it over-looks Departure Bay and has a fantastic view of the ferries as they come around Newcastle Island. I'd wanted to move to the same neighborhood, but nothing was for sale when Evan and I were house-hunting. We ended up in a newer subdivision, but I love our home. It's a West Coast contem-porary with cedar plank siding, earth-toned granite counter-tops, and stainless steel appliances.

Greg's still in the process of restoring their house, but it's going to be beautiful when they're done. Lauren's bright-ened it up a lot over the years with handmade curtains, pastel walls, vases full of fresh flowers. I'm constantly pilfer-ing from her vegetable garden.

I rapped on the back door, then pushed it open. "Hey, it's Sara."

She yelled down from upstairs, "Brandon's room!"

When I got to the room—decorated in hockey motif—I found Lauren putting away laundry. I curled up on the quilt with its Canucks logo and hugged the pillow as I watched Lauren, envying how content she is with her life.

She paused with a pair of socks in her hand. "What's wrong?"

"I don't really want to talk about it."

Her voice was teasing as she said, "You have to tell me now." She held a sock up like she was going to throw it at me.

"I'm okay. I just wanted to hang out for a bit."

"Are you still upset about your birth mother?" She turned and put the socks away, opened the next drawer.

I hadn't planned on telling her, just wanted to be around her warmth for a while, but before I knew it the words were coming out.

"I found out who my real father is."

She turned around, a small blue T-shirt clutched in her hand.

"You don't sound happy. Who is he?"

I was torn between my fear of what Lauren might think and my need for her to tell me it was okay, to make me feel better like she always does. I remembered Evan's warning not to tell anyone. I remembered my vow to Julia not to tell anyone. But this was my sister.

"You can't tell *anyone* about this—not even Greg."

She placed her hand across her heart. "Promise."

My face felt hot as I said, "You've heard of the Campsite Killer, right?"

"Everyone's heard of the Campsite Killer. Why?"

"He's my father."

Her jaw dropped open and she stared at me with a stunned

expression for what felt like hours. Finally she sat beside me on the bed.

"That's just . . . Are you sure? How did you find out?"

I sat up, the pillow in my lap, and told her about the private investigator and everything that had happened since. I searched her face, waiting to see all the horrible things I've been thinking mirrored in her eyes. But she just looked concerned.

She said, "Maybe Evan's right and it's just a coincidence?"

I shook my head. "The way she spoke to me today—she hates me."

"I'm sure she doesn't hate you. She probably—"

"No, you're right, it's worse than that, it's like I disgust her." My voice was thick as I tried not to cry.

Lauren rubbed my back. "I'm so sorry, Sara. The people who matter love you. Does that help?"

Except Dad didn't love me, and the fact that she wouldn't see it made it even more painful.

"You don't understand what it feels like to be adopted, to have your birth mother give you away like you're a piece of garbage, then reject you again. I've been waiting to meet her for years, and now . . ." I shook my head.

"I know it hurts, but you can't forget all the good in your life."

Lauren was about to say something else when we heard a voice downstairs.

"Hello, hello, hello, witches." Melanie.

Lauren said, "We're up here." I gave her a look and she made a zipping motion across her mouth.

Melanie came around the corner and dumped her purse on the floor.

"Thanks for hogging the whole driveway with your Cherokee, Sara."

"Not like I knew you were coming over."

She ignored me and turned to Lauren. "Thanks for your help the other day. Kyle and I appreciated it."

Lauren waved her hand in the air. "No problem."

I said, "What's going on?"

"Not everything's about you and the wedding." Melanie smiled like she was joking, but it didn't meet her eyes. Melanie looks Italian like our mom, but she wears her dark hair in a short spiky cut and favors bold red lips and kohl-circled eyes. When she's not glaring at the world or sulking about something, she's a knockout.

Dad loved taking her to all his logging camps with him when she was growing up—he was convinced she was going to be an accountant and help run his business. But as soon as she hit her teens the only thing Melanie wanted to spend time counting was boyfriends. And she found plenty of them at the pub where she tends bar. It used to be Dad's favorite hangout, but he hasn't stepped foot in the place since she started working there when she turned nineteen.

Lauren said, "Kyle needed a place to rehearse so I let them use the garage."

Melanie turned to me. "You book anyone for your wedding yet?"

"Evan and I are still talking about it."

"Perfect, because Kyle wants to do it for your wedding gift." She smiled big.

It was far from perfect. I'd heard Kyle's band a few months ago and they were barely in tune. I glanced at Lauren. She was looking back and forth between Melanie and me.

"That's an interesting suggestion, but I have to talk to Evan. I'm not sure what he has in mind."

"Evan? He's so easygoing, he won't care."

"Maybe, but I should still talk to him first."

Melanie laughed. "Since when do you wait for Evan's approval?" She paused, then her eyes narrowed. "Oh, I get it. You don't *want* Kyle to do it."

Here we go. Melanie was spoiled by all of us when she was a kid, but especially by Dad. If Mom was sick I was in charge and that's when the problems really began. Lauren was easy, I could tell her to pick up her toys and she'd do it right away, but Melanie would just stand there with her hands on her hips, glaring at me. Lauren or I would just end up doing it for her.

"I didn't say that, Melanie."

"*Unfuckingbelievable.* Kyle's band's gotten really good and he's willing to do this nice thing for you, but you're going to say no?" Before I could respond, Melanie shook her head and said, "I told you she'd shut it down, Lauren."

I said, "You've already talked about it?"

Lauren said, "No, well, just a little. Melanie mentioned last night that Kyle could use the exposure, and—"

"And you said he could probably meet some people at the

wedding," Melanie said. "You said it would be a good opportunity for him."

My face felt hot and my pulse sped up. Melanie wanted to use my wedding as an audition for her boyfriend? And Lauren *gave* her the idea?

Lauren said, "But I didn't know if Sara already had other plans."

"She *doesn't*," Melanie said. "It's just because she doesn't like Kyle."

Melanie stared at me, her chin out, daring me to deny it. I wanted to tell her exactly what I thought: *he's not good enough for you and he sure as hell isn't good enough to play at my wedding.* But I counted to ten, took a couple of deep breaths, and said, "I'll think about it, okay?"

Melanie said, "Suuuure you will."

"You will. Right, Sara?" Lauren's face was pleading as she looked at me, worried there was going to be a fight. And there was going to be a big one if I didn't get out of there fast.

"Right. I should get going." I stood up.

Lauren said, "You can't stay for a coffee?" I knew she wanted me to stay so we could work everything out, or at least pretend nothing was wrong, but if I heard one more thing out of Melanie's mouth I was going to blow up. I forced a smile.

"Sorry, I have to get Ally. Next time, okay?"

I didn't look at Melanie as I walked out.

That night I tossed and turned. Finally I got up and made notes—the only way I could calm down. First item was to call Lauren in the morning and apologize for leaving so abruptly. Then I wrote a letter to Melanie, saying all the things I'd wanted to tell her earlier but never would. Four years of therapy and I'd finally learned how to manage my anger—counting to ten, writing letters, leaving a room to cool off—but Melanie could push my buttons faster than anyone. I hated how quickly she could make me lose my temper. How out-of-control I felt when I did. But mostly I just felt sad. I'd loved her so much when she was little, loved how she looked up to me and followed me everywhere. Then I lost her in the mall when she was four.

We were Christmas shopping and Dad told me to watch her while he went into a store. Melanie wanted to walk around, but I knew Dad would be furious if we moved an inch, so I held on to the back of her coat. The tighter I gripped, the harder she fought, pulling and clawing at me, until she broke away and ran into a crowd of shoppers. The next twenty minutes were the most terrifying of my life. I started screaming her name frantically. Dad came running out of the store, his face white. When we finally found her—playing on a mechanical pony—Dad dragged me to the parking lot and spanked me behind his truck. I still remember trying to break away from him, crying so hard I could barely breathe, his hand coming down again and again.

Most of my worst childhood memories are of my getting into trouble because of Melanie. One Halloween Lauren and I were dressing up as cheerleaders. Melanie wanted the same costume, but we had made only two, so I told her she could be a princess. She grabbed my pom-poms and ran out of the room, saying she was going to throw them in the fire. I chased her, slipped in the hallway, knocked over a lamp, and broke the shade. When I told Dad, he was furious—not because of the lamp but because I should have included Melanie. I wasn't allowed to go trick-or-treating, and he let Melanie wear my costume. The worst part was he made me walk with them from house to house. I still remember watching Melanie skip up to the door in the costume I'd spent weeks making, the little skirt swinging with each step, my heart breaking when people told her how cute she looked.

When we hit our twenties—and neither of us was living at home—we started getting along better. After I had Ally, Melanie would come over sometimes and hang out, watching movies with me, laughing and eating popcorn. It was great, like we were finally sisters. We still argued once in a while, but the only times we really fought were if I tried to give her advice about her friends or some of the guys she was seeing. When she started dating Kyle I told her I was worried he might be using her because she worked at a bar. She flipped out and we didn't speak for a while. Then I met Evan and Dad began inviting us over for dinner—he called only when Evan was home—and arranging family brunches and barbecues.

Melanie missed a lot of these dinners because she was working, but when she did make it to one, she started taking shots at me—especially if her boyfriend was there. I didn't know if she was just pissed off that Dad liked Evan more than Kyle, or because I didn't like Kyle either, but she was hell-bent on making me look bad. And if I did lose my temper, Dad would come down hard on me and wouldn't say squat to Melanie. The more I tried not to react, the harder she hit. Now anytime we talked about the wedding it felt like a setup for a fight.

Lauren always ended up in the middle and I knew she was probably feeling awful about what had happened earlier, which made *me* feel awful. But guilt still gnawed at me for another reason, and I made a note to remind her not to tell anyone about my birth father.

The next morning I slept late and ended up rushing around to get Ally off to school. Then a client called and needed an emergency repair on a hall stand that was going into an antique show. I never did get a chance to call Lauren, and I collapsed into bed swearing I'd deal with it the next day. But I didn't, and as the days turned into a week I slid back into a depression.

The simplest task seemed insurmountable and my body ached all over. Even the idea of going to therapy was exhausting. So I slept too much, ate too much, and stayed on the couch all afternoon watching movies. I had to force myself out for walks with Moose, steering him away from his preferred path through the woods to the safer, more populated nearby park. Usually I love watching him chasing bunnies all over the fairgrounds, the earthy scent of hay and animals still lingering in the air. But now the buildings just looked old and abandoned as my feet slogged through puddles.

The only other times I dragged myself out were for Ally, using any energy I had left to hide what I was feeling. But I didn't do a very good job. One day we were driving home in a downpour, not unusual for March, or any month on the coast, but it added to my already dismal mood. We stopped at a red light and I was staring out the windshield.

Ally said, "Why are you sad, Mommy?"

"Mommy's not feeling well, honey."

"I'll take care of you," she said. She was so sweet that night, trying to make me soup and telling Moose he had to be quiet. She also spent the night in my bed. We snuggled together as she read me stories, lending me her favorite Barbie for comfort, the rain pattering against the window. The next morning I finally called Lauren to apologize for leaving so fast, but she beat me to it.

"I'm sorry I said anything to Melanie about Kyle playing at the wedding, Sara. But you two are always fighting and it makes it hard to say anything to either of you."

"Melanie drives me nuts."

"I wish you two weren't so jealous of each other."

"I'm not *jealous* of her, I just hate that she gets away with everything."

"Dad's just as hard on her, you know."

I laughed. "Yeah, right."

"He is—you just don't see it. He's always on her case about her job, telling her how well your business is doing and how big your house is and how successful Evan is. I think sometimes you two clash because you're so alike."

"I'm nothing like Melanie."

"You're both really strong people, and—"

"*Nothing*, Lauren."

She was silent.

I sighed. "I'm sorry. I'm just going through a hard time."

Her voice was gentle. "I know, hon. Call me anytime you want to talk." But I didn't, because as much as I loved my sister, there were some things she couldn't help with, some things that would always separate us. She knew where she belonged.

When another week slipped by and I was still moping around, I decided it was time to make some changes. I stopped Googling the Campsite Killer ten times a day, stopped reading about genetics and deviant behavior, which only led to nightmares, and bought material for a birdhouse—something Ally had wanted to build for ages. We had so much fun working on it together, Ally giggling while she painted, waving the brush around and splattering paint all over her fingers and the table. And slowly the darkness started to lift. Evan and I even managed to have a nice dinner over at Lauren and Greg's one weekend. Or at least it was nice until Dad showed up to go over some work stuff with Greg.

I felt terrible for Greg, listening to Dad berate him downstairs—when he knew we could hear in the kitchen. It was especially bad considering Dad came up after and told everyone he'd just hired a new foreman. Greg has been waiting years for Dad to promote him. Dad stayed for a beer and spent the entire time talking to Evan about fishing. It disgusts me that he plays favorites, but I was also disgusted at myself for feeling proud that he likes my fiancé.

By the first week of April, I finally felt like my depression was behind me. I was sleeping through the night and staying awake during the day. I was spending hours in my workshop again and getting caught up on projects. I'd been feeling so good I even got up early this morning and went on a shopping bender for Ally. I dropped a ton of money on craft supplies and a Netbook, telling myself it would help her learn. I love buying her things: costumes, books, games, paints, clothes, stuffed animals. If Ally's happy, I'm happy. As I walked back into my house carrying all the bags, the phone rang.

"You better come over tonight." It was my father. And his tone told me I was in trouble—big trouble.

"What did I do wrong?"

"I got a call. . . ."

Dad paused for an excruciating minute. I held my breath.

"It says on the Internet that your father's the Campsite Killer." His voice was tight with anger, *demanding* an explanation. I tried to make sense of what he'd just said, but it felt like the wind had been knocked out of me.

"Did you know about this? Is it true?" His words hammered into me again, sending my pulse skyrocketing. This was the last way I wanted them to find out. I thought of Mom, of how hurt she was going to be. I dropped onto the hall bench, closed my eyes, and got it over with.

"I found my birth mother a couple of months ago." I

took a deep breath, then spat out the rest. "And it looks like my birth father is probably the Campsite Killer."

Dad was silent.

I said, "Who called you?"

"Big Mike."

Dad's head foreman? How did he find out about this? The man is barely literate. Dad answered my questions for me.

"He said his daughter found it on *Nanaimo News for Now*."

"You mean that gossip Web site?" I was already running upstairs to my computer.

Dad's voice was hard. "You found your birth mother two months ago, but you didn't say anything? Why didn't you tell us you were looking for her?"

"I wanted to, but I just . . . Hang on, Dad."

I typed in the Web site address and found the article. *Karen Christianson found in Victoria . . .*

"Oh, no."

I tried to read the article, but shock made the words jumble. I caught snippets. *Karen Christianson . . . Only survivor of the Campsite Killer . . . Julia Laroche . . . Professor at the University of Victoria. Thirty-three-year-old daughter Sara Gallagher . . . Family-run business Gallagher Logging in Nanaimo . . .*

It was out, everything was out.

Dad said, "How did they know she was your mother?"

"I have no idea." I stared at the screen as panicked thoughts careened through my head. How many people had seen the article?

Dad said, "I'll call Melanie and Lauren. I want everyone here by six. We'll talk about it then."

"I'll e-mail the site right away and tell them—"

"I've already called my lawyer. We'll sue their asses off if they don't take this article down right away."

"Dad, I can handle it."

"I'm taking care of it." His tone made it clear he didn't think I could handle anything.

After he hung up I realized he'd said, "Your father's the Campsite Killer." Not your *birth* father, just your father.

Now you know why I'm so stressed out, Nadine. After I got off the phone with my dad I read the rest of the article, wanting to throw up the whole time. It had a ton of pictures of Karen Christianson—they even posted her staff photo from the university. I couldn't believe how much detail was in it about me too, what I do for a living, stuff about Evan's lodge. The only thing it didn't mention was that I had a daughter—thank God.

Even though Dad had called his lawyer, I sent the Web site an e-mail asking them to remove the article and phoned every extension listed on the site, but no one called back. Yet again I was left feeling like an idiot who couldn't do anything right. I tried to call Evan, but he was out on one of the boats with a group and wouldn't be in until after dinner. Lauren wasn't answering her phone, and she's a stay-at-home mom. She was probably hiding out in her garden. I'm sure she's dreading tonight's meeting as much as I am—Lauren hates it when people are upset.

Now I'm wondering if Melanie could've heard Lauren and me talking. But bitchy as Melanie can be, I just can't see her doing something this mean. Of course, if she told Kyle . . . he looks like the kind of guy who'd sell his kid sister if he thought it would get him ahead. There's no way Lauren or the PI would have said anything.

I haven't been this scared about a family meeting since I had to tell my parents I was pregnant. Dad got up in the middle of that speech and left the room. I took Moose for a walk, hoping to get rid of all the nervous energy humming through my body, but I just ended up rushing back home to my computer. The article was still up when I had to leave for our appointment. I'm trying to calm down by reminding myself this can't go anywhere if I don't confirm anything. Dad's lawyer works at one of the top firms in Nanaimo. He'll have the article pulled off that site by the end of the day. People might gossip for a while, and then something else will take its place. I just have to wait things out.

But I have a feeling something worse is waiting for me.

SESSION FOUR

Thank God you can fit me in—I know I was here yesterday, but when I panic like this everything in my
head just spins around and around. All I could think was
that I had to come here. You have to help me calm down
because if one more thing happens today I'm going to lose
it completely.

By the time I left my house for the family powwow I was in
an even worse mood. It didn't help that I'd had a heated debate with a six-year-old who did *not* like the change of plans.

"You said we can make pancakes for dinner. In different
shapes like Evan makes them." Her voice was anxious. Ally
has a methodical streak and all decisions require much de-
liberation, which is adorable when she sticks her little tongue
out of her mouth and contemplates what to buy Moose with
her birthday money but an absolute nightmare if we have to
do anything in a hurry.

"I don't have time tonight, Ally Cat. We're going to have chicken soup."

Fists balled on her hips. "You promised." The second part of Ally's orderly nature is that she needs to know our plans for each day and what she can expect in every situation. If I deviate off course, or God forbid rush through any step of the process, she'll come unglued.

"I know. I'm sorry, but we can't today."

"You *promised*." Her high-pitched whine set my teeth on edge.

I whirled around. "Not *today*."

She ran back to her room with her dark curls bouncing around her head and slammed the door. I heard something thump against it. Moose sat outside her door looking at me reproachfully. I didn't hear her crying, but Ally rarely cries—she'd throw something before she ever shed a tear. I once saw her stub her toe, then turn around and kick the offending table leg.

I tried the handle. It turned, but something was against the door. Ah. Evan taught her to brace her chair under the knob if there's an intruder.

"Ally, I'd like you to come out so we can talk about this, please."

Silence.

I took a deep breath.

"When you come out we can pick another night this week to make pancakes—I'll teach you how to make the batter from scratch. But you have to come out at the count of three."

Silence.

"One . . . two . . ."

Nothing.

"Ally if you don't come out here *right now* you're not watching *Hannah Montana for a week*."

She opened the door, walked past me with her arms crossed and her head bowed, then tossed a sad look over her shoulder.

"Evan *never* yells at me."

Things didn't get any better at my parents'. When I pulled in front of their log house on the outskirts of Nanaimo, Melanie's car and Lauren's SUV were in the driveway. Ally was already out of the Cherokee, Moose at her heels. I marched up to the front door, armor in place, knowing it wasn't going to help one bit.

They were all in the living room. Melanie didn't look at me, but Lauren gave a tentative smile. Dad's face was an iron mask. He was in his armchair in the middle of the room, dressed in his usual steel-toed work boots, black T-shirt, and red strap jeans that every self-respecting logger on the island lives in. Barrel-chested and brawny, full head of hair a snow-white crown, with his wife and daughters flanking him, he looked like a king.

"Nana!" Ally ran toward Mom and hugged her legs, her pink goose-down coat squishing up around her ears.

For a moment I wished I could run to Mom and hug her too. Everything about her is soft—her dark hair now threaded with silver, the powdery perfume she always wears, her voice, her skin. I searched her face for anger but just saw fatigue. I looked at her, my eyes pleading. *I'm sorry, Mom. I didn't want to hurt you.*

She said, "Let's go in the kitchen, Ally. I have a cinnamon bun for you. The boys are already in the back." She took Ally's hand and led her away.

As they passed me I said, "Hi, Mom." She touched my hand and tried for a reassuring smile. I wanted to tell her how much I loved her, that this wasn't about her, but before I could gather the words she was gone.

I threw myself into a chair facing my father, chin up. We held gazes. I looked away first.

Finally he said, "You should've talked to us before you found your birth parents."

Years of working in the sun have emphasized the deep grooves around his mouth, which was set in a hard line. Even though he's over sixty, it was the first time I'd seen my dad look old, and shame washed over me. He was right. I should have told them. I was trying to avoid hurting their feelings—and this conversation. But I'd made the whole thing worse.

"I know. I'm sorry, Dad. It made sense at the time."

He raised his left eyebrow in the way that always made me feel like a colossal failure. This time was no exception.

"I want to know how that Web site got this information."

"I'd like to know that myself." I stared at Melanie.

She said, "What are you looking at me for? I didn't even know about it until Dad told me."

"Sure you didn't."

Melanie twirled her finger by her temple and mouthed, *Crazy.*

My blood surged with a hot rush of anger. "You know, Melanie, you can be a real—"

"*Enough.*" Dad's voice boomed.

We were all quiet. I met Lauren's eyes. I could tell by her expression—part guilt, part fear—that she'd told Dad she already knew about my birth parents.

I turned to Dad. "The only other people who know are Evan and the private investigator I hired—but he was a retired cop."

"Did you check his credentials?"

"He gave me his card and—"

"What do you know about him?"

"I told you, he's a retired cop."

"Did you call the police and verify that?"

"No, but—"

"You didn't check him out." Dad shook his head and my face burned. "Give me his number."

I wanted to tell him that he wasn't the only person capable of doing something, but as usual he had me doubting myself.

"I'll e-mail it to you."

From the corner of my eye I noticed Mom standing in the doorway with a plate.

"Does anybody want a cinnamon bun?"

She sat on the couch and set the plate on the coffee table with some napkins. No one reached for a bun. Dad looked hard at Melanie and Lauren, who both took one. I followed suit even though there was no way I could choke anything down. Mom smiled, but her eyes were red-rimmed—she'd been crying. Crap.

She said, "Sara, we understand that you wanted to find your birth family, we're just disappointed you didn't tell us. It must have been very upsetting when you found out who your real father was." Her pale cheeks told me she was still pretty upset herself.

"I'm sorry, Mom. It was just something I needed to do for myself. I was trying to work through it first before I talked to anyone."

Mom said, "Your mother—the article said she's a professor?"

"Yeah. She doesn't want anything to do with me." I looked away, blinking hard.

"It's not personal, Sara." Mom's voice was gentle. "Any mother would be proud to have you as her daughter."

Tears filled my eyes. "I'm *really* sorry, Mom. I should've told you, but I didn't want you to think I was ungrateful or something. You're an amazing mother." It wasn't lip service. Mom loved every art project we dragged home, every costume she had to make at the last minute, every pair of torn favorite blue jeans only she could fix. Mom loved being a mother. I'd never asked, but I was sure she was the one who wanted to adopt. I'd bet money Dad just did it for her.

I said, "You'll always be my real parents—you raised me. I was just curious about my history. But when I found out about my biological father, I thought maybe you guys wouldn't want to know." I looked at my dad, then back at her. "I didn't want to upset you."

Mom said, "We're worried and scared for you, but it would *never* change how we feel about you." I looked at Dad again. He nodded, but his face was distant.

I said, "Evan's out on the boat, but I'm going to tell him it's on the Internet as soon as I get home."

Dad said, "The article's gone, but we're still going to sue the bastards."

I dropped my head to rest against the back of the chair and let out my breath. It was going to be okay. For a moment I felt protected—Dad was actually sticking up for me—but then he said, "The dumbasses never should've used my company name," and I knew what he was really protecting.

I felt another stab of guilt when I saw Mom's hand press against her belly as she grimaced. Dad also noticed and his eyes turned hard as they locked on to mine. He didn't have to say the words. He's said them many times, many ways. But the silent ones always hit the hardest. *Look what you did to your mother.*

Mom started talking about the wedding, but the conversation felt forced. Melanie and I steadfastly ignored each other.

Finally I said, "I should get Ally home to bed." When I went outside to call her in, Lauren followed and closed the door behind us.

"Sorry I told Dad, but he asked if I knew and I didn't want to lie to him."

"It's okay. Was he mad at you for keeping it a secret?"

She shook her head. "I think he's just worried."

"Is that why you ignored my call today?"

"I didn't want to get caught in the middle." She looked miserable. "I'm sorry."

I didn't want her caught in the middle either. I wanted her to take my side, but that was never going to happen. When we were kids and Dad went on a tirade against me, Lauren hid in her room. Later she'd come out and help me with my chores, but somehow I just felt more alone.

"You didn't tell Melanie about my real father, did you?"

"Of course not!"

So Melanie had overheard and probably told Kyle, and then he told God only knows who. Nothing I could do about it now.

On the drive home, I was feeling a little calmer but still worried about how many people saw the article before it got pulled off. Then I remembered Mom saying they were worried and *scared* for me. I stopped at a red light, focusing in on that moment. Dad's tense face, the concern in Mom's eyes, something they were both thinking but didn't say. What had I missed? Then it hit me.

The Campsite Killer could have read the article.

I didn't know I was still sitting at the light until a car honked behind me and Ally said, "Mommy, go!" I drove the rest of the way in a daze. I'd been so caught up in defending myself, so terrified of my father's anger, I'd missed the thing I should be most afraid of. If the Campsite Killer found that article, he not only knew I lived in Nanaimo, he knew my name.

As soon as we got home Ally had a bath, then I read her a story, but I kept stumbling over words and losing my spot on the page. I had to talk to Evan. After Ally fell asleep I tried to call him, but he wasn't answering his cell. I bundled up in a blanket on the couch, watching mindless TV and waiting for Evan to call back. Just as I was about to give up and go to bed, the phone rang. Before he could ask what I'd been up to, I asked him how his day was.

"We found a pod of humpbacks, so the group was happy." Evan built his lodge on the remote west coast of the island, so it offers guided kayak tours and whale watching not just fishing charters.

"That's awesome."

"Sure looking forward to coming home this weekend, though. . . ." He growled and I tried to join in but couldn't pull it off. So I took a deep breath and spit it out. First I told him about leaving Julia a message and her awful call back, then about telling Lauren, and finally that it hit the Internet. He took it better than I thought, a lot better than I would—no surprise there.

"It won't go anywhere," he said.

"But people are obsessed with serial killers—half the books and movies made are about them. If they find out I'm his daughter . . ."

"You know where the shotgun is and the key for the trigger lock—"

"The shotgun!"

"You'll be fine. That site can't have that many readers."

"What if *he* reads it?"

"The Campsite Killer?" He paused for a moment. "Nah, there's no way he's reading a Nanaimo blog."

"You really think it'll be okay?"

"Yeah, I do. Let your dad's lawyer handle it."

"I'm just freaked out."

He softened his voice. "I'll be home soon."

Before I dove into bed last night I couldn't help peeking at the Web site and was happy to see the article was still gone. I also did a quick Google search and nothing came up. I went to sleep convinced Evan was right—it wasn't going to go anywhere. In fact, it was good this happened because it forced things out in the open with my family—keeping things under wraps is not exactly a talent of mine.

This morning Ally sang Moose a song in between bites of toast and peanut butter. Ally and I are both peanut butter fiends, you wouldn't believe how many jars we go through. After I dropped her off at school I grabbed a coffee and headed out to the shop to attack a new armoire. I was in the zone within minutes and didn't stop for lunch. Finally, in the afternoon, I decided to grab a snack and refill my coffee. Before I headed back out to my shop, I snuck upstairs for another peek at the *Nanaimo News for Now* site. The article was still down. For peace of mind I did another Google search for Karen Christianson. This time a bunch of new hits popped up.

I set my cup down so fast coffee sloshed over the rim, and clicked on the first link. It was for a serial killer fan club in the States. In the forum someone named "Dahmersdinner" had posted that Karen Christianson was hiding in Victoria and using the name Julia Laroche. Her daughter, a woman named Sara Gallagher, lived in Nanaimo. I stared at the screen, my heart thumping loudly in my ear. There was nothing I could do, no way to delete it. Then I noticed there were comments—lots of them. I clicked on the tab and expanded the page. First they were along the lines of "I wonder if it's true" and "Can you imagine what his kid looks like?" But then more members joined in.

Someone had gone to the university site and found Julia's office information. Then they linked to articles she'd written and Web sites that had photos of Karen Christianson. One commenter actually Photoshopped her picture to make it look like the Campsite Killer was standing behind her with a bloody rope in one hand and his other on his penis. They talked about Julia's looks, complimenting the Campsite Killer's taste. One jerk said he wondered if I was as twisted as my father. Another compared me to Ted Bundy's daughter, saying they should hunt these "bitches" down before they could spread the disease. I read every vile comment, sick with shame and fear. I felt ripped open, exposed to the world.

I clicked from site to site as fast as I could—the majority of hits were coming from true crime blogs and a couple of Web sites devoted to serial killers, including the one I'd already found on the Campsite Killer. The more legitimate sites were careful to just say that Karen was "rumored" to have a daughter. It was the commenters, always anonymous, who added my name and that I lived in Nanaimo. Then I noticed a University of Victoria Student Forum was one of the hits. My stomach in knots, I clicked on the link but couldn't get in without a student ID number.

A wave of panic came over me. *What do I do now? How do I stop this?* The cordless beside me rang and I jumped.

Lauren said, "I have to tell you something."

"Is it about the Internet buzz?"

"You're online?"

I stared at the screen. "It's *everywhere*."

Lauren was quiet for a moment, then said, "What are you going to do?"

"I don't have a clue. But I think I should talk to Julia."

"Do you really—"

"If she hasn't heard, I should warn her. And if she has, she's going to think I told everyone. But if I call to explain, she'll probably just hang up on me." I groaned. "I've got to go. I need to figure out what to do."

Lauren's voice was gentle. "Okay, hon. Call if you need me."

After I hung up the phone, I collapsed onto the couch. Moose joined me, grunting and snuffling into my neck. My mind spun in a million panicky directions. The whole world is going to know the truth about my father. The Campsite Killer could find Julia—and me. Evan's business could be ruined. My business could be ruined. Ally's going to be teased at school.

The phone rang. I checked the call display. Private number. Julia?

I answered on the third ring.

"Hello?"

A male voice said, "Is this Sara Gallagher?"

"Who's speaking?"

"I'm your father."

"*Who* is this?"

"I'm your real father." His voice sped up. "I read about it on the Internet."

A jolt of fear ran through me. Then I realized the voice was too young.

"I don't know who you really are or what you read, but—"

"Are you hot like your mommy?" I heard laughter in the background, then another young-sounding voice called out, "Ask her if she likes it rough too."

"Listen, you little—"

He hung up the phone.

I phoned Evan right away, but his cell went straight to voice mail. I thought about calling Lauren, but she'd be scared for me—hell, I was scared, which made me even angrier. Some teenagers were calling me and pretending to be my father just for kicks. What if Ally had picked up the phone? I was pacing around, fuming, when the phone rang again. I was hoping it was Evan, but it was Ally's teacher.

"Sara, do you have time to talk when you pick Ally up today?"

"What's going on?"

"Ally had a . . . disagreement with a classmate who tried to use some of her paints and I'd like to discuss it with you." Great, just what I needed right now.

"I'll talk to her about sharing, but maybe we can meet another time—"

"Ally pushed the girl—hard enough to make her fall."

That's when I called you. There is no way I can meet Ally's teacher without talking to you first. I need to wrap my head around the fact that everything's blown wide open. I can't shake those sick comments, that awful phone call. And I know her teacher's going to suggest that Ally meet with the school counselor again to learn how to handle her issues. She's had problems before—yelling at other children, arguing with her teacher—but that's just when she feels rushed. Her teacher also said Ally has difficulty transitioning from one subject to the next, and that's when she stresses out the most. I tried to explain there's nothing wrong with her— she just doesn't like change. But her teacher kept asking if there were any problems at home. Let's just hope she hasn't heard about the Campsite Killer being my father.

I hate it when I get this upset, hate how my body reacts. My throat and chest get so tight I can barely breathe, my heart rate skyrockets, my face feels hot, I start sweating, and my calves ache with unused adrenaline. It feels like a bomb exploded inside my head, and my thoughts are flying everywhere.

We used to talk about how my anxiety was caused from growing up adopted and having a distant father: my subconscious was afraid I'd be abandoned again, so I never felt safe. But I think it's more than that. When I was pregnant with Ally I read that you need to be calm or your baby will pick up on your negative energy. I spent nine *months* inside a woman who was constantly terrified. Her anxiety flowed into my blood, into my molecules. I was born in fear.

SESSION FIVE

When I first started therapy and was trying to avoid talking about my childhood you said, "To build up a future you have to know the past." Then you told me it was a quote from Otto Frank, Anne Frank's father, and that you'd toured her house in Amsterdam. I remember sitting here—you'd gone to get us a coffee—looking around at the photos on your wall, the art you brought back from your trips, the carvings and statues you collected, the books you wrote, thinking you were the coolest woman I knew.

I'd never met anyone like you before, the way you dressed, all artsy elegance, sort of a bohemian intellectual, a sweater shawl tossed over your shoulders, your hair cut in all those crazy chunks of gray, like you not only embraced your age—you were *proud* of it. The way you pulled your glasses off when you leaned in to ask me something, your finger tapping on your crooked mug—which you made in pottery class because you were bored and you told me it was important to never stop learning. I studied every move, drank it all in, and thought, *This is a woman who isn't afraid of anything. This is who I want to be.*

That's why I was so surprised when you told me you were also from a dysfunctional family and that your father had been an alcoholic. What I admired most was that you didn't have any resentment or anger—you'd dealt with your crap and moved on. You'd built up a future. I left here feeling so hopeful that day, like anything was possible. But then later I thought about what you said— about knowing your past—and it hit me that I'd never be able to build a *real* future because I didn't know my *real* past. It was like building a house on no foundation. It might stay up for a while but eventually it would start sinking.

When I got home Moose snorted and jumped all over me like I'd been gone a million years. After I let him out for a pee—poor guy only made it a foot out the door—I thought about calling the cops to report the prank call but decided to wait and talk things over with Evan. When I scrolled through the call display to see if he'd phoned while I was out, I noticed two private numbers. I checked my voice mail and they were from newspapers.

For the next hour I paced around the house with the cordless gripped in my hand, praying Evan would call soon. The phone rang in my hand once, making me jump, but it was just another reporter. After a while I made myself call Dad and tell him what I found online and about the calls.

He said, "Don't answer the phone if you don't know the

number. If someone asks about the Campsite Killer, deny everything. You were adopted but your birth mother wasn't Karen Christianson."

"You think I should lie?"

"Damn right. I'll tell Melanie and Lauren the same. And if any punk calls again, just hang up."

"Should I go to the police?"

"They can't do anything. I'll deal with this. Send me the links."

"Most of them are just forums."

"Send them."

I did as he said, then tortured myself by reading the comments again. There were ten new ones, each sicker than the last. I checked the other Web sites and the comments were just as bad. It shocked me that people could be so mean about someone they didn't know—and it terrified me that they knew my name. I wanted to monitor the sites, wanted to defend myself and Julia, but it was time to go meet with Ally's teacher.

It wasn't as bad as I thought. Turns out the other little girl had been harassing Ally for a while—messing up her desk, taking paints while Ally was still using them—and Ally finally lost it. Of course, I said I'd explain to her that pushing wasn't the way to deal with disagreements and she should tell an adult if she's having problems, but I'd have said anything to get out of there. What Ally did was wrong, and I did talk to her about it, but frankly it didn't seem like such a big deal compared to the fact that I'd just ruined Julia's life, not to mention my own. Then I dragged my whole family into it. It was the last one that hurt the most.

The phone finally rang at eight. As soon as I saw Evan's cell number I answered in a rush, "We have to talk."

"What's going on?"

"That Web site—it spread somehow, maybe they didn't do a Google sweep. But now it's on other blogs. It's mostly about Julia, but there are all these disgusting comments— some of them mention my *name*. Then this teenager called and said he's my father. Reporters are calling, but I'm not answering, and Dad said—"

"Sara, slow down—I can't understand half of what you're saying." I took a deep breath and began again. At the end Evan was silent for a minute, then said, "Have you called the cops?"

"Dad said they can't do anything."

"You should still tell them what's going on."

"I don't know . . . he said he'll deal with it." The last thing I wanted was Dad pissed at me for going against him.

"So let him, but get something on record."

"He's right, though. They can't do anything about some-one playing a joke."

"You asked for my advice. Call the police in the morning— and don't comment on any of these blogs."

"Okay, okay."

After I hung up the phone, I climbed into bed and watched late-night TV until I fell into a restless sleep. Early the next morning the phone rang. Without looking at the call display I reached over and picked it up.

"Hello?"

A male voice said, "Good morning. I understand you restore furniture?"

I sat up. "I do. What can I help you with?"

"I have a few pieces, a table, some chairs. I don't think they're worth much, but they were my mother's and I'd like to give them to my daughter."

"Value isn't always what you can sell something for—it's what it means to you."

"This table means a lot. I spent most of my time there—I like food." He laughed and I laughed back.

"Kitchen tables tell the story of a family. Sometimes people just want me to clean them up a little but preserve marks their children made, things like that."

"How much do you usually charge?"

"Why don't I have a look and give you an estimate." I climbed out of bed and threw on a robe as I headed to my office for a pen. "I can come to your house, or a lot of my clients just e-mail me photos."

"You go to strangers' homes?"

I paused in my hallway.

He said, "Do you go alone?"

Okay, there was no way I was taking this job. My voice flattened, turning cold. "I'm sorry, I didn't catch your name?"

He was silent for a moment, then said, "I'm your father."

That explained it, just another jerk playing a prank.

"*Who* is this?"

"I told you—your father."

"I *have* a father and I don't appreciate—"

"He's not your father." The voice turned bitter. "I wouldn't have given my kid away." He paused and I heard traffic in the background. I almost hung up, but I was too mad.

"I don't know what kind of sick joke you're playing—"

"It's not a joke. I saw Karen's photo and recognized her. She was my third one."

"Everyone knows Karen was his third victim."

"But I still have her earrings."

My stomach climbed into my throat. What kind of person pretends to be a murderer?

"Do you think this is funny? Calling someone and trying to scare them? Is this how you get your kicks?"

"I'm not trying to scare you."

"Then what do you want?"

"To get to know you."

I hung up. The phone rang back right away. The call display showed a BC area code, but I didn't recognize the prefix. Finally the ringing stopped, only to start up again. My hands shook as I unplugged the phone.

I raced down the hallway, woke Ally up, told her to get ready for school, and jumped into the shower. Out in minutes, I made her some peanut butter and toast while she brushed her teeth, slapped her lunch together while she ate, then tore out of the house.

When I walked into the police station two older men in plainclothes were manning the front desk. As I headed toward them a policewoman came through the door behind the counter and picked up a file off a desk. I guessed her to be First Nations, with high cheekbones, coffee-colored skin, big brown eyes, and thick, straight dark hair pulled back in a tight bun.

At the counter I said, "I want to talk to someone about some calls I'm getting."

One of the men said, "What kind of calls?"

The policewoman said, "I'll take it," then led me to a door with a metal plate reading "Interview Room" and motioned me in. It was bare except for a long table and two hard plastic chairs. On the table was a pad of paper, a phone book, and a phone.

She settled in a chair and leaned far back. Now that she was facing me I saw her name badge: "S. Taylor."

"How can I help you?"

It occurred to me that what I was about to say was going to sound crazy as all get-out. I was just going to have to give her the facts and hope she believed me.

"My name's Sara Gallagher. I'm adopted and I recently found my biological mother in Victoria. Then I hired a private investigator and he found out she's Karen Christianson. . . ."

She stared at me blankly.

"You know, the Campsite Killer's only living victim?"

She sat up straight.

"The private investigator thinks the Campsite Killer's probably my father. Then the Web site *Nanaimo News for Now* somehow got hold of the information and it spread all over the Internet. Yesterday I got a prank call from teenagers pretending to be my father. Then this morning a man called, also saying he was my father. But this time he said he had her earrings."

"Did you recognize his voice?"

I shook my head.

"What about the phone number?"

"He called from a 250 area code, but the prefix was 374 or 376, something like that. I wrote everything down but I forgot the paper and—"

"Did he tell you why he was calling?"

"He said he wanted to get to know me better." I made a face. "I know it's probably just a joke, but I have a daughter, and—"

"Has your birth mother confirmed you were conceived in the process of a sexual assault?"

"Not in so many words, but yeah."

"I'd like to record your statement."

"Oh, okay. Sure."

She stood up. "I'll be back in a moment."

While I waited for her I glanced around the interview room and fiddled with my cell phone.

The door whipped open. She sat down, set a small recorder on the table in front of me, and pulled her chair close. She said her name, my name, and the date, then asked me to repeat my full name and address. My mouth went dry and my face felt hot.

"In your own words, I'd like you to tell me why you think the Campsite Killer is your biological father and the details of the phone calls you received recently." Her serious tone made me even more nervous and my heart sped up.

She said, "Go ahead."

I did the best I could, but I occasionally meandered off course and she brought me back with a quick "And what did he say next?" She even wanted to know Julia's address and any information I had on her. I felt weird giving it, considering I basically got the information by stalking her. I also told her we'd been trying to reach the PI and that he's a former cop. Her neutral expression never changed.

When we were done I said, "So what happens now?"

"We'll look into this."

"But you don't think it's *actually* the Campsite Killer calling?"

"When we have more information we'll let you know. Someone will be in touch soon."

"What if he calls again? Should I change my number?"

"Do you have call display and voice mail?"

"Yeah, but I have a business, and—"

"Don't answer any calls from unfamiliar numbers and let it go to voice mail. Make note of the number and time, then let us know ASAP." She handed me her business card, then moved to stand by the door.

In a daze, I followed her down the hallway.

To her back I said, "But do you think it's just someone

trying to scare me? And you have to take it seriously because of the Campsite Killer connection?"

She glanced over her shoulder. "I can't really say until we look into it, but be careful. And thanks for coming in. If you have any questions give me a call."

Out in the parking lot, I sat in the Cherokee and stared at the business card in my hand. My body was shivering. I'd hoped the police would tell me I had nothing to worry about, but Constable Taylor had passed up every opportunity to reassure me. Now I was terrified it really was the Campsite Killer calling.

Were the police going to talk to Julia? How long was it going to take before they got in touch with me? How was I going to make it through another couple of days not knowing? I thought about what the man had said about Karen's earrings. Wasn't that the quickest way to prove him a liar? But if I called Julia, she'd just hang up before I could ask her anything.

I glanced at the clock. It was only nine in the morning—time enough to get down to Victoria and still be back to pick Ally up from school.

Because it was Friday and not yet lunchtime I thought Julia might be at the university, so I headed straight to the campus. I spent the entire drive rehearsing ways to tell her what was going on, but first I had to actually get her to talk to me. I hoped showing up at her workplace would mean she couldn't slam the door in my face. But when I called her office from a pay phone, an assistant told me she didn't have any classes that day and she didn't know when she'd be back.

I was going to have to go to her house.

As I drove down Dallas Road, I started to second-guess the brilliance of my plan. I was crazy. Julia was going to flip at the sight of me. I should just leave it to the police. But still I found myself parked on the road in front of Julia's house, staring at her front door.

I had to let her know what was going on. She was the only person who knew about the earrings. I had a right to ask— the safety of my family depended on it. *Her* safety depended on it.

When I knocked on her door my heart kicked into high gear and my throat tightened. She didn't answer, but her car was in the driveway. Had she seen me walk up to the house? What should I say if Katharine's home? This was a bad idea. Then I heard voices from the back of the house.

As I came around the corner I saw Julia and an older man standing by a basement window at the far end of the house. The man was carrying a clipboard and Julia was pointing at the window, her face pale and strained. I stopped, wondering if I should leave. I picked up part of their conversation, something about steel bars. Now I remembered seeing a van for a security company on the street. The man said something as he shook Julia's hand, but she seemed distracted. She was still staring at the window as he walked past me with a nod. I waited until he was down the driveway, then cleared my throat. Her head snapped in my direction.

"Hi, I need to talk to—"

"That's it. I'm calling the police." She stalked toward a back deck.

"That's why I'm here—it's *about* the police."

That stopped her. She turned around.

"What do you mean?"

"I've been getting calls from newspapers and—"

"What do you think *my* life is like?" Her face was flushed and angry. "I had to cancel classes today because reporters are harassing my students and waiting in the parking lot. My home number and address are unlisted, but it won't take them long to get that information. Or did you already tell them that too?"

"I never—"

"Are you trying to make *money* off this? Is that what you're here for?" She started to pace in short jerky directions like she wanted to run but didn't know where to go.

"I didn't have anything to do with it getting out. That's the last thing I wanted. I only told a private investigator, and then my sister because I was upset, but I don't know how it got leaked."

"You hired a private investigator." She shook her head and squeezed her eyes closed. When she opened them, they looked desperate.

"What do you *want*?"

"I don't want anything." But it wasn't true. And now she'd never give me what I really wanted.

"Do you know how long it took for me to build a life here?" she said. "You've ruined *everything.*"

Her words crashed into me and I almost stepped back from the blow. She was right, I had ruined everything. And it was about to get worse. The next part would terrify her even more, but it had to be said. I braced myself.

"I came here today because I thought you should know a man called me this morning. He said . . . he said he's my real father. He recognized your photo and he said he had your earrings."

She was completely still, the only movement her pupils dilating. Then she began to shake as tears leaked from the corners of her eyes.

"They were a gift from my parents. Pearls. Pink ones with silver leaf backings, for my graduation." Her voice caught and she swallowed hard. "I was worried about wearing them camping, but my mother said beautiful things were to be enjoyed."

He *did* take her earrings. I remembered the man's voice, the way he spoke about his daughter. My blood *whooshed* in my ears as I stared at her, trying to think of what to say, trying not to think about what this meant.

Finally I found some words. "I'm . . . I'm sorry he took them."

Her eyes met mine. "He said *thank you.*" She looked away again. "The police never revealed to the public that he took my earrings. They told me they'd catch him." She shook her head. "Then I found out I was pregnant. But I couldn't kill it. So I changed my name and moved away. I just wanted to forget it ever happened. But every time he murders someone, the police find me. One of them told me I was the lucky one." She laughed bitterly, then looked back at me.

"I've lived in terror for thirty-five years that he's going to find me. I haven't slept one night without waking up from a dream that he's still chasing me." Her voice quivered. "You found me, *he* can find me."

For once her expression wasn't guarded and I could see the raw pain in her eyes. I could see *her*. Every broken piece. This poor woman had lived in fear for so long—and now she had even more because of me.

I stepped closer. "I'm really—"

"You should go." Her face had closed down again.

"Okay, sure. Do you want my number?"

She said, "I have it." The patio doors closed behind her with a solid click.

That night Evan came home and I told him we needed to talk, but we didn't get a chance until Ally and Moose were in bed and we'd collapsed on the couch. Evan sat with his legs up on the coffee table, and I sat at the opposite end with my arms wrapped around my knees. He was upset about the second call but glad I'd gone straight to the police. When I told him I'd also gone to see Julia he just shook his head. But he *really* didn't like hearing about the earrings.

"If he calls again—don't answer it."

"That's what the cops said too."

"I don't like that this is happening and I have to leave on Monday. Maybe I should get one of the other guides to take this group."

"I thought everyone was away."

He rubbed his jaw. "Frank might be able to do it, but he's only been out once on his own and it's a big group. They come back every year."

Evan had worked for years to build his lodge's reputation to the point where he was booked every summer. But one bad trip with an inexperienced guide or, worse, an accident, and his business was toast.

"You *have* to take them."

"Maybe you should stay at your parents' or Lauren's."

I considered the idea for a moment, then said, "I don't want to tell Dad about the call yet, not until we know more. He'll just take over and stress me out. And I don't want to worry Lauren either. Greg's at camp, so I wouldn't be any safer over there. She's got kids to think about too."

Evan still looked unsure, but he said, "Okay, I'll put the shotgun under the bed and a baseball bat by the front door. Make sure you lock up every night, and take your cell if you go for a walk—"

"Baby, I'm not stupid. I'm going to be careful until the police figure out what's going on."

Evan ran a warm hand up my thigh. "I'm here to protect you tonight. . . ."

I raised an eyebrow. "Trying to distract me?"

"Maybe." He smiled.

I shook my head. "I have too much on my mind right now."

Evan pounced on me, growling into my neck. "Let me help with that." As he tried to kiss me I moved my face to the side, but he held my head in place by the back of my hair, teasing my mouth with his. My thoughts started to settle and my body began to relax. I focused on the feel of his shoulder muscles flexing under my hand. Of our mouths open, tongues playing. I unzipped his jeans and used my foot to drag them down. We laughed as they caught on his ankles, but he kicked them free. He hooked his hand into my pajama bottoms and peeled them off, giving my ass a quick smack that earned him a fake yelp. I lightly punched his shoulder. We kissed for a few minutes.

Then the phone rang.

Into my neck Evan said, "Leave it." And I did, but as I nuzzled his ear and grabbed at his butt, my mind was busy. Was it the Campsite Killer? The police? Did Julia call? Evan stopped kissing my collarbone and rested on me for a moment. I could feel his heart beating fast. He leaned up on his elbows and gave me a slow kiss, then said, "Go see who called." I made denial noises. He gave me a look as he sat up and reached for his pants. "I know it's killing you."

I gave him a sheepish smile, then dashed to the kitchen.

It was just Lauren, calling to chat about the boys, but for the rest of the weekend we both jumped every time the phone rang. Evan left Monday morning, but not until he lectured me on safety again. That afternoon I got a call from a private number. My body tense, I waited until it went to voice mail. Staff Sergeant Dubois wanted me to call back as soon as possible.

Staff Sergeant Mark Dubois turned out to be extremely tall—at least six foot four—and genial, despite his intimidating height and deep voice.

"Hi, Sara. Thanks for coming in." He sat behind an enormous L-shaped desk and waved me into the seat in front. "Have you received any more strange calls?"

I shook my head. "But I saw my birth mother on Friday and she said the earrings the Campsite Killer took were pearls. They were a grad gift from her mother."

The sergeant said, "Hmm . . . ," then clicked his tongue against his teeth. "We'd like to interview you, but this time we're going to audio- and videotape it. Is that all right?"

"I guess."

The sergeant led me down the hallway and into another room. This one was friendlier, with an overstuffed sofa, a lamp, and a painting of a seascape on the wall. There was also a camera in the upper corner. I settled at one end of the couch and the sergeant sat at the other, throwing a long arm up to rest on the back.

The questions were basically the same as the policewoman asked on Friday, but his tone was pleasant—conversational— and I opened up more. I even told him about my last visit with Julia and her emotional reaction.

"Good job, Sara," he said with a smile after I was done.

"This is going to be a big help to us." His face turned serious. "But I'm afraid we need to tap your phone and—"

"So you *do* think it was him?" I cringed at the desperate tone in my voice.

"We don't know yet, but the Campsite Killer is a high-priority case and we need to take every lead seriously. Until we can confirm it was just a prank, our first concern is your safety. We'll have a DVERS installed in your house as soon as possible."

"A what?"

"Domestic Violence Emergency Response System. It's an alarm system we use when we feel the victim's at risk."

I'm a victim now.

"The private investigator you hired is a retired policeman, but we haven't been able to locate him yet for an interview. We'd prefer you not have any contact with him about this case. In the next couple of days, two members of the Serious Crimes Unit in Vancouver will come over to the island and talk to you."

"Why can't Nanaimo just deal with it?"

"The Serious Crimes Unit has more members and greater resources. The suspect is potentially responsible for some horrific crimes. If that's who's calling you, then obviously we'd like to apprehend him, but we need to make sure we don't jeopardize you or your family while we're doing it."

Fear shot down my legs. "Should I send my daughter somewhere?"

"He hasn't made any direct threats and we try not to

separate families, but I suggest you go over some basic safety rules with her. Your husband's away right now?"

"Fiancé—we're getting married in September. He already knows about the call, but should I tell my family?"

"It's very important you not discuss this with anyone—including family—and your fiancé also needs to keep it to himself. We can't risk a leak to the media and the suspect finding out about the investigation."

"But what if my family's in danger too?"

"At this point he hasn't indicated he wants to harm anyone. If there's a threat, we'll take the appropriate measures. Someone will be at your house tomorrow morning to tap your phone, and ADT will wire it for the alarm. In the meantime, if he calls, don't answer, and contact me immediately." He handed me his card. "Do you have any questions?"

"I guess not. It's all just so . . . surreal."

He stood up and gave my shoulder a quick squeeze.

"You did the right thing by talking to us."

I nodded like I believed him.

That night, while Ally played outside with Moose, I kept watch through the sliding glass door as I peeled carrots and listened to the TV playing behind me. When the local news came on, I almost cut myself. Sure enough, their lead story was Karen Christianson. They showed shots of the university—bunnies nibbling grass on the front lawn, noisy students in the cafeteria, a classroom door—while a newscaster said a professor had been identified as Karen Christianson, the Campsite Killer's only surviving victim. They didn't give my name, just said that Karen was rumored to have a daughter living in Nanaimo who couldn't be reached for comment. The newscaster's closing line was delivered in a somber voice. "As the days grow warmer, we can't help but wonder where the Campsite Killer is now, and where he'll be this summer." That's when I turned the TV off.

When Ally came back inside I told her we were going to play a game of "let's pretend" and went over our safety rules. Evan and I had done this with her before, but this time every little detail mattered. Ally soon tired of the game, but I made her go over everything twice. What our code word is: Moose. That she's not to go anywhere with an adult who doesn't know it. What number on the phone is programmed to dial 911, what things the operator might ask, especially our address. And a new rule: she's not to answer any phone, or open the door until an adult looks first. My heart stopped every time she forgot something.

When I snapped at her for answering the phone twenty minutes later, which turned out to be Lauren, she shut herself in her room and refused to talk to me. I made pancakes for dinner and wrote *I'm sorry* in blueberries. She got over it, but I still felt bad dropping her off at school this morning.

When I got home the police were waiting to tap my landline, and ADT arrived soon after to wire the house. They also showed me how to use the small personal alarm, which I'm supposed to wear around my neck. I don't want Ally to ask about it, so I carry it in my purse. After everyone cleared out I stared at the alarm and my now-tapped phone, trying not to panic. How long is this going to last? I can't even have a private conversation with Evan anymore—

The phone rang.

Just go look. It's probably not even him.

It rang again.

It might be the police.

Evan's cell number. I let my breath out in a rush.

He said, "Hi, baby, I—" then broke off. Dead air. When I called back I got voice mail. Great, another dropped call. I slammed down the receiver. When it rang again I almost picked it right up, but at the last minute I noticed the call display. It was a pay phone. I held my breath and waited for it to stop ringing. He called back five times.

This time I phoned the police right away, Nadine, but the man didn't leave a message, so we aren't any further ahead. Sergeant Dubois said I still shouldn't answer the calls until I talk to the Serious Crimes Unit people, and they can't be on the island until tomorrow. They want me to come in first thing and give a DNA sample. That's why I resched-uled our appointment for this afternoon. Well, that and because I can't think straight.

I tried some of the techniques you suggested: going for a run, writing in a journal, meditating, humming to release the tight feeling in my throat—I even tried humming *while* meditating. The worst part about all of this is that I can't tell my family, can't talk to Lauren. You know me—I dump everything out, *then* figure out what to do. Thank God for

Evan. We talked last night and he's being super supportive, but I miss him so much. When he's around I feel more focused, settled, like everything's going to be okay.

Today Julia's lawyer released a statement that she wasn't Karen Christianson and had never given a child up for adoption. Anyone claiming otherwise would be faced with legal action. This morning after I dropped Ally off at school a reporter and a cameraman were waiting in my driveway. Taking my dad's advice, I told them the statement was true, neither Julia Laroche nor Karen Christianson was my birth mother, and I'd sue if they printed anything about me or my family. Then I closed the door in their faces.

I understand why Julia lied—she's trying to protect herself. In my case I'm trying to protect Ally, but it was weird reading that Julia denied she'd had me. It made me feel like I don't exist or something. But that's not such a bad thing right now. I'm not looking forward to the DNA test. If it matches with the DNA they have on file from the crime scenes, then all of this will be real. I keep hoping it won't match. Maybe there was a mix-up with the adoption records and I'm not Julia's daughter after all. I could only be so lucky.

SESSION SIX

I can't remember the last time I picked up a tool. I snapped at Lauren the other day, and all she asked was whether I'd sent out invitations yet. But if I even *think* about making a guest list, my mind blanks.

When I tried to talk to Evan about it he said we might want to consider postponing the wedding until things settle down. You can imagine how well that went over. He does have a point—the timing is a nightmare—but I waited my whole life to feel the way I do when I'm with Evan. I didn't know men like him even existed. He's so nurturing, bringing me food when I'm in my workshop, pouring baths when I have a headache, yet he's strong enough to handle my intensity. And we're both homebodies, preferring to watch movies on our couch rather than go out in the evening. We rarely fight, but when we do we work it out fast. He's so good and kind that it makes me want to be the same way.

I can't stand the idea of waiting to marry him. The way things are going lately, though? I may not have a choice.

Last Wednesday morning I headed straight to the police station. My hands gripped the wheel as I sat in the parking lot for a couple of minutes. *It's going to be okay, whatever I find out, I can handle it.*

Inside I gave some blood for a DNA sample, then Sergeant Dubois took me back to the room with the couch to wait for the Serious Crimes people. Just as I sat down there was a knock on the door and a man and woman entered.

I expected haggard-looking older men in black suits and sunglasses, but the woman was somewhere in her forties and dressed in loose-fitting, navy dress pants, a plain white blouse, and a brown, blazer-style leather jacket. Her short dirty-blond hair was streaked by the sun and her skin glowed with a tan. The man was younger, maybe late thirties, wearing stylish black pants and a black dress shirt with the sleeves rolled up, revealing Asian symbols tattooed down both forearms. His olive skin tone, shaved head, and hooded eyes gave him a Mediterranean look. When he flashed a friendly smile I caught a dimple—and the impression he didn't lack for female attention.

Sergeant Dubois said, "Sara, I'm going. I'll leave you to Staff Sergeant McBride and Corporal Reynolds," then left the room. The woman sat at the other end of the couch while the man pulled up a chair in front of me.

"So you're from the Serious Crimes Unit in Vancouver?" I said.

He nodded. "We came over last night." I couldn't place his accent, maybe somewhere on the East Coast. He handed me his card and I saw he was Corporal B. Reynolds. So the woman was the sergeant. I was impressed.

She handed me her card. "You can just call me Sandy." She motioned to the corporal. "And this is Billy."

"Bill," he said, shaking a fist at Sandy.

She laughed. "I'm older and wiser, that means I can call you whatever I want." I smiled, enjoying their banter. Sandy turned to me. "Can we get you a coffee or water, Sara?"

"I'm good. I'll just need to pee a million times."

Sandy shook her head and said, "Isn't it annoying? I made Billy stop twice on the way here." He nodded and rolled his eyes.

I said, "It got worse after I had my daughter. Do you have children?"

"Just a dog."

Billy snorted. "Tyson's not a dog. He's a human in a Rottweiler suit."

Sandy laughed. "He's a handful." She met my eyes. "And I'm sure Ally keeps you busy." For a moment I was surprised they knew Ally's name, then I realized they probably knew everything about me. My bubble popped. This wasn't a social call. These people were here to catch a serial killer.

Billy had a thick file in his hands and started to flip through it. He dropped it, and I moved to help him gather the papers, then recoiled when I saw a photo of a woman's pale and bruised face.

"Oh, my God, is that . . ." I looked at Sandy. She was watching beside me but made no comment. I glanced back at Billy, who was casually placing photos back in the file.

"Sorry about that," he said. I sat back in my chair and stared hard at him, wondering if he'd dropped it on purpose, but he looked genuinely apologetic.

Sandy said, "This must be very overwhelming for you."

"It's pretty crazy." They were both watching me now, so I added, "It's not quite the situation I was hoping for when I decided to find my birth mother."

Sandy's eyes were sympathetic, but her fingers tapped on her knees.

Billy said, "Have you heard from him again?" He leaned forward and his biceps bulged as he rested his elbows on his chair. The lamp in the corner cast a glow on the right side of his face and his eyes looked almost black in the dim light. I pressed farther into the couch, fiddling with my engagement ring.

Sandy cleared her throat.

I said, "Just the calls I got Monday night. I already told Sergeant Dubois about them—I gave him the phone numbers."

Billy looked at Sandy, then back at the file in his hands. It made me nervous, which made me mad.

I said, "I didn't answer because Sergeant Dubois said you guys were going to coach me on what to say, but the number's still on the call display if you want to check."

"You handled it perfectly." Sandy's voice was calm. "The

next time he calls we'd like you to answer. Let him guide the conversation, but if there's an opening, try to see if he'll give you any information about the earrings, the victims, where he's calling from, anything like that. Even small details can help us determine whether he's actually the Campsite Killer. But if he becomes agitated, change the subject."

"What if it's really him?"

Sandy said, "Then you might be able to establish a relationship with him and—"

"You want me to *keep* talking to him?" My voice rose in panic.

Billy said, "Let's just take this one step at a time. We're not going to ask you to do anything you don't want to do."

Sandy said, "That's right, for now we just need to know who this person is and why he's calling."

My body relaxed, slightly. "Do you have any idea where he might be?"

Billy said, "The calls have been coming from the Kamloops area, but the pay phones he used were in remote locations and wiped clean, so he's being careful." I was relieved to hear he was an hour and a half ferry trip and a few hours' drive from my home.

"Billy and I are staying in town," Sandy said. "We'll give you our cell numbers so you can call us the minute you hear from him—any time of day."

We were all quiet for a moment, then I said in a hushed voice, "Summer's coming. Do you think he's still, you know . . . active?"

Sandy said, "We never know when he'll hit, but as long

as he's out there it's always a possibility. That's why this lead is so important."

"You have a lead?" They stared at me. "Oh, you mean me." My face was hot.

"The profiles show someone familiar with the woods," Billy said. "He's cunning and used to living by his wits, probably a loner. Someone who spends a lot of time hunting." I shuddered as an image of a terrified woman running through the woods flashed in my mind. Billy continued, "The description we got from Julia yesterday—"

"You saw Julia?"

Sandy said, "We interviewed her in Victoria. Based on her original description the suspect was probably in his late teens or early twenties at the time of her attack. He'd be in his early to midfifties now. Methods have changed in the last few years, so we had her sit down again with a police artist from the Behavioral Science Unit."

Billy handed me a sheet of paper. "This is a composite sketch of how the suspect might look today."

I sucked in my breath. No wonder Julia freaked out at the sight of me. Even in this rough drawing I could see the resemblance—same cat eyes, left eyebrow that arched higher than the right, Nordic bone structure.

I stared down at the drawing. "His hair . . ."

Sandy said, "Julia described it as a deep, reddish-brown color . . . and wavy." I looked up just as her gaze flicked to my hair. My stomach rolled. Billy took the sketch from me as Sandy said, "Julia was attacked in the middle of July, but another woman was killed in Prince Rupert later that August.

This is the only time he hit twice in the same summer, so it was probably because he failed with Julia. He's very careful and leaves virtually no evidence. That's why we need you to play along with this caller, so we can find out if he's really the Campsite Killer. It's all we have to go on right now."

I looked back and forth between Billy and Sandy. Their gazes were steady on mine. I took a deep breath, and then nodded reluctantly.

"Okay, I'll try."

As soon as I left the station I phoned Evan. He didn't answer his cell, so I left him a miss-you-and-need-you message. I wasn't ready to go home and face the possibility of another phone call from my supposed father, so I picked up a vanilla latte and walked along the seawall—obsessing about everything Sandy and Billy had said. We wouldn't see the results on the DNA test for another three to six weeks, but I got the feeling the police were sure I was the Campsite Killer's daughter.

Before I left them I'd asked about the other cases, what kind of evidence they had, but they wouldn't give me details—not even on Julia's. They said it was better I didn't know too much so I wouldn't accidentally reveal anything. They also told me to call them right away if I saw anyone who looked suspicious. Problem was, now everyone did.

When I'm out for a walk I generally stop and talk to anyone and everyone, but now I avoided eye contact and watched middle-aged men warily. Was it him? What about that tall man under the tree? Was that man on the bench staring at me?

It was sunny for a change, but still cool for the middle of April, and the wind off the ocean was biting. After I walked the seawall twice, my cheeks stung and my hands felt like ice cubes. Evan hadn't called back yet and I couldn't avoid home any longer—Moose needed out and I had a ton of things to do before I picked Ally up from school. I took a deep breath and headed to the Cherokee. If he called I was just going to have to deal with it.

But nothing happened for the rest of the week. By Friday evening I was starting to wonder if the call was a hoax after all. Sandy or Billy checked in every day, their voices more falsely casual with each call, and I wondered if they thought I'd made it up. The initial flurry of calls from reporters died down, and when I checked online there were no new comments on any of the blogs. A few people asked Evan and Lauren about it, but they told them it was just a rumor. No one dared ask me. But I caught a few odd looks from parents at school when I dropped Ally off. I'm sure people are still gossiping, which drives me nuts, but as long as it doesn't get back to Ally, I can deal with it. I talked to Dad, and the private investigator hadn't called him back either. He was still talking about suing that Web site, but it sounded like he was losing interest as everything died down and his lawyer bill went up.

It was all going away. I'd never been more relieved.

———

By Saturday morning I was missing Evan like crazy and couldn't wait for him to come home Monday. While Ally played over at Meghan's, I hit my shop for a few hours and got more done than I had in a week. Still riding the high of getting so much accomplished, I took a quick shower before I picked up Ally.

While I soaped sawdust out of my hair, I made mental plans for the rest of the day. Maybe we'd tie-dye some T-shirts and go to a movie later. We hadn't had a girl's night for a while. When I was single we used to get dressed up and go on dates together every weekend. As much as I loved my life now, I missed our special times. After she was asleep I could make a rough guest list for Evan to go over. How long had it been since *we'd* done anything special together? While I pulled on some jeans and one of Evan's T-shirts, stopping to sniff for any lingering traces of his scent, I daydreamed about a candlelight picnic, then a bubble bath for two, followed by—

The doorbell rang.

I peeked through the side blinds and spotted a delivery truck. The name painted on the side was a local company, but I kept one hand gripped on the baseball bat Evan had tucked in the corner and cracked the door.

A short man with black hair and droopy jowls stood on the steps, a small box in one hand and a clipboard in the other.

"Sara Gallagher?" I nodded. He thrust the clipboard toward me. "Please sign at the bottom."

I rested the baseball bat on the wall behind the door, signed the clipboard, and took the box. As he started backing down the driveway I glanced at the return address.

Hansel and Gretel Antiques
4589 Lonesome Way
Williams Lake BC

It was addressed to my business, Better Than Before, Furniture Refinishing and Antique Restoration, but I didn't recognize the other store. In the kitchen, I cut the tape down the center of the package. As I rummaged through the foam kernels my hands touched something square. I pulled out a blue velvet box and opened it. Resting on satin was a beautiful pair of—

Pearl earrings, they were *pink* pearl earrings.

I dropped the box.

Sandy answered on the first ring.

"I think he just sent me her earrings. . . ." I struggled to get my breath. "But there's no note or—"

"He *sent* you something?" Sandy's voice was too loud, then she caught herself and it smoothed out. "Just leave everything as is—don't touch anything, we're on the way."

I stared at the box on the counter, my entire body shaking.

"The address said it's from Hansel and Gretel Antiques."

"Do you recognize the company?"

"No, but 'Hansel and Gretel' was one of Ally's favorite stories." My mind filled again with an image of a woman running for her life. "The children, they were lost in the woods."

Sandy paused for a moment, then said, "Just hang in there, Sara, we're on our way. Are you home alone?"

"I'm supposed to get Ally. She's at her friend's, and I was just going to—"

"Call and arrange for her to stay longer, we'll be there in a few minutes."

Ten minutes later tires crunched on gravel. I peeked out the front window—I'd been lurking in the living room, as far from the box as I could get—and watched as a black Chevy Tahoe pulled up, with Billy at the wheel. It was barely parked before Sandy climbed out. Even though it was cloudy, they were both wearing sunglasses.

I whipped open the front door. "You have to get that box out of here."

Billy said, "We'll be as quick as we can."

Inside the house, they pulled on gloves and examined the box and the earrings while I sat at the table. Moose rested his round bottom on my feet, growling at the police under his breath.

My cell phone rang on the table. Sandy and Billy turned and looked at me.

"It's probably Evan." I picked it up and checked the

call display, then jumped to my feet. "I think it's *him*." I held the phone out like I was hoping one of them would answer.

Sandy's voice was clipped. "Is it the same number as before?"

"I don't think so. But the prefix looks the same—I don't know how he got my cell number."

The ringing stopped.

I said, "What do we—"

Sandy grabbed the phone out of my hand and checked the call display.

"Pen?"

"Drawer behind you."

She yanked open the drawer, found a pen and paper, and scribbled something down. She handed Billy my cell, then went into the other room with her phone. She was talking quickly into it, but I couldn't hear the words. Her hand moved in the air in rapid jerks.

I sat back down with a thud and stared at Billy. "It's him. I know it."

Now Billy checked the call display on my cell. "Let's just wait and see if he calls back."

"What if he senses you're here and flips out and—"

"One step at a time. Looks like he might've called from a cell this time, so right now Sandy's contacting a service provider. Hopefully, they'll be able to triangulate the call."

"Triangulate?"

"If he's in a populated area near multiple cell phone towers we can narrow down his location to within a two-hundred-meter radius, about the length of two football fields. But if he's in a remote area where there's only one tower, or on the move, that zone could be several miles. If he calls back, just take a deep breath, pretend we aren't here, and let him do the talking. It's going to be fine. You can handle this, Sara."

Sandy moved farther into the living room. Her voice sounded angry.

I said, "Those are Julia's earrings. They have silver leaves, just like she said. He took them from her when he—" I covered my mouth with one hand.

Billy said, "You okay, Sara?"

I shook my head.

"Take a couple of really big breaths in through your nose, try to imagine the air going deep into your lungs, then blow out through your mouth until there's nothing left."

"I know how to *breathe*, Billy. What if the earrings have blood on them and—"

"Take a deep breath." His voice was firm.

I took a quick one. "I'm just saying he might have ripped them from her and—"

"Right now your body is going into fight-or-flight. You need to calm down or nothing I say will register. Put your hand on your chest and focus on it lifting as you breathe. Don't think about anything but your hand. It will help, Sara."

"Fine." I did as he suggested, holding his gaze while my chest rose and fell, my eyes conveying *I'm only doing this because you're making me.*

He smiled and motioned for me to do it again. Finally he said, "I was right, wasn't I?"

I actually did feel a lot better, but I said, "Just give me a minute." In the downstairs bathroom I splashed cold water on my face. Then I stared in the mirror at my watering eyes and flushed face, at my hair. His hair. I wanted to shave it all off.

Sandy and Billy were waiting in the kitchen. Sandy paced, Billy leaned against the counter with Moose in his arms. Moose squirmed at the sight of me and Billy let him down, saying, "All right, all right."

Sandy smiled. "Feel better?" But the smile didn't reach her eyes and her body radiated tension.

The earrings were in a plastic bag on the counter beside Billy. So was the box.

Evidence.

Billy got me a glass from the dish tray and ran me some water. As he handed it to me I said, "Thanks."

He nodded and crossed his arms across his chest and leaned back against the counter. Sandy's phone rang again and she picked it up.

"What?" Her face flushed as she said into the phone, "That's not fucking good enough." She frowned as she listened, running her hand through her hair until it was sticking up.

With my arms wrapped around my body, I leaned against the counter near Billy.

"I can't believe this is happening."

Billy said, "It's a lot to take in."

"Ya think?"

Sandy flashed us a look, then stalked off to the living room.

Billy lowered his voice and said, "We'll also have someone check into the depot the package was sent from. Now that we know he has your cell number, we'll tap it as well. Someone will be monitoring any calls to your landline or cell twenty-four hours a day."

As Billy filled me in on the process, giving me lots of details and facts, my mind began to settle and I felt my confidence come back. Billy was right, I could handle this. Then my cell rang.

Billy grabbed the phone. Sandy closed hers and ran back.

Billy said, "Same number." Sandy nodded and Billy handed the phone to me.

Sandy said, "Okay, Sara. You can answer it now." But I couldn't.

It continued to ring. They stared at me.

Sandy raised her voice. "*Answer* the phone."

Billy said, "It's okay, Sara, just like we talked about. You've got it in the bag, you're ready to go."

I looked down at the phone in my hand. Every ring clamored in my head. All I had to do was pick it up. Pick it up. Pick—

The ringing stopped.

Sandy said, "Shit! We lost him."

Billy said, "Sandy, let's just give her a moment, okay? He'll call back."

"If he doesn't, we lost our only chance to stop him."

"I'm sorry. I just—I panicked."

Sandy looked like she was forcing herself to sound patient. "That's all right, Sara, most likely he'll call back." She tried to smile, but I was sure she wanted to slap me. She held out her hand for the phone. "When he calls I'll pretend to be you."

Billy said, "Do you think that's a good idea, Sandy? He's heard her voice." Sandy glared at him, but he just said, "Don't worry, you'll get your chance to rip him apart. When we catch him I'll leave you alone in the room with him for a couple of hours."

To my surprise, Sandy started to laugh, then pretended to throw her phone at Billy, which made me laugh. The tension faded from the room and I leaned back against the counter. It was okay. If we could still laugh, it was okay.

Billy turned to me. "Sara, I know you're scared. But I also know you can do it, or we wouldn't ask. You just have to get over the initial fear—once you start talking you'll do great. Got any coffee?"

Just as I pointed to the stainless-steel flask behind them on the counter, the cell rang. They spun around.

"Remember, you can do this." Billy's voice was low and steady and rang with conviction. "Now pick up the phone!"

I took a deep breath and answered my father's call.

"Hello?"

"Hi, Sara. How are you?" He sounded excited—eager.

"Why do you keep calling me?" My body began to vibrate and I sat down at the kitchen table. Sandy and Billy eased themselves into chairs across from me.

"Because I'm your dad."

"I *have* a dad."

He was silent. Sandy's hand balled on the table like it was taking all her strength not to rip the phone from my hand.

"You can call me John for now."

I didn't say anything.

He said, "You got my present?"

"Yes. How did you get this number?"

"It was on the Internet." Of course, my business was listed on a Web site directory. That must've been how he found me in the first place. Too late I remembered Evan's warning, *You sure you want your cell number on there?*

"Do you like the earrings?"

"Where did you get them from?" I knew I sounded angry, but I couldn't stop the emotion from leaking into my voice. I glanced at Billy and he mouthed, *Keep going*. I didn't look at Sandy.

John said, "Karen gave them to me." I closed my eyes against the image his words created. He said something else, but it was drowned out by a roar from a vehicle going by.

He said, "Sorry about the background noise. I'm in my truck."

"Where are you?"

He paused for a moment, then said, "It won't work like that, Sara. I know you've probably called the cops and your landline's tapped. But I won't reveal anything they can use. Even if they trace this call, I know the Interior like the back of my hand. They'll never find me."

I stared at the two cops sitting at the table with me. Did he really know I'd called them or was he just bluffing? My pulse beat loud in my ear. I had to answer fast. "I didn't tell anyone. I thought it was just a prank."

He paused for a moment, then said, "I guess you probably got a few prank calls. Your family must be upset. Is that why you told the papers Karen Christianson wasn't really your mother?"

My stomach muscles tightened at the intimate tone in his voice, his casual way of speaking about my family. Then I realized I'd found my way out.

"She's *not* my mother. It was just a rumor someone started. I told you—"

"I saw your Facebook photo. You're my daughter."

My *Facebook* photo. How many others did he see? Did he know about Ally? My mind scrambled, trying to remember my profile settings.

He said, "And I saw Julia's photo in the paper. I know she's Karen Christianson. She hit me in the head." The last sentence he said with grudging respect.

"Is that what this is about? You're trying to find her?"

"I have no interest in her anymore."

"Then what do you *want*?"

"I have to talk to you whenever I have the urge. It's the only way I might be able to stop."

"What . . . what will you stop?"

"Hurting people."

I sucked in my breath as my thoughts scattered.

He said, "I have to go now. We'll talk more next time—keep your phone with you."

"I can't always answer when you—"

"You have to answer."

"But I may not be able to. Sometimes I'm busy and—"

"If you don't answer, then I'll have to do something else."

"What do you mean?"

"I'll have to find *someone*."

"No! No, don't do that. I'll keep my phone on—"

"I'm not bad, Sara. You'll see." He hung up.

He hasn't called since. I know I should be happy—no news is good news, right? But I walk around in a constant state of anxiety. The first thing I did was check Facebook. Thankfully he could only see my profile picture because the rest was set to private, but I still removed everything. Billy and Sandy stayed until I'd calmed down, or as calm as I could be given what had just happened, and we went over what to do if he calls again. They want me to continue denying I told the police anything. Billy said the more confident John is, the more likely he'll make a mistake. But I think he has good reason to feel confident.

The police weren't able to triangulate the call because he'd made it from somewhere west of Williams Lake and they could only get a signal from one tower. It took almost an hour for the local police to get there, and by then he could've been anywhere. All they could do was patrol the main highway and back roads, stopping vehicles, asking homeowners if they'd seen any strangers in the area. But without a vehicle description they don't have much to go on. He was also using a stolen phone, which sent them on another wild goose chase as they tried to track down the owner.

I've traveled through BC and I know the more populated towns are in the southern part of the Interior, the Okanagan region, but when you're in the Central and Northern Interior, most of the towns are small. They're also hours apart, with nothing but mountains and valleys surrounding them. You don't have to drive far to disappear into the wilderness. And if the remoteness of the terrain wasn't bad enough, Billy said there can be delays getting information from the service provider, and sometimes the signal even pings off the wrong tower. I asked about GPS, but apparently he can just turn that feature off.

Billy thinks John knew exactly how long it would take for the police to get to the area. Even the pay phones he'd called me from were all remote locations like old campsites and rest areas, which meant no witnesses or cameras. They also think he makes sure there are multiple routes to the location, so he's never fenced in. The police still seem sure they'll find him, but I'm having some serious doubts. They don't think he realizes they can tap my cell, but he said it himself, it doesn't matter what I told them or if they traced the call, he knows the Interior like the back of his hand.

He's been getting away with this for over thirty *years*. What's going to stop him now?

When I told Evan what happened he freaked out and wanted me to tell the cops I wouldn't do it. I told him they thought I was their only chance to find him, and if they didn't he'd keep killing. Finally we agreed I'd take it one day at a time. He came home on Monday—God, I was happy to see him—but I still couldn't relax. We finally sat down and did the guest list, but then Billy called to see how I was doing. I left the table so I could talk to him out in my shop and when I came back in Evan said, "One of your boyfriends?"

"Ha, ha. It was that cop I met the other day. Sorry for taking so long—we were talking about John."

"No worries."

But I *was* worried. I couldn't stop thinking about what I should say next time John called. We went for a long walk with Ally and Moose that night and rented a comedy, but I couldn't tell you one thing that happened in that movie.

Evan said he hates seeing me so scared and upset, but I can't help it. While I'm making dinner for Ally, while I'm tucking her in at night, while we're brushing our teeth in the morning, all I'm thinking about is whether the police will catch John before he kills someone.

I've read every article on his victims. I know about Samantha, the pretty blond nineteen-year-old who was camping in a provincial park with her boyfriend. He was shot twice in the back as he tried to escape. They found Samantha's body a couple of miles into the park. Her arm was broken in three places from a fall, and as she fled through the woods something jabbed straight through her cheek. The Campsite Killer covered her face with her Nike T-shirt, then raped and strangled her. I used to have the same shirt.

I know about Erin, the brunette softball player who decided to go camping by herself and was found two weeks later by someone's dog—he brought her hand back to the campfire where his owners were roasting marshmallows. The police had to use dental records to identify what was left after the animals got to her.

Sleep has become my nighttime nemesis. I wander the house or watch late-night TV while the clock ticks. I have baths, showers, drink warm milk, and lie on Ally's bed stroking her curls while she sleeps. If Evan's home I curve my body around his, try to match my breathing with his, and daydream about how beautiful our wedding will be. Nothing helps.

When I'm not reading about John online, I'm researching serial killers: Ed Kemper, Ted Bundy, Albert Fish, the Green River Killer, BTK, the Hillside Stranglers, the Zodiac Killer, Canada's Robert Pickton and Clifford Olson, and too many more. I study their patterns, their triggers, their victims, every detail of their horrific crimes. That's in addition to the books by FBI profilers and psychologists.

I compare theories and arguments—psychopath, mental defect, chemical imbalance, dysfunctional childhood? I take pages and pages of notes and when I finally do fall into an exhausted sleep, I have nightmares of women leaping off diving boards onto pavement or running through fields of broken glass. I hear their screams. I hear them beg, but they're begging me to stop chasing them. In the dreams they're running away from *me*.

SESSION SEVEN

It was my birthday on Friday, but I wasn't in the mood to celebrate. Evan tried so hard to cheer me up. He'd obviously taken Ally shopping—she gave me a beautiful green cashmere cardigan—and he spoiled me with a new mountain bike. I made sure to exclaim over their gifts, forced down three pieces of the pizza they made, and laughed in all the right places at the movie we rented. But my head was filled with thoughts of Julia.

Growing up I often wondered on my birthday what my real mother was doing, if she even remembered the date. Now I wondered if all these years I'd been celebrating, Julia had been tortured with memories of me forcing my way out of her body, of John forcing his way in.

When I first held Ally in my arms after she was born, I couldn't imagine ever letting her go. I'd been scared I wouldn't be a good mother, would screw it up somehow, but as soon as her little fingers grabbed mine, I fell head over heels. I also became fiercely protective, watching carefully if anyone held her, taking her back if she fussed. It was hard being a single mom—money was tight and I had to carry Ally in a Snuggie on my back when I worked in my shop—but I loved that it was just her and me against the world. Before Ally, I never felt like I had roots, and in my darkest depressions I thought it wouldn't matter if I died, no one would miss me. But when I had her I finally had someone who loved me unconditionally, who *needed* me.

She's growing up so fast—gone are the days when she'd play imaginary fairy games with me like wiz-a-boo and pansy ears. I don't want to miss one moment of her life. I don't want to be distracted when she tells me stories about her teacher, Mrs. Holly, whom she idolizes because she has straight, long blond hair and can tap-dance, or about a bug Moose just ate, or when she sings all the songs from *Hannah Montana*. I don't want to rush her to bed at night or out of the house in the morning. But I'm so afraid John will call and hear her in the background.

We managed to stop the media spread because nothing was confirmed, and was in fact denied, but rumors are still floating around. Hopefully the gossip will fade before it gets to Ally or any of her friends. I've started casually asking how things are going at school. Nothing seems to have changed. But what if it comes up later, like when she's a teen? And if the truth ever does get out, how would people treat Ally once they knew who her grandfather was? Would they be afraid of her?

I watch her play with other kids or roughhouse with

Moose, and all the things that just seemed like part of her personality before frighten me now. The way she gets so angry sometimes that her face flushes and her hands ball. The way she kicks or slaps or bites when she's frustrated or overtired. Is it just part of her spirit, a normal six-year-old learning to cope with her emotions, or something more serious?

I find myself looking in the mirror, studying my features, thinking about the man who shares them. Wondering what else we share. Then this morning I realized why I keep dreaming of women running away from me, why studying those serial killers freaks me out so much. When I read about them, I see *my* traits. Serial killers have grandiose fantasies—my whole life I've daydreamed and fantasized. They're obsessive-compulsive—when I'm into something, the rest of the world disappears. They have tempers, mood swings, depressions—check, check, check. They also tend to be solitary, and I've always been a loner, preferring to focus on Ally and work. I've never wanted to kill anyone, and as far as I know murder isn't hereditary, but sometimes when I get really angry, I've broken things, pushed or shoved people, thrown objects, had fantasies about driving my car straight into a wall, of hurting myself. What would it take to turn that rage outward?

Of course, it's easy for me to zero in on my negatives and heap them all on John's genetic doorstep. But like you just pointed out, how do I know those traits didn't come from growing up adopted, or even from Julia? And I probably won't know because she'll never let me close enough to find out. Billy said she confirmed the earrings were hers. Knowing how much the sight of them messed me up, I can only imagine how she felt. I wish I could talk to her. I even picked up the phone once, but this time I dropped it.

Evan left Saturday morning. He was excited because he has a big fishing charter coming up from the States, but he was also concerned about leaving me like this. He told me to stop reading books about serial killers, but there's no way I can just stop researching. I have to find something, some insight or clue, that might help stop John.

But lately I just feel tired. Not sleepy tired, wired-up and strung-out tired. Most evenings I just pace from window to window waiting for the phone to ring. That's where I was when John finally called again on Monday: standing at my bedroom window upstairs, watching Moose and Ally chase each other in the yard below, thinking how happy they looked, remembering how happy I used to be.

My cell rang in my pocket. I didn't recognize the number, but I knew it was him.

"Hi, Sara." His voice was cheerful.

"John." My mouth went dry and my chest tightened. The police had my cell tapped now, but I didn't feel any safer.

We were both silent for a moment, then he said, "So . . ." He cleared his throat. "Your business, do you like making furniture?"

"I *refinish* furniture, I don't make it." Sandy told me to be friendlier next time he called, but I was having a hard time even being polite. My body tensed as I heard Ally down in the kitchen.

Please, please, just stay there.

He said, "I bet you could make stuff if you wanted to."

Ally was coming up the stairs, jabbering to Moose.

I moved toward my door. "I'm happy doing what I do."

Ally was at the entrance to my room. "Mommy, Moose wants his dinner and—" I gestured for her to be quiet.

John said, "What's your favorite part?"

"Can we do crafts now?" I gave Ally a firm look and pointed back down the stairs, mouthing, *I'm on the phone.*

"But you *promised*—" I closed the door and locked it. On the other side, she began to slam her hands against the wood while she yelled, *"Mommy!"*

I covered the phone's speaker and sprinted to the farthest side of the room.

John said, "What's that racket?"

Crap, crap, crap.

"I meant to turn the TV off and accidentally turned it up."

Ally slapped the door again. I held my breath. Now they were both quiet.

Finally he said, "I asked what your favorite part is."

"I don't know. I just like working with my hands." There were lots of things I loved about woodworking, but I wasn't sharing any of them with him.

"I'm good with my hands too. Did you like building things when you were growing up?" No sounds from the hall. Where was Ally?

"I guess so. I used to steal my dad's tools."

Silence from both of them. I held my breath again, strained my ears. Finally a cupboard slammed in the kitchen. She was downstairs. I let out my breath and dropped my forehead onto my knees.

"I would have given you tools," he said. "It's not right that I didn't know I had a kid."

My anger flared. "I guess the circumstances of how I was conceived sort of took away that option."

He was silent.

"Why do you do it? Why do you hurt those people?"

No answer.

My blood roared in my ears, warning me I was going too far, but I couldn't stop.

"Are you angry? Do they remind you of someone, or—"

His voice was tight. "I *have* to do it."

"Nobody has to kill—"

"I don't like this." He was breathing fast into the phone. *Back off, back off NOW.*

"Okay, I just—"

"I'll call you tomorrow." And he was gone.

I called Billy right away. While we talked, I threw together some dinner for Ally and dumped food in a bowl for Moose. This time John called from north of Williams Lake and it took the police forty minutes to get there. They patrolled the area again: stopping vehicles, talking to locals, showing John's sketch at gas stations and stores, but so far no one has seen anything. I asked Billy how they were ever going to catch John if he keeps calling from rural locations and he said they have to just keep doing what they're doing and hope they eventually get a lead. They did find the private investigator, though—on a Caribbean cruise with his wife.

When I finally hung up the phone I went to find my daughter, who was slumped in front of the TV. I felt so bad for ignoring her I told her she could sleep in my bed that night, a treat that usually brings squeals of delight. But she was quiet as I tucked her in and read *Charlotte's Web*—Ally's only interested in a book if it has an animal in it. When she whispered something into Moose's ear, I stopped reading.

"What's wrong, Ally Cat?"

She whispered something else to Moose. He flicked his bat ears and looked at me with round, moist eyes.

"Do I have to tickle it out of Moose?" I held my hands out and pretended to go for him.

"Don't!" Her cat eyes glared.

"Then I guess you'll have to tell me."

I smiled and made a silly face, but she wouldn't look at me.

"You closed the door."

"You're right, I did." How was I going to explain this? "That wasn't very nice of Mommy. But I have a new client and he's very important. He's probably going to be calling a lot and I have to give him all my attention, so you need to be really quiet, okay?"

Her brow furrowed and her cheeks flushed. One of her feet began to kick under the blanket.

"You said we could do crafts."

"I know, sweetie. I'm sorry." I sighed, feeling bad for letting her down again and hating that John was the reason. "But it's like when I'm working in the shop or Evan goes to the lodge. We still love you, more than anything, but we have to take care of grown-up things sometimes." Now both feet were kicking. Moose stood up and walked to the end of the bed. Ally kicked at him under the blanket. A jolt of anger shot through me.

I held her leg in place with my hand. "Ally, stop it."

She yelled in my face, *"No!"*

"That's enough. You don't speak to—"

She kicked again. Moose yelped and fell off the side of the bed, landing on the floor with a thump.

"Ally!" I leaped out of bed.

Moose grunted and wriggled over to me when I knelt on the floor. I stroked his ears and turned to Ally.

"That is *not* okay. We don't hurt animals in this house."

Ally glared at me, her mouth mean and small.

I stood up. "Back to your bed—*right now*." I pointed to her room. She grabbed her book and held it up as though she were going to throw it at Moose.

"Don't you dare, Ally!"

A look I'd never seen before crossed her face—hatred.

"Ally, if you throw that book, you're going to be in big trouble."

We held gazes. Moose whined. She looked at him, then back at me. Her face was red and her eyes almost slits.

"I'm serious, Ally, if you—"

She threw the book as hard as she could. Moose dodged and the book slammed into the wall.

My blood surged with rage as I grabbed her wrist and hauled her out of bed. My hands gripping her shoulders, I yelled into her face.

"You never, ever, *ever* hurt an animal! *Do you hear me?*"

She stared at me, bottom lip out, defiant.

Still gripping her wrist, I dragged her to the door and down the hall to her room. I let go and pointed to her bed.

"I don't want to hear another thing out of you unless it's an apology."

She stomped into her room, slammed the door behind her.

I wanted to go in, wanted to explain, wanted to make it all better, wanted to give her holy hell and then some, but I didn't know what to say. It was the first time I'd been afraid of my daughter. It was the first time I'd been afraid of how angry I was at her.

Moose stayed in bed with me. I couldn't believe Ally had lashed out at him like that. He'd always been able to calm her quicker than I could. When I got him I was living on my own and wanted company while Ally was at preschool. He brought laughter to my day and protection at night, but best of all, the little meatball had a stabilizing effect on Ally. If she was scared to try something new, I'd tell her Moose liked it. When I needed her to focus on something or listen to me, I could use Moose as a threat or a bribe, and when she was really sick or upset, simply for comfort. But that night I was the one who needed comfort. I pulled Moose under the covers and tucked his big head into my neck.

The next morning Ally was singing into her cereal and blowing bubbles in her juice like nothing had happened. She even drew me a picture of some flowers with her crayons and gave me a hug, saying, "I love you, Mommy." Usually I go over things with her when we've had a conflict. After growing up in a house where one parent yelled while the other stayed in the bedroom, I swore I was going to talk things out with my children. But this time I was just happy the bad night had passed.

After I dropped her off at school, I came home to stain the headboard I was still struggling to finish, but I kept waiting for my cell to go off at any minute. Finally I gave up and took a coffee break. I was just pouring a cup when I heard a knock.

Moose rushed barking and snorting to the front door. My stomach jumped into my throat. I walked down the hallway, my body hugging the wall. I grabbed the baseball bat Evan had left behind the door and peeked through the blinds at the side window, but I couldn't see a vehicle.

I yelled, "Who is it?"

"Damn, woman, you trying out for the marines?" Billy.

I opened the door and Moose was out like a rocket, a compact mass of wiggling snorts and snuffles. Billy laughed and picked him up.

"Hey, squirt."

"What's going on, Billy? Why are you here? Did he kill someone?"

"Not unless you know something we don't. I was just coming over to see how you were doing after that last call."

"Come on in. Where's Sandy?"

"Coordinating with some of the other departments involved in the investigation."

"And you're in charge of me?"

He grinned. "Something like that." He followed me to the kitchen, sniffing the air. "Is that coffee?"

"Can I pour you one?"

"Sit, I'll get it."

I collapsed at the kitchen table. Billy tossed his suit jacket over the back of a chair, then made himself at home in my kitchen, getting a mug out of the cupboard, opening the fridge for milk. He stopped and stared.

"What?"

"Your fridge is as bad as mine. Don't you have anything to eat?"

"Are you raiding my refrigerator?"

"Trying to, but I think I just saw a tumbleweed go by. You need to go shopping ASAP."

"I've had a few things on my mind."

Billy closed the fridge and started making peanut butter sandwiches. He glanced over his shoulder. "Want one?"

I shook my head, but he took out two more slices of bread.

I said, "What do you mean, as bad as yours? Aren't you married?"

"No sirree, Bob. I'm divorced. My ex is still back in Halifax." That explained the East Coast accent I caught in his voice.

He let Moose outside, then sat at the table. He handed me a sandwich as he took a huge bite of his. His eyes rolled back.

"Man, that hits the spot." He took a swill of his coffee and watched me as I nibbled my sandwich. "You look like hell."

"Thanks a lot."

He grinned, then his face turned serious.

"How you holding up? This is some heavy stuff you've got going on here."

"I'm doing all right. But I'm putting in some serious couch time with my psychiatrist. Can I send the RCMP my receipts?" I smiled.

"There are resources you can apply for through the Victims of Crime Act. I'll get you the forms. But I'm glad you're talking to someone, Sara. This is a lot to deal with."

"I just feel like it's all on me, you know? I want to help, but most of all I just want this all to go away—I want my life back."

"The sooner we catch him, the sooner that will happen. You did great last night."

"I don't know, Billy, I thought maybe I pushed too hard."

"You backed off at the right time. 'To a surrounded enemy, you must leave an escape.'"

"Huh?"

"It's from *The Art of War* by Sun Tzu."

I started to laugh. "Isn't that from that movie with Michael Douglas?"

He shook his head. "*Wall Street*. I know, I know, I'm a cop cliché." He smiled. "Sandy gives me a hard time about it too. In my defense, it's the most successful book on military strategy ever written."

"I'm not in the military!"

He laughed. "You don't have to be. It's just about strategy and applies to lots of things in life. I don't go anywhere without a copy. You should check it out. It'll help you deal with John."

"It's just so weird."

"What's weird?"

"Talking to him. In that one conversation he asked me more about my work than my real dad ever has." I caught myself. "I guess *he*'s my real dad—I meant my adopted dad."

Billy set his sandwich down and leaned forward, his eyes intense.

"Most killers don't seem like killers, Sara. That's what makes them so dangerous. You have to be careful not to—"

A tap on the sliding glass door sent our bodies jerking back in their seats. I spun around. Melanie was standing at the door with Moose in her arms. She must've come through the side gate. Billy was on his feet, his hand hovering near his sidearm.

"It's my sister."

His hand dropped. Melanie slid open the door and strolled in.

"Did I catch you at a bad time?" Her smirk said it all. I knew my face was red, but I shot her an as-if look.

"Melanie, this is Billy. He's . . ."

Billy jumped in. "Sara's going to restore some furniture for me."

"I see." She leaned against the counter and reached for the jar of peanut butter. She stuck her finger into the jar and brought it to her mouth. As she licked the peanut butter off, she said, "What's with the gun, Billy?"

Billy just grinned. "I'm an RCMP officer, so you better be nice to me."

Melanie's face said she'd love to be very nice to him.

I said, "We were just wrapping up. I'll walk you out, Billy. Melanie, grab a cup of coffee." She nodded, but her eyes were on Billy.

Outside, I said, "Sorry about that, my sister . . ." I shook my head. "We don't get along—like at all."

He grinned and shrugged. "No biggie. Just stick with the cover and it should be fine." His face turned serious. "When John calls again, remember he doesn't really care about you, Sara. This is a man who takes what he wants, and he thinks you belong to him."

Melanie was waiting by the front door. "Evan know you're hanging out with hot cops?"

"He knows about all my *client*s. What are you doing here, Melanie?"

"I'm not allowed to come visit my big sister?"

She sauntered into the living room and sprawled on the couch. Moose hurled himself on top of her and licked her face as she scratched his head. Traitor.

"I have to get back to work. What's up?" I remembered my cell was on the kitchen table. *Please don't let John call.*

"Dad wants us to talk before Brandon's birthday party on Saturday. He said we have to get along. Mom's not feeling well." Her chin jutted out at an angry slant. With everything happening I forgot Lauren was having a party for Brandon, and I hated to hear Mom was sick again, but I wasn't about to share either fact.

I waited her out.

She said, "I never told that Web site your real father's a serial killer, you know."

"I didn't really think you did—I was just upset."

"Yeah, right."

I sighed. "I didn't, Melanie." Her face was stony and I knew there was no way I could ask if she'd told her boyfriend—she'd take my head off. "Just tell Dad we worked everything out."

"Sure. If that's how you want to play it."

"I'm not *playing.*" I wanted her out of the house fast. "I believe you. I do, okay? I'm sorry I overreacted."

Her eyes narrowed.

I said, "So how's Kyle?"

She was watching me. I forced myself to keep an interested look on my face.

"He just got a regular gig at the pub."

"That's good."

"Yeah."

We stared at each other.

I said, "So . . . listen, I haven't had a chance to talk to Evan about Kyle playing at the wedding, but I will when he gets home."

Melanie sat straight up on the couch. "What's going on?"

"I'm just trying to get along with you, okay?"

"Why?"

"Because we're *sisters*."

"You're never this nice. Are you worried I'm going to tell Evan about the cop?"

I stared at her. My hands itched to smack the smirk off her face.

Don't take the bait, don't take the bait.

I said, "I really should get back out to the shop."

She stood up. "Don't worry, I'm going. So when are we supposed to do this bridesmaid-dress-shopping thing?" Lauren and Melanie are my bridesmaids and Evan's two younger brothers are his best men. Lauren and I have been talking about a shopping trip for a while, but I put it off because of John and because I dread having to deal with Melanie's attitude. Every fiber of my being wants to tell her she isn't in the wedding party anymore, but I know that's exactly what she wants.

"I'm not sure yet," I said. "I'll let you know as soon as possible."

"Whatever."

I stood up and followed her out of the living room but

stopped near the door to the garage. She was almost through the kitchen and at the sliding glass door where she'd left her shoes when the cell rang on the table. She paused and turned around.

I lunged toward the phone, almost knocking a chair over.

A number I didn't recognize. It had to be John.

Melanie was staring at me, one eyebrow raised.

"I'm waiting for a call from a client, but it's just one of those stupid 800 numbers." I shrugged.

She gave me a funny look. "Okay . . ."

I forced my face into a neutral expression.

She was slowly sliding the door open. The phone was still ringing. My heart fluttered in my chest. Melanie glanced over her shoulder. I smiled and gave a little wave. She was still looking at me. *Walk away, walk away.* Finally she turned around.

When she was past the window, I answered the phone in a breathless rush. "Hello?"

"What took you so long?" His voice was annoyed.

"I was in the bathroom."

"I told you I need you to keep the phone with you at all times."

"I'm doing my best, John."

He sighed. "Sorry, I've had a hard day."

"That's too bad." It almost killed me to keep the sarcasm out of my voice, but I still ended up sounding abrupt. I walked to the front window and watched Melanie drive off. For a moment I wondered what she would do in my situation. Probably just tell John to screw off.

"Some people I work with, they think they're better than me."

"Where do you work?"

"I can't tell you that."

"Can you tell me what you do?"

He paused. "Not yet. So what kind of things do you like to do for fun?"

My body tensed. "Why?"

"I'm just trying to get to know you better." His tone picked up. "I like being outdoors."

"Yeah? Like camping and stuff?" I couldn't bring myself to ask if he liked to hunt. I thought he'd pick up on my lack of genuine interest, but his voice was cheerful when he answered.

"I camp all over—spots most people are scared to go. There's not too much of BC I haven't seen. You could drop me at the top of a mountain and I'd still find my way out. But I stick to land."

I racked my brain for something to say. "Why's that?"

"I can't swim." He laughed. "Do you like camping?"

"Sometimes."

John's tone flattened. "Do you go with your boyfriend?"

I hesitated for a moment. Was it better he knew about Evan? He'd think I have protection living with me. "He's my fiancé."

"What is his name?"

I hesitated again. I hated the idea of him having Evan's name, but what if he already knew? "Evan."

"When are you getting married?" A hint of something in his voice.

Time stretched out as I tried to think how to answer.

"Um, we're not sure yet, still trying to work all that out. . . ."

"I have to go." He hung up.

I called Billy right away. This time John was somewhere between Prince George and Quesnel, which is even farther north of Williams Lake. As soon as he was done talking to me, he turned the phone off and essentially vanished. He could be standing right behind a cop and still they wouldn't be able to get his exact location, only a general area. Billy assured me John was going to slip up soon, but when he said it again I wondered who he was trying to convince.

It doesn't help that we don't know what kind of truck he's driving—*everyone* has a truck in the Interior—or whether he's changed his appearance. I asked about roadblocks, but Billy said it's a waste of resources unless they can pinpoint his exact location. Their best bet is to keep showing his photo around and talking to the locals. At least everyone usually knows everyone in rural locations. The police are also working with conservation officers, so they can stop hunters or anyone driving on the Forest Service roads. Hopefully they get a lead soon, because I'm not sure how much more of this I can take.

I wonder what he does after our talks. Does he go home

and make himself a nice dinner, then sit in front of the TV and laugh at sitcoms while he cleans his guns? Maybe he stops at the pub and orders a hamburger and beer, bragging to the waitress about his daughter like a typical father. Does he go over and over our phone call like I do, or forget all about it like I wish I could?

SESSION EIGHT

I *am* trying to calm down. But I don't know where to start. I'm just sick with worry. Not to mention tired and hungry, I have so much going on right now I shouldn't even be here, but I didn't want to cancel again. I *know* I'm talking too fast, my blood sugar's crashing, which is why I'm forcing myself to eat this disgusting granola bar I found in my glove box. Fine, I'll slow down and start at the beginning.

After our last session I tried that technique you gave me for staying in the present. I sat on our couch and closed my eyes, using all my senses to focus on the smooth fabric under my hands, the dryer thumping in the background, the cool hardwood under my bare feet, but my mind always went back to John. He hadn't called for three days and I was working really hard on reminding myself I have zero control over what he does. But I couldn't stop thinking about how he hung up so abruptly. Wondering if it was because I'd mentioned Evan, wondering if he sensed I lied when I told him we didn't have a wedding date yet, wondering what he might do.

Thank God Evan came home for the weekend. No matter how bad I'm freaking out, he can usually bring me back to some semblance of calm, or at least to the point where I'm not hyperventilating. Before we went to Lauren's for Brandon's birthday we had a talk about how to handle it if John called, and I was feeling better about the whole deal. I was even kind of looking forward to the party. I've always had a soft spot for Brandon and couldn't believe he was already turning ten. I'd practiced changing *diapers* on him. Not that my trial-and-errors with him helped when it came to dealing with a strong-willed little girl.

Just trying to take Ally shopping for a present was insane. First she had to walk up and down every aisle. Then we finally settled on a Nintendo game, but she wouldn't stop looking at the ones still on the shelf. "Maybe he'd like hockey better, Mommy." I said Brandon would be happy with any of them, but she started picking up one after another again. When I finally snapped and grabbed the one she'd already picked, she screamed, "It's the wrong one, Mommy!" like her life depended on it. Then she stood in the middle of the aisle, her arms crossed in front of her, and refused to budge no matter what I said. At the end of my rope, I said, "Fine, you can just stay here all day," and started walking away. After a moment she followed along behind, her little shoulders slumped and her lips tight as she struggled not to cry.

A few miles down the road she was still staring out the passenger window. Now that I was calmer, I felt bad for rushing her and said, "Brandon's going to be so excited when he sees your present." She still wouldn't look at me, so I started singing along to the radio, making up my own words. "Sugar pie, Ally Cat, you know I love *you*. I can't help myself, I love *you* and nobody else, except for Evan, and Moose, and Nana, and Auntie Lauren, and—" I sucked in a big breath of air. The corner of Ally's lips twitched as she tried not to laugh. I started singing louder. By the time we picked up Evan, she was also singing—in between giggles, which got me laughing too. Then she tilted her head to one side, smiled at me, and said, "You're so pretty, Mommy." God, I love that kid.

We were still having fun when we pulled into Lauren and Greg's driveway. This year the party was a Transformers theme, so I knew the whole house would be decorated top to bottom, and they had all kinds of games for the kids. I probably would've had a great time if both my fathers hadn't ruined it for me.

Dad was getting a case of beer from his truck when we got out of the Cherokee. As Ally ran ahead with Moose to find the boys, I followed my father and Evan to the backyard while they talked fishing. Greg hovered over a gas grill, apron tied around his neck. He grinned at the sight of us. A big teddy bear of a man, he pulled me, then Evan, in for a rough hug. After he released us he opened a cooler near his feet and handed Evan a beer. Judging by Greg's rosy cheeks he'd already helped himself to a couple.

"You want anything, Sara?"

"I'll grab a coffee inside, thanks."

In the kitchen, Lauren was dumping chips into a bowl while Mom finished up the dishes. Lauren has a dishwasher, but Mom won't use one. She doesn't think they get dishes clean enough.

"Can I help with anything?" I said.

Lauren turned around with a smile and blew a wisp of blond hair off her face.

"I think we're okay for the moment."

I gave Mom a kiss on the cheek, noticing her face seemed thinner since I last saw her. She smiled, but her eyes were tired and she'd definitely lost weight. I poured myself a cup of coffee and felt my good mood slipping away.

As I took my first sip I spotted Melanie and Kyle coming around the side of the house. Dad barely acknowledged Kyle, who was dressed in skinny black jeans and a tight black T-shirt, before turning back to his conversation with Evan.

Lauren came up behind me and rested her chin on my shoulder. We watched the men for a moment. Greg was telling a story—beer in one hand, tongs in the other. Evan and Melanie laughed when he finished. Greg's eyes darted to Dad to see if he was laughing too—he wasn't.

I said, "Beer and logging. Greg's two favorite subjects."

"Be nice." Lauren poked my back.

While the kids dove into the food at their table, the adults settled around the log picnic table Greg built. I was just taking my first bite of burger when my cell rang in my pocket. I pulled it out and casually glanced at the call display. Another strange number. It had to be John.

It rang again. As I stood up, everyone around the picnic table stopped talking. The only sound was from the kids' table.

I said, "Excuse me for a minute." Dad's face was a thundercloud. Trying not to break into a run, I walked around the corner until I was out of sight, then answered the phone.

"Hello?"

"I needed to hear your voice."

His words made me cringe, but I said, "Is everything all right?" How was I going to get him off the phone?

"I'm glad I found you." His voice was tight, like it was hard to get out the words. "Knowing . . . knowing I have you . . . helps." I heard a noise in the background but couldn't make it out.

"What's that sound? Where are you calling from?"

"It's not too late."

"What's not too late?"

"For us."

I didn't say anything for a moment, trying to focus on the sounds in the background. Animal or human?

"*Tell me* it's not too late."

"No, no, of course not."

He exhaled into the phone. It sounded labored, like he was breathing through clenched teeth.

He said, "I have to go."

After I closed the phone I tried to compose myself, but my throat was so tight I felt like I was strangling. My vision blurred. I pressed the heel of my hand against my temple and closed my eyes. How was I going to deal with this? I couldn't let my family see how upset I was. I wanted to call Billy, but everyone would wonder if I was gone much longer. *Don't think about John, just shut it out and focus. Pull it together, Sara.* As I walked back to the table I caught Evan's eye and gave a slight nod.

"That the client you were waiting for?" he said when I sat down.

Thank you, baby.

"Yeah." I avoided my dad's stare from across the table and picked my burger up. "Sorry about that, guys. This client is really high-maintenance."

Dad said, "It could've waited."

"He has limited time, so I have to—"

Dad had already turned his attention back to Evan. On the other side of the table Kyle picked at his food. His nails were painted black.

Melanie caught me staring. "Was it that good-looking cop?"

Evan's body tensed beside me.

I shook my head. "No, a different client."

Melanie said, "What was his name again? Bill?"

I nodded, then forced myself to take another bite of my burger. "These are great, Greg."

"He didn't look like the antique-collecting type," Melanie said. Now everyone was watching me.

Mom looked confused. "You met one of Sara's clients?"

Melanie said, "Yeah, when I stopped by the other day they were having lunch."

Shut up, Melanie.

Evan stopped eating and was looking at me.

"He just came over to see my shop and I was making a sandwich, so I offered him one." Not quite, but close enough.

Melanie said, "So what *are* you doing for him?" I wanted to smash my burger into her smirking face.

Think, think.

"His mother just passed away and she had a basement full of antiques. I'm trying to sort through them for him and clean them up so he can sell them. There are quite a few pieces." I warmed to my lie. "Could take me awhile." I glanced at Evan. He was staring down at his plate.

Before I could say anything further my cell rang.

Dad dropped his burger on his plate and looked disgusted.

I checked the call display. It was John again. My pulse sped up.

I groaned and got to my feet. "I'm so sorry."

Dad said, "Sit down."

"It's my client again—"

"Sit *down*." Dad's hands balled into fists by his plate.

"Sorry, I have to take it."

As I left the table Dad shook his head and said something to Mom. I glanced back over my shoulder and tried to catch Evan's eye, but he didn't look up.

Around the corner of the house I said, "What's wrong?"

"The noise." He groaned into the phone. I heard something slamming.

"Are you hurt?"

"You *have* to talk to me—you have to help."

Traffic sounds.

"Are you driving?"

Screeching tires. A car honked. Were those the noises that were upsetting him?

"Maybe you should pull over and—" Ally came around the corner of the house. *Oh, crap.* Why didn't Evan stop her?

I covered the speaker just as she said, "Grandpa said you have to come have cake now."

"Okay, sweetie. I'll be there in a minute. Go ahead."

As she trotted off I said, "John? Are you still there?" Only sounds of traffic.

I was about to hang up when he finally said in a desperate voice, "I need you to talk to me."

"What do you want to talk about?"

"Tell me—tell me your favorite foods."

I wiped sweat from my forehead. I was missing my nephew's birthday because he wanted to hear what I like to eat?

"Can't you just tell me what's wrong? I'm at a family party and people are—"

"I thought you said you didn't tell anyone about me." His voice was hard.

"I didn't! But it's going to start looking odd that I'm talking on my phone and people are going to ask questions and I don't—"

He'd hung up.

For the rest of the party every nerve ending in my body vibrated with unanswered questions. What were the sounds in the background? Why was he talking about a noise? What was he going to do now? My whole system was in overdrive—my face burned, my armpits were soaked with sweat, my legs screamed to get out, to go home, talk to Billy, *anyone* who could make this horrible feeling go away. I tried to focus on the conversation around me, but I couldn't follow the threads. Every kid's voice grated, every shriek sent a bolt of anger through me. I glanced at my watch constantly, my phone tight in my hand.

It didn't help that Dad gave me hell right in front of Ally for answering the phone, calling me selfish and rude. I apologized, like I always do, but he kept giving me the evil eye after we returned to the party. Mom's smile flickered in and out as she looked back and forth between us. Melanie and I simply avoided each other. At least Lauren didn't seem to be angry, but she sure was distracted. Every time I looked at her she was watching Greg. One time I caught her giving him a dirty look when he went for another beer—not that it stopped him. But I was having my own relationship problems. Evan was laughing and joking with everyone, putting his arm around my shoulder when Brandon opened our present, but he wasn't meeting my eye. Finally it was time to go. My good-byes were short, earning a concerned look from Mom, but I was focused on getting Ally and Moose to the Cherokee. I practically dragged Ally down the driveway, snapping when she complained. Evan was silent.

We were backing out when my cell chirped, alerting me I had a text message.

Billy: *How was the party? Call when you get home.*

"Who's that?" Evan said.

"The police want to go over John's calls." I was already dialing Billy's number, but it went straight to voice mail. "Crap, he must be out of range."

Evan stared at the road ahead.

The rest of the drive was silent. When we finally got home, Ally threw herself in front of the TV to watch *Hannah Montana*. I tried to call Billy again and this time I left a message. After ten minutes, which I spent washing our dishes from breakfast, I went looking for Evan. He was in the backyard cleaning up Moose's poop.

I said, "I know what you're thinking, but it's not like that."

"I'm thinking you should clean up after your dog."

My dog? That pissed me off.

"I try to stay on top of things, Evan, but I have to take care of everything when you're gone."

"It takes five minutes."

"You know how busy I've been lately."

"Yeah, too busy to tell me you're having lunch with other guys."

"It was *nothing*. Melanie was just trying to stir up trouble."

He jabbed the shovel at the ground, scooping in short, jerky movements. "Well, she did a good job. Greg kept giving me weird looks all afternoon."

"What was I supposed to say? You know I'm not allowed to talk about it."

"Why didn't you tell me he was here?"

"By the time we talked, John had called again and I was freaking out. I didn't even think to tell you Billy came over because I didn't think it mattered. He's probably going to have to come by a lot, and—"

"Now it's *Billy*?" Evan stopped the shovel and looked at me.

"Oh my God, Evan, that's just what Sandy calls him. He's not even my type, okay? He dresses superslick and he's got tattoos and—"

"That's supposed to make me feel better?"

I wanted to grab the shovel out of his hands and thump him over the head with it.

"You know what? I don't need this. If Billy can find this guy, I'm going to talk to him every day because I want him out of my life—you should too. I would think you'd be happy someone is checking on me when you're gone. If you don't trust me, maybe we shouldn't be getting married." I spun around and stormed back into the house.

As I passed the living room I peeked in on Ally. She was wrapped in a blanket on the couch with Moose in her lap, sleepily staring at the TV.

"You should go to bed soon, Ally."

"Noooo . . ." Tired of fighting, I left it for now and headed upstairs to my office.

To try and calm down, I wrote out everything I remembered from the calls—making a note to ask Billy if they have the technology to isolate the sounds in the background. I closed my eyes and tried to focus. What were those noises? My eyes flew open—what if he'd abducted a woman? Maybe he was taking her somewhere in the truck and the sounds were her trying to get out!

Just as I picked up the cordless to call Billy again, I heard the sliding glass door open downstairs, then footsteps. Evan was in the kitchen.

I hesitated for a moment. Maybe I should wait until the morning. But this was important.

Billy answered on the first ring.

I said, "I was thinking the sounds in the background could be a woman. Maybe he's taking her somewhere and he's going to—"

"Whoa, whoa, hold on. That's not his MO and we haven't had any reports of missing women."

"Then what were the sounds?"

"We're still working on isolating them, but so far we don't have anything usable."

"Maybe you need some more people on the task force."

"We have every available member of Serious Crimes in Vancouver and some in Nanaimo—"

"Can't you bring in members from Toronto?"

"It doesn't work like that, Sara. Most of the files are old and have already been investigated. We have access to lots of resources and this case is top-priority, but until John makes a move, or someone sees something, we can't do much."

"It doesn't seem like they're doing *anything*."

"I'm sure it seems that way, but they're following up leads, coordinating with the lab and other departments. Right now we're trying to find out who owns the cell phone he used."

I knew I sounded cranky when I said, "Do you at least know where he was calling from?"

But Billy just said, "He's moved west of Prince George, probably somewhere near Burns Lake. It's possible he's heading toward Prince Rupert, so we've notified the local detachments and they'll circulate the sketch to truck stops, gas stations, any places he might stop along the way."

I took the heat out of my voice. "What do you think was wrong with him? He was complaining about a noise?"

"We're hoping the next time you talk you can get him to elaborate."

"I don't want there to be a next time. I'm sick of this."

"You have to do what feels right to you, Sara. But I won't lie—we really need your help. You're likely our only chance of ever finding him." I closed my eyes against Billy's words and dropped my forehead onto my desk.

He said, "I know it feels like he has all the power, but he wants a connection with you. That's why he keeps calling back. No one knows how far we can push this. But like Sun Tzu says, 'The opportunity of defeating the enemy is provided by the enemy himself.' Eventually he'll give us something to go on."

Evan was coming up the stairs.

"I have to go."

"Okay, we'll be in touch. Get some rest."

Just as I set the cordless down, Evan walked in behind me and dropped into his chair. I spun around.

He said, "Was that Bill?"

God, he could read me like a book. "I had to debrief. Jesus, Evan."

His face was blank. Part of me wanted to argue and defend, to storm out in righteous anger. My face felt hot and I was on the edge of losing it. *Pull back. Flipping out won't solve the problem.*

I took a breath. "I'm sorry I lost my temper. It's just all this stuff is so big, I really need you on my side."

"I am on your side."

"It sure doesn't feel like it. I hate that you're mad at me."

Evan heaved a sigh, then grabbed my foot and pulled it into his lap. As he massaged it he said, "I'm not mad at you, I'm mad at this situation. It's a nightmare."

"You don't think I know that? God, he could be killing some woman right now—and there's nothing I can do about it."

"If he kills someone it's not your fault. He's a killer, it's what he does."

"But it would be my fault because I didn't stop him." I remembered Billy's words. "I'm pretty much the cops' only chance at catching him."

"The cops are using you as bait! You don't have to talk to him, you know. I think you should just get yourself out of this."

"I can't sit here and do nothing while he's out there looking for his next victim."

"Sara, you're always stressed out and your emotions are all over the place." He held up a hand. "You have every reason to be upset. But I'm worried about you."

"Are you worried about *me* or about Billy?"

He gave me a look. "I'm sorry I'm being a jealous prick, okay? If you say I have nothing to worry about, then I believe you. I just hate the idea of some other guy protecting you. You're my girl."

I crawled into Evan's lap and wrapped my arms around his shoulders. As I nuzzled his ear, I said, "Baby, he's got nothing on you. And right now, he's the one who has to deal with all my paranoid meltdowns. You get the good stuff."

"Hmm . . . keep talking."

I traced my mouth along his collarbone. Licked his earlobe. Whispered against the warm flesh of his neck, "Ally?"

"Asleep on the couch with Moose. I was going to carry her up later. But I can get her now if—"

I put my face close to his and grabbed the back of his hair. He raised his eyebrows. I rested my lips on his and kissed him slowly, softly, then harder—grinding my lips against his, snaking my tongue into his mouth. As he tried to suck on it, I pulled away and smiled at him. He grabbed a length of my hair and wrapped his fist around it, then brought my face close and kissed me hard. I got up and made a come-here motion with my finger, strolling out of the room with an exaggerated sexy walk.

He laughed and followed me into our bedroom. I slid onto the bed, then tossed my hair over my shoulder and said in a bad Southern accent, "Lordy me, sailor, you've been out to sea for such a long time, I'm not sure if I re-member what to do. . . ."

Evan did his own sexy walk over to the bed, then pulled his shirt off over his head, one-handed—the way I love. He dangled the shirt from his finger, then dropped it to the floor as he wiggled his eyebrows.

I smiled. "I think it's coming back to me."

He laughed and climbed into bed beside me. We kissed for a while, our anger long gone. He scraped his unshaven cheeks against mine, laughing as I complained.

He pinned my hands down for a moment. I flashed to John. Had he done that to Julia? How did he hold the women down when he was raping them? I pushed away the violent image. Now Evan was looming over me. I saw John looming over a woman.

Evan looked down into my face. "What's wrong?"

"Nothing." I pulled him on top of me, hiding my face in his neck. And for the next while, I almost believed it.

After breakfast the next morning we took Ally and Moose for a walk out to Neck Point to watch the sea lions, then Ally went over to Meghan's to play. I was working hard on keeping John out of my mind, but Evan was working harder. I'd mention something about the case and Evan would give me a kiss, I'd mention something else and he'd nuzzle my neck, I'd try to push him away and finish my thought and he'd nibble my ear. I'd try to wiggle away and somehow my bra was coming off.

Afterward Evan and I lazed around in bed and made plans for what to serve at the wedding rehearsal dinner. Now that I'd allowed myself to relax for a moment, I started looking forward to the big event again. But it also reminded me I still needed to arrange a day to go shopping with the girls. The idea of putting up with Melanie for hours made me want to grind my teeth, but there was no way around it.

Evan and I were discussing decorations and I was getting excited about the idea of fairy lights strung through fir trees when my cell rang in the office.

I looked at Evan. He said, "Go ahead."

A blanket wrapped around my naked body, I sprinted down the hall and grabbed the phone off my desk.

It was the number John had called from last time.

As soon as I answered he said, "Are you having a nice day?" There was a tone in his voice I hadn't heard before—a coolness.

"It's going all right. How about you?" I tried to sound pleasant, but I was even angrier than usual that he'd called and ruined what had been a nice afternoon.

"Is Evan there?"

Still unsure of his tone, I said, "He's here . . . but he's not in the room, if you're—"

"Have you been honest with me, Sara?"

My stomach dropped. "Of course."

"Have. You. Been. Honest?"

I sat down in my chair. Did he know I've been talking to the police? Oh, God, did he find out about Ally?

"What's wrong?"

"I saw the Web site."

My mind raced. Had there been another article?

"I'm not sure what—"

"It's *all* there." What was he talking about? I decided to wait him out.

After a few beats he said, "You have a wedding date—you're trying to trick me."

"I don't know what . . ." Then I remembered Evan had made a wedding Web site a couple of weeks ago. How was I going to get out of this?

"We *had* a date set. But lately we've been talking about changing it. That's why I said we weren't sure. I wasn't lying to you. I wouldn't do that." I held my breath.

He hung up.

I was still sitting there a couple of minutes later when Evan came in and sat behind me at his desk.

"Was it him?" he said.

I nodded.

Evan spun me around in my chair to face him. "You okay?"

"He found our wedding Web site. I'd told him I didn't know the date. He sounded *really* mad."

"Did he threaten you?"

"No, it was just . . . his voice."

"I'll put a password on the site right away. You should call Bill."

"This is bad, Evan."

"It'll be okay. He's not going to kill anyone over a Web site." He was already signing on to his computer.

That night I tossed and turned while Evan slumbered beside me—or tried to. When I rolled into him for the hundredth time he murmured, "Go to sleep, Sara." I forced my body to be still, but my mind spun in dizzying circles, sending horrific snapshots of John ripping a woman's clothes off, his hands tight around her throat, her scream rending through the air as he forced himself into her.

As soon as Evan left in the morning, I met Billy and Sandy at the station. Hungover from lack of sleep, I clutched a coffee in my hand while talking a mile a minute. I finally started to calm down when Billy said I'd handled the call with John perfectly, that you have to "know when to fight and when not to fight." Sandy smiled and nodded, but I got the distinct feeling she was pissed off. I wasn't feeling too happy myself. I'd been hoping John's using the same phone might help us somehow, but they told me he was using a prepaid cell, which he'd bought for cash. No one at the store remembered what he looked like. All he had to do from now on was buy a SIM card to top up his minutes.

The call came from near Vanderhoof, so he was heading east again, which meant he might be making his way back to the junction at Prince George. My first thought was that he could be coming to the island—if he drove all night he could be in Vancouver already. I asked them if I was in danger and Billy said they didn't think so, but to be on the safe side they'd have an officer patrol by our house several times a day.

Even with those reassurances and Billy texting later to say, *Hang in there, you're doing great*, it took hours before I stopped jumping at every sound. When John still hadn't called by Tuesday night, I started hoping he was gone for good. But I couldn't shake the feeling he was just warming up.

After I dropped Ally off at school yesterday, I came home and let Moose into the backyard. Feeling more settled than I had in a while, I decided to burn off some steam in my shop before our session that afternoon. I got totally caught up in refinishing a cherry table and before I knew it a couple of hours had flown by. Then I remembered Moose was still out in the backyard. I expected him to be waiting at the sliding glass door, wet nose marks smeared all across the glass, but he wasn't there. I opened the door and whistled. Nothing.

"Moose?" When he still didn't come running, I walked out to the backyard. Was the little bugger stuck in the woodpile again? But when I checked he wasn't there.

Maybe he was messing around in the compost. I followed the stepping-stones around the side of the house. He wasn't there either. I walked closer to the gate and checked it out. It wasn't latched.

I ran into the driveway yelling, *"Moose!"* at the top of my lungs. A dog barked, and I held my breath. It barked again—too deep to be Moose. I ran all the way to the end of the driveway where our mailbox is. *Please, oh, please, be here.* But he wasn't.

He wasn't at any of my neighbors' houses either. That's why I had to cancel our session. After I phoned you I spent the afternoon calling the pound, the SPCA, the vet's—*everyone.* No one has seen him. I called Evan in near-hysteria—totally flipping out and accusing him of leaving the gate unlatched when he'd cleaned up the backyard. He just kept raising his voice and repeating, "Sara, calm down for a minute. Sara, *stop!*" until I shut up long enough for him to tell me he was positive he'd closed it.

After we got off the phone I called Billy, sure John had taken Moose in retaliation. Right away Billy checked with the patrol car that was keeping an eye on my place. The officer said he didn't see anything suspicious when he drove by that morning, but Billy still came over and checked around the house. Not that there was much to see. The gate would be hard to open from the outside, but if you were tall enough you could reach over and do it.

When Billy finished looking around, he made me sit and write out a list of who to call next, where to put up signs, what Web sites to post on. At first I balked, wanting to just get out and start searching, but Billy said it would save time and that "running around like a chicken with its head cut off" wasn't doing Moose any favors. Finally I just grabbed a pad of paper and started the list. My heart rate slowed with each new item I added.

Billy suggested I try to call John to see if he was on the island. We didn't know if he was using the same phone anymore, but I gave it a shot. I just got a "this customer is out of range" recording. Billy said if John had taken Moose, he'd probably call soon. The police were going to park a car on the road until we found out if John was on the island. After Billy went back to the station I called Lauren. She rushed over and we made signs, then posted them everywhere. But no one's called.

When it was time to pick up Ally from school, I didn't know what to say. I try not to lie to her, but the one other time we lost Moose, at a park, she freaked out and bit Evan when he tried to stop her from running across the road after him. I was hoping against hope I'd find Moose this time before I had to tell her the truth. If he doesn't come home . . . I can't allow myself to even go down that path. I don't know if I did the right thing—I *never* know if I've done the right thing—but I told Ally that Moose had to get a checkup and was staying over at the vet's. She wanted to visit him, but I talked her out of it and distracted her with movies and games all evening.

Ally fell right to sleep, but I stayed awake for hours worrying about where Moose could be, terrified of who might have him. And why.

SESSION NINE

I'm so depressed today, but I'm hoping talking to you will help. Other than Evan or Billy, you're the only person I *can* talk to these days, at least about anything that's really going on. I've been sitting around my house all morning waiting for our appointment. Time on my hands is not a good thing.

I can't stop going to that Web site about John and looking at all the pictures of his victims and their families. Afterward I think about them, wondering what their lives were like, what they could've been. I fixate on little details, like the shell necklace one girl wore that was never recovered. I wonder if John has it. Her boyfriend, whom John shot in the back of the head, had just gotten a new dirt bike for graduation. The kid could fix anything, loved restoring old cars. His dad still has the one he'd been working on when he was murdered. The dad refuses to finish it and it sits in the garage, all the tools still around it where he left them. I cried and cried at that image, of a car up on blocks and a family that will never be put back together.

I think about the moment their families were told the news. Then I torture myself with thoughts of something horrible happening to Evan or Ally. I'm sure the pain would kill me. How do the parents of these victims get out of bed every morning? How do they keep on living?

Everywhere I go I see death—a side effect of reading nonstop about serial killers. But the thing that haunts me the most is how quickly it happened to these people. I don't mean just John's victims. I mean all the murdered people I've been reading about. They were just going about their lives, sleeping, driving, jogging, or maybe just stopping to help a stranger, then just like that their life was over. But sometimes it wasn't, sometimes they lived for days. Some of the things these killers did . . . I can't stop thinking about their victims' last moments. How terrified they must have been, how much pain they endured.

I used to enjoy true crime shows. "It was a hot summer day in the Rockies when the young blond reporter decided to go for a jog. . . ." I *liked* the tingle of fear I'd get down my back and the way I'd sit on the edge of my seat during dramatic reenactments, clutching the pillow, my body tense. It was fascinating, this look into the dark side of human nature.

Evan's always trying to get me to think more positively, or at least more rationally, which requires calming down first—always a challenge, and I've been working really hard on it. But when the car makes a weird noise I automatically think the brakes are going, when Ally gets a cold I think it's pneumonia, and when Moose disappeared . . .

As soon as I got home from our last session I made the rounds of calls again—the pound, SPCA, all the vets in town—but still no sign of Moose. Billy came over to help, carrying a greasy bag of burgers and fries I practically inhaled. He said he had a feeling I hadn't eaten all day and he was right. We drove around and put posters up at all the gas stations and stores in my area. My house is close to the base of Mount Benson, so we even drove up that way, stopping a few times to get out and call Moose.

It was nice to have company, especially when I started spiraling into fear-based rants about who might have Moose. Billy would just ask a question or give me a task that forced me to concentrate. At one point I started talking so fast I was almost hyperventilating and he said, "Whenever you feel yourself panicking, just breathe, regroup, and focus on your strategy. Trust me, it works." Then he made me look at my list of places where I wanted to hang posters and tell him what I'd crossed off, interrupting if I rushed through any. It was frustrating as hell, but the tight band around my chest gradually began to loosen.

When Billy had to go back to the station, I kept driving around by myself for another hour. I was almost back at our house when I rounded a sharp bend and nearly ran into some ravens in the middle of the road, fighting over what looked like entrails. Then I spotted the trail of rust-colored blood leading to the ditch, where a raven stabbed at a small dark mound. After I pulled over onto the gravel shoulder, I walked toward the ravens. My eyes pricked with tears.

Please, God. Don't let it be Moose.

The ravens flew up when I got closer and cawed as they perched on the power line. With my eyes riveted on the trail of blood, I took the last few steps on shaky legs and looked down into the ditch at the mangled corpse.

It was a raccoon.

When I got back in the Cherokee and started down the road, the ravens swooped back to their treasure. I shuddered as they stabbed at it again and again, sorry for the raccoon, relieved it wasn't Moose.

I was almost home when my phone chirped with a text message from Billy to give him a call. My DNA results were back.

It wasn't until after I'd walked in my house—it felt so empty without Moose's snorts and grunts—poured myself a cup of coffee, and called Evan, that I had enough courage to phone Billy. I sat in my favorite chair in the living room, wrapped Ally's Barbie quilt around me, and dialed Billy's cell. Just my luck, Sandy answered.

"Thanks for calling back, Sara. Billy's on the other line right now, but I can fill you in."

"You have the results?"

"They came in an hour ago." She was trying to keep her

tone neutral, but it vibrated with excitement. "You're definitely a match to the DNA we have on file."

The Campsite Killer *is* my father. This is real. I waited for the emotion to hit, for the tears to come. But they didn't. It felt like Sandy had simply told me my own phone number. I stared out the window at my cherry tree. It was all in bloom.

Sandy was still talking. "We weren't able to collect biological samples from every scene, but when DNA testing came into effect we conclusively linked him to many of the victims."

"How do you know he's responsible for the other murders?"

"The MO is consistent."

"What about women who are still missing?"

Her voice was forced patience. "The Campsite Killer is only triggered in the summer and he doesn't try to hide the bodies, so he's not considered a suspect in any other disappearances."

"But isn't it unusual that he only attacks in the summers? I know about cooling-off periods between kills, but his are—"

"It's not unheard-of for a serial killer to have a long cooling-off period. Once their needs are met, they can often hold off for a while, reliving the crime over and over."

"And that's why they take souvenirs."

"For some of them, yes. John probably uses the jewelry to keep himself connected to the victim. But we still don't know what triggers him in the first place, or why his kills are so ritualized—which is why your conversations with him are that much more important."

"I'm trying my best, Sandy. I didn't know he'd see the Web site."

"Of course, a perfectly understandable mistake."

I gritted my teeth. "It wasn't a *mistake*. I don't want him knowing details of my family, of my life."

"We don't ever want you to do something you feel puts you at risk." But I knew it wasn't true. She wanted to catch John—more than anything. And she hated that she needed me to do it.

"He has to trust you, Sara."

"So you've mentioned. A couple of times now. I should get going—I still have a missing dog to find." I hung up before she could say anything else.

But I didn't find Moose. And when Ally came home from school I finally broke the news that he was missing.

"You lied! You said he was at the vet's!" Then she started hitting my legs and screaming "Why, why, why!" until she was hoarse. All I could do was hold her furious, trembling body away from mine until she'd worn herself out. Finally she just dropped to the floor and wept. It broke my heart when she wailed, "What if he doesn't come *home*, Mommy?" I promised I was doing everything I could to find him, but she was inconsolable and sobbed in my arms while I fought to hold back my own tears. That night she crawled into my bed and we held each other close. I stayed awake for hours, staring at the clock.

The next morning Ally and I shared a solemn breakfast. When she said, for what felt like the hundredth time, "You *have* to find Moose, Mommy," I told her I would. But as every day passed I was losing hope. I even tried to call John again, rehearsing ways to ask if he'd taken my dog, some threatening, some pleading, but still no answer.

After I took Ally to school, I did load after load of laundry and vacuumed the house top to bottom. The sight of Moose's stuffie—its tail stiff with dry drool—just about broke my heart. Usually I wash it every week, but I couldn't bring myself to erase any sign of him and instead simply set it in his dog basket.

I was just about to take a shower when the cordless rang in the kitchen. Hoping it was someone calling about Moose, I raced downstairs, but when I checked the call display it was just Billy.

"Got some good news for you, Sara."

"You found Moose!" My heart was in my throat as I waited for his answer.

"I asked all the guys to keep a lookout for the little guy when they were on patrol. One of the officers pulled over some teens at the skate park and he was getting their vehicle information when he saw a French bulldog in the backseat. He checked his tag, and sure enough it was your dog."

"Oh, thank God! How did they get him?"

"They said they found him running down the road and were going to return him soon, but the officer said the kid's girlfriend was crying when she handed him over, so you might not have gotten him back."

"Ally's going to be *so* happy."

"He's at the station with me. I'll bring him over ASAP."

"That would be great. Thank you so much, Billy."

"Hey, we always get our man—or dog." We laughed.

I called Ally's school and they said they'd let her know. Evan got the call next and he was thrilled. It took some serious self-control on my part not to make a snarky comment about the gate, but as usual he read my mind.

"I still think I shut the gate, but maybe I'm wrong." I was just happy we had Moose, so I dropped it. When I told him Billy was bringing Moose over right away he said, "That's nice of him."

"Yeah, he's been a huge help," I said. "And not just with finding Moose. He's also teaching me how to calm down and focus when I'm upset."

Silence from the other end of the phone.

"Hello?"

"How exactly is he teaching you?"

"I don't know, lots of ways. Like he gives me tasks so I have something to channel my energy into."

"I tell you to do the same thing."

Evan's tone was starting to piss me off. "It's different when he does it. He's a cop, not my fiancé. You get annoyed."

"I don't get *annoyed*. I just think you get yourself freaked out over nothing sometimes."

"And you make me feel like I'm just some crazy stress case." I knew I should pull back, knew comparing him to Billy was going to backfire big time, but anger pushed the words out of my mouth. "Billy doesn't make me feel like crap."

"Well, I don't like you hanging out with him."

"He's the cop handling my case!"

"So what's he doing driving around looking for Moose, then?"

"I can't believe you're being like this—"

The doorbell rang.

Evan said, "Is someone there?"

"I told you Billy was bringing Moose over."

"Then I guess you better let him in." He hung up.

Moose was wriggling so much that Billy almost dropped him handing him over. Once Moose and I finished our joyous reunion, which involved a lot of grunting and snuffling on his part, I offered Billy a coffee.

"Sure, I'll take a quick one."

I poured us both a cup and we were heading toward the living room when he stopped at the door to the garage.

"Is this where your shop is?"

"Yeah, we keep talking about building one in the back, but I like being closer to the house."

"Can I see it?"

"Sure, but it's a mess." I opened the door.

I showed him some of my equipment, laughing when he

turned on the sander and revved it up. A typical guy, he had to try all Evan's power tools. After he shut the last one off, he walked over to the cherry lamp table and ran his hand across the surface.

"Is this what you're working on?"

"Yup, I just stripped it yesterday." I came over to stand near him and rested my hand on the table. "It's still rough in spots."

I looked up at the sound of heavy boot steps in the kitchen. The door swung open. We both jumped back. Billy's arm pushed me behind him.

My dad's large frame filled the doorway. His eyes focused on Billy, then at Billy's hand protectively in front of me.

"Dad! You scared the bejesus out of me." I held my hand over my heart. The tools must've drowned out the sound of his truck.

"I knocked. Door was open." He stepped into the shop.

"This is Billy, Dad. One of my clients."

Dad nodded his head in greeting but didn't smile. He gave Billy the once-over, then turned to me.

"Lauren said Moose was missing, so I came to see if you needed help."

"Thanks, Dad, but he was returned this morning."

He grunted. "I see that." His gaze focused back on Billy. "You're with the RCMP?"

"Yeah, almost fifteen years now."

"You know Ken Safford?"

"Not sure I do. . . ."

"What about Pete Jenkins?"

"Don't think so. I just transferred over from the mainland, so I'm still trying to get to know everyone." I was impressed with how smoothly Billy was able to lie.

"Well, I should get going," he said. "Thanks for the coffee. Just e-mail me the new quote when you have it ready, Sara."

"Okay. Want me to walk you out?"

"Nah, I'm good. Visit with your dad."

Dad didn't move, forcing Billy to step around him. Dad and I were left alone. I shivered in the cold garage.

"See the table I'm working on?" He glanced at it and nodded. "Did you want a cup of coffee?" Dad never sat around and drank coffee, but he surprised me.

"If it's fresh."

He was standing at the sliding glass door staring out into the backyard when I handed it to him. He nodded, then said, "You guys need some more wood?"

"I think we're okay. It's warming up."

"Ask Evan next time he calls. If he needs some he can let me know." Of course I should ask Evan—God forbid a woman would know anything.

He took a gulp of coffee. Still staring into the backyard he said, "Evan's a good man."

"That's why I'm marrying him, Dad."

He grunted and took another sip. "You better get your head screwed on straight, Sara, or you're going to lose everything."

Tears stung my eyes. "My head *is* screwed on straight. Is this because of what Melanie said about Billy? I told you, he's just a client. Evan knows him, and—"

"I've got to get back to camp." He turned around and set his cup on the counter. At the door he said, "It doesn't look good, Sara—another man being here when Evan's away."

"It doesn't *look* good? For who?" But he was walking to his truck. I followed him. "Dad, you can't just come over and say stuff like that, then leave."

As he climbed into his truck he said, "Tell Evan your gutters need to be cleaned, looks like the left one's been overflowing."

Before I could say anything else, he closed his door and started backing down the driveway. I stared after him until the sound of his diesel truck faded in the distance.

As I walked back into the kitchen my cell rang. I checked the call display. It was John. Was he still mad about my wedding date? What if he found out I lied about something else? *Stop. Calm down. Just answer the phone or he'll be really angry.* I swallowed hard and took a few breaths.

"Hello?"

"You can't lie to me again."

"I wasn't—" *Don't argue.* "You're right, I'm sorry."

We both paused. He said, "What's wrong?"

"I'm fine." I fought the urge to cry.

"You don't sound fine." His voice was concerned.

I said, "It's just work stuff."

"What are you working on?"

"Just a lamp table right now."

"What kind of wood is that made from?"

"This one's cherry."

"Cherry's beautiful. Nice rich tones."

Surprised at his insight I said, "Yeah, it really is."

"What kind of tools do you use?"

"Mostly smaller tools, planes, sanding clamps, drills. But for work like this it's usually done with brushes." I eyed mine. "I have to get some new ones soon. They're getting kind of ratty, but I want a new jack plane too."

"Evan should get you what you need."

"I can buy things myself. I just get distracted."

"I saw his Web site—he's one of the guides, so he's away all the time. A husband should be there for you." Great, one father thinks my fiancé is too good for me and the other one thinks he's not good enough

"He makes it home often." Except for the next couple of weeks, when he has back-to-back bookings.

"Is he home now?"

My eyes flicked to the door. Had I locked it when Dad left?

"He's coming home soon." I sprinted to the alarm and made sure it was set. "And my brother-in-law stops in all the time." Greg had never stopped over once.

"But Evan leaves you alone and unprotected?"

I caught my breath. "Do I need protection?"

"Not anymore. I have to go, but I'll call soon."

When Evan called that night he apologized for getting pissed off earlier and said he was glad Billy was helping me.

I knew he was just saying that so we could move on, but I was more than happy to go along with it. I didn't tell him I'd just gotten off the phone with Billy, who told me John had called from somewhere between Prince George and Mackenzie. They still didn't get there in time, but I was happy he was at least heading in the opposite direction of me.

Later, when I was lying in bed, I thought about my phone call with John, about how concerned he sounded when he thought I was upset. Then I realized I'd never heard that tone in my dad's voice. Not once. If John wasn't the Campsite Killer, I probably would've been happy I finally had a father. I didn't know which thought was worse, but they both made me cry.

On Monday another package arrived—same delivery driver, same address. When I saw it was from Hansel and Gretel I called Billy right away. He was over in Vancouver with Sandy, meeting with the rest of the task force, and told me not to open it. It was still sitting on my counter when John called later that afternoon.

"Did you get my present?"

"I haven't had a chance to open it." The package was larger and heavier than the last one, but I still asked, "Is it jewelry again?"

His voice was excited. "Open it now."

"Right now?"

"I wish I could see your face."

That was the last thing I wanted. "Hang on, I'll open it."

With John still on the phone, I pulled on a pair of garden gloves from my shop, then took a knife to the seal, feeling guilty about not waiting for Billy.

John said, "Is it open yet?"

"I'm just taking the paper out." He'd packed whatever it was carefully. I lifted the object out and unwound the bubble wrap.

It was a brand-new jack plane.

"It's beautiful." And it was. The handle was hardwood and stained dark chocolate, the steel blades gleamed. My fingers itched to try it out, but I only allowed myself to pick it up, to feel the weight of it, to imagine it gliding over wood, shavings falling to the floor, lifting off years of— Stop. Put it back in the box.

"You *really* like it? I could get you a different one—"

"It's perfect. That was thoughtful." I remembered how Dad would watch Lauren and Melanie on Christmas morning, how he'd smile when they opened their presents, how he'd leave the room to refill his coffee when it was my turn.

We were both silent.

"John, you seem like such a nice guy. . . ." *When you're not killing people or threatening me.* I gathered myself for the next part. "I just don't understand why you hurt those people."

No answer. I strained to hear his breathing. Was he mad? I eased forward.

"You don't have to tell me today. But I'd like it if you were honest with me."

"I am honest." His voice was cold.

"I know, of course. I just meant that if I understand you,

it will help me understand myself. Sometimes . . ." I imagined Sandy and Billy listening. Tuned them out. "Sometimes I have terrible thoughts."

"Like what?"

"I lose my temper a lot. I'm working on it, but it's hard." I paused, but he didn't say anything, so I kept going. "I feel this darkness come over me and I say awful things, or do really stupid stuff. It's better now that I'm older, but I don't like that side of myself. When I was younger I even got into drugs and alcohol for a while, just trying to block it all out. And I did some things I really regret, so I started seeing a psychiatrist."

"You still see one?" Would he think it was bad or would it encourage him to get help? As I continued to hesitate he said, "Sara?"

"Sometimes."

"Do you talk about me?"

The tone of his voice told me how to answer. "No, I wouldn't do that unless you said it was okay."

"It's not."

"No problem." I tried to keep my voice casual. "So can you tell me anything about your parents? That's one thing about growing up adopted—you never know your history." Both sets of my grandparents are gone now, but I still remember Mom's gruff German father and how her mom barely spoke English, just scurried around the kitchen like she was afraid to stop moving. Dad's parents were blue-collar, his dad a carpenter and his mom a homemaker. They were nice to me, but *too* nice. They tried so hard to make me feel like part of the family, they made me feel different. My grandmother always watching me with concerned eyes, the extra hug and kiss at the door.

John said, "What do you want to know?"

"What was your dad like?"

"He was Scottish. When he spoke, you listened." I pictured a large man with red hair yelling at John in a thick accent. "But I learned how to survive."

"Survive?" He didn't elaborate, so I said, "So what did he do for a living?"

"He worked in logging, a faller right up to the day he died. He was having a heart attack and still took down a hundred-and-fifty-foot Douglas fir." He laughed and said, "He was a mean son of a bitch." He laughed again and I wondered if it was something he did when he was uncomfortable.

"What about your mother? What's she like?"

"She was a good woman. Things weren't easy for her."

"So they've both passed on, then?"

"Yes. What kind of movies do you like?" Thrown by the abrupt change of subject, I took a moment to answer.

"Movies . . . I like lots of different ones. They have to be fast-paced—I get bored easily."

"Me too." He was quiet for a few seconds, then said, "Enjoy the rest of your day, Sara. We'll talk more soon."

I phoned Billy immediately, but he wasn't able to call back for ten minutes, which I spent pacing. He told me John was somewhere around Mackenzie now, which is northeast of

Prince George. The area is all provincial parks and mountain ranges, so he'd disappeared again, but Billy said I handled the call perfectly and it seemed like John was really connecting with me. He didn't give me a hard time about opening the package either, just said he understood John had put me on the spot and that they'd be over soon to pick it up. They think he probably shipped it from Prince George. Makes sense, it's the largest city in the North, so there are more depots and less chance of him standing out. Then Billy reminded me to call them right away if John sent another one. Later Billy e-mailed me a cool quote:

> Know the enemy,
> Know yourself,
> And victory
> Is never in doubt,
> Not in a hundred battles.

He must've been sitting right at his computer, because when I e-mailed him back, asking what the heck it meant, he responded in seconds. *Means you did a great job today, kid. Now go to bed!*

I laughed and sent him a quick *You too!* then turned off my computer. As I was heading to bed, the landline rang again. I thought it was Evan calling to say good night, but it was John.

"Hi, John. Everything okay?"

"I just wanted to hear your voice again before I shut down for the night."

I cringed. But I said, "That's nice."

"I really enjoyed our talk today."

"Me too. I liked it when you told me about your family."

"Why's that?"

"Well . . ." I hadn't expected him to ask for details. "Other kids in school, my friends growing up, they all knew where they came from. But my past was just a black hole. It made me feel cut off from regular people, like I was different or weird. I guess finally hearing some stories made me feel normal."

"It's nice getting to know you." He paused for a moment, then said, "When I was having my dinner, I thought about what you told me earlier."

"Which part's that?"

"About losing your temper . . . I get angry too."

Here we go. "What kinds of things make you angry?"

"It's hard to explain. You might not understand."

"I'd like to try. I want to get to know you better too." I meant it. Not just because he might reveal something that would help the cops catch him, I also wanted to know just how much we had in common.

He didn't say anything right away, so I continued.

"The other day when you called, you sounded like you were in pain?"

"I'm okay. Did I tell you we had a ranch when I was kid?"

Frustrated that he'd changed the subject on me again, I took a breath and said, "No, but that must've been a great way to grow up. How much land did you have?" I said, hoping he'd mention where he was from.

"We had about ten acres at the base of a mountain." His voice sounded excited. "Neighbors would bring sick animals to my mom all the time. She only used natural medicines, comfrey for coughs, things like that. She'd keep chicks and kittens in her shirt to keep them warm and she could almost bring them back from the dead." He gave a happy laugh. "We had a lot of farm dogs when I was growing up, they were always having puppies. The smallest one, Angel, was mine. She was part husky and part wolf—I hand-reared her with a bottle. She went everywhere with me. . . ." His voice turned flat. "But she ran away. My mother said it was in her nature. I tried to find her but never could."

"I'm . . . I'm sorry."

"I'm glad I found you, Sara. Good night."

I stayed awake for hours.

I hoped I'd feel better after talking to you. But I'm beginning to think nothing is going to do that. I'm also beginning to think they're never going to catch John. The second call came from north of Mackenzie, near Chetwynd, which is in the foothills of the Rocky Mountains. They thought they had something when a local rancher reported a truck on the side of the road, but it turned out to be just a couple of hunters. I marked a map with all the spots John had called from, each one taking him farther away from me physically but deeper into my mind, skewing my perceptions, like someone was turning me sideways and making everything look different, feel different.

184 · Chevy Stevens

I'm sure it makes sense to you that I'd be off-kilter, all things considered, but it feels deeper than that. More of a core upheaval. Like those volcanoes that have been brewing for years, then one day they just *explode*. I'm not saying I'm going to explode, although it's possible, just that it feels like something big has burst inside. Maybe because for so many years I've used the fact that I had real parents out there somewhere in the world as a way of comforting myself over anything I didn't like about my family.

It's like thinking you were handed the wrong life and you just had to get to the *right* one and everything would be okay, then finding out that there isn't a right one. Or the right one was actually the wrong one after all, or—never mind, you know what I mean. But then I think about my temper, my urges to lash out with tongue or fist, I think about Ally's tantrums, the line we both cross sometimes when we lose control, and I wonder if we do belong in that other life, with that other family.

When I first told you I found my mother, I said it was like standing on cracking ice. This is like falling straight through into the freezing water. You struggle back to the surface, your lungs burning, everything focused on that patch of light above you. And you finally make it there, but the hole's frozen over.

SESSION TEN

I've never been so scared in my life. I still can't believe I actually thought I was in the driver's seat with John. I'm such an *idiot*. You warned me about getting overconfident. Did I really think just because he asked me about my tools and my work, because he told me about his *dog*, that I had any control over him? He has all the power, and do you know why he has the power? Because I'm terrified of him and he knows it.

The day after our last session another box was delivered. I knew I should wait until Sandy and Billy opened it, but I wanted to know if he'd sent me another tool, wondering for a moment why it mattered, then brushing off the thought. This box was smaller and lighter than the one the jack plane had arrived in. I gave it a little shake but didn't hear anything. After I found some gloves, I carefully sliced open the package and lifted out a smaller box from inside. What if it was another victim's jewelry? I debated for half a second about calling Billy, then lifted the lid off the box.

A small rustic metal doll, maybe four inches tall and a couple of inches wide at the shoulders, lay nestled in cotton batting. The body seemed to be made from some sort of dark, heavy metal, like iron or steel. Its arms and legs were thick and straight down like a toy soldier's. The feet and hands were just round metal balls. It was wearing a little denim skirt and a yellow T-shirt. The clothes were delicate, the stitching intricate. The head of the doll was also a round ball of metal. But it had no face. No mouth or eyes.

Long straight brown hair, parted in the middle, was attached to the top of the head. Faint traces of glue were visible through the strands, but you had to look closely. Why had John sent this? I looked back in the main box to see if he'd included a note, but it was empty. I looked back at the doll again. Marveled at the clothes, the hair.

The hair.

I put the doll back in the box and called Billy. He and Sandy were at my house twenty minutes later—I was waiting in the driveway, pacing back and forth with Moose in my arms, when Billy stepped out of the driver's side of the SUV.

"It's in the kitchen," I said.

"You okay?"

"I'm *freaking out*."

"We'll get it out of here as soon as possible." He gave my shoulder a quick squeeze and scratched the top of Moose's head.

Sandy's first words as she exited the SUV were "I thought we agreed you would contact us the next time a package arrived."

"I changed my mind." I headed toward the house.

"Sara, this is an investigation." She was following close on my heels as we reached the front steps.

"I know what it is." I fought the urge to close the door in her face as I walked into the house.

"You could damage evidence."

I spun around. "I wore *gloves*."

"That still doesn't—"

Billy said, "Come on, Sandy. Let's have a look." She brushed past and headed straight to the kitchen. Billy shook a scolding finger at me behind her back. I gave a couldn't-help-it shrug. He smiled, then focused in on the box.

Sandy set a soft briefcase on the kitchen counter, took out some gloves, and handed Billy a pair. Their backs were to me as they examined the box. A minute crawled by, then Sandy lifted the smaller jewelry box out and gently took off the lid.

I said, "It's real hair, isn't it? Do you think it's from one of the victims?"

Neither of them turned around. Sandy put up a hand. "Sshhh . . ."

If I didn't already dislike her, that would have sealed the deal.

Finally, after a few moments that felt like hours, she murmured something to Billy. He nodded. Sandy slid the jewelry box into a plastic bag while Billy bagged the larger box.

Sandy turned and said, "We're going to take this back to the station."

"So the hair's from one of the girls?"

"We won't know anything conclusive until the lab runs some tests." She walked past me with the evidence bag. "We'll be in touch." She stopped with her hand on the front door handle and frowned at Billy, who was still in the kitchen. "Let's go, Billy."

"Right behind you."

She gave him another look and went outside.

I turned to Billy. "What's her problem?"

"She's just frustrated because none of the leads are going anywhere."

"You don't seem frustrated."

"I have moments, but I stay focused. I'm building the case brick by brick. If one falls out, I move on to the next. But I look for the *right* brick—if I shove them together without making sure each one fits, the structure's going to collapse. Even after we catch John, there's still a trial. That's why it's important to be patient." He gave me a stern look. "We can't risk losing trace evidence or contaminating it with a fiber from your clothes. One mistake and he gets away forever. Trust me, it's happened."

"I get it. I shouldn't have opened the box."

He nodded. "I know you were careful and wore gloves, but it's one of those department regulations we can't get away from. Remember, I'm on your side. We both have the same goal—to put John behind bars. The right piece of evidence and we've got him."

"What about the boxes? Did anyone see him sending them?"

"A clerk in Prince George thought he remembered the person who shipped the first box, but his description was of a man with a dark beard and sunglasses with a baseball cap pulled low. He's probably wearing a disguise. We'll follow up on this package right away, but unless the depot has a camera, or someone saw his vehicle, we're no further ahead."

"What about the jack plane—can't you find out where he bought it?"

"We've notified any stores in the Interior that sell them, but there are literally hundreds."

"That sucks, and I get that you guys are frustrated, but I wish Sandy would lose her attitude."

"She's formed friendships with a lot of the victims' families, so every time he slips through our fingers she feels like she's letting them down. Sandy releases her tension out loud. But that has nothing to do with you—you're doing great. That call last night was perfect."

"I still don't feel like I'm getting enough out of him."

"Remember, brick by brick. Anything he reveals is more than we knew before. 'Do not pursue an enemy feigning flight.' If you pressure him too much, he could become suspicious."

"I don't know, maybe . . . Sometimes it feels like he's a little off mentally, you know? Not just violent, but sort of disconnected from reality. He doesn't seem worried at all."

"He's confident and arrogant. But that doesn't make him any less dangerous. Remember that." Outside a horn honked.

Billy smiled. "I better go before she drives off and leaves me here."

As I walked him to the door I said, "I was reading an article the other day about how some killers keep trophies and souvenirs. You said the jewelry is his souvenir, so what's the doll?"

"That's what we need to find out. But feel free to e-mail me any articles that trigger something for you—any questions too. Even if it's just random notes. We're used to viewing everything from our perspective, but you might have a fresh take."

"I'll keep that in mind. I've been doing a lot of research. I don't know if it's helping me much, though. Just scares me, then I can't sleep for hours."

"Did you pick up a copy of *The Art of War*?"

"I keep forgetting. But I'll try to get one this week."

"It will help. I'm usually up late going over my notes or reviewing the file again, so feel free to call anytime you need to get something out of your head." He held my gaze. "We're going to catch him, Sara. I'm doing everything I can, okay?"

"Thanks, Billy. I really needed to hear that."

John called later that night. Thankfully Ally was already in bed, but I stayed downstairs to make sure she didn't hear me.

"Did you get my gift?"

"It's really nice, thanks. Did you make it?" As I thanked him, I realized it was the first time I'd done that.

"Yes."

"The detail on it was incredible. How did you learn how to do that?"

"My mother taught me how to sew. She taught me how to work with leather too."

"That's really cool. She must have been a neat woman. You never told me what her background was."

"Haida, from the Queen Charlotte Islands."

"I'm part First *Nations*?"

His tone was proud now. "The Haida believe in passing their stories down through each generation, and now I can share mine with you. I've got some good hunting stories. I could write a book." He chuckled. "Did you know a bear looks similar to a human when it's skinned? The hands and feet especially. Except the feet are backwards, and the big toe is on the outside."

"No, I didn't know that." I didn't *want* to know that. "Do you hunt bear?" I kept my tone interested while I tried to wrap my head around the fact that my grandmother was First Nations.

He said, "Moose, elk, bear."

Remembering that Sandy told me to find out anything I could about his guns, I said, "Do you have a certain gun you like to use?"

"I have a couple, but my favorite is my Remington .223. I shot my first one when I was four." He sounded pleased with himself. "Bagged my first deer when I was only five."

"With your dad?"

"I'm a better shot than he was." His voice turned serious.

"And I'll be a better father." Before I could ask him what he meant he said, "What was your favorite ice cream when you were a kid?"

The rest of the phone call he asked more questions along those lines: What was my favorite soda? What kind of cookies, chocolate with peanut butter or plain? The questions were so rapid-fire I didn't have a chance to think up lies. I was getting the feeling that he was a serious junk-food hound. But the only specific thing he revealed about himself was that he loved McDonald's—Big Macs, mainly. I wondered if that little detail would make Sandy happy or if she'd just be frustrated she couldn't stake out every McDonald's herself.

We'd only been on the phone for ten minutes, but I was exhausted, drained from his questions and the effort to gauge his reaction to every answer. Forcing myself to sound polite so I didn't lose any ground I'd just gained, I said, "John, it's been great talking to you, but I really have to go to bed."

He sighed. "Get some rest, we'll talk soon."

Billy called a few minutes later to tell me John was traveling south on the Yellowhead Highway. They think he was in McBride, a small town between the Rockies and the Cariboo Mountains. The population is under a thousand, but no one noticed anyone who fit John's description. The police were starting to wonder if he'd frequented these areas before. He might not be turning up on anyone's radar as a stranger because they *know* him. Hoping he'd continue south on the same highway, they were making sure all gas stations, truck stops, and stores had his description. When we finally hung up I went straight to bed, but I didn't sleep. I just stared at the ceiling, wondering if John was on the highway right now, if he was getting closer with every minute that ticked by.

The next day another box arrived. This time I called Sandy and Billy right away. I thought they'd just grab it and go, but they opened it with me there so if John called I'd know what was inside.

This doll was blond.

I wanted to cry at the silken curls, at the little polka-dot tank top and white shorts, wondering which woman's hair it was, wondering if it had been her pride and joy.

They thought he'd sent the package from Prince George and were going to check all the depots in the area, but I already knew he was smart enough to wear a disguise. After Sandy and Billy left, I went upstairs and checked out the Campsite Killer's Web site again. The pictures of his first victim showed a woman with black hair. Then I pulled up the photos of his next one. Suzanne Atkinson had straight brown hair—parted in the middle. His third, the woman he killed after Julia escaped, Heather Dawson, smiled broadly in her photo, her heart-shaped face framed by lustrous blond curls. She'd been proud of them.

She was last seen wearing a polka-dot blouse.

I called Billy right away. "You *knew* he took pieces of their clothing and hair."

He was quiet for a moment, then said, "We knew, but we didn't know what he did with them."

"What else are you holding back?"

"We try to fill you in as much as possible without jeopardizing the investigation."

"What about jeopardizing me? Shouldn't I—"

"We're *protecting* you, Sara. This is a man who can read people really well. The less you know, the better. If you inadvertently reveal something that only the police would know, we could lose him—or worse."

I took a deep breath and let it out slowly. Like it or not, I could see some of the sense in what he was saying.

"I hate being left in the dark. *Hate* it."

He laughed. "I don't blame you one bit. I promise to tell you everything you need to know, when we know it. All right?"

"Can you tell me why he leaves their faces blank?"

"My guess is he's depersonalizing them. Same reason he puts the victim's shirt over her head—he can't look them in the face."

"That's what I thought too. Do you think he feels shame?"

"If you ask him, he'd say yes. He's a psychopath—he knows how to mimic emotions. But I don't believe he truly feels them for one minute."

John called again that night and I managed to thank him for the doll. But this time I said, "Can you tell me about the girl?"

"Why?" So he wasn't going to deny it was from one of his victims.

"I don't know, I just wondered about her. What she was like?"

"She had a pretty smile." Her picture flashed in my mind. I thought of John touching her. I thought of her pretty mouth begging him to stop. I closed my eyes.

"Is that why you killed her?"

He didn't answer. I held my breath.

After a moment he said, "I killed her because I had to. I told you, Sara. I'm not bad."

"I know, but that's why I don't understand why you *had* to kill her."

He sounded frustrated as he said, "I can't tell you yet."

"Can you tell me why you made a doll with her clothes? I'm really interested in your . . ." What should I call it? "In your process."

"Then she stays with me longer."

"And that's important? That she stays with you?"

"It helps."

"What does it help with?"

"It just helps, okay? We'll talk more about it another time. Did you know pine beetles make blue wood?"

I didn't get the feeling he changed the subject to avoid anything. More like another thought occurred to him so he went with it. I hated how much he reminded me of myself.

"I've read about it, but I've never worked with any of it."

"It's not the beetle that kills the trees, you know. It's the fungus they carry." He paused, but I didn't know what to say and he went on. "I've been reading about different woods and tools so we can have things to talk about. I want to know everything about you."

I shuddered. "Me too. So what about you? Do you make things other than the dolls?"

"I like working with different materials."

"But you're obviously talented with metal. Are you a welder?"

"I can do lots of things." It wasn't a direct answer, so I was about to repeat the question when he said, "I have to get going, but I've got a question for you."

"Okay. Sure."

"What do you call a grizzly with no fur?"

"Um . . . I don't know."

"A bare bear!"

He'd called from Kamloops, one of the major cities in the Interior, and about five hours from his last location. But the fact that he was in a more populated area wasn't working to our advantage—there was a three-day rodeo and he called from somewhere in the middle of it. Billy sounded confident when he told me they were searching the crowd, but I could read anger in his clipped tone, his short sentences.

John called three times the next morning. The first thing he asked was where the dolls were and what I was doing with them. His voice was tight, so I quickly said, "I made a special shelf in my shop for them—that's where I spend most of my time."

"Okay, that's good." But then he said, "Are you sure they're safe there? What about sawdust? Or chemicals? Do you work with chemicals?"

I grasped at the first thing that came to mind. "It's a locked display case, so they're protected by glass." John didn't say anything, but I heard traffic. I said, "Would you like them back? I understand if you—"

"No. I have to go."

He called back twenty minutes later, asking again if I liked the dolls. Ten minutes after that he called again. His voice sounded more anxious with each call. Finally he said he had to go, he wasn't feeling well.

I wasn't feeling so great myself. I'd barely slept since he started sending me things. When I did, my dreams were haunted by screaming women being chased by metal figurines. I'd hoped to sleep in that morning because it was Saturday and I didn't have to drive Ally to school, but no chance of that after John's calls. Billy phoned right away to tell me the last couple of calls came from the outskirts of Kamloops and every available officer in the area was patrolling the roads. Ally and I fought all morning—I swear she senses when I'm at my least patient and picks that moment to drag her heels on *everything*. The more I tried to rush her, the more upset she got. She even grabbed my cell out of my hand and threw it across the living room. Thank God it just hit the couch. But I did mess up—I nearly forgot she had to go to a birthday party that afternoon, so we had to stop on the way there to grab a present.

Ally wanted Spider-Man walkie-talkies for the birthday boy, but the store was out and we didn't have time to go to another one. I assured her Jake would like the science kit, feeling like the worst mother in the world when I saw how disappointed she was. After I came home from dropping Ally off, I planned on getting some work done. But then I got a call from Julia.

I didn't recognize the number showing on the cordless, but the area code was Victoria and it could be a client.

The first words out of Julia's mouth were, "Has he called you again?"

"Ah . . ." The police warned me not to tell anyone, but she was in the same boat as I was. Didn't she have a right to know?

"He has, yes."

"He sent you my earrings—I had to *identify* them."

I didn't have a response, but I had a feeling she didn't want one.

She said, "Has he said anything about me?"

John's voice rang in my head. *I saw Julia's photo in the paper.*

"Nothing."

"I want to move, but Katharine thinks we should stay. I can't sleep." Her tone was bitter. Blaming.

"They're going to catch him—"

"That's what Sandy says, but I've been told that so many times. . . ."

"You've talked to Sandy?"

"The police keep me updated." How nice. "I have to go."

"Do you want me to call you if . . ." If what?

But she'd already hung up, leaving me wondering why she'd phoned in the first place. Then I wondered if even she knew why.

I dialed Sandy's cell and as soon as she answered said, "I just talked to Julia."

"Did you call her again?"

Why did she assume I'd called Julia, not the other way around? My face was hot.

"She called *me*."

"I hope you didn't discuss the case with her?"

"She asked if he called again and I said yes. That's it."

"Sara, you have to be careful with—"

"She already knew he'd call and she knows he sent me her earrings. If I denied everything she would've wondered more. She said you've been filling her in yourself anyway."

Sandy didn't say anything, so I jumped in with my own questions.

"What have you found out about the dolls? It's the victims' hair, isn't it?"

"We're still waiting for the DNA results."

"Have you notified their families?"

"Not at this point. We need to be careful how we approach

this—they don't know the Campsite Killer is in contact with someone."

"After all those calls today, please tell me you have a lead."

"Not yet." Her voice was curt. "The calls were getting closer to Cache Creek, moving west of Kamloops. There are a lot of provincial parks in the area, so he's probably traveling on back roads."

"Maybe he's heading back up north?"

"Try not to speculate, Sara." Her schoolteacher tone was bugging the crap out of me.

"Isn't that what police work is?"

I was proud of my comeback until she said, "No, it's a careful analysis of data and facts, then the drawing of a conclusion based on hard evidence."

"Well, then. Are there any *facts* or *data* that might give us an idea of what he does for a living? He seems to be on the road a lot, so I was thinking he could be a truck driver or a deliveryman or—"

"All possibilities. I'm about to step into a meeting now. Can I have Billy call you back so you can discuss it further with him?"

"No, I'm fine." I hung up the phone, frowning. What did I ever do to that woman?

I worked in the shop until it was time to pick up Ally. I was still trying to finish the cherry lamp table, but my heart wasn't in it. It didn't help that John's comment about "rich tones" kept flickering through my brain. Of course he liked the wood—it probably reminded him of blood. I shuddered at the macabre thought. I was used to being away from Evan for long stretches of time, especially during the summer, but it was never easy. Today I missed him terribly and wished I could call him, but he was out on the boat all day.

We'd been talking every night—we had a long call after I found out I was part First Nations. Evan thought it was great. But it was weird knowing Sandy or Billy, or whoever else, could listen whenever they wanted. It was also hard when Lauren and I talked on the phone because she'd say something personal and I knew she was being taped but she didn't. I usually tried to stick to the subject of our kids or the wedding. But not telling her what was really going on was killing me.

We'd finally made plans to go dress-shopping on Sunday. We were all going to meet at my house in the morning and drive to Victoria in my truck. Lauren was already baking something and I knew she'd have a thermos of coffee. Melanie, well, I was sure she'd bring her attitude. I was hoping like crazy this would be one of the days I didn't hear from John.

The rest of the afternoon passed quietly and I picked up Ally, who was so burned-out she fell into bed after her bath. When I tucked her in she informed me Jake already had two science kits. I felt so bad I told her I'd take some of her friends to a matinee soon, but she said, "You'll just forget, Mommy." I swore I wouldn't, my heart breaking that she doubted me. When I kissed her good night and whispered that I loved her, she didn't say it back. I told myself she was just tired. Evan called later and we managed to have a nice talk right up until I heard my cell ring.

"Hang on a sec, baby." I checked the display. "It's John."

"Call me back."

I picked up the cell. "Hello?"

"Sara . . ." There was a long pause.

I said, "You still there?"

"Did you like the dolls?" He slurred the last words and I wondered if he'd been drinking. In the background I heard traffic.

"Are you driving?"

"I asked you a question."

It was a phrase my dad used often when I was growing up, guaranteed to make me not want to answer at all, but I said, "Yeah, I like them. I told you that."

"I wasn't sure . . . wasn't sure you would." The slurring again.

What do I do with this? I waited him out.

"This is how it should be. Father and daughter . . . talking."

"For sure."

All I heard was breathing.

I said, "It meant a lot to me when you sent the dolls. I know they're important to you." I paused, but he was still quiet. "And I like talking to you. You're an interesting guy." It killed me to let him believe I liked anything about him.

"Yeah?"

"Absolutely. You have some great stories."

"Remind me to tell you about the time . . . I killed a bear with just my .22—only took one shot. Sucker had been tracking me. . . . Did you know grizzlies will track and kill other bears?"

I was about to answer when a car honked on his end.

"We'll talk more soon." He hung up.

I called Evan back and told him what had just happened.

"That's weird."

"No kidding. I'm going to Victoria with the girls tomorrow and I don't know what I'm going to do if he calls."

"Treat him like you would a normal person—tell him you're busy."

"But he's *not* a normal person."

"Let's talk about something else. How was Ally's birthday party today?"

"We almost missed it because John called three times this morning—it was awful. And I forgot Jake's birthday party so we had to get a present on the way there. Ally was so upset."

"Poor Ally. She feels neglected."

"Excuse me? Are you saying I'm *neglecting* my daughter?"

"I didn't mean it like how you're about to take it. Let's not go there."

"You already took it there, Evan. I feel bad enough without you getting on my case too."

"I'm sorry I said anything. I know you're having a hard time."

We were both silent for a moment. I imagined Sandy in a

room somewhere, headphones on, listening to my relationship problems, smiling that condescending smile.

I said, "I appreciate that you're looking out for me—"

"I am."

"I know, but I can take care of myself."

He laughed.

"Hey! I've managed just fine for years."

His voice teased, "Just admit you were a mess before you
fell in love with me." This time I laughed, not even caring
if Sandy was listening.

The next morning the girls arrived around nine-thirty, just
after I dropped Ally off at Meghan's. We took my Cherokee and Lauren brought fresh-baked scones and a thermos
full of coffee. The drive down was fun, with everyone talking at once and Lauren cracking runaway bride jokes. Melanie was even in a good mood, although we had a close call
when she asked to use my cell phone because she'd forgotten hers. When I hesitated she kept looking at me, so I
grabbed it out of my purse and handed it over. I was terrified John would call while she was on the phone, but she
just made a quick call to Kyle.

The morning flew by as we hit the downtown boutiques.
We were planning to have an outdoor wedding, so Evan
and I were trying to stick with a natural theme. We found
a bridesmaid dress that was perfect. It was this strapless tea-
length chiffon in a gorgeous silvery green, almost a sage, like

the flat side of fir needles, and it looked great on both girls. After we ordered the dresses we had a late lunch at an Irish pub overlooking the inner harbor. It was nice to have a day when I could just laugh and talk about familiar, everyday things. Normal things. But I forgot my life was anything but normal.

After the girls came back to my place and got their vehicles, I picked up Ally. As soon as we walked into the house I dug my cell phone out of my purse to put it on the charger.

Twenty missed calls.

I scrolled through the list of numbers. They were all from John and Billy. I checked my voice mail, but there was just one message from Billy to call him ASAP, then five hang-ups. Why hadn't I heard it ring?

I grabbed the cordless and called my cell. It vibrated in my hand. On its side there's a button that changes it from ring to vibrate, but I hadn't touched my cell since that morning. It must have gotten bumped in my purse when I dropped my wallet back in.

I called John right away, but his cell was off. Then I phoned Billy and got his voice mail. I left a message.

For the next hour I paced around my house, glancing at the phone, willing it to ring, worried about why Billy hadn't called back yet, and all the while struggling to stay calm so Ally didn't sense something was wrong. Finally, just after I put her to bed, John called.

As soon as I picked up I said, "I'm so sorry I missed your calls. The phone was set on vibrate and I didn't know—"

"You *ignored* me."

"That's what I'm trying to explain. I didn't ignore you, the phone was in my purse and I didn't know it was on vibrate. It was in the very bottom—you wouldn't believe the junk I have in there—and there was a lot of noise around me." Not a lie. Three excited women do make quite a racket.

I paused and held my breath.

"I don't believe you, Sara. You're lying."

"I'm *not*. I swear. I wouldn't do that to—"

But he'd already hung up.

And that's where it's still at. My next call was from Billy, who was as close to pissed off as I've ever heard him sound.

"How did this happen, Sara?"

After we spoke for a minute or two his tone changed and he said I shouldn't beat myself up—it was an accident. I'm pretty sure Sandy didn't agree, though. She called as soon as I hung up from Billy, asking the same question. I told her I hadn't ignored John on purpose and I think she believed me, eventually, but I could tell she was still angry. She said John's cell had pinged off towers in Kamloops each time it connected with my phone, but he'd been staying in high-traffic areas. They pulled over a bunch of vehicles, running checks on anyone who looked suspicious, but they still didn't have a suspect.

Sandy told me they'd have a patrol car parked outside,

just in case John decided to hop on a ferry and talk to me in person. When I asked if she actually thought he'd do anything, she said, in her tense voice, "We'll find out soon, but if he *is* stupid enough to try something, we'll get him."

But I haven't heard from John since. Not once. I wish I could be happy about that.

SESSION ELEVEN

I *can't* sit still right now. I have to keep moving, have to walk around. My legs ache with frustration, with the unbearable agony of waiting. It must be driving you nuts, my bouncing around your office. You should see me at home—I pace from window to window, pulling up blinds, dropping them back down. Sweep up dirt, only to abandon the half-filled dustpan in the corner. Put half the dishes into the dishwasher, then start doing laundry. I stuff my mouth with peanut-butter-laden crackers, then race upstairs to Google, find a thread of something on one site, and follow it from site to site until my eyes are blurry.

Next I call Evan, who tells me to do some yoga, go to the gym, take Moose for a walk, but instead I pick fights with him over stupid stuff—because that makes so much more sense.

I make notes, charts. I have graphs for my graphs. My desk is peppered with Post-its, rapid thoughts scrawled in a jerky hand. It's *not* helping. I ignore work e-mails or barely answer. I'm trying to buy myself time on some projects, trying to hang on to it all, but I'm losing my grip on everything.

As soon as I got home after our last session, Billy and Sandy pulled into my driveway. When I opened the front door and saw their grave faces, my stomach flipped.

"What's wrong?"

"Let's go inside," Billy said.

"Tell me what's going on first." I searched his eyes. "Is Ally—"

"She's fine."

"Evan—"

"Your family's all fine. Let's go inside. Got some coffee?"

After I handed them theirs I leaned against the counter, the hard edge biting into my back, my clammy hands curled around the warm mug. Billy took a gulp of coffee; Sandy didn't touch hers. She'd spilled something on her white shirt and her hair was a mess. Dark circles shadowed her eyes.

I said, "Did he kill someone?"

Sandy looked at me hard. "A female camper was reported missing this morning from Greenstone Mountain Provincial Park near Kamloops. Her boyfriend was found dead at the scene."

I dropped my coffee mug. It shattered and I watched coffee splash up on Sandy's jeans. But she didn't even glance down, she was still staring at me. None of us moved to clean it up.

My hands went to my face. "Oh, God. Are you sure? Maybe—"

"He's the main suspect," Sandy said. "The shell casings found at the scene are consistent."

"This is my fault."

Billy said, "No, it's not, Sara. He made the choice." But Sandy didn't say anything.

"What are we going to do now? What about the girl?"

He was quiet for a few seconds. "Right now we're searching the surrounding area for the female victim's body."

"You think she's dead?"

Neither of them answered.

"What's her name?"

Billy said, "We haven't released that to the media yet—"

"I'm not the *media*. Tell me her name."

Billy looked at Sandy, who turned to me and said, "Danielle Sylvan. Her boyfriend was Alec Pantone."

My mind filled with images of a young woman fleeing through the bushes, John chasing after her with a rifle in his hands. I wondered when I'd get her doll.

I stared down at the broken mug, the pool of coffee.

"What color's her hair?"

They were both silent. I looked up. Dread passed over me.

"What *color* is her *hair*?"

Billy cleared his throat, but before he could say anything, Sandy told me.

"Auburn—long and wavy."

The room spun. I gripped the back of the counter with

my hands. Billy stood up and in one big step was at my side, clasping my shoulders.

"You all right, Sara?"

I shook my head.

"Do you want to get some air?"

"No." I took a couple of breaths. "I'll . . . I'll be okay."

Billy leaned against the counter beside me. His arms were crossed in front of his chest and he massaged his biceps through his black Windbreaker over and over. From across the table coils of anger radiated off Sandy.

I turned to her. "You think it's my fault."

She said, "It's no one's fault. He's a killer, we never know what's going to set him off."

"But he's never killed this early before—never in May."

She stared at me. Her eyes were bloodshot and the pupils dilated, turning the cool blue almost black. Her skin looked windburned.

I said, "You think because I didn't answer his calls he went out and killed someone."

"We don't know what—"

"Just say it, *Sandy*—admit you think it's my fault."

She gazed at me steadily. "Yes, I think having his calls ignored triggered him to find a victim. No, I don't think it was your fault."

For a moment I felt victorious—I'd forced her to admit what she was really thinking—then the horror of the situation washed back over me.

I turned to Billy. "How old were they?"

"Alec was twenty-four and Danielle twenty-one." *Twenty-one*. I thought of their parents getting the news and pressed the heels of my hands hard into my eyeballs.

Block it out. Block it out.

"What do we do now?"

Billy said, "We're not getting a signal from his cell phone, but just in case, we'd like you to try to call him again." He took my cell off its charger on the counter and handed it to me.

Before I started to dial I said, "How am I supposed to act?"

Billy said, "Good question. You should have a plan before you—"

Sandy said, "Just start off expressing how sorry you are, show lots of remorse, then gauge his reaction. Wait and see if he brings up anything, but don't say you know about the woman. It won't hit the news until tonight."

I glanced at Billy for confirmation and he nodded, but his neck was flushed. He didn't look at Sandy and I wondered if he was pissed she had interrupted him.

As I dialed John's number Sandy's hand curled into a fist on the table. Her nails were chewed to the quick. John's phone was off.

I shook my head.

Sandy stood up. "We're going to fly out to Kamloops this afternoon. Keep trying to reach him. We'll call you if we learn anything further from the crime scene."

I walked them to the door. "She could still be alive?"

Billy's face was tense. "Of course, and we'll try our best

to find her." But I saw it in their eyes—they were going to Kamloops to find a body.

That night I tossed and turned for hours, thinking about everything Sandy had said. My guilt segued into anger when I thought more about the police—why hadn't they staked out all the parks? They knew he was in the area. But when I got out of bed and Googled, I learned the park was one hundred and twenty-four hectares. How were they ever going to find her? How were they going to find *him*?

I called John several times, but his phone was never on. I thought of what I'd say if he did answer. *Why did you do it? Did she die quickly?* It was the second question that haunted me the most. I could taste Danielle's fear. It gnawed at my skin, burrowed into my muscles, screamed in my head: *You did this!*

Evan called that night after Ally was in bed and I cried through the entire phone call. I tried my best not to sound blaming, but it leaked out when I said, "You'd been giving me a hard time about checking my phone all the time, so I was trying to just relax and have fun like you said, and—"

"I didn't know he'd—"

"I *told* you, but you kept saying I was worrying too much and now two people are dead."

"Sara, I was just trying to help you—you're my priority, not him. And it's awful what he did, but it's not your fault. You do see that, right?"

"If I'd answered the phone, they'd still be alive."

"And if you went back in time and killed Hitler, millions of—"

"That's not the same thing. I have no control over what happened then, but I could've stopped this."

"All of this is outside of your control, but you're going to blame yourself no matter what."

"I wish you could understand why I'm so upset."

"I do—it's horrible what happened, and you're taking it even harder because you get so involved in everything. But it stresses *me* out when you get yourself all worked up. You have to try to step back a little."

"It's not that simple, Evan. I can't just close my eyes to everything like you." I flinched at my harsh tone. Then waited out the silence that followed. Finally Evan broke it.

"I'm not the bad guy here."

I groaned. "I'm sorry. This is just so awful and I miss you."

"I miss you too—I'm coming home this weekend, okay?"

"I thought you have a big group."

"I'll call Jason in. You need me right now."

"God, Evan. I want to tell you to stay, but I really do need you." I rubbed my nose on my sleeve. "I keep seeing her face, you know, seeing her having fun with her boyfriend. Then John's there—with a gun, and she's watching her boyfriend get shot, then she runs away, and . . ." I was crying again now, trying to get my breath.

"Baby . . ." Evan sounded helpless. "You've got to stop thinking about stuff like that, *please*."

"I can't help it. I think about what if it was *you*, then I just—"

"Mommy?" Ally was at the top of the stairs.

I cleared my throat and tried to keep my voice pleasant.

"What's wrong, sweetie?"

"I can't sleep."

"I'll be up in a minute."

Evan and I said our good-byes, then I washed my face in cold water, hoping Ally wouldn't notice my puffy eyes. As I cuddled in bed with her, Moose at our feet, I stroked her hair and gently tickled her back. Then I thought of another mother out there who just found out her daughter was missing. I wondered what she did to soothe her to sleep when she was little. I wondered what this woman would think if she knew her daughter was gone because my cell was on vibrate.

When Ally drifted off, I eased out of her bed. Moose's head popped up, but I motioned for him to stay and he dropped it back onto Ally's Barbie quilt. In my office I pulled up Google and typed in "Danielle Sylvan." I hoped there wouldn't be anything, but I found an article in the paper where she'd volunteered for a literacy program. The photo of her face beaming as she held out an armful of books to some children just about killed me. The deep red of her hair was vibrant against her pale skin. I imagined that skin even paler in death, and my stomach flipped. I sent the article to

Billy, knowing he had a BlackBerry and would get it instantly. My message said, *Did you find her?* I waited and waited—hitting send/receive every second. Finally, ten minutes later, he answered: *not yet.*

I turned off the computer and climbed into bed, cell on the night table. I tossed and turned for hours.

It's your fault, all your fault. Your fault.

The next morning Ally was cranky: "I don't want to wear my raincoat." "I want to wear the blue socks, no, the yellow ones." "When will Evan be home?" "Why can't Moose come?" "I'm tired of cereal." Finally I got her dressed and we were on our way. We were a mile from her school when my cell rang in my purse. Ally, who was singing in her seat and moving her head back and forth in time with the windshield wipers, began to sing louder. I reached into the console and grabbed my cell. As soon as I saw John's number, I panicked.

"Ally Cat, this is an important client, so you have to be quiet, okay?"

She kept singing.

I raised my voice as the phone rang again. "Ally, that's *enough.*"

She looked at me. "You're not supposed to answer the phone while you're driving, Mommy—it's not safe."

"You're right, that's why Mommy's pulling over." I quickly turned onto the soft shoulder of the road and stopped the Cherokee. "He really needs my help, so you have to be super quiet, okay?" Rain thundered down on us as Ally stared out the window, drawing shapes in the condensation. She was pissed at me, but at least she was quiet.

I answered the phone in a rush. "Hello?"

"Sara." His voice was low and raspy. Like he'd been yelling.

I said, "I'm really sorry about what happened. I made a mistake, but it won't happen again, okay? I promise."

I held my breath and braced for a barrage, but he was silent.

So Ally couldn't hear, I turned to the window and lowered my voice. "John, there was something about a missing woman on the news last night?"

He was still silent. In the background I could hear traffic, but there was another sound—a persistent thump. I strained my ears. Beside me Ally's legs started to kick. Still waiting for John to answer, I flipped open the glove box and found a notepad and a pen. As I handed it to Ally, I motioned for her to draw me a picture. She ignored the pad and crossed her arms over her chest. I gave a warning look, and she stared out the window.

I said, "Are you still there?" The thump in the background was louder.

"You shouldn't have ignored me. I needed you."

"I'm sorry. But I'm here now. Can you tell me where she is?"

His voice was flat. "She's with me."

Hope surged—until I realized he didn't say she was alive. "Is she okay?"

Beside me Ally kicked at the dashboard. I grabbed her foot and gave another warning look. She pulled her foot out of my hand and started bouncing up and down in her seat. I clamped my hand down on the phone's speaker. "Ally, stop it this minute or—or you're not going to Meghan's sleepover on Sunday." Ally gave a shocked gasp and sat back in her seat.

On the phone John said, "I don't know what to do."

I had to say something fast. *Think, Sara, think. He depersonalizes them. He doesn't want to think of them as people. Make her real.*

"The news said her name is Danielle. She has people who really care about her, John. Her parents, they just want her home, and—"

"I wanted *you*. The noise was getting bad—nothing was working. I couldn't wait any longer."

I glanced at Ally. She was drawing on the window again.

"Well, you can talk to me now, so you can let her go home, okay?"

His voice was flat. "It's not that simple." I cringed as I remembered saying the same thing to Evan.

"It is—you can do it. I know you can. You just have to take a step back and think about it for a minute." The thumping stopped in the background. Was it Danielle? Had she passed out?

The rain had eased. Ally was still drawing on the window. I covered the speaker on the phone and said, "I'm just stepping outside for a minute, honey."

Her eyes were wide. "Mommy, no. Don't leave—"

"I'll be right here." I opened the door and stood at the side of the road, smiling at Ally through the window as I said to John, "You could blindfold her, then drive somewhere and just leave her on the side of the road." In the vehicle Ally's face was pinched. I drew little faces on the window. She unbuckled herself and crawled onto my seat. She started to smile as she drew teeth on my happy face.

John said, "It won't work."

It was starting to rain harder again. I was getting soaked as cars passed me.

"It *will*. By the time someone finds her you'll be long gone. They'll never catch you."

"This wasn't how it was supposed to happen." A loud *smack*, like he'd punched a wall.

"Are you okay?" All I could hear was heavy breathing. I tried a different tactic. "I know you don't really want to hurt Danielle. I saw pictures of her on TV and she looked just like me. She's someone's *daughter*—you have to let her go."

Silence.

"John?"

A click, then a dial tone.

I climbed back into the Cherokee and cranked the heat while I watched my windshield wipers swish back and forth. The cell phone was hot in my hand. Beside me Ally was saying something, but I couldn't think straight. Was he killing her right now? Did I say something wrong? I should have—

"Mom! I'm going to be late for school."

The phone was ringing again. "I know, sweetie, I'm sorry. Mommy just has to take this, then we'll get going, okay?" She groaned beside me. I gave her a little smile, but my heart raced as I glanced down at the phone. It was Billy. I let out my breath. Ally was kicking at the dashboard and singing again, but this time I didn't try to stop her.

"Billy, thank God."

"We got a good signal off the call." His voice was clipped. "He's in Kamloops and we're doing a sweep of the area—every available officer is on the road. But I don't want you to get your hopes up."

"She's alive—I *know* it."

I heard voices in the background, then Sandy was on the phone.

"If he calls again you have to try to keep him on the line as long as possible. Let him do the talking. If by any chance he hasn't killed her, we want to keep it that way."

"But what do I say? I'm scared I'll say something wrong and he'll—"

"Just proceed cautiously."

"What does that mean? Do I ask about her or not?"

Sandy sighed. "Just stay calm when you're talking to him. He needs to hear you care about him, that you're interested in him, that you're sorry. He probably felt rejected when you ignored his calls—"

"I didn't ignore—"

"Sara, do you really want to argue over semantics? A woman's life may depend on this next call. What are you doing right now?"

I gritted my teeth against all the ways I wanted to tell her off and simply said, "I have to drive Ally to school."

"She's *with* you?" Her voice rose.

"I was driving her to school, but he didn't hear her."

"If he finds out you never told him you have a child—"

"I don't want that either, Sandy—she's my *first* priority. And right now she's late for school."

"Drop her off, then call us."

I bit out, "Fine."

As I pulled back on the road Ally said, "Is the woman okay, Mommy?"

Still going over Sandy's call in my head, I said, "What woman, honey?"

"The one you were talking about with your client. You said she was missing."

Crap, crap, crap.

I tried to think back over what she might have heard. "Oh, she just got a little lost when she was walking home. But the police are going to find her soon."

"I don't like it when you talk on the phone so much."

"I know, honey. And I really appreciate how good you were."

She stared out the window.

In front of the school I got out and gave Ally a hug and a kiss. Her shoulders were slumped and her little face pinched. I pulled back and looked her in the eyes.

"Ally Cat, I know I haven't been the best mommy lately,

but I promise I'll try harder, okay? This weekend Evan's coming home and we'll do something as a family."

"With Moose too?"

"Of course!" I was relieved this earned a small smile at least. As Ally started to run to the doors of the school, she stopped and turned. "I hope the police find the lady who's lost, Mommy."

Me too.

As soon as I got home I called Billy. "What do you want me to do?"

"If he phones again, just remember what Sandy said, stay calm and let him talk. Don't forget he's calling because he's trying to reach out. He's in a highly emotional state and you seem to be the one person he feels can help him. He'll probably call soon."

But he didn't. I paced around my house, then tried to work in my shop but couldn't focus. So I drank countless cups of coffee—which didn't exactly help take the edge off—and spent hours Googling serial killers, hostage negotiation, all the while thinking about what could be happening to Danielle. I e-mailed Web page after Web page to Billy, feeling calmer each time I sent something and each time he answered, even if it was just a quick message: *you're doing great, keep them coming.* Then I thought about John, about how he said he couldn't wait any longer, the pressure just built until he had to do *something.* The sudden realization that I understood exactly how he felt scared me more than anything.

Later that evening Ally and I were just sitting down to dinner when my cell rang. It was John.

Ally made a face as I got up from the table.

"I'll just be a minute, sweetie. If you finish all your dinner we'll watch a movie together after, okay? But you have to promise to be quiet as a mouse."

She sighed but nodded and dug her spoon into her mashed potatoes.

I raced into the other room and answered the phone.

"John, I'm really glad you called back. I was worried." I was still worried. I didn't know if he was calling for help, or to tell me it was too late.

He didn't answer.

"Is Danielle okay?"

"She won't stop crying." The frustration in his voice terrified me.

"It's not too late. You can let her go. For me, *please*. She didn't do anything wrong. I was the one who messed up." I held my breath.

He was quiet.

I said, "Can I talk to her?"

"That wouldn't be good for you." His tone was parental. A father telling his daughter she can't have another cookie.

"What are you going to do?"

"I don't know." He sounded frustrated again.

"You don't have to do anything right now. Do you want to talk for a little bit? You asked me what I like to eat the other day. I was wondering what kind of stuff you like. Are you allergic to anything?"

"No, but I don't like olives?" His voice rose at the end.

"I'm not a fan of them either—or liver."

He made a disgusted noise. "Liver is the body's filtration system."

"Exactly." I laughed, but it sounded hollow. "John, the other day you said the noise was getting bad. What did you mean? Is it bad now?" If I could figure out what the problem was, maybe I could use it to make him let Danielle go.

"I don't want to talk about it."

"Okay, no problem. I just wondered if it's something you can get help for."

"I don't need help."

"I didn't mean it like *that*. I just thought if you talked to me about it, maybe I could help."

"This conversation isn't going anywhere." He sounded exasperated. "I'll call you another time."

"Wait, what about Danielle—"

But he was gone.

I threw the cell onto the couch and put my head in my hands. The phone rang a minute later. I looked at the call display. It was Billy.

"Good work, Sara. He's still in Kamloops, but we got a better location on him, so we've set up a couple of roadblocks on the main highway."

"But if he sees a roadblock right after talking to me, won't he suspect something?"

"We have counterattack vehicles set up so it just looks

like we're out to get drunk drivers. I think we're close, Sara. I don't think he wants to hurt her, but he doesn't know what to do with her either. There's a chance you can convince him to let her go."

"Do you honestly think so, Billy? Do they ever let them go?"

"It depends on how much of a risk he thinks she is. But odds are in our favor. We just have to exploit the enemy's dispositions to attain victory."

"What the heck does *that* mean?"

"You need to flatter him, convince him you think he's a nice guy. That you know he'll do the right thing. He wants to be your father. Treat him like one." My stomach coiled in on itself and my guts cramped.

"I'll try. I have to go—" I made it to the bathroom just in time.

But I didn't hear from him again that night. Billy checked in later and told me the roadblock hadn't turned up anything except a couple of impaired drivers. The next morning, Saturday, Evan came home. The minute he walked through the door I hugged him so tight he had to practically peel me off. As he unpacked I followed him from room to room, telling him everything that had happened, every conversation I'd had with Billy or Sandy since. I was keyed up, jumping at every noise and talking a mile a minute, but just knowing he was home and could distract Ally if John called again was a huge relief.

Ally hadn't forgotten my promise to do something as a family that weekend, and she made sure she told Evan about it while he made us grilled cheese sandwiches and tomato soup. I'd already reassured her as soon as we woke up that we'd go to the park later, but she'd looked at me doubtfully. It didn't help that I'd been on the phone all morning right up until Evan got home. First with Billy, then Lauren called. I hadn't talked to her since we went shopping, so I had to chat for a bit or it would look odd, but acting normal on the phone took so much energy I was exhausted by the time I hung up.

After lunch we headed down to the seawall and Maffeo Sutton Park—Ally loves the playground there and we usually take her to the ice-cream parlor on the promenade. I did my best to enjoy some precious time with my family, but I kept taking out the cell in my pocket, making sure it wasn't on vibrate.

When we got to the ice-cream parlor we ordered hot chocolates and a small bowl of ice cream for Ally, who insisted we get a bowl for Moose. We were sitting at an outdoor table near the marina, watching people walk past on the boardwalk with their baby carriages and dogs, when my cell rang. Evan froze and my stomach clenched, but when I saw who it was I mouthed, *Billy*, to Evan, who nodded and headed inside to the bathroom.

Billy told me they were now searching campsites and motels, hitting grocery stores and every gas station they could with John's sketch, checking surveillance cameras. We hung up just in time for me to see Ally spill hot chocolate down her coat. As I walked toward the shop to grab a napkin, I heard my cell ring on the table.

I spun around.

Ally lifted the cell to her ear.

"*Ally, no! Don't answer it!*"

I sprinted toward the table. I was almost there—my hands reached for the phone.

She said in a singsong voice, "Mommy can't come to the phone right now 'cause she's spending time with *me*," and hung up.

She handed me the phone, then went back to eating her ice cream. I grabbed her shoulders and spun her toward me. She dropped her spoon.

"Ally, you're *never* supposed to touch my phone."

Her eyes filled with tears. "But you're always talking on it." The woman at the next table gave me a dirty look and whispered to her friend. I let go of Ally and flipped open my phone.

Evan ran out of the shop. "I heard yelling, what's going on?"

I scrolled through received calls. *Please, please, please let it have been Billy.*

The last call was from John's number.

Evan said, "Sara, what happened?"

I tried to answer, but I was frozen.

Ally sobbed. "I told the man Mommy was busy."

Evan's face paled as he looked at me. Hand over my mouth, I nodded. He tried to put his arm around me, but I shrugged it off.

"I have to think."

Stop. Breathe. He might not have turned his cell off right away. He might be as shocked as I was.

I walked a few paces from Evan and Ally and dialed John's number. I had to start over twice.

He answered on the first ring.

"John, I'm so sorry, but—"

He said, "You lied," then hung up.

I turned and looked at Evan. He was sitting beside Ally with his arm around her shoulders. Our eyes met and I shook my head. He stood up and started to clear the table as he said something to Ally. They walked over to where I was leaning against the railing, my hand gripping the cold metal. Ally wouldn't look at me.

Evan said, "Let's head back to the car, your mom's turning blue, Ally."

I smiled at her and pretended to shudder as I rubbed my hands up and down my arms. But she still wouldn't look at me. As we walked toward the parking lot, Evan grabbed my hand in his and held tight. We stared at each other while Ally walked ahead with Moose on his leash. All I could think about was Danielle. Did I just sentence her to death?

I said, "Billy and Sandy will probably—"

My cell rang and my heart stopped. I grabbed it, looked at the call display, and let out my breath.

"It's Billy."

Evan said, "I'll go ahead with Ally." He caught up to her and took her hand. Following behind, I answered the phone.

"God, Billy, what are we going to do?"

It was Sandy. "Billy's on the other line. What happened? How did Ally get the phone?"

"It was on the table, I just turned my back for a second."

"Sara, we went over this. You knew if he caught you in a lie he'd probably kill Danielle."

"I didn't know Ally was going to answer it—she's not supposed to, but I've been on it so much lately she just—"

"It shouldn't have been out of your hands for a *second*."

I raised my voice. "I'm going to hang up if you keep talking to me like this, Sandy."

She was silent for a moment, and when she spoke again her voice was calm.

"The calls came from Clearwater, which is north of Kamloops, but we'll put a patrol car on your street tomorrow and have someone follow you when you leave."

"You think he's coming *this* way?"

"We don't know where he's going."

My heart was going nuts in my chest. "What about Ally? She has school and—"

"Talk to her teachers, tell them there's a custody issue. Make sure they know she's not to go with anyone. Take her right to her class, and tell her to wait with her teacher until you pick her up. Don't let her out of your sight."

"You don't think—he wouldn't hurt Ally, would he?"

"All we know is that he's very angry and a woman's probably dead by now because of this."

"Stop blaming me, Sandy. Maybe if you were doing your job, he wouldn't be calling in the first place. Why aren't there more men on this?"

"We have every member of Serious Crimes on this now, but it's a process—"

"Well, your *process* isn't working."

This time I hung up the phone and stalked toward the car with self-righteous anger spurring me on. But then I thought of Danielle and my mind filled with images of her dying on a forest floor, clawing at mounds of earth, begging for her life. And the truth burned like acid in my gut. It was my fault.

The ride home was silent, Evan's face tense when he reached over and held my hand. Grateful for the warmth, I stared out the windshield, blinking back tears.

Evan said, "Do you think you should talk to your family?"

I shook my head. "Sandy would have a bird, but I don't want to drag anyone else into this anyway."

"They might start wondering why you're so distracted."

"They're pretty used to me being obsessed about something. I'll just say I'm busy with the wedding or behind with work, which I am." Another wave of anxiety swamped me when I thought of all the e-mails I'd been ignoring.

"Maybe you should think about taking some time off."

"I've spent years building my business—I can't just drop everything."

"You can build it back up."

"I'm just a little behind—I can handle it." I was a lot more than a little behind.

"Then maybe you and Ally should come up to the lodge with me for a while."

"Ally's already struggling in class. I can't pull her out now. And the lodge is so remote. If anything happened up there . . ." I used to love going to Evan's lodge and hanging out in Tofino: the West Coast hippie lifestyle mixing with five-star resorts, organic coffee shops with hemp-seed muffins, the rustic art galleries, and kayak shops. But now all I could think about was the small police station, the hours of driving on a winding road through the mountains with no cell coverage.

"Then I'll take some time off."

I gave him a look. "And how are you going to do that? You just told me yesterday the lodge was booked for the rest of the summer."

He groaned. "I hate not being here for you. I should be taking care of you and Ally."

Even though Ally was in the back listening to Evan's iPod, I lowered my voice.

"We'll be *fine*. The police are watching the house and we have an alarm. Besides, you'll be home for the next couple of days. But I can't see him coming to the island—he always ignores me when he's pissed off."

"I want you to be extra careful."

"No kidding."

We lapsed into silence.

After a while I said, "Maybe he already let her go. You know, before he called."

"Maybe." Evan gave my hand a squeeze. But he didn't look me in the eye.

That's why I didn't want to wait until Wednesday to see you. I *couldn't* wait. All I've been doing is waiting. The whole weekend Evan and I watched the news religiously. We jumped out of our skin every time the phone rang, but my cell never went off except when Billy eventually called and told me the same stuff as Sandy, minus the part where she made me feel like I'd just signed Danielle's death warrant. When I said everything felt totally out of control, he told me again to get a copy of that book he's always quoting from. He said, "It's the only thing that helps me when I'm worried about the investigation. I review the files and focus on strategies. 'The skillful warrior does not rely on the enemy's not coming, but on his own preparedness.' I think of every possible scenario or direction the case might take, then I prepare for each event."

I said, "Wow. When do you sleep?"

He laughed. "I don't." I was surprised because I figured him for the type to hit the sheets and be out in ninety seconds like Evan. It was nice to know I'm not the only one who gets obsessed and can't sleep.

When I told him Evan was home for the weekend, he sounded relieved and told me to hang in there. I asked him when he was going to be back on the island and he said Monday, which is today, so I'm sure I'll hear from him soon. Sandy's staying behind. I guess until they find Danielle . . .

Evan stayed home as long as he could, even Sunday night, which is when he normally leaves. Poor guy had to get up at four this morning to head back to the lodge. We held each other at the door for a long time. After he left, I climbed into bed with Ally and snuggled next to her until it was time to get up for school.

I saw Danielle's parents on TV a couple of times. Evan told me to stop watching, but I couldn't. Her mom doesn't look very old. Maybe she had Danielle when she was young like me with Ally. I wondered if she warned her to be careful before she left on her camping trip or if she told her to have fun.

SESSION TWELVE

Thanks for fitting me in. You'll hear about this tonight on the news, but I wanted to tell you myself.
If I can, that is. All the way here I practiced saying
the words out loud, but . . . it's just so hard. I haven't
even told Evan yet—he's out on the boat. But I *have* to
tell someone. I have to get this feeling out of me. I feel
like Lady Macbeth trying to wash the blood off her
hands.

This morning Billy arrived at my door with his BlackBerry
gripped tight in his hand—and a look in his eyes that made
my stomach drop.

"She's dead, isn't she?"

"Let's talk."

We went into the living room. Even though it was sunny
my body started to shiver. As soon as Billy sat in the armchair beside the couch Moose leaped into his arms. This

time Billy just gave him a quick pat and put him back on the floor. He met my eyes, his face serious.

"They found her body this morning."

I tried to process what he'd just told me, but my brain felt sluggish.

"Where?"

"Wells Gray Park. It's the closest to Clearwater, so we'd searched there first, but it's over five hundred thousand hectares. We might not have found her if some hikers hadn't wandered off a trail. Looks like Danielle was killed within a few hours of his call."

Hearing Danielle's name made her death brutally real. I thought about John depersonalizing his victims—if only I could do the same.

"Was she . . ."

"She wasn't raped, but she was strangled." Billy's voice was steady, but he kept flipping his BlackBerry around and around in his hand.

I frowned. "That's not his usual way—"

"We don't know why he deviated from his pattern—the situation with you may have made it difficult for him to complete his ritual—but we're sure it's him. We're still investigating the scene. Looks like he let her out at the side of the road, then chased her into the woods."

A sick feeling washed over me. "Oh, God. I told him to leave her at the side of a road."

"He may have been trying to do just that. But then she started to run and it excited him, or something else triggered him."

"He didn't rape her, though."

"And that may have had something to do with you humanizing her—or because of the similarity between the two of you."

"You mean because we have the same hair?"

"She was probably chosen because of her resemblance to you, so this attack wasn't sexually motivated. It was an attempt to connect with you."

"And now she's dead."

Tears were leaking out of my eyes. Billy reached over and gripped my shoulder.

"Hey. Stop. This isn't your fault."

"But it is, really. And I'm sure Sandy thinks it is."

He let go of my shoulder. "Sandy knows you're not to blame."

"Where is she?"

"Talking to the family."

Anxiety hummed in my chest. "Will they know what really happened?"

"They'll know the Campsite Killer's the main suspect and we're doing everything we can to catch him."

I put my hand over my mouth, trying to hold back a sob. Billy set his phone down on the side table and leaned close.

"You okay?"

I shook my head. "This is horrible. I just wanted to find my birth mother and now two people are dead because of me."

"They're dead because of *him*. And when we catch him you'll have helped save who knows how many women, Sara."

"But we probably won't catch him now. He's never going to call back."

"Actually, there's a pretty good chance he will. After a murder the killer enters a state of calm, it's a release—some describe the feeling as euphoric. He can't talk about it with anyone else, so he may try to share it with you."

"He doesn't trust me anymore."

"He's angry you withheld something, but we believe his curiosity and desire for a family is going to win out. He's going to want to know about his grandchild."

"What do I say if he calls again?"

"Just apologize. We don't want him sensing another lie, so confess and ask for forgiveness. This will give him the feeling he has control over you again."

"He *does* have control."

"You can pull the plug anytime, Sara. No one will think any less of you if you do. We'll get him one day—he has to make a mistake eventually."

This was my chance. I could walk away from the nightmare and move on with my life. My mind filled with images of how life was a few months ago, relaxed, easy, full of fun and laughter. Everything in me wanted to go back to that time, wanted to unload this enormous burden, this desperate trapped feeling. All I had to say was yes, one simple word and it was all over.

For *me*.

"Sara?"

It was too late. I'd already gone too far.

"No. We have to catch him—I don't want him to hurt anyone else."

He nodded a couple of times and picked up his phone. "We're going to make sure he doesn't."

I gave him a shaky smile. "Are you sure you want such a stress case on your team?"

"You're not so bad." He smiled and stood up. "But I better get back to the station."

I walked to the door with him. "Did anyone see him in the area?"

"We don't have any witnesses, but we're still working on finding out where he bought the jack plane and trying to learn everything we can about the dolls."

"Did the DNA . . ."

"The hair samples match two of the victims, yes."

I took a deep breath. "Do you think I'm in danger?"

"We want to make sure you're safe—that's why there's a car on the street—but every time he's made a threat it's been aimed at other people, never at you. If he comes after you or your family, the dialogue will stop."

Outside on the front step I said, "I can't believe she's *dead*. This is just so awful." I blinked back tears.

"I'm sorry, Sara. I know how much you wanted a happy ending for Danielle. Trust me—I did too." His voice was tense and frustrated. He rested both hands on my shoulders and looked me straight in the eye. "You have to shake this off and focus on how we're going to stop him. It's the only thing we can do for Danielle now."

Billy still had one hand gripping my shoulder when we

heard a car come ripping down the driveway, radio blast-ing. Billy stepped away from me immediately.

As soon as I saw the car I said, "It's my sister."

Melanie smirked through the window as she parked in front.

Billy walked toward his SUV. As he passed by Melanie she said, "Howdy, Officer. What's your hurry?"

He gave her a big smile and a wink. "Oh, you know, catching bad guys. Boring things like that." He stopped at his truck door and over the hood of the SUV said, "I'll let you know about the other pieces tomorrow, Sara."

"Sure, no problem."

As he drove off with a honk of his horn, Melanie saun-tered up the front steps and raised her eyebrows. I rolled my eyes, turned, and walked into the house. This time I didn't wait for her innuendos.

"God, Melanie, I am not messing around with Billy. He's a client and a *friend*. I'm in love with Evan and marrying him, remember?" I walked to the kitchen with Melanie hot on my heels.

"I remember, but I'm not sure your *friend* Billy does. He's into you."

I poured myself a fresh cup of coffee but didn't offer her one, hoping she'd leave soon.

"You don't have a clue what you're talking about. You've seen him twice and both times he was flirting with you."

"But I'm not the one he likes." She shrugged. "Look, I don't know why he'd be into you either, but he is." She sat at the kitchen table.

"Nice. And he's not 'into me.' What are you doing here anyway?" I leaned against the counter.

"You said you'd talk to Evan about Kyle playing at the wedding?"

I slapped my forehead. "Oh, crap. I didn't get a chance this weekend and—"

"Of course you didn't. That's why I brought you one of his CDs." She took one out of her purse and set it on the table.

"I'll try to listen to it."

"Why do you have to try? Why can't you just say, Sure, Melanie, I'd love to?"

"Why are you always picking fights with me?"

She said, "Because you're always looking down on *me*."

I shook my head and opened my mouth to tell her she needed to get over herself. Then I remembered there was a dead girl. A girl who had a sister named Anita who pleaded on TV last night for her return.

"I'll listen to the CD." I glanced at my shop door. "But I have a lot to do, so . . ."

"Don't worry, I'm leaving." I didn't try to stop her when she got up and headed to the door. I just followed behind and stood on the steps, waiting for the parting shot.

At her car she turned and said, "You should go see Mom sometime. Or did you forget about her too?"

"I've been really busy."

"You haven't gone over in a long time."

Guilt spread through me and was quickly followed by anger. Melanie didn't have a clue what was going on in my life—she never had.

"Worry about your own relationships, okay?"

She slammed her car door and backed up, spraying gravel all over the driveway.

After she left I walked inside and slammed *my* door behind me. I checked my cell, but no calls. I didn't even know what I'd say to John if he did call.

I was going to phone Lauren and bitch about Melanie, mostly because I couldn't talk about what was really bothering me, then decided to wait until Greg was back in camp. I know, me waiting—what a shocking concept. But it's not the same talking to her when he's home. Lauren got together with Greg when she was so young, I wonder sometimes if she missed out. But she usually seems happy and doesn't complain about him, so I guess it doesn't matter what age they met. Then again, Lauren never says if something's bothering her unless I hound her, and even then it's like pulling teeth to get her to talk about it.

I asked her why once, holding back being so completely foreign to my own nature, and she said she doesn't like to dwell on the negative parts of life. I wish I could say the same. Maybe then I could forget that a woman is dead because of me. Maybe then I could forgive myself. At this point I'd settle for forgetting. But my guilt is like a canker sore in my mouth and I can't stop my tongue from running over it and over it and over it again.

SESSION THIRTEEN

I'd like to say I'm doing better. Mostly because I love the way you smile when I tell you things worked out or that something you said helped. A lot of what you and I talk about *does* help. But lately stuff is coming at me so fast and furious I don't have time to get over one thing before I'm thrown headfirst into the next.

Every day I Google Danielle's name to see if there's another article. Her family started a memorial Web site and I can't stop looking at her photos and reading the little facts that made up her life. She was supposed to be a bridesmaid in her friend's wedding this summer and they'd just had their dresses fitted. I cried, thinking of her dress hanging in a closet somewhere. You asked if I might be obsessing about the victims because I'm trying to come to terms with my own worst fears of losing my daughter, but I don't think that's it. I don't know why I put myself into Danielle's pain, why I conjure poignant images, each more painful than the last. Why I can't stop wanting to know everything about her life.

You taught me years ago that we can't choose how we feel about something; we can just choose how we deal with those feelings. But sometimes even when you have a choice, the things you're choosing between are so horrible it doesn't feel like much of a choice at all.

Saturday morning I was at the grocery store with Ally when my cell finally rang. I didn't recognize the number, but the area code was BC. I answered with a cautious, "Hello?"

"You didn't tell me you had a daughter."

I stopped in the middle of the aisle as fear gripped tight around my chest. A few paces in front of me, Ally was pushing a small buggy, with her red purse slung over her shoulder. She stopped and examined a bag of pasta, her lips pursed.

I said, "No, I didn't."

"Why?"

I thought about Danielle. If I didn't say the right thing I might be next. My face felt hot and my vision blurred. I forced myself to take a breath. I had to sound calm—had to keep *him* calm.

"I was being cautious. You hurt people, and—"

"She's my granddaughter!"

Ally wheeled her cart back toward me. I pressed the phone against my chest.

"Sweetie, why don't you go to the end and pick out some cereal?" She loves examining all the boxes for their various prizes. Picks one, puts it back, picks another. Normally I hated it.

John said, "Is she with you right now?"

Crap. He heard me. "We're grocery shopping."

"What's her name?"

Every fiber of my body wanted to lie, but he might already know.

"Ally." She glanced up. I smiled and she went back to debating cereal options.

"How old is she?"

"Six."

"You should have told me about her."

I wanted to tell him he had no right to know anything about my life, but this was not the time to piss him off.

"I'm sorry, you're right. But I was just protecting my daughter. Any mother would've done the same thing."

He was silent. A woman walked down the aisle. I moved to the side, wondering what she'd think if she knew who I was talking to.

He said, "You don't trust me."

"I'm *scared* of you. I don't understand why you killed Danielle."

"I don't either." When we first started talking his voice was angry and tense, but now he seemed almost defeated. My heart rate slowed slightly.

"You have to stop hurting people." It came out as a plea.

I held my breath, expecting him to flip out, but he just

sounded defensive when he said, "Then you can't lie to me again. And you have to keep talking to me when I need you to."

"I won't lie, okay? And I'll try to talk to you when you call, but sometimes people are around me. If I can't answer, you could just leave a message and I'll call you—"

"That won't work."

I wondered if he still suspected the cops were tracing his calls.

"If you keep phoning a bunch of times in a row, my friends and family are going to start asking questions."

"So tell them."

"They won't like me talking to you, and—"

"You mean the cops don't want them to know we're talking." He said it causally, but I wasn't fooled for a minute. He was testing me.

My pulse sped up again. He had his suspicions, but suspecting and knowing were two different things. I had to stick with my lie.

"No, I mean my family wouldn't understand. And they'd tell the police—"

"You've already called the police."

"I *didn't*—I told you before. I didn't believe who you were at first, then I was scared you'd come after my family. Evan would be worried and—"

"So leave Evan—you don't need him."

My body tensed. He sounded angry again. Had I just put Evan in danger? At the end of the aisle Ally had picked out a box of cereal and was now doing wheelies with her cart. If

I didn't distract her soon, she was likely to crash into one of the displays. I motioned for her to follow me to the vegetable section, trying desperately to think of something to say to calm John down.

"I'll try to talk to you whenever you want. But I love Evan and we're engaged. If you want to be part of my life you have to understand that."

I held my breath at my daring. How would he take this?

"Fine, but if he gets in the—"

"He won't." I let out my breath, sagging against the cart. Ally was trying to get my attention. I handed her a plastic bag and motioned for her to pick out some apples.

John said, "I want to talk to Ally."

I stood up straight.

"That's not a good idea, John."

"She's my *granddaughter*."

"But she might say something to someone, then it will raise questions like I told you, and—"

His voice was frustrated. "If I can't talk to her, then I want to meet you."

My blood roared in my ears. I never thought he'd want to meet, never believed he'd take that risk. I had to scare him off—and fast.

"But what if the police are watching me?"

"You said you didn't tell them. I believe you—I'd know if you were lying."

For a moment I wondered if he was the one lying. I shook off the thought. He had no way of knowing I was working with the police.

"But that stuff about you being my father was in the newspapers and on TV. What if they're following me?"

"Have you seen someone following you?"

"No, but that doesn't mean they—"

"I'll phone you tomorrow."

Billy called my cell right away, but Ally was bumping her cart into the backs of my legs and I knew she'd reached her limit. She wasn't the only one.

"Give me a bit, Billy. I'll call you as soon as I get home." I rushed through the rest of my shopping, then made Ally a quick lunch back at the house and let her pop in a movie.

I called Billy from my landline. "Did you get him?"

"He was using a pay phone at a campsite near Bridge Lake, west of Clearwater." Billy sighed. "By the time they got there, he was gone. He probably had his vehicle parked below and cut through the woods. The tracking dogs lost the scent."

"What are we going to do? I don't want him to talk to Ally, and obviously I can't meet him."

"We don't want you to do anything that puts you at risk, but—"

"There's *no way* I'm meeting him."

"I don't blame you."

"So what should I do?"

"He's going to keep upping his demands, so we want you to be ready for that." Billy's voice was casual, but something felt off.

Then I got it. The police wanted me to meet with him, but they couldn't ask me to do it.

Sandy got on the phone. "Sara, why don't you come into the station this afternoon and we'll discuss it?"

"Fine."

I dropped Ally off at Meghan's again—grateful her mom loved having her—and headed to the police station. Sandy and Billy took me into the room with the couch again. This time Billy sat down beside me and I studied the side of his face. Was Melanie right? Did he like me? He turned and flashed a quick smile, but I didn't see a hint of anything other than friendliness. I had bigger things to worry about right now. Sandy paced back and forth in front of the couch.

I said, "You want me to do it, don't you?"

Sandy said, "We can't ask you to put yourself in danger."

"What if I wanted to meet him?"

She jumped on it. "You need to pick the spot before he does, but do it casually, you don't want him suspicious. Location is paramount—we have to consider the public's safety."

"What about *my* safety? Aren't you supposed to be worried about that?"

"Of course your safety is our primary concern. We'll make sure—" She caught herself. "If you decided you wanted to do this, we'd be there the entire time."

"Oh, perfect, so he can spot you and then kill me?"

"He'd never know we were there. We'd pick a location

that doesn't have a lot of people around, but nothing too remote, and we'd have undercover officers covering you every minute."

Billy said, "We'll plant a wire device on you, but the plan is for us to arrest him *before* he has a chance to get close to you."

"Wait a minute. You have a plan already? When did I agree to do this?"

They stared at me.

Finally Billy said, "Nobody's planning anything, we're just talking. But if this is something *you* choose to do so we can arrest John, we'll do everything in our power to protect you. Like Sandy said, your safety is our main concern."

I eyed Sandy. "I'm not so sure about that."

Sandy pulled a chair close in front of me and sat down. She grabbed a file off the table at her side, pulled out a picture, and thrust it in front of my face.

"I want you to take a good look, Sara."

It was a photo of Danielle's corpse. Her face was pale, her neck bruised. Her eyes bulged out and her blackened tongue stuck out of her mouth.

I jerked back in my chair and closed my eyes.

Billy grabbed the photo out of Sandy's hand.

"What the hell, Sandy?"

"I'm getting a coffee." She shoved the file at him and walked out of the room. The door banged shut behind her.

"I can't believe she did that." I pressed my hand against my heart. "Her eyes and her *tongue* . . ."

Billy sat on the couch near me. "I'm really sorry, Sara."

"Aren't there rules about that sort of stuff? She's a sergeant!"

"I'll talk to her. She's just in a bad place today. Losing Danielle was really hard on her. She wants to catch John before he kills someone again—we all do."

"I understand, but I have a daughter. If something happened to me . . ." My voice broke.

Billy leaned back in the couch and let out a big breath.

"And that's another reason we need to catch him soon—so you can stop living in fear. But if it makes you feel any better, you're probably the one person who's not in danger from John. You've done a great job at gaining his trust."

"Does he trust me, though? He still makes sure he doesn't stay on the phone long. So why is he willing to risk meeting me?"

"It's possible he's setting up a meeting so he can do countersurveillance and see whether you're working with the police. He's a hunter, so he either stalks his prey or flushes them out. But I think he really does trust you. He's arrogant enough to believe you would never betray him."

Prey, that's exactly what I was to John. But I felt more like a sitting duck. My stomach rolled.

"But I *am* lying, and when he realizes—"

"He'll be in handcuffs. But maybe you shouldn't meet him, Sara. Not if you're this scared."

"Of course I'm scared, but that's not it. I just . . . I need to think about it."

"You *should* think it over."

"And I've got to talk to Evan."

"Sure, if he has any concerns I'd be happy to talk with him."

That would go over great. But I said, "I'll let you know."

Billy walked me out of the station. There was no sign of Sandy, who I hoped was getting reamed out by a superior.

At the Cherokee he said, "I won't lie to you, Sara. Meeting with John is risky, but you already know that. But I also know you'll make the right decision in the end." Then he closed my door.

I picked up Ally and made my way home, still trying to figure out what had just happened back at the station. Was I actually considering meeting John? Had I totally lost my mind? For the rest of the afternoon, Ally and I played at the park with Moose, but only part of me was there. My cell phone was mercifully quiet, but my head spun. Should I do it? Was I a horrible person if I didn't? What if he killed another woman? But what if he killed *me*?

My mind conjured images of Ally and Evan weeping at my funeral, of Lauren raising Ally and Evan taking her for ice cream when he came home on weekends. But then there were the images of me standing bravely in a park, spotting John and speaking cryptically into a wire device. A SWAT team swarms in and wrestles him to the ground. Families of the victims call with tearful thanks, saying they've finally found peace.

No matter where my thoughts took me, I couldn't get

the image of Danielle's face out of my head. I hated that Sandy used her photo to manipulate me. I hated that it worked.

Later, while Ally had her bath, Evan and I talked on the phone. When I told him John wanted to meet, his first response was, "No way, Sara. You can't do it."

"But what if this is the only chance to catch him?"

"You can't risk your life like that—what about Ally?"

"I said that too, but the cops don't think I'm in any real danger, and—"

"Of course you're in danger. He's a *serial killer* and he just murdered a woman. Isn't he already breaking his pattern or whatever they call it?"

"They said they could protect me and they'd arrest him before we even spoke, and—"

"This isn't your responsibility."

"But think about it, Evan. This could get him out of our lives for good. Catching him would make me feel like I did *something* right. I'm in constant limbo, wondering what he'll do next, when he'll call, what he'll say. You know what this is doing to me—to us. If they arrest him everything can go back to normal and we can just enjoy planning the wedding."

"I want you *alive*. Nothing else matters if he kills you."

"What if the cops used another girl as a decoy or—"

"He's seen pictures of you. If he realized it wasn't you, he could go nuts and hurt lots of people, including you and

Ally. I told you before, the police are just using you as bait. I won't let you risk yourself like that."

"You won't *let* me?"

"You know what I mean. You're not doing it, Sara."

Part of me wanted to argue, the part that hated being told what to do, but a bigger part was relieved he'd made the decision for me.

"I was going to say I'll tell them tomorrow, but they're probably listening anyway."

Evan shouted into the phone, "She's not doing it."

After that call I thought I'd hear from Billy or Sandy, but the phone was blissfully silent. The next day John called.

"Did you think about meeting me?"

"Yeah, and I still don't think it's a good idea. It's too risky."

"You said the cops don't know."

"But I told you last time, they might be following me."

"They have no proof you're my daughter and no idea we're talking."

God, he was smart. I was running out of ways to say no. I went back to the police excuse—it was all I had.

"They still might be watching, and—"

"Don't you want to meet me?"

"Of course I do. But if the police are following me it could turn into a big shoot-out."

"I'll protect you."

I almost laughed at the irony. The police wanted to protect me from him and he wanted to protect me from the police.

"I know. But I have a daughter—I just can't risk my life like that."

"What's Ally doing right now?"

"She's in bed."

"Do you read stories to her?"

"All the time."

"What's her favorite?"

I hesitated. The police said not to lie to him, but I couldn't stand the idea of him knowing intimate details about Ally.

"She loved *Where the Wild Things Are*." She hated it.

"What's her favorite color?"

"Pink." Ally loves candy-apple red. Brighter the better.

"I have to go. I'll think about our meeting."

"No, John. I'm not going to meet you—"

But I was talking to air.

John was making his way back down south—toward me. A trucker thought he'd seen someone near the pay phone around the time of the call, but he couldn't describe him and hadn't seen what he was driving. I barely slept that night, feeling John drawing near, hearing his tires on the pavement. The roads deserted as he traveled in the dark.

The next day, Monday, another package arrived. Billy and Sandy came over within a half hour of my phone call. Sandy and I hadn't spoken since she'd ambushed me at the station, so when I opened the door I only greeted Billy. Sandy, marching to the kitchen with her briefcase in hand, didn't seem to notice.

I held my breath while she carefully sliced open the box and lifted out a white jewelry box with her gloved hands. A small yellow envelope was taped on top. She set the box down on the counter and gently removed the envelope. Then she used a penknife to slice into the top, leaving the sticky part untouched. With tweezers she slid a card out of the envelope.

In bold blue pen it said, *For Ally, love from Grandpa.*

I stepped back in horror.

"You okay, Sara?" Billy said.

"That's *disgusting.*" How dare he write to my child! I wanted to rip him apart from limb to limb, wanted to rip the card up in a million pieces.

Billy gave a sympathetic smile.

He held open a bag and Sandy carefully slid the envelope and card into it. Next he slowly lifted the lid off the jewelry box. Both Sandy and Billy were crowding over it, so I couldn't see the contents.

Sandy shook her head. "What a sick bastard."

"Let me see," I said.

They moved to the side as I came closer. Nestled in white cotton was a doll dressed in a pink sweater and blue jeans. I remembered Danielle's sister sobbing on TV as she described what Danielle was wearing the last time she was seen alive. But it was the sight of the auburn hair glued to the faceless head that hit me the hardest. As I stared at the smooth metal my brain superimposed the image of her face agonized in death. I turned away.

Sandy said, "You need to have a good look in case he asks you anything."

"Just give me a minute." I sat down at the table and took a few deep breaths. "I keep seeing her face in that photo."

"Have you given any more thought to meeting with him?" Sandy spun around, still holding the jewelry box.

"Evan won't let me. He's too worried."

Billy nodded. "He wants you to be safe."

"It's so risky." I stared at the box in Sandy's hands. "But if I did it . . ."

"We arrest him and this all ends," Billy said. "The gifts, the phone calls . . ."

"Women being murdered," Sandy said.

"You know, Sandy, the guilt trip doesn't help. What you did with the photo was horrible."

She glanced at Billy, who cleared his throat. Her jaw tightened, but she said, "You're right, Sara. That was over the line."

For a moment I was startled, but as I met her eyes and she looked away, I knew there wasn't one speck of sorry in her. I shook my head and turned back to Billy.

"I thought about the exact same things, Billy, but if I do it Evan's going to be really upset."

"Do you want me to talk to him?"

"No, it would just make it worse if he felt you were pressuring me. He doesn't think I should be helping at all, it's too dangerous. And he's right. I'm risking Ally, especially now that John knows about her."

"We don't believe your family is at risk, but—"

"But he wants something from us. You said it yourself a couple of times—his demands keep increasing. What's next? He demands to meet Ally?"

"That's one of our concerns too. If we don't act fast he'll keep escalating."

"But if I meet him so much could go wrong."

Billy nodded. "Yes, it could. That's why we're not asking you to do it—even though this may be our only opportunity to stop him."

"What if he got away? He'd know I tipped you off."

"You've already set up a good explanation for that—the media coverage. You've warned him we could be following you."

"But he might not believe it, and then he'd either disappear again or decide to punish me." We were all silent. After a moment I said, "What are your chances of catching him any other way?"

"We're trying everything we can, but . . ." He shook his head.

"Maybe he'll stop, he's getting older."

But I already knew how unlikely that was before Billy said, "Serial killers don't just stop. They get caught, usually for other crimes, or they die."

Sandy held out the jewelry box. "I hope you like these, because you're going to be getting a lot more of them."

I glared at her. "That's really nice."

"It's reality."

Billy's voice was firm. "Sandy, give it a rest." I expected her to tell him off, but she just studied her cell. He turned to me. "Are you ready to have a closer look at the doll?"

I took a deep breath and nodded. Sandy handed me a pair of gloves. After I slid them on, she passed me the box.

"Just hold it by the edges and don't touch anything else."

As I examined the doll carefully, I tried not to think of Danielle, how pretty she was, how her hair was the same color as mine, how she died with my father's hands around her throat.

John called later that day from his cell when I was making a cup of coffee.

"Did she get it?"

"The doll arrived, yes. Thanks." I almost choked on the last word.

"Did you give it to Ally?"

"No, she's just a little girl, John. She wouldn't understand—"

"You won't let me talk to her, and now you won't let me send her presents? I made it for *her*."

"I'll save it until she's older. She's so young—I was worried she'd lose it."

He was breathing heavy into the phone.

"Are you okay?"

It sounded like he was talking through clenched teeth when he said, "No—the noise. It's bad right now."

I stood motionless, my hand still on the coffeepot. What noise? I strained my ears. Did he have another girl? I heard something. Laughter? Then chopping sounds. An axe hitting wood?

I forced myself to take a slow, deep breath.

"John, where are you?"

The sound stopped.

"Can you *please* tell me where you are?"

"I'm at a campsite."

My heart went into overdrive. "Why are you there?"

He hissed into the phone, "I told you—*the noise.*"

"Okay, okay. Just talk to me. What are you doing at the campsite?"

"They're *laughing.*"

"Drive away. Please, I'm begging you, just drive away."

The sound of a truck door opening. "They have to stop—"

"Wait! I'll meet you. Okay? I'll meet you." *God help me.*

Now you know why I had to see you a day early. It took me a few minutes to get John back in his truck and away from the campsite. I just kept telling him how great it would be to meet him, basically getting him to focus on something else. It was hard at first—he kept talking about the noise, then about the campers laughing. Then I'd say something like, "I can't believe I'm finally going to meet my dad." Eventually he calmed down and said he'd phone soon so we could arrange our meeting. I'm supposed to go see Billy and Sandy after I'm done here—they want to go over everything in case John wants to set up something right away. He'd called from just north of Merritt, a small town only four hours from Vancouver. He was heading in this direction.

When I told Evan last night he said, "They're just manipulating you, Sara."

"They who?"

"All of them—the cops and John."

"Don't you think I'm smart enough to know when I'm being manipulated?"

"Meeting with John is reckless when you have a child. Did you even think about her? You had no right to agree to something this big without talking to me first."

"Are you *kidding* me? I put Ally above everything—you know that. And where do you get off telling me what *I have a right to do*?"

"Sara, you need to stop yelling or I'm—"

"You need to stop being a *jerk*."

Now his voice was raised. "I'm not going to talk to you if you keep yelling."

"Then you shouldn't say asshole things like that."

He was silent.

"So now you're not going to speak at all? And *I'm* the immature one."

"I'm not discussing anything with you until you take it down a notch."

I gritted my teeth and took a few big breaths. Forcing myself to speak calmly, I said, "Evan, you have no idea what it was like talking to him, knowing he was picking out his next victim. If I didn't say the exact right thing, someone was going to *die*. Can't you understand how horrible that felt? Billy said the faster we catch him, the faster he's out of our lives. And it's true. Even if the cops are manipulating me, it doesn't change the facts."

Evan was silent for a long moment, then finally said, "Shit. I hate this, Sara."

"Me too. But can't you see I didn't have any other choice?"

"You had another choice—you just didn't take it. I get why you felt you had to say yes, but I still don't like it, and I don't agree with it. If it's going to happen, then I want to be home. I'll shut down the lodge if I have to, but I want to ride with the cops when it goes down."

"I'm sure they won't have a problem with that."

We talked for a little while longer. He apologized for accusing me of being reckless, I apologized for calling him names, then we said our good nights. But I don't think either of us actually had one. I spent hours staring at the ceiling. All I could think about were the campers John had been watching. They didn't know how close to death they'd come. Then I wondered how close I was.

SESSION FOURTEEN

Right now, I'm a train wreck. The more Evan tries to calm me down, the more upset I get. Then I hate myself, which makes me lose it even more, so Evan tries even harder to calm me down or goes all take-control-alpha-male, so then I turn into an irrational bitch from hell.

But when I finally get a reaction from him, when his face flushes and he raises his voice or walks off, *that's* when I calm down. Then I look over everything I'd just said or did and feel horribly ashamed, so I suck up, trying to squirm my way out of whatever mess I'd just caused. Thankfully he doesn't hold a grudge for long and in typical Evan fashion drops it and moves on, but I'm the one who can't let it go.

This isn't the first time we've talked about my overreactions, and then my overreaction to my overreaction. It's funny I can even use that term with you, because if anyone else in my life even hints I'm overreacting it's guaranteed to make me see red. You've told me it's never about the situation at hand—that's just the switch. It's the currents between people sparking off each other that cause the problem. You have to deal with the way you're fighting, not what you're fighting about. How many times did you try to hammer that into me? You'd think I'd have gotten the hang of it by now, but in the moment? It all goes out the window. At least now I know where I got it from.

After John's initial excitement about meeting I thought he'd want to set something up right away, but when he called after I got home from our last session he just wanted to talk about Ally. I kept trying to change the subject, but when I mentioned the meeting he said he was still considering how best to go about it, then he brought up Ally again. I hated talking about my daughter with him, hated wondering what he was doing with the information.

Sandy and Billy, who I saw every day once I agreed to meet John, didn't understand why he was stalling either but agreed it would look odd if I started pushing and said I should let him bring it up. Now that I'd made the decision to meet, I couldn't wait to get it over with. Especially because it didn't look like we were going to get him any other way.

He'd called from near Cranbrook, which was a surprise. They'd expected he'd keep heading south, not eight hours east. His next call came from a pay phone even farther east, almost to the Alberta border. I spent hours staring at the map, trying to figure out what he was thinking, why he was heading in the opposite direction.

Every call he wanted to know more and more about Ally, and I was walking a tightrope between truth and lies. I didn't know how Internet-savvy he was, so on things I thought he could verify, like birth dates or school info, I was careful to tell the truth, but when he asked about her likes and dislikes, I lied my butt off. Ally now hated cheese and red meat, was easygoing, shy with strangers, and terrible at sports. I had to make notes so I wouldn't forget the details about this new daughter I was creating.

Evan was happy John hadn't picked a date and was hoping he'd changed his mind—but he didn't like that John was asking so many questions about Ally either. He again suggested she come up to the lodge with him, but I told him it wouldn't be good for her—she'd get too far behind in school. Of course, he told me she'd be fine and that I worry too much. But I know my daughter. It doesn't take much to throw her off. Her teacher's been all over me since she pushed the other little girl. I don't know if she's heard the rumors, but I noticed an extra note of concern in her voice when she spoke about Ally. I didn't want to give her more fuel.

Finally, Friday night, John called—this time from his cell.

"So how's Monday?"

"To meet?" My heart started to race. "Okay."

"I've been looking over a map."

I heard Sandy in my head. *You have to pick the spot. Location is paramount.*

"I know the perfect place. It's one of my favorite parks and I take Ally there all the time."

"Where's that?"

"Pipers Lagoon." I held my breath. *Please, please, say yes.*

The police initially chose Bowen Park, but there was an outdoor arts festival. Pipers Lagoon Park was remote enough that there wouldn't be any crowds, just people out for walks, especially on a weekday. A narrow gravel dike led from the parking lot out to the twenty-acre park with its rock bluffs, arbutus trees, and Garry oaks. The dike was bordered by ocean on each side and lined with park benches, so I'd be able to sit in the open and the police could keep an eye on me from several vantage points. But the best part was that there was only one road in, so they could block John's escape.

On the phone he said, "Sure, let's meet there at twelve-thirty."

I tried to match his enthusiastic tone. "Perfect!" But my stomach climbed into my throat. In three days I was going to be bait for a killer.

Billy called right away to let me know John was still near the Alberta border and that we'd go over everything in the morning. Once I told Evan it was set up he said he was coming home Sunday night. I don't think Billy really wanted him to ride with them, but I told them I wouldn't do it if they didn't allow it. Sandy said as long as Evan understood he wasn't to interfere, he could sit in the command vehicle.

John called the next morning, Saturday. He was in high spirits, saying how much he was looking forward to meeting me, then asked what I was doing that day. I said I was taking Ally for a walk later.

He said, "It's nice you spend so much time with her."

"Life gets in the way sometimes, but I try."

He was quiet for a moment, so I took advantage of his good mood.

"Did your parents spend time with you?"

"My father worked a lot, but my mom did, until she left."

"Where'd she go?"

"Don't know. She left when I was nine. She missed her people, so I think she went back to the reserve." That was interesting. I wondered if his mother leaving was what started everything.

"That had to be really hard—you must have missed her a lot. Did you ever try to find her?"

"A few times, but no luck."

"That's so sad, John."

"It was tough. But she waited until she knew I was old enough to take care of myself, then one night she was gone."

"Why didn't she take you with her?"

"I think she knew if she did, he'd hunt her down."

"God, I can't imagine leaving Ally."

"My dad was a hard man."

"Did she leave you a note or anything?"

"She left a spirit doll to protect me." The dolls!

"Like the dolls you gave me?"

"Similar. They're for protection." He made dolls from women he killed so he'd have *protection*? Too bad the women didn't have protection against him.

"What are they protecting you from?"

"The demons."

Was he into witchcraft? Was that what this was all about?

"Are these First Nations demons?"

His voice wasn't angry, more bored, when he said, "I'll tell you another day."

"Can I ask about your dad? You mentioned before that he was strict."

"He was a violent drunk. He knocked out my front teeth for telling a joke."

"No sense of humor, huh?"

John laughed. "You could say that. But he taught me everything I know about guns. When you're in the woods, though, you can't just rely on firepower—that's one thing he never understood. But my mother did. If it wasn't for her teachings he'd have killed me the first summer."

"What do you mean?"

"When I turned nine he started taking me up into the woods and leaving me there."

"Like for an afternoon?"

"Until I found my way home." He laughed again.

"That's *horrible*." My shock was genuine. "You must have been terrified."

"Being out there was better than being at home with him." He laughed for the third time and I knew he must be uncomfortable. "I used to stay out for weeks on end. He'd beat me because it took me so long to find my way back, but I could've come home sooner. Sometimes I'd be living right on the outskirts of the ranch and he didn't know. I'd line up his head in my gun's sights, and *pow*."

"What stopped you?"

"How's Ally today?"

Not surprised by the abrupt subject change, I said, "She's great."

"Little girls all seem to like Barbie dolls, so I was going to—"

"Ally doesn't like Barbies." Last thing I wanted was for him to send another doll. "She's more into bugs and science stuff." Ally would own every Barbie in the world if she could, and if I ever gave her a science kit she'd probably burn down the house.

He said, "Better get going. I have some packing to do." He paused, then said, "I'm really looking forward to this."

"It's going to be awesome."

"I'll call you soon." I was about to hang up when he said, "Wait, I got a joke for you. You'll like this one."

"Sure."

"One man says to another man, 'Did you ever hunt bear?' and the other man says, 'No, but I went fishing in my shorts.'" He laughed loudly.

I said, "That's a good one," and forced a laugh.

"Tell Ally." His voice was excited. "She'll love it."

You have no idea what my daughter would love.

"Sure, she'll crack up."

———

Sandy called as soon as I hung up and her excitement radiated through the phone so strongly I wanted to hold the receiver away from my ear. They thought he was traveling west along the border—toward Vancouver. Even though he'd talked longer, the signal connected with a tower in Washington State and threw them off his trail. They wanted to meet me at Pipers Lagoon so we could walk the area and make sure we were all on the same page. I dropped Ally off at a friend's and headed over to the park.

Dressed in blue jeans and with her perpetual windblown appearance, Sandy looked like she was in her element. Billy was wearing a baseball cap pulled low, a Windbreaker, and dark denim jeans with hiking boots, which gave him a rugged look that wasn't wasted on a couple of women who checked him out as they walked by. He and Sandy scoured the area for the best vantage points. We decided which bench I should sit at and they pointed out a few locations where they'd have undercover officers.

Sandy wanted Billy stationed in the parking lot, but he said, "I worked out a plan last night. I think we need to take him down *before* he gets to the parking lot. 'On enclosed terrain, if we occupy it first, we must block it, and wait for the enemy.' We can put a car at the base of the hill and one at the top where—"

"I don't have time for one of your quotes," Sandy said. "I want him in the parking lot when we arrest him. I'm not losing him into one of the driveways bordering the road."

"Understood, but I just think—"

"I don't like it." She walked away with her cell to her ear.

I'd have told her off, but Billy just stared after her for a moment. If it wasn't for the red wave crawling up his neck, I wouldn't have known he was even pissed.

I said, "See, her attitude sucks."

He smiled. "Come on. Let's walk the route again."

The rest of the weekend I never heard from John once, which was terrifying because I had no idea how close he was. If he kept driving after his last call he could already be on the island. And if that wasn't stressful enough, we don't know *how* he might come over—there are two ferry terminals in Vancouver, but he could also take the ferry from Washington to Victoria, then drive up the island to Nanaimo. I was driving myself crazy imagining every possible scenario, wondering where he was every minute. Thank God Evan came home on Sunday. I'd cleaned the house from top to bottom that morning, then made him chicken cordon bleu in an effort to keep myself sane, or at least busy. But neither of us could eat much. After dinner Evan called Billy and asked how the meeting was going to go down. His tone was polite as they talked, but his expression told me he wasn't happy about the conversation.

Later we snuggled on the couch. Evan was quiet while I babbled about Moose's new organic food, my suspicion that one of our neighbors is growing pot, what to do with Ally this summer—everything and anything to stop myself from thinking about what was going to happen the next day.

When I finally paused for breath he pulled me in tight against him.

"Sara."

"Hmm?"

"You know how much I love you, right?"

I turned to him. "You think something's going to happen to me tomorrow!"

He didn't meet my eyes. "I didn't say that."

"But that's what you're thinking."

This time he looked at me, his face serious. "You sure you don't want to call this thing off?"

"Nope, tomorrow they're going to arrest John and he'll be out of our lives once and for all." I tried for a big smile, tried to believe what I was saying.

"This isn't funny, Sara."

My smile faded. "I know."

That night in bed we held each other close as we went over everything again. Finally we fell asleep, but I dreamed I was being hauled away to prison. Ally cried through the glass and Evan came and visited me with Melanie—his new wife. I woke up at five-fifteen a.m., glanced at the clock, then stared at Evan's sleeping form, thinking for the hundredth time, *Am I doing the right thing?*

The next morning Evan made pancakes. We were joking around with Ally while Moose grunted and snorted his way through his own plateful, but Evan and I kept meeting eyes over our coffees, and I checked my cell phone over and over. Was John already on the island? Was he close? Did he know my address? What if he showed up here? I checked the alarm and caught Evan rechecking it.

After we dropped Ally off at school, where a patrol car would be parked outside all day, we headed to the police station. Evan waited while they fitted me with a wire device. I was to drive down to the park, walk to the bench, sit, and wait. Evan was to go with the police in the main vehicle so John wouldn't see us together. If for some reason he did get close, I was to make sure I didn't go near any car, mine or his, and to keep lots of space between our bodies. All these commands were couched as cautions and followed by "if you still want to go through with this." The message was clear: if the shit hit the fan and I got hurt, the police wanted it known I was doing this of my own free will.

Once I got to Pipers Lagoon, Sandy would park down the road in the command unit with Evan. Billy would be one of the undercover agents acting as workmen installing new signs in the parking lot. Other police officers would be scattered around as dog walkers and birders. One female officer was going to push an empty stroller with a strategically placed blanket and another was stationed on the hill above my bench, sketching the ocean. I was relieved they were bringing in so many members—they weren't taking any chances. But I was.

About half an hour before I was supposed to meet John I left the station. On the way there the sun broke through the clouds, bouncing off cars and shining into my eyes. My head started to pound and I realized I hadn't taken my pill that morning. I reached into my purse and hunted for an ibuprofen, but the bottle was empty. Perfect.

The closer I got to Pipers Lagoon, the more my heart climbed into my throat. Why had I ever agreed to this? My mind was filled with images of all the things that could go wrong: John grabs a hostage. John grabs me. Evan jumps out to help and gets shot. The urge to call everything off was huge.

I parked and looked around at the other vehicles. No trucks. What if he'd rented a car? I didn't see any license plates for a rental company. I wiped my sweaty palms on my legs. *Okay. All I have to do is get out and walk to the bench.*

I took a deep breath, climbed out of the Cherokee, and started along the graveled path, holding my coat tight as the wind off the ocean grabbed at it. For a moment I panicked when a young couple hovered near the bench I was supposed to sit at. Thankfully, they moved on.

As I waited, my head started to pound harder and my eyes began to water. My migraine was coming in fast. I glanced at my watch, then looked around the parking lot again.

Twelve-thirty arrived, but no sign of John. I watched every vehicle that pulled in. The wind whipped my hair around, obscuring my vision. I pushed it back. A man got out of a small car. I held my breath. He stood for a moment and glanced around, then took off his baseball cap. I caught a flash of reddish hair. *Oh, God, it was him.* He closed his car door and started walking down the path. Where were the police? They were supposed to grab him right away.

Closer, closer, closer.

Finally the man was close enough for me to see his face. He was too young. I let out my breath. He gave me an odd look as he passed by. I focused back on the parking lot. Had I missed someone? No new vehicles. I checked my watch. Another five minutes had passed. Where was he?

My heart was beating so fast I was worried something was wrong, but I put it down to nerves. Even though it was sunny, the wind was cold and my body felt like it had been dipped in ice. I shuffled my legs back and forth and tucked my hands into my armpits.

Another ten minutes passed. Still nothing. I took the cell phone out of my pocket and dialed the last number John had called me from. No answer. What was going on? Was he even on the island?

I stood up and looked around. The female policeman on the rocks above me was sketching and gazing out at the ocean. I sat down, feeling my head spin as the migraine clenched at the base of my neck. I looked at my watch again: a half hour after our meeting time. I was still considering what to do when the cell in my pocket rang.

I picked it up and flipped it open. I didn't recognize the number.

"Hello?"

"Are you there?"

"John, I was starting to wonder. Is everything okay?"

"I don't know, Sara, you tell me." Dread oozed over me.

"What's going on? I'm waiting for you like we agreed."

"You seem to have a problem telling the truth."

I glanced around. Was he watching me? Was anyone watching me? A shiver slid down my spine.

"I don't know what you're talking about, John."

"You haven't been telling me the truth about Ally." My mind scrambled over everything I'd told him. What could he have possibly found out?

I said, "I've always tried to be as truthful as possible."

He chanted, "Ally loves Barbies. Ally's good at sports. Ally doesn't like science."

I sucked in my breath. "Have you been watching me?"

"You lied."

I was scared, but I was also angry. "Ally is my daughter, John. My job is to protect her. You shouldn't have been asking those questions."

"I can ask whatever questions I want."

Get a grip, Sara. Remember who you're talking to.

"Let's both calm down and start over, okay?"

"It's too late."

"It's never too late with family—that's what being a family is about."

He was silent.

My heart was going nuts. I pressed my hand against it.

Finally John said, "Check the bathroom stall—the last one. I've left something for you."

"Right now?"

"I'll call you back." He hung up.

I got to my feet and headed down the path toward the out-door bathroom at the far end of the parking lot. My eyes frantically searched the hills, the beach, decks of the houses overlooking the lagoon. *Was he watching me?* I glanced back over my shoulder. The policewoman on the hill was pack-ing up her things and talking into a cell phone. Once I reached the parking lot I passed by Billy and the other cops. Billy was talking into his phone too, but he gave me a nod. Did that mean I should keep going?

On my right, I spotted the policewoman with the stroller heading to the bathroom. She almost made it to the entry before me, but an older woman leaving the bathroom started talking to her—gesturing like she was asking for directions. I hesitated at the entrance, but if I waited any longer it was going to look weird. I took a deep breath and went in.

Thankfully no one was in the bathroom, so I went to the last stall and eased open the door. At first glance there was nothing unusual—it must be in the toilet tank. I wondered if I should wait before checking, but I didn't know how long I had until John called back. With shaky hands, I lifted the lid off the tank. A Barbie doll floated facedown in the wa-ter. I knew I shouldn't touch it. I flipped it over with my pinky nail.

The face was melted off.

I tore out of the bathroom, almost bumping into the police-woman, and raced to the Cherokee. My hands shook as I fit my key in the door lock. Finally I was racing down the road—my cell rang. I caught my breath, but it was just Billy.

"You okay, Sara?"

"Ally, she's at school and—"

"We have someone watching the school right now."

"I want to talk to Evan."

"We need to go over some things with you—"

"Now, Billy." I hung up.

Evan called right away. "You okay?"

"No." I told him about the Barbie.

"Jesus. Billy said he was a no-show, but he didn't—"

"I don't feel good."

"What do you mean?"

"I have a migraine and my heart's beating really fast. It's hard to breathe and my chest feels all tight."

"It's probably just from the anxiety and—"

I raised my voice. "It's *not* a panic attack, Evan. Jesus. I think I know what a panic attack feels like. I forgot my pills."

His tone was calm. "Sara, just pull over." I heard voices in the background

"I can't—what if he's following me?" When Evan didn't answer right away, I said, "Did Billy say where he's calling from?"

"He . . ." Evan cleared his throat. "He said John's in Nanaimo."

I was silent with dread, waiting for Evan to finish.

"They said it looks like he was driving around the north end when he called, but his phone's shut off now."

"So the whole time he could've been *watching* me."

"Maybe you should drive to the station. We can meet you there and—"

"I'm going to check on Ally."

"The police already—"

"I'm going to check on *Ally*, then I'm going home."

He was quiet for a moment. "Okay, I'll tell them."

I got to Ally's school just as she was heading back in from recess. She was thrilled to see me, wanting me to say hello to all her friends. I told her I'd come by to give her a hug, and I did—a long one. Over her shoulder I spotted Sandy's Tahoe parked at the end of the block. When Ally went back to her classroom I talked with the officers sitting outside in the car, who assured me John wouldn't get by them. Fifteen minutes later I turned onto our street and Sandy passed me in the Tahoe. When I pulled into our driveway she was parked in front of the house. Evan met me at the door and grabbed me for a hug.

"There's been a patrol car on the road watching the house the whole time. Sandy's checked everything inside—it's all clear."

"Thank God. I have to get my pills."

I kicked off my shoes and raced up to the bathroom. When I came out Evan was already closing the blinds in the bedroom and had a cool cloth in a bowl of ice on the night table. I turned off the lights and lay on the bed, my hand pressed against my still-racing heart.

Focus. Breathe. It's okay. You're safe now.

Evan whispered, "Want me to stay with you?" but even his soft voice burrowed like daggers into my temple.

I shook my head and pulled the pillow over my face.

"I'll check on you in a while." He gently closed the door behind him.

A few minutes later I heard Evan and Sandy talking downstairs. Sounds of a vehicle outside, then another male voice. I rolled into a fetal position, focused on my breathing, and let the pills take me away.

When I woke up it was the middle of the night. Evan was lying beside me.

"Want some water, baby?"

I murmured a yes and he warned me to cover my eyes when he turned on the lamp. He filled up a glass in the bathroom and carefully handed it to me in the dim light.

I sat up. "Thanks."

Our voices hushed, he filled me in on everything that happened after I fell asleep. Billy stayed at the house with me while Sandy and Evan picked up Ally from school. Evan told Ally that Sandy and Billy were friends from the lodge and were going to be staying with us for a while. Ally didn't seem to mind and in fact loved Sandy, of all people. Now Billy was sleeping on the couch downstairs and Sandy in the spare room beside Ally.

I said, "Sandy must be so pissed about what happened today."

"She's okay. She kind of reminds me of how you get when you're obsessed by something."

"Gee, thanks."

He laughed softly.

"What are we going to do, Evan?"

"We'll just have to play it safe for the next couple of days and see if he calls again. This is exactly what I was afraid of, though."

"What?"

"That something wouldn't go right and he'd be even more of a threat."

"They would've got him if he hadn't found out I was lying about Ally."

"I didn't think you should be telling him anything about Ally in the first place."

"I had to tell him *something*, and I really don't need the I-told-you-so."

"Sorry." Evan took a deep breath. "I just don't ever want to go through another day like today."

"Me neither. The thing that worries me the most is, *how* did he know I was lying?" We were both silent for a moment. "You don't think he's been talking to someone we know?"

"None of our friends are stupid enough to share personal details about your daughter with a stranger, Sara."

"It could be someone from her school—a teacher or one of the other parents, even one of the kids or something. Or . . ."

"What?"

"Melanie works at a bar," I said. "What if he came in and said he had a six-year-old daughter or something? She might've started talking about her niece."

"That's a stretch—she's more apt to be talking up Kyle's band."

"Oh, crap." I sighed. "I said we'd listen to his CD, for the wedding."

"We'll do it soon."

"We better, or she's going to be pissed."

"Melanie's the least of your problems right now."

We were quiet again, then he said, "No, I have a feeling he's been to the island and he's been watching you." His arm tightened around me. "Keep an eye out. Look for any vehicles that may be following and pay attention to your surroundings."

"I always do."

"No, you don't. You get distracted. Promise you'll be careful."

I spoke slowly, exaggerating each word. "I promise to be more aware of my surroundings."

He kissed my temple and gave me a squeeze. Tucked into Evan's arm, with the warmth of his body against my side and the steady sound of his heart beating in my ear against his chest, I started to drift off.

He murmured in the dark, "I don't want you to talk to him again, Sara."

I whispered into his shoulder, "I won't. I'm done."

———

But I haven't heard from John since. Evan stuck around the last couple of days. So did Billy and Sandy, which is why I didn't come for my session yesterday. It wasn't so bad having them there, I guess. Usually one of them went to the station during the day, and it was nice having someone escort Ally to school with me, but I missed my alone time with Evan—I missed *my* alone time.

Billy was the one who usually hung out at the house during the day, which was *not* helping my relationship. A couple of times Evan walked by when I was grilling Billy about the case or his theories on John, and Evan got this *look*. One night after he went to bed, Billy and I stayed up talking about different cases he'd worked on. When I finally crawled into bed Evan rolled over and put his back to me. I asked what was wrong—twice—and he said, "I don't like how friendly you're getting with Billy."

"Um, he's staying in our house. What am I supposed to do, ignore him?"

"He's a cop. He's supposed to be professional, not chatting up my fiancée."

"You've got to be kidding. We were talking about old cases."

"I don't like the guy."

"That's obvious—you were rude to him at dinner."

"Good. Maybe he'll get the hint and go sit in the fucking squad car."

"I can't believe you're being such a jerk. He's like a *brother* to me, Evan."

"Just go to sleep, Sara."

This time I turned my back on him.

Part of me sees Evan's point—can't say I'd like it if he started hanging out with Sandy all the time—but I meant what I said: Billy's become like an older brother to me, a *really* protective older brother who carries a gun. One time when I had to meet him at the station I saw him walking a woman to her car. As she got in I caught a glimpse of her bruised face. When I asked Billy about her, he shook his head and said, "Another abusive husband on a bender."

"Was she getting a restraining order?"

He snorted. "Yeah, but they're a waste of paper. Half of the abusers go after the women anyway. And they usually get away with it." He stared at the woman's car as it drove off. "She'll end up in the hospital next time. Her husband needs a taste of his own medicine."

Something in his voice prompted me to ask, "Have you ever done that? Taken things into your own hands?"

He turned to me, his face serious. "Are you asking if I've broken the law?"

I tried to laugh off my impulsive question, then said, "I don't know, I can see you as the masked crusader type."

He looked down the road again. " 'The skillful strategist cultivates the way and preserves the law, thus he is master of victory and defeat.' " He turned to me. "Come on, let's get a coffee."

Even though Billy blew off the question with yet another quote, I had a feeling he might have done a little street justice in his time. It doesn't bother me if he did. In fact, I like it. That's the kind of person I want on my side. He told me once he's still close to a few victims he worked with, that for him "the case doesn't stop until someone's behind bars or dead." I hope he adds John to that list—in either category.

There was a call on my cell this morning, but it only rang twice, then stopped. Not that I was going to pick it up anyway—I'd already told Sandy I'm not answering if John calls again. I thought they'd give me a hard time, but they both kept their opinions to themselves. They probably think I'll change my mind. Not a chance. The number was from a pay phone near Williams Lake, so it looks like he's off-island. Maybe I well and truly pissed him off this time and I won't ever hear from him again.

I wonder what that would be like after so long. Will I spend the rest of my life looking over my shoulder? Waiting for the phone to ring? Can something like this ever really be over?

SESSION FIFTEEN

When I got home from our last appointment Evan told me he'd decided to stay for the weekend. I wondered if his decision was motivated more by concern about Billy than about John, but it was nice having him home for a change. Not that it helped me get anything done. I can't tell you how many times I've picked up a tool and just set it back down. Most of the day I just sit at my computer.

Now I'm resorting to Googling things like "how to know if you're being followed" or "self-defense moves that could save your life." One article had suggestions for what to do if you're attacked by a serial killer or rapist, like fighting back or screaming. It even listed what might trigger each one. But it seems like the only way of knowing for sure which kind you've got on your hands, or rather has his hands on you, is when you've messed up and he's killing you.

I still printed everything out—just in case. Then I added the pages to the enormous file I've already got going for all my other John stuff. I've been keeping a logbook, back from when he first started calling. I make note of the time of day he calls, his moods, tone of voice, speech patterns, *anything*.

When I'm not Googling, I'm e-mailing Billy little *How's it going out there?* messages. He always answers back. Sometimes just, *Don't worry.* Or *Hang in there, I'll call later and touch base.* Evan would freak if he knew how much we're in contact. I don't like doing it behind his back but I can't explain why I need the reassurance, at least not in a way Evan would understand. He's great at shaking me out of my funks and balancing the roller coaster of emotions I'm generally on. But that's when I'm operating at a level five. Once I've hit ten, all his just-don't-think-about-it advice pisses me off. Billy's we've-got-it-under-control attitude is what I need.

Last Friday night was brutal. Even though Evan was home and I hadn't heard from John since Monday, I didn't feel any more relaxed. My cell phone was quiet, but my mind was *loud*. All the books say that serial killers can be superimpulsive. If John gets an urge to talk he just might pick up the phone regardless of how angry he is, just to tell me how angry he is. Or he might decide to do it in person. But the thing is, people of John's type—*my* type—are just as obsessive as they are impulsive. What kept me up all night was wondering what was keeping *him* up. Then on Saturday morning the calls started again.

My cell rang while we were making breakfast—well, Evan was making it, I was talking and getting in the way. The number was new, but the area code was still for BC.

Evan said, "Don't answer it."

"It's a different number."

He turned back to the stove. "If it's not him, they'll leave a message." They didn't. "They" called back three more times—always stopping after the fourth ring. Halfway through setting the table, I was frozen with a fork in my hand, waiting for the phone to ring again.

Evan glanced over his shoulder. "Just turn it off."

Moments before, I'd been thinking how glad I was Sandy and Billy were gone so I could have Evan all to myself, but now I wished they were here so they could tell me what to do. All my tough talk—and resolve—about ignoring John was slipping away.

I said, "But what if he has another girl?"

Evan spun around with the spatula in his hand. "Turn off the phone, Sara."

I stared at him as it rang again.

Eggs sizzled in the frying pan behind Evan as he said, "I thought you said you were done."

"But what if he has someone or he's at a campsite and—"

"If you don't talk to him, he can't manipulate you."

Ally came around the corner. "What stinks?"

Evan spun back around. "Christ, the eggs." As he moved the pan to another burner he looked back over his shoulder. "Do whatever you want, Sara. But you know exactly what's going to happen."

I turned off the phone and set it on the table.

Evan grabbed my hand. "It's the only way you're going to get your life back." I sat down, pulling a squirming Ally into my lap and burying my face in her hair, feeling sick with dread—and guilt. Whose life had I just destroyed?

After we drove Ally to Meghan's we came home and Evan did some work around the house. I finally finished the headboard I'd been struggling with, but it felt like climbing uphill with rocks tied to my ankles. Billy had phoned to tell me John called from a pay phone near Lillooet, about three hours south of his last call—and three hours from Vancouver. While I worked I kept wondering if while I was sanding something John was looking for his next victim.

The police have a patrol car cruising by Ally's school at all her breaks. The teacher thinks I'm involved in a bitter custody battle with her real father—luckily I never told the teacher he's dead—but I wondered if I should've kept Ally home. Evan and I had talked about it but decided we should keep things as normal as possible for her. The trick was keeping *me* as normal as possible. I've run an inch below manic for most of my life, revving into high gear at a moment's notice, but now? I don't even know what normal is anymore.

When Evan and I stopped for lunch, I tried to look interested as he told me how he'd reorganized the woodshed, but he noticed I was picking at my sandwich.

He said, "Why don't you go see Lauren for a bit?"

"I don't know." I shrugged. "We haven't talked much lately because I feel like I'm lying all the time. And I haven't told anyone you're home. They'll wonder why I didn't mention it."

"Just tell them I had a cancellation and wanted to spend some time with you so we could get some wedding stuff done."

"God, the wedding. We still have to order the cake, the flowers, rent your tux, get the wine, make the labels." I threw my hands into the air. "We still haven't even sent invitations."

"It's going to be fine, Sara."

"The wedding's in three and a half months, Evan. How is that fine?"

Evan raised an eyebrow. "Hey, Bridezilla, you might want to be a little nicer to the groom."

I sighed. "Sorry."

"What's the biggest thing on your list?"

"I don't know. . . . The invitations, I guess."

He thought for a moment. "You go visit Lauren, and I'll find a template for a cover e-mail and update the site. When you get back we'll fine-tune it, then tomorrow we can go through our e-mail addresses and send the link out."

"But . . ."

"But what?"

"Once the invites are out there . . . I don't know, maybe you're right. What if things get worse with John and—"

Evan said, "They're not going to. He's out of our lives.

And you're going to keep him out, right?" I nodded. "So unless you're having second thoughts about marrying me?"

I tapped my chin. "Hmm . . . let me think."

He grabbed my hair and pulled my face close for a kiss.

"I'm not letting you get away. Not when there's a cop waiting to take my place."

I smacked his shoulder. "Billy doesn't like me that way. And right now he probably hates me for screwing their case up."

Evan just grunted and said, "Good. Now go see your sister."

When I got home—feeling a lot better about life after inhaling half a dozen of Lauren's peanut butter cookies and a whole pot of coffee—Evan told me he'd gotten a couple of calls from the lodge. I said I was worried about him losing business, he said he was more worried about losing me.

Once John realized I wasn't going to answer my cell phone he tried the landline a couple of times. When Ally came home she wondered why we weren't picking it up, so we told her that it was just salespeople and she was *not* to answer it. We turned the ringer off at night and gave the police Evan's cell number because my cell was also off. John tried a couple more times on Sunday. All the calls came from around Cache Creek, and I felt safer knowing where he was, or at least the general area, but Evan said it just made me more insane trying to predict his next move. He had a point. I agreed to call the phone company on Monday to change our number. Then I got the e-mail Sunday night.

Evan was about to show me the wedding Web site he'd spent all weekend updating when I decided to check my e-mail. As soon as I saw the address HanselandGretelAntiques@gmail.com I knew it was from John. The message was in all caps.

SARA,
THE PRESSURE IS BAD. I NEED YOU.
JOHN

The walls of my office closed in as I stared at my screen. Behind me Evan was talking, but I couldn't make sense of the words. My body felt hot all over, my legs heavy with dread.

Evan said, "What's wrong?"

"John just e-mailed."

Evan spun his chair around, asked me something else I didn't catch. I opened the window above my desk, needing air, but I still felt like I was suffocating. Billy, I had to get in touch with Billy. I forwarded the e-mail and he called right away to say the RCMP would try to find out where John had sent it from, but I was sure he'd used a public computer.

When I showed Evan the e-mail he told me to just ignore it. I tried to focus on the wedding site, but I couldn't get John's words out of my head.

I said, "What if he kills someone?"

"The police have warnings out to all the campsites. But he's going to end up killing *you* if you keep communicating with him, Sara." He scrolled through another page on the Web site. "Come on, this will take your mind off it. See, I changed the format and added our horoscopes and links to a map—there's a little quiz too. And people can RSVP right online."

"That's cool—and thanks for trying to distract me. But not communicating with John is what's pushing him over the edge."

"So let him get pissed off. I'm here, the house is wired, and we have cops patrolling by. If you're going to talk to him at all, that's what you should tell him—that the police know he's been contacting you and they'll catch him if he steps foot on the island again."

"That might make him go totally ballistic."

Evan turned from the screen. "What do *you* want to do, Sara?"

"I just want this to all go away."

"Then let the police do their job."

"But they can only do so much and I can't stand not knowing what he's doing."

"Sara, if you talk to him, I'm going to be really pissed off."

"Now *you're* threatening me? That's not fair."

"It's not fair that I have to worry about you. You said you were done."

"But he's not done. We can change our numbers—I can

change them a million times—but as long as he's out there he's going to find new ways to contact me."

Evan's face was stony. "So what do you want to do?"

"I think—I think maybe I should try to meet with him again. If—"

"No, Sara. You can't do it."

"Evan, just think about it. Please. I don't want to do it either—it's terrifying. But we have to catch him. It's the only way this is ever going to end. How are we going to be able to have a wedding with this hanging over us?"

"If you do this, I don't want any part of it."

"What does that mean?"

"It means I'm not sitting in that truck, wondering if you're getting yourself killed. You're risking Ally too, you know."

"That's so unfair—I'm trying to protect Ally. She's not going to be safe until he's caught."

"If you do this, she should come to the lodge with me."

"Ally's staying here."

"So you want her in town where he can snatch her from school?"

"She's safer here with police protection than up at the lodge. The drive there is deserted, there are only like three policemen in the entire town—and he knows where the lodge is, Evan. If anything happened up there—"

"I could protect her better up there."

"Billy can protect her—" I pulled back as I realized what I was about to say.

"So you think Billy can take better care of Ally?"

"He's a cop, Evan."

"I don't care what he is, if you do this I'm taking Ally to the lodge or I'm telling your parents and she can stay there."

"You're not taking my daughter *anywhere*."

"Your daughter? That's what it comes down to? She's not mine so I don't have any say in what happens to her?"

"Evan, that's not what I meant!"

He closed down his computer and headed for the office door.

"Do what you want, Sara. You will anyway."

That night Evan slept on the couch. I tossed and turned for hours, still arguing with him in my head, but by midnight most of my anger had burned off. I *hated* that he was mad at me. I turned onto my back and stared at the ceiling. Why couldn't Evan see that meeting with John was the best chance—like Billy said, probably the only chance—of getting him out of our lives?

In the dark I turned over everything we'd said. *My* daughter? Evan was more of a father than she'd ever had in her life. Did I really think because she wasn't biologically his that he shouldn't have a say in what happens to her? Now I realized that subconsciously I'd always considered Evan's opinions second when it came to Ally.

Maybe he was right. Maybe it was time to cut John completely off. I'd done everything the police had asked, endured all of John's calls to the point where I was a walking panic attack, finally agreed to meet him—and he still hadn't been caught. He'd said he wouldn't hurt anyone as long as I talked to him, then killed Danielle even after I pulled off to the side of a highway to answer his call. And how did I know he wouldn't have attacked her even if he had reached me in Victoria? If I made the slightest misstep he used it as an excuse to do what he was going to do anyway. Now the stakes were higher. He knew he could use Ally as leverage—if I was willing to lie to protect her, he might wonder what else I'd be willing to do for her.

I could've explained my feelings to Evan better, but why was he being so dominating? I ran back through the fight and this time tried to put myself in his shoes. Then I got it. Evan was scared. And he had every right to be. How would I feel if he was going to do something that terrified me but I couldn't stop him? The last thing I wanted was a marriage like my parents'—Mom in the kitchen and Dad calling the shots—but Evan wasn't bossing me around; he was just worried.

I crept downstairs and into the living room. Evan was on his back, one arm thrown up over his head. I knelt by his side and admired his features in the moonlight. I love his high cheekbones and the way his upper lip is slightly fuller on one side. His hair was messed up, making him look even more boyish. I moved my face close to his.

"What are you doing?" he murmured.

"Sucking up."

He grunted in the dark and wrapped his arm around my shoulders, pulling me up and on top of him so my head rested on his chest.

He said, "You weren't very nice."

"I know. I'm sorry. But you were being all alpha-male guy."

"I *am* alpha male. You just need to accept that." I heard the smile in his voice.

He grunted into my neck. I grunted back. It had been a long time since we'd done that. I smiled against his cheek. His left hand crept down and grabbed my butt.

"You know, you could make it up to me. . . ."

I giggled into his shoulder.

"Evan?"

"Yeah, baby."

"I won't meet him, okay?"

"Good, because I have to go back to the lodge in the morning and I don't want to worry about you."

"First thing in the morning, I'll change all the phone numbers."

He pulled me in tight and gave me a kiss, then our bodies relaxed against each other, my head on his shoulder, his arms loose around my back as he drifted off to sleep.

The next morning after Evan left I changed my cell and my landline. I gave the police the new numbers. My family would wonder why I changed them, so I just told them that since the article had come out we'd had a lot of newspapers and wackos calling. When I talked to Melanie she said, "I heard Evan was home."

"Yeah, for a bit."

"What'd he think of the CD?"

"Um . . ." Before I could make up an excuse Melanie said, "You're unbelievable. Some sister," and hung up.

When I tried to call her back and apologize, her phone just rang. Then my guilt turned to anger—I didn't need this crap. I had a serial killer messing with my life. Okay, so she didn't know that, but she could just wait for once.

Since I changed my numbers the calls from John have stopped. The first couple of days were hard—I checked my locks and the alarm constantly—but when nothing happened I started to relax. Evan was right, I should have done this a long time ago. No more jumping up, no more checking my cell every ten seconds. I haven't watched the news or Googled anything. I'm even getting caught up with some projects—yesterday I returned a ton of e-mail quotes. It's like I was addicted to some horrible drug, and now that I'm sober I can't believe how much it had taken over my life. But this is it. I've quit for good.

SESSION SIXTEEN

You know what really bugs me? From the outside look-ing in, everyone thinks Evan is the calm rational one and I'm the crazy one. I even go along with it. I think, *God, I shouldn't have flipped out like that, why do I always overreact so much?* It's not until later when I trace it back to try to figure out why I blew up that I realize Evan tossed a lit match at my feet when he already knew I was standing in a pool of gasoline.

Like this morning. I'm trying to get Ally ready for school and she's going through all her clothes trying to decide what to wear. She finally picks a red shirt, but then she's worried her headband doesn't match, so she has to go through all her clothes again. Then Moose, who decided this is a great time to get some sort of bacterial infection that requires antibiot-ics three times a day, will not eat anything that has a pill in it no matter how cleverly disguised. So I'm chasing him around the kitchen, trying to get the thing down his throat, while

Ally's screaming, "You're hurting him!" Food is landing on me, on the dog, on the kid, and on the floor. Then Evan, my sweet, kind, *rational* fiancé, walks in, looks at the mess, and says, "Jeez, I hope you're cleaning that up."

Are you *kidding* me?

So of course I lose it. "Get the hell off my back, Evan. If it bothers you so much, clean it up yourself." Then he storms outside, pissed at me for yelling at him. He didn't talk to me for an hour, which isn't like him at all. I can't stand it when someone gives me the silent treatment, so I end up apologizing, then later I'm like, wait a minute—why didn't he apologize for picking the worst time in the world to get on my case?

We talked about it right before I came here and he said he was sorry for his comment, but I know he's still pissed off. Then on the way here I remembered what you said last session, that Evan might be feeling resentful of all the time I'm spending on the John situation. I didn't think so then because we'd been getting along great, but this week something changed, and now everything's changed. No one's having much fun right now—except maybe John.

The day after our last appointment I got a call from Sandy.

"Julia would like to talk to you. She tried to call you but you've changed your numbers."

"What does she want to talk about?"

"I don't know, Sara." She sounded annoyed. "She just

300 · Chevy Stevens

asked me to give you her home number." I could imagine how much Sandy loved playing messenger. The thought made me smile.

"Thanks. I'll call her right now." But I didn't. Instead I made a cup of coffee, then sat at the table with the phone in front of me. The woman could make me feel horrible and I had enough of that going on. Maybe I shouldn't call her back at all. Give her a taste of her own medicine. I lasted two minutes.

She answered on the first ring.

"Sandy said you wanted to talk to me?"

"I'd like to see you in person so we can talk privately."

"Oh. Okay. I, um, can't really go anywhere today, I have to pick up Ally soon, and—"

"Tomorrow's fine. What time can you be here?"

"Maybe around eleven?"

"I'll see you then." She hung up, leaving me with no explanation and the urge to call her back and tell her I wasn't coming. But there was no way I could do that, which pissed me off. She probably knew it too. That pissed me off even more.

Evan wasn't keen about me driving all the way down to Victoria when we still didn't know where John was, but he understood I had to find out why Julia had called. I promised I'd be careful, then proceeded to speculate about a million possible reasons she might want to see me, until he finally said, "Sara, you'll find out tomorrow. Go to bed."

"But why do you think she—"

"I have no idea. Now go to bed. *Please*."

I did, but I stayed awake for hours, wondering what to wear, how to speak. This visit felt so different. She'd asked to see me. She *wanted* to see me.

The next morning I headed straight down to Victoria after I dropped Ally off at school. I was almost a half hour early, so I grabbed a coffee from a shop near Julia's house, remembered there's a public beach close to her place, and drove down that way. As I passed by her house I noticed a woman coming out the side door. She ran her hand through her hair.

No way.

I pulled into a neighbor's driveway, then watched in my rearview mirror as Sandy crossed the street and got into an unmarked police car. What was she doing in Victoria? She called yesterday and never mentioned it. Of course, I didn't mention my upcoming visit either. After Sandy drove by I pulled out and continued to the beach. For twenty minutes or so I stared out at the ocean, sipping my coffee and thinking about what I'd just seen. They might've been going over the case, but the timing seemed odd.

I drove back to Julia's house. She smiled briefly as she answered my knock, her lips tight against her teeth. Even though it was the middle of June, she was dressed all in black in a long skirt and a sleeveless tunic. She looked pale and her bangs were a sharp line against her forehead. I smiled back and tried to make eye contact. *See how harmless I am? How lovable?* But her eyes flicked away as she ushered me in with a quick movement of her hand.

"Would you like some tea?"

"No, thanks."

She didn't offer anything else, just gestured for me to follow her to the living room. As we passed through an enormous kitchen with gleaming marble countertops and cherry cabinets, I spotted two mugs on the counter. I wondered if one had been for Sandy.

The living room was more formal than my taste and as I eyed the white couch and matching love seat I tried to imagine Ally there. The Himalayan cat reclined on a leather ottoman in the middle of the room, glaring at me as it flicked its tail. I sat on the love seat, Julia perched on the couch in front of me and smoothed her skirt down her legs. She gazed out at the ocean for a long time before she spoke.

"I heard you won't talk to him anymore."

Where was she going with this?

"That's right," I said.

"You're the only one who might be able to stop him."

My body tensed. "Would *you* want to talk to him?"

"That's different."

I felt bad for my comment and said, "Evan, my fiancé, we decided it's too risky."

She looked hard at me. "I want you to meet with him, Sara. For me."

I gasped. "What?"

She leaned forward. "You're their only chance of catching

him. If you don't talk to him, he's going to kill more people. He's going to rape and kill another woman this summer."

We stared at each other. A pulse beat at the base of her throat. The cat leaped off the ottoman and stalked off.

"That's why Sandy was here today, isn't it?"

Her eyes widened in surprise and she sat back.

"I saw her leaving, Julia. Did she tell you to say this stuff to me?"

She said, "She didn't tell me anything."

We held gazes. I knew she was lying, but she didn't even blink.

I said, "What about *my* life? What about *my* child?"

Her hands shook in her lap. "If you turn your back on this, then *you're* a murderer."

I stood up. "I'm leaving."

She followed me to the door. "It disgusted me that I had you inside me for nine months, it sickened me knowing you were out there in the world—that something of his *lived*."

Her words froze me at the door and I stared at her, waiting for the pain to hit, like when you cut yourself and first see the blood, but your mind doesn't realize yet how badly you've been hurt.

"But if you stop him," she said, "it will have been worth it."

I wanted to tell her everything she was saying was unfair and cruel, but my throat was tight and my face hot as I tried not to cry. Then the anger left her face, her body sagged, and when she looked at me her eyes were desperate, defeated.

"I can't sleep. As long as he's out there I'll never be able to sleep."

I threw myself out the door, slamming it behind me, ran crying to the Cherokee, and jammed into reverse. I tried to call Evan as soon as I was back on the road, but he didn't answer. After a few miles my hurt and anger had segued into guilt. Was she right? If I didn't set up another meeting and John killed someone, was I a murderer?

Normally when I drive up the Malahat Highway from Victoria I take it slow and focus on the road—with one side a sheer drop and the other a rock wall, there's no room for error—but today I was speeding around the corners, my hands gripping the wheel. When I reached the summit and started down the other side where the road opens back up into two lanes, I called Sandy.

"That was low, even for you."

"What are you talking about?"

"You know damn well." As I came too close to another car on a sharp bend I forced myself to slow down.

"Did something go wrong?"

"You can drop the act, Sandy. I saw you leave her house." She was silent.

"I'm not dealing with you anymore." I hung up.

I tried to call Evan, but he still didn't answer. I *had* to talk to someone. Billy answered on the first ring.

"I want Sandy off the case. I won't work with her."

"Uh-oh. What's going on?"

"I just drove all the way down to Victoria to see my birth mother—because I stupidly thought she might actually want to visit—but it turns out she was just trying to talk me into meeting John. I got there early, and saw Sandy leaving her house. She talked Julia into it! Did you know about this?"

"I know Sandy's been speaking to her, Julia's a very important witness. But I don't believe she was trying to set up—"

"Don't you think it's pretty convenient she just happened to be there on the same day?"

Billy was quiet for a moment. "Would you like me to speak to her?"

"What's the point? God, I feel like such an *idiot* for thinking Julia really wanted a visit. But she just . . ." I stopped as tears threatened again.

Billy said, "Where are you right now?"

"Coming back from Victoria."

"Why don't I grab some coffee and sandwiches and I'll meet you at your house? We can talk about it, okay?"

"Really? You don't mind?"

"Not at all. Call me when you're closer to Nanaimo."

The rest of the drive I rehearsed all the things I wanted to say to Sandy, but Julia's voice kept breaking in. *If you stop him, it will have been worth it.*

When I pulled in my driveway, Billy stepped out of his SUV with a smile, holding a tray with two Tim Hortons coffee cups and a brown paper bag.

"There's not much Timmy can't fix."

"Not so sure about that." I smiled.

"Well, we can try." After I let Moose into the backyard, Billy and I sat on the back patio and tucked into our sandwiches.

I studied him across the table. "Do you think I'm a murderer if I don't meet with John?"

"Where did you get *that*?"

"That's what Julia said."

"Ouch." His eyes radiated sympathy.

"Yeah. Evan said it wouldn't be my fault if he kills someone."

"Of course it isn't. As a police officer I always feel responsible when a suspect gets away, but I just try to learn from it and do a better job next time."

As we worked on our sandwiches I thought about what he'd said. But Billy wasn't done with the subject.

"You don't have to do anything you don't want to, Sara. But if you choose not to meet him, you can't blame yourself for the rest of your life when he does something."

"The thing is, if it was just up to me I would try to set up another meeting. I was going to call and tell you that, but Evan flipped out. There's no way he'd let me do it again."

"He's just trying to protect you."

"I get that, but he doesn't torture himself like I do. I know it sounds nuts, but it's like I can feel everything those victims feel, what their families feel. Don't you ever feel like that when you work a case? Like you're losing yourself?"

"It's hard, but you learn to compartmentalize."

I sighed. "That's my problem. I can't separate from *anything*. Even when I was a kid I had a one-track mind. Dad used to hate it because I'd be right into something for a while and I'd go on and on about it for days, then the next week it was something else." I laughed. "What were you like as a kid?"

"I got into trouble all the time—fighting, drinking, stealing. My dad kicked me out when I was seventeen and I had to live at a friend's."

"Wow! That's awful."

"It worked out for the best." He shrugged. "I joined a gym near my house, and this old cop who taught kickboxing took me out on a few ride-alongs. He talked me into being a cop or I'd probably be behind bars."

"I'm glad you decided to be one of the good guys."

"Me too." He was grinning.

"Are you and your dad close now?"

"He's a pastor. All he cares about is church and God, in that order."

"Really? What was that like growing up?"

"If you think I have a lot of quotes, my dad could preach the Bible word for word." He smiled, but I saw a flash of something hard in his eyes before he looked down at his empty coffee cup.

"Was he strict? You know, 'spare the rod' and all that?"

He nodded. "Not violent or anything, but he believes in penance." He gave a short laugh. "When I was a kid, I got in a fight at Sunday school because I was trying to stop a boy from beating up a smaller kid. Dad made me apologize to the whole congregation—then kneel at the front of the church and renounce my sins and beg the Lord's forgiveness. That was just for starters."

"But you were just trying to protect someone. Didn't you explain what happened?"

"There's no explaining anything to my father. But I know what I did was right. I'd do it again in a heartbeat."

"It's weird thinking of you having a dad like that. You're so calm and logical."

"Now, sure. But it took me awhile to get there."

"Really?"

"I had a bad temper when I was in my twenties. When I first joined the RCMP I wanted to take down every criminal myself."

"Back that up. *You* had a temper?"

A mischievous grin. "I may have bent a few rules."

"Or a few faces, right? I knew it!"

His expression grew serious. "A case got thrown out because of me and I was suspended—almost got kicked off the force. It was a hard lesson, but I learned to work within the system."

"But don't you get frustrated? Like when someone keeps getting away with crimes?" I shook my head. "If John got off on a technicality, I'd go nuts. It would be pretty tempting to take matters into my own hands."

Billy's face was intent, troubled. I didn't fill in the silence.

"That case I just told you about?" he said finally. "It was a serial rapist. After months we had a lead on where he might be staying and I decided to check it out. When I got there I saw a man leaving who fit the suspect's description. The rapist always took his victims' clothes, so I climbed in a window looking for evidence—and sure enough, there was a bag in the closet filled with women's clothing. I was about to leave when the suspect walked in the front door. When he saw me, he took off running and I gave chase. . . . It didn't end well."

"What happened?"

He met my eyes. "Let's just say I let my emotions rule my head and I made a mistake."

"But you always seem so in control." I was intrigued that Billy might have another side to him. One a lot more like myself.

"*The Art of War* changed my life—kickboxing helped too. When you're in the ring you find out fast that if you lose your cool, you lose your coordination."

"Huh, interesting. Are your tattoos from the book?"

He pointed to his left arm. "This one says, 'Weakness stems from preparing against attack.'" He pointed to his right arm. "And this one is, 'Strength stems from obliging the enemy to prepare against an attack.' I got them when I joined Serious Crimes."

"They're really cool."

He smiled. "Thanks."

We finished our sandwiches, then Billy's BlackBerry dinged. He unclipped it from his belt and glanced down.

"Looks like you got another e-mail from John." I'd almost forgotten the police were forwarding all my e-mails to themselves. Billy's face was tense as he scrolled down.

"What does it say?"

He handed me the phone.

IF YOU WON'T TALK TO ME,
I'LL FIND SOMEONE WHO WILL.

Fear slammed through my body, forcing the air out of my chest in a rush. He was going to do it—he was going to kill someone else. I tried to say something to Billy, but my whole body felt like it was pulsing with the blood roaring in my ears.

Billy said, "Are you all right?"

I shook my head. "What . . . what's going to happen?"

"I don't know. We'll trace where this came from and make sure the detachments across BC increase their patrols at campsites."

"What do I do now?"

"What do you want to do?"

"I don't know—if I start talking to him again Evan's going to be *really* upset, but if John . . ."

"Only you can make that decision, Sara. But I have to go make some calls. I'll let you know if I hear anything."

As soon as he left I went upstairs and stared at John's e-mail, my heart and thoughts going a mile a minute, then it was time to get Ally. Thank God she chattered about her day all the way home, because my mind spun around and around.

What was I going to do about John? Hours later I wasn't any closer to an answer.

To distract myself I Googled Billy and found an article about the case he'd mentioned. What he didn't tell me was that after he chased the rapist they got into a fight. He grabbed Billy's gun and as they struggled for it the thing went off, injuring an old lady walking her dog. Because Billy had unlawfully entered the house, the judge wouldn't allow the evidence into court and the rapist got a stay of proceedings. No wonder Billy did everything by the book now. Even though he broke some major rules, I was impressed he went after the guy on his own like that.

After Ally was in bed Evan finally called back. I told him about John's e-mail and what had happened at Julia's.

"That's a pile of horseshit. I can't believe she did that to you. Just write that woman off, Sara. You don't deserve that."

"But you kind of have to see things from her point of view. I know what it feels like to live in fear of what's going to happen next. If there was someone who could stop me from feeling that way right now—"

"There is—the *police*. You have to let them do their job."

"Billy's trying."

Evan was quiet.

I said, "What?"

"I just think it's weird that he brought you lunch."

"I was upset—he was trying to make me feel better. And I'm glad he was here when I got that e-mail."

"Seems like Billy's always trying to make you feel better."

"He's a policeman—he's just doing his job. At least he never makes me feel pressured like Sandy does."

"Don't kid yourself. He's probably just playing good cop."

"He *is* a good cop."

There was a long pause, then Evan said in a flat voice, "You want to talk to John."

"I don't want to talk to him, I want to stop him." He didn't say anything, so I continued. "Do you know how hard it was to hear that from Julia? That I'm the one person who can make her feel safe again? The same person who went looking for her and started all—"

"He raped your mother, that's how this started."

"I know, but I'm the one who can stop it."

"What are you saying?"

"I think . . . I think I should try to meet with him."

"No, I already told you. No way."

"What if I just start talking to him again? Maybe I can coax him to reveal more, or at least take his attention away from the campsites."

"Why can't you just let it be?"

My voice broke as I said, "Because I can't. I just can't."

Evan's voice was gentle. "Baby, you know this isn't going to make Julia love you, right?"

"This isn't about trying to get her to love me. But if you love me, Evan, you should understand why I have to do this."

"I think there's a part of you that likes being the only one who can stop him—that's why you can't let it go."

"That's a *horrible* thing to say. You actually think I like that my father is a serial killer and he already killed a woman because of me?"

"I didn't mean it like that, I mean you just don't know how to—"

"Stick my head in the sand and pretend everything is okay? Like you?"

"Now, that's a horrible thing to say."

We were both silent.

Finally Evan sighed and said, "We're just going around in circles. If you're going to talk to him again, just be prepared that he's going to try and set up another meeting."

"I don't know what I'm going to do yet, Evan. I just need to know I have your support."

"I'm not happy about you talking to him, but I understand why you feel you have to. But I mean it, Sara—I don't want you to try to meet him again."

"I won't do anything without talking to you about it first, okay?"

"You better not."

"Or what?" I said it in a teasing tone, but Evan's voice when he answered was serious.

"I'm not kidding, Sara."

Over the weekend I thought about what I should do and talked to Billy about it again. He said Sandy told him she never coerced Julia into speaking to me, it was something she wanted to do on her own. Maybe, but I have my doubts.

Sandy's so driven I think she'd do just about anything to get John. As time went on and I still hadn't made a decision, I wondered if I could get away with never having to. Then Julia called on Monday.

"I heard he e-mailed you again, Sara. Are you going to talk to him?"

"I haven't decided." I braced for her anger.

"Well, while you're *deciding*, maybe you should consider this—the police said I might be the next person he tries to contact." Her voice quivered on the last word and I realized how scared she was. "This time I hope he kills me."

Then she hung up.

It took a full five minutes for my heart to stop pounding. I called Evan, but he didn't answer. I knew I should talk to him before I made a decision and I did wait another hour, but when he still didn't answer an odd kind of calm settled over me. I knew what I had to do.

I went upstairs and typed out an e-mail to John. All it contained was one sentence—*How can I help you, John?*—and my new phone numbers. Then, before I could allow myself to think about it any longer, I hit send.

But I still haven't heard from him. It just about killed me not to ask Sandy if she told Julia I'd e-mailed him back. *Does she like me now? Now that I'm risking my life and my family? Now that Evan's pissed off at me?* Then I told myself over and over again that I don't care what she thinks. I'm getting so good at lying, I almost believe it.

The thing is, though, it's not just for her. This will never end unless I find a way to make it end. And in my gut I know the only way to do that is to meet with him—you even agree with me. I know it's crazy for me to think I can do something the police can't. But sometimes, on a deep kinetic level, as much as I don't understand what John does, something inside me *does* get it. I do think I have the power to stop him. And Evan is right, I like it.

Then I think of John, of that moment when he's standing over those women, or lining someone up in his gun sights. I wonder if this is how he feels.

SESSION SEVENTEEN

Have you ever felt like you had it all in your hands, everything you ever wanted, but then you dropped it, or maybe you just squeezed too hard? The whole way here I was trying to come up with the perfect analogy for what's been going on. And isn't that just the story of my life? I'm always trying to make it perfect.

You know what my past relationships were like—epic dramas I discussed with anyone willing to listen. Either I was completely obsessed with my ex-boyfriends or they were completely obsessed with me. And as your thick file can attest, things didn't end well.

God, when you used to say, "You'll know when it's the right person. . . ." I wanted to throw things at you. But you'd just give me that all-knowing smile of yours and say, "Trust me, Sara, real love doesn't feel like that." If I was currently entangled in a relationship that was heading straight for a cliff, even if deep down I *knew* it, I'd argue with you until I was blue in the face that he was The One!

I never understood just how wrong they all were and just how right you were until I met Evan. My past relationships were like a brutal hockey game—a brawl could break out at any minute, we were never on the same side, and no one ever won. Evan and I were *always* on the same team. I never had to look behind me or question where he was—I knew he was skating beside me, working in tandem with the same goal in sight. But it's like all of a sudden I looked up and now he's on the opposite side of the rink, we're both playing defense, and someone's going to get slammed into the wall.

What's been happening between Evan and me lately, all this fighting, isn't good. It scares me as much as John does. But it's my own reactions that scare me the most. Because when someone pushes me, I push back harder.

John finally called the day after our last session.

"I missed talking to you."

I didn't answer right away, wasn't sure I could without calling him every name in the book.

"I'm glad you e-mailed," he said. "I was worried."

He was worried? That was interesting. Billy and most of the books I'd read said serial killers don't feel remorse but knew how to emulate it, so I figured they must understand the principle behind it. I decided to test my theory.

"What you did was horrible, John."

"What I did?"

"Leaving the Barbie with its face burned off, then sending

e-mails you know are going to upset me. You made me feel awful."

"You *lied* to me."

"You were asking unfair questions. You might be Ally's biological grandfather, but I don't know what you want from us—or from her. I'd have to be crazy to give you personal details about my child."

"I just wanted to get to know you better." He sounded unsure, like he was thrown off guard by my confident tone.

"But you're not sure if you can trust me yet, right? It's the same for me. If you *genuinely* want to get to know me, you can't flip out like that. And if you get mad you can't just threaten me. You have to tell me what's bothering you and we'll try to deal with it, okay?"

He was quiet for a bit, but I waited him out. Finally he said, "I can't stop it."

"Can't stop what?"

"Losing my temper. It just happens."

I tried to think of something to say, but how could I give advice on something I can't control in myself? Then I wondered why I wanted to help him. Did I actually think there could be a man in the monster? And what would that prove? That I wasn't a monster? I pushed the thought away.

"It's the same for me, John, but I—"

"It's *not* the same."

"Because you kill people?" My pulse sped up at my daring, but he didn't answer. I stepped farther out on the limb.

"Sometimes when I lose my temper I hurt people too. I've done some crazy things."

"I'm not *crazy*."

"I meant sometimes I can understand what you might feel like when you do it. How you just want to control them and how angry they must make you feel." I thought back to that moment on the stairs with Derek, the smug look on his face. The thud when he hit the floor. I did understand, more than I wanted to.

John was silent again, but his breathing had sped up. Probably time to pull back, but something in me wanted to push harder, wanted to make *him* squirm.

"You said your dad was violent. Did he ever touch you sexually?"

"No." His voice was disgusted, but I couldn't stop the next words coming out of my mouth.

"What about your mother?"

His voice was loud in my ear. "Why are you doing this, Sara? Why are you saying these things?"

"This is how it felt when *you* asked questions about Ally."

"Well, I don't like it." He sounded nervous, worried.

"Well, I don't like it either." When he didn't respond, I opened my mouth to launch another verbal attack. *Stop, think.* What was I doing? My breath was coming fast, my face hot. I'd been so caught up in the moment, so alive with power, I forgot who I was talking to. I just wanted to hurt him.

Then it hit me: this was how John felt.

I was frozen for a moment, coming back into myself, wondering how much damage I'd done. I imagined Billy and Sandy freaking out in a room somewhere. I was supposed to be gathering information, not provoking him. John hadn't hung up, though. There was still a chance to get things back on track.

I lowered my voice, struggling to sound calm. "Look, I don't think this is easy for either of us. Maybe we could play a game?"

His voice was cautious. "What kind of game?"

"Kind of a truth-or-dare thing. I ask a question, you have to answer it honestly. Then you ask a question and I'll answer it honestly. You can even ask about Ally." I closed my eyes.

"You already proved you lie."

"You lie too, John."

"I'm *always* honest with you."

"No, I don't think you are. You want to know everything about me, but you have this whole other world you won't talk about. Maybe I'm more like you than you think."

"What do you mean?"

What *did* I mean? I thought back to a few minutes ago, how heady and exciting it felt walking that dangerous edge between reason and emotion. All my senses heightened, my body keyed up and ready to fight.

"I told you, I've hurt people when I'm mad. I even pushed someone down the stairs." If I made it sound worse, would he open up more? "He broke his leg and there was blood everywhere. I don't like feeling that out of control, and something tells me you really don't either."

He was silent.

I said, "I'm willing to go first. . . ."

After a moment he said, "We can try it."

"Okay, ask me anything you want."

There was a long pause. I held my breath.

Finally, he said, "Are you scared of me?"

"Yes."

He sounded surprised. "Why? I've been nice."

I didn't even know how to begin to answer that.

"It's my turn now. Why do you make dolls with the girls' hair and clothes?"

"So they stay with me. Were you happy with your adopted family?"

His question caught me off guard. No one had ever asked before. And there had been moments of happiness, but always wrapped in worry of when it would be taken away. I flashed to a memory of baking a meat pie with Mom when I was thirteen. The kitchen was warm and fragrant with the scent of meat cooking, garlic, onion. Her hand soft on mine as we rolled out the crust, laughing at our mess. We had just popped the pie in the oven when she rushed to the bathroom. She emerged pale and weak, saying she needed to lie down and asking me to watch the pie. I carefully took it out when the top was golden brown, excited to show Dad.

When he came home an hour later he glanced at the stove, then slammed his hand down on my shoulders and spun me around. "How long has the stove been left on?" His face was red, his neck corded.

I was so scared I couldn't answer. From the corner of my eye I saw Lauren take Melanie's hand and leave the kitchen.

"Where's your mother?"

When I still didn't answer, he shook my shoulder.

"She's . . . she's sleeping. I forgot about the stove. But—"

"You could've burned the house down."

He released my shoulder, but I could still feel where his hand had been. I rubbed at it. His voice was mean and hard as he pointed down the hall. "Go."

But I didn't tell John any of that now.

"I was happy sometimes. My turn. Why do you want the girls to stay with you?"

"Because I get lonely. Did you wonder about me when you were younger?" He started to say something else, then stopped and cleared his throat, like he was uncomfortable. "Am I what you wanted for a dad?"

He couldn't be serious. But he was.

"I wanted to know who my real father was, what he was like, yeah." How was I going to answer the second part? "You . . . you have a lot of the qualities I would've liked in a father." As I said the words, I realized they were partly true—he had given me something I'd wanted from my dad most of my childhood, something I didn't want to admit I still needed: attention. *Change the subject, Sara.* "Why do you always kill people in the summer?"

He was quiet for a little while. Then, his voice cautious, he said, "The first time it happened, I was hunting. I came across this couple in the woods and they were . . . you know. The man saw me." His voice sped up. "And he comes at me, and he's swinging. So I have to fight back, and we're down on the ground and he's hitting *really* hard with these sucker punches, and he got a couple of good ones in, but I had my knife and *smack* it goes in right up under his rib cage."

"So you killed him?"

"One more thrust did it. But the girl, she's screaming. Then she sees me looking at her and she starts to run—I only ran after her because *she* ran. So she's running harder, but I just wanted to explain that it's not my fault, it was self-defense. Then when I caught up to her . . ." A long pause, then he said, "Maybe a father shouldn't talk to his daughter about this kind of stuff."

I didn't want to hear any of what he was telling me, but I said, "It's okay, John. It's good to talk about it." I kept my voice casual. "What happened?"

"I didn't want to do it. But I had her pinned down and she kept screaming. I wasn't feeling well that day—it was really hot out. But after she was dead I felt better."

He paused, waiting for me to say something. But I was mute.

"I stayed with her for a while. But when I left, the noise came back, so I visited her again and it went away. But then they found her. . . ."

I pictured a decomposing body in the woods, John staring down at her. I closed my eyes.

"So you started making the dolls?"

"Yeah." He sounded relieved, like he was pleased that I understood. "With your mother I didn't get to finish." His voice turned angry. "I had to do it again with another woman, then the noise left. That's when I knew for sure." He was quiet for a few seconds. "But I'm glad I didn't finish or I wouldn't have you."

This time I was the one who changed the subject. "This noise, John. Do you hear voices?"

"I told you, I'm not crazy." He said it like I was the crazy one. "My head just hurts. And my ears won't stop ringing."

Then it clicked.

"Do you get *migraines*?"

"All the time."

"They're worse when it's hot out, aren't they?" Now I was the one who sounded excited.

"Yeah, that's when they're really bad."

How did I miss this? All the signs were there. His groaning, the slurred voice, his irritation with noise. Heat-induced migraines.

"I get them too, John."

"Really?"

"Yeah, they're awful. And they're worse for me in the summer too."

"Like father, like daughter, huh?"

His words snapped me back to reality. This wasn't a bonding talk with a long-lost father.

"They started when I was a teenager," I said. "When did they start for you?"

"When I was kid."

"Do you take anything for them?" If he had a prescription the police might be able to track him down that way.

"No, my mother made me things for my headaches. She said the pain was spirits haunting me."

"Do you think if you kill someone the spirits go away?"

"I know it. But I should go. I've got to watch my minutes. We'll talk soon."

He had to watch his *minutes*? Was that why he usually cut his calls short? I almost laughed.

"Okay, take care."

After he hung up, I realized what I'd just said. *Take care?* It was just habit, something I often said to friends or family, but John was neither. Was I getting so used to talking to him that my subconscious no longer knew the difference?

When Billy phoned to tell me John had called from off the island, somewhere north of Prince George, before vanishing into the mountains, he sounded excited about how much I'd gotten him to reveal. I was excited too. So much makes sense now. All the literature says serial killers often feel euphoric after they've murdered someone, and for John that probably manifested into a belief that it made his headaches go away.

Billy also said that the first time John killed someone he was probably in his late teens. Since it was likely his first sexual experience too, it would've been even more intense. His mother, who abandoned him, probably spent his childhood filling his head with myths, which could easily explain why his kills are so ritualized. Serial killers tend to create elaborate fantasy worlds to protect themselves from isolation. I can only imagine what a young boy left up in the mountains who has to hunt to survive starts daydreaming about.

When Evan called that night I tried to share everything with him, but his answers were short and he asked me about other things, like work, or Ally, or whether I'd sent out the e-mail wedding invitation yet, which was odd because usually he's the last to nag about stuff like that.

I said, "I haven't had time to go through my e-mail addresses, but I'll do it tomorrow."

"Haven't had time or didn't want to?"

"I ran out of time, Evan. I was kind of busy, remember?" Realizing how bitchy I sounded, I softened my voice. "I'll do it tonight, okay?"

We lapsed into silence, then I said, "It totally makes sense why he doesn't have any boundaries. He probably didn't get much socialization. And I bet if I looked up the weather around each time John attacked someone, there was a heat wave that summer or barometric pressure change—that can really affect migraines. You know how hot it gets in the Interior."

Evan sighed. "Sara, can we talk about something else for a change?"

"Don't you think it's interesting he gets headaches like me?"

"It doesn't change his being a killer."

"I know that, but it helps me to know *why* he kills."

"Does it really matter why? He just does it because he likes it."

"Of course it matters. If we know why, we have a better chance of—"

"We? You know you're not a cop, right? Or did you join the force while I was gone?" He was making a joke, but I sensed an undercurrent of tension. Anger rushed through my system.

Stop. Think. Breathe. He was just taking shots because he was upset. *Don't react. Go to the root of the problem.*

"Evan, I love you more than anything. I hope you know that. This John stuff just takes up a lot of time. But it doesn't mean I've forgotten about you."

"If it's not this, it's something else. There's always a new obsession."

"I'm *obsessive*—you know that!"

"I just miss the days when you used to obsess about me." He laughed.

I laughed too, relieved the tension had passed.

"Well, the sooner we get this guy out of our lives, the sooner I can go back to obsessing about your life, okay?"

"Sounds like a plan. Has he mentioned meeting with you again?"

"Not yet, but he probably will. I think next time he'll show up, though."

"Next time? There's not going to be a next time." And the gloves were back off.

"Holy cow, Evan. Dominate much?"

"I'm almost your husband. I should be allowed to have a say in this."

"But you're *wrong*. I told you before, the only chance we have to get him out of our lives is if I set up a meeting and they arrest him."

His voice rose. "And if they don't? If something goes wrong again? Then what?"

"That's not going to happen. He's starting to trust me. I can feel it. He told me more in the last call then he ever has before, and I—"

"You think because he told you about his headaches that you're safe? That you know everything he's thinking? You're not a cop and you're not a shrink. Or is Nadine telling you to do this too?"

"She's been helping me figure out what I want to do."

"What about what I want you to do?"

"What are you saying, Evan?"

"I'm saying that if you meet with him, I'd have to really think about our relationship and how important it is to you."

"You're not serious?"

"You're endangering your life, Sara."

"You endanger your life every time you go out on the boat."

"That's not the same thing and you know it."

"I can't believe you just threatened me."

"I didn't threaten anything, it's just how I feel—"

"Well, maybe I need to think about this relationship too." And I hung up. I stared at the phone for a long time, waiting for Evan to call back.

But he didn't. So I called Billy.

He came over right away, bearing coffees and donuts.

"Cops and donuts? Isn't that some sort of cliché?"

He patted his trim waist. "And me watching my diet."

I laughed, pulled the donut box close and looked in, didn't take one.

He said, "You want to talk about it?"

"I just hate all of this. Feeling like I have to choose."

"It's a tough choice."

"I know it's selfish of me to want Evan to support everything I do, but he practically threatened to end our relationship."

Billy's eyebrows shot up. "Yikes."

"I mean, am I wrong here?"

"You're the only one who can answer that question, Sara. I think it comes down to what you can live with. Or whether you can live with yourself."

"That's the thing. I couldn't stand it if John kills another person. So how do I live through the summer—or any summer? Every weekend I'm going to be a mess wondering if he's done it again. And how am I supposed to have a wedding if I'm looking over my shoulder every ten seconds?"

He nodded. "I hear you. It was the same for me with my ex. She wanted an average guy, but I couldn't just cuddle on the couch watching TV when there was a killer on the loose. I always had to see it to the end."

"That's totally how I feel. I started this, so it's up to me to end it." I felt another wave of anger at Evan. Why couldn't *he* understand?

Billy said, "I brought a copy of *The Art of War* over for you—it's in the truck. But maybe you just need to take a break from everything for a little while."

"How am I going to do that?"

"We could start by going for a drive? Get out and talk for a bit?"

"I don't know, Ally's at school and I have so much to do around here. . . ."

"Are you actually going to do any of it?"

"Probably not." I sighed. "Sure, let's go."

We drove around for close to an hour, just drinking coffee and talking about nothing in particular. We didn't discuss my fight with Evan. It's got to be hard when they know he's trying to stop me from helping them, but all Billy said was that he could understand why Evan was having such a hard time. On the way home, I flipped through *The Art of War* and noticed he'd highlighted some of the quotes—a few were even circled.

He glanced at me. "The strategies can be used for everything—politics, business, managing conflicts, you name it. And they can be applied to any investigation. John's case is a perfect example. This book could be the key to finally stopping him."

"It just looks like a lot of quotes."

"But each one is brilliant. To give just one example, 'It's not about planning; it's about quick and appropriate responses to changing conditions.' That's exactly how a cop needs to think." His dark eyes glowed as they met mine. "If more members of the RCMP read this book we'd have a lot more convictions."

"You should write your own book."

"I've actually been working on something for a few years— how *The Art of War* can be used in police work. 'Victory belongs to the man who can master the stratagem of the crooked and the straight.'"

"That's so cool!"

He glanced at me. "Yeah?"

"Totally." If he was going to use military strategies to get John out of my life, I was all for it. This case needed someone who was willing to go the extra mile. Then I thought about Sandy. How far would she go to catch John?

The rest of the way home Billy told me all about his book. By the time he dropped me off, my anger had cooled and I was feeling horrible about my reaction to Evan on the phone earlier. I was also feeling pretty bad about taking off with Billy. I knew it was nothing, but would Evan?

My mind filled with panicky images of Evan moving out, of having to sell the house, of canceling the wedding, of Ally sobbing and having weekend visits with Evan, of lonely nights filled with the knowledge that Evan was the best thing that ever happened to me and I lost him. As soon as I walked in the door I e-mailed all our wedding invitations. Then I tried to call Evan, but his cell was off. I didn't leave a message—I didn't know what to say.

When Evan called later that night I was working in the shop. My stomach lurched and I took a deep breath before answering. Here we go.

He said, "Hey, baby. I'm sorry about earlier, I was being a dick. It's just that this guy is bad news and I don't think you get how dangerous he is."

I let out my breath. We were going to be okay.

"I do, Evan. Of course I do. And I really hope you didn't mean what you said about our relationship, because I sent out our invitations." I laughed.

Evan was quiet. My chest tightened.

I said, "Okay, now you're scaring me."

"You scare me, Sara. I want to marry you and make a life with you—I love you—but you're putting yourself and Ally in danger. I want to protect you, but you don't listen to me."

"Since when do I have to obey everything you say? I'm not a dog." I laughed, but he didn't.

He said, "You know that's not what I mean. I don't want you to meet with him again. I don't know how much clearer I can make it. I didn't even want you to talk to him in the first place."

"I know that, Evan. But I'm trying to tell you I can't keep living my life in limbo. It's killing me."

"Sara. Just do it. Meet with John. I don't care anymore. But I have to go to bed. I have a long day tomorrow."

"Wait, Evan. I want to talk about this—"

"No, you don't. Your mind is made up and you just want me to be okay with it. But it doesn't matter how many different ways you say it, I'm not okay with it. Talking about it is a waste of energy."

"I need to know *we're* going to be okay, if I do this."

"I don't know, Sara."

I was crying now. "You and Ally are the most important people in the world to me, Evan. I don't want to lose you, but I'm losing myself. I can't eat, sleep, anything. I'm a mess. Can't you see that?"

"Just make a decision." He sounded resigned.

He said good night and I whispered it back through my tears, then pulled on one of his T-shirts and climbed into bed. I couldn't imagine a life without Evan—didn't *want* a life without him. But if I didn't end this thing with John soon my relationship was going to die regardless because I was spiraling out of control. Either way I was ruined.

Evan was right, I had to make a decision and I knew what it was going to be. There was only one way out. Then my life could return to normal. I just prayed Evan was still going to be a part of that life.

The next morning John called my cell when I was taking Ally to school. This time I tried something different.

"Hi, John, I'm just driving Ally, but I'll call you back as soon as I can."

"But I want to talk." He sounded startled.

"Great, because I really want to discuss some of the stuff we talked about the other day."

"I can't leave the cell on. But I need—"

"Okay, just give me a call back in a half hour on my home line." I hung up.

I held my breath, expecting him to call right back, but he didn't. Billy called to tell me John was near Williams Lake again and they had every available officer out on the roads. Exactly a half hour later John called my landline. While he bragged about tracking a black bear through a marsh that morning, I debated whether I should wait for him to mention another meeting or bring it up myself. As he started describing how he gutted the bear, then dragged the two-hundred-and-fifty-pound carcass out of the bushes without breaking a sweat, I interrupted.

"It's got to be hard to shoot a bear. I'd be scared I'd miss and he'd come after me."

"I never miss." His voice turned angry. "Every year I come across injured bears out in the woods because of some amateur. If I can't get a solid shot right behind the ear and straight into the brain, I don't pull the trigger. Most hunters, they get excited, then they jerk up at the last minute and—"

"Wow, that's really interesting. It's too bad we didn't get to meet. I would sure like to hear some of these stories in person."

"Great minds think alike! I was just going to suggest another meeting—you can bring Ally."

"I don't know. . . . Maybe it should just be me the first time. She might say something to Evan. But I can bring pictures of her?"

"Yeah, yeah, bring pictures. That would be great." I shuddered at the idea of him touching a photo of Ally.

He said, "So when do you want to meet?"

"When were you thinking?" My mouth went dry.

"I need to get away. It's getting warm out." His voice was

angry again. "People are starting to camp and they throw their trash into the woods and turn their radios up so loud you can't hear yourself think."

"Soon, we can meet soon."

"Okay. Tomorrow."

That's why I called for an emergency session. I know you don't normally do evening appointments, so I really appreciate this. Trust me, I wanted to come earlier, but I've been at the station all afternoon. Billy said he'd watch Ally—can you believe he's taking Ally to Boston Pizza and he wouldn't accept any money? Evan's supposed to call later tonight and I don't know how I'm going to tell him or if I even should. I'm just sick about it. But I'm sure after we catch John, Evan will forgive me. Who was it that said it's better to beg for forgiveness than ask for permission?

You're the only person I can tell this, but when I was at the station listening to Billy and Sandy—I'm meeting John at Bowen Park this time, so they wanted to go over a new plan—I had a really weird moment. I think what triggered it was something Billy said about John's headaches, about John using them as an excuse. I caught myself for a second wanting to defend him—to defend *myself*. My entire life people have looked at me like I was faking it when I had a migraine. But I know how much they hurt, how the pain almost makes you insane.

When I was in school one of my friends fought with her mom constantly and when her mom would say, "You're just like me when I was your age," my friend would go on and on about how she was nothing like her mom. I didn't understand it. For one, they were a lot alike, and two, I thought it was a lot worse not being able to see yourself at all in your parents—like me. Definitely not in Mom, who is the sweetest, most patient woman on the planet, and Dad, well, we'd need another hour to cover all the ways we differ.

That's one of the reasons I was so disappointed when I met Julia. I still didn't see myself. It scares me how much I'm like John—his impulsiveness, his short attention span, his temper. Now even with the migraines. But I'm terrified I'm becoming *more* like him. Every time he says something that reminds me of myself I fantasize about killing him, taking a knife to the meeting and stabbing him over and over again. But the best part is when he's lying there, bleeding—when I can see he's finally dead. It feels good.

SESSION EIGHTEEN

I thought about everything you said, and considering what I'm going through I guess I could be doing a lot worse. You get some of the credit. No matter what I tell you, no matter how weird I'm feeling, you make me *look* at it. And you always help me figure out where it's coming from. Then I can deal with it, or at least try to make sense of it. Evan accepts all my quirks and craziness—well, that might be up for debate at the moment. But I don't think he really understands why I do the things I do, or maybe he just doesn't need to know why.

Me, I've always questioned everything—a trait that drove my dad nuts. Okay, most people in my life. But you were the first person who told me it was okay to have questions, who encouraged them. Actually you were the first person who told me *I* was okay. Even Lauren sometimes tells me to stop being so . . . so *Sara*. But not you.

You said my obsessions were passions, that my intensity was a powerful gift, that my determination was admirable.

That what I considered my weaknesses could also be my greatest strengths. If John is a mirror that reflects back my worst distortions of myself, then you're a mirror that reflects the good. Sometimes I wonder what would happen if I didn't have you holding it up.

When I got home from our last session Evan had left a message saying he was exhausted and was turning his cell off and going to bed. I felt bad he didn't know I was planning to meet John at noon the next day but relieved I didn't have to tell him. I left a message saying I was sorry I missed his call and wished him a good night. Then I hung up before I blurted out everything.

After Billy brought Ally home he waited while I put her to bed, then we went over the logistics for the meeting again. The police had counterattacks set up on the main highway from Williams Lake to Vancouver and conservation officers stopping people on the back roads, but for all they knew they'd already let John through. We had to continue with our plan.

This time Billy was posing as a park landscaper working near the bench where I'd be sitting. I felt a lot better knowing he'd be close. He's so big and solid, definitely someone you'd want by your side if you were going into a dark alley—or meeting a serial killer. A couple of times I cracked a joke and he always smiled, but then he'd point back to his sketch of the park. His belief that their plan was going to work shored up my belief that I was doing the right thing. All I had to do was sit on a bench for a little while and this whole nightmare would be over.

After Billy left around ten I collapsed into bed and sank into a dreamless sleep. But the next morning I woke on Evan's side of the bed and as I cuddled his pillow, breathing in his scent, my confidence began to ebb. What if something happened to me? What if that last conversation I'd had with Evan was our *last* conversation ever? I had to let him know how much I love him. But when I tried his cell, he didn't answer. For a moment I was tempted to phone Billy and call the whole thing off. Then I thought about what would happen if I did.

Ally wanted to make me breakfast, pancakes the same way Evan makes them. I let her make a total mess of the kitchen—she looked so cute in her little apron and chef's hat as she served me—then sat at the table with her instead of rushing around to clean up. As I listened to her morning chatter, smiling at her story about what Moose did to his stuffie, I prayed this wouldn't be her last memory of me. I tried to remind myself that John had never threatened me, but I couldn't forget that he was a killer. When we got to Ally's school I walked her to her classroom, then dropped to my knees in front of her.

"Ally, you know how much Mommy loves you, right?"

"Yup."

"How much?" I said in a teasing voice.

"More than Moose loves his bunny!" She giggled and I

pulled her in for a hug, squeezing so tight she said, "Mom-meeee!" and I had to let go. She joined a couple of friends and, giving me a little wave over her shoulder, she entered the classroom.

On my way to the station for a final briefing with Sandy and Billy, I tried to call Lauren, but she didn't answer. Desperate to talk to *someone*, I almost called Melanie, then remembered I still hadn't listened to Kyle's CD. When I tried Evan's number again I just got his voice mail. This time I even called the lodge's direct line to his office, which I don't like doing because he's rarely there, and his receptionist, who I don't like because she has no sense of humor, said he was working on one of the boats.

After the meeting at the station I was on my way home to kill an hour when I passed a store with bundles of flowers outside. I picked the biggest bunch I could and drove to my parents' place. When Mom opened the door, her face lit up.

"Sara, what a lovely surprise. Have you eaten?"

As I sat there drinking coffee, playing with my cinnamon bun, wondering if I'd live through the day, Mom touched my hand every two minutes.

"I'm glad you came by, sweetie. It's been so long since we've had a chance to visit."

"Sorry, Mom, it's just been crazy between wedding plans and work."

"I'm always here if you need help." As she smiled I noticed she'd put blush on her cheeks, but the makeup just sat on top of her pale skin. I wanted to brush it off and replace it with a kiss. She did always try to be there for me, despite her illness. But she couldn't help with this. She couldn't help with any of my problems growing up—not that I ever asked. I loved my mom for her sweet and gentle soul, but it was those same characteristics that stopped me from sharing anything real. I'd do anything to protect her from pain.

"I know, Mom. You're awesome."

She smiled again. She was so easy to please. All she wanted was for her children to be happy. The thought of all the lies I'd told her over the last couple of months, was still telling her, made tears prick at the back of my eyes.

"Dad never wanted to adopt me, did he?" I couldn't believe I'd asked, and judging by Mom's flushed cheeks, she couldn't either.

She looked around like he was going to walk in right that minute. "Of course, he just . . ."

"It's okay, don't worry about it." I already had my answer. Guilt was written all over her face. I always knew why Dad was so distant, but to have it finally confirmed hurt more than I'd expected.

I switched the talk to Ally until it was time to go meet John. I gave Mom a hug and a kiss at the door, letting myself sink into it for a moment, inhaling her powdery cinnamon scent. Then, with a promise to bring Ally over soon, I got going. As I neared the park I tried to call Evan's cell one more time. Still no answer, so I left him a message. I didn't know what to say, so I just told him I love him and, "I'm sorry I'm such a pain in the ass."

———

At Bowen Park I found the bench near the outdoor tennis court where I told John I'd wait, then watched every truck and car pulling in. My gaze roamed the park in case he walked in from a different direction, and I held my breath every time I spotted someone, letting it out in a rush when it turned out to be a false alarm. Billy, weeding a garden bed on my right, met my eyes a couple of times, giving me a hang-in-there smile. When I wasn't watching for John, I was monitoring the whereabouts of the undercover officers.

Ten minutes passed. To occupy my hands I spun my coffee cup around and around and around. Another ten minutes and still no sign of John. The gallons of coffee I'd drunk had me needing to pee, bad. Images of my bladder exploding filled my head. Thank God I remembered to take my pill this time. I was about to risk speaking into the wire device when my cell rang. It was John.

"John! Where are you?"

"Sorry, Sara, but I'm not going to be able to meet today."

"You've got to be kidding. I've been sitting here for almost a half hour." I forced myself to calm down. "I'm just confused. Yesterday you were really excited about getting together, so why are you—"

"I changed my mind." He sounded pissed off.

You don't think I wanted to change my mind, you jerk?

"That's too bad, John. I've been really looking forward to meeting you."

"I'm sorry, I wanted to, but it just won't work out."

"Where are you right now?"

"Vancouver."

"You're almost here. Why don't you see if you can catch the next ferry?"

"No, we'll have to meet in a couple of days."

"Unfortunately that's not going to work for me. Evan's coming home tomorrow." Two can play that game.

"So?"

"So I'm going to be busy."

His voice rose. "I don't want to meet today. When I woke up, it didn't feel right."

Of course it didn't feel right, you murdering son of a bitch—the cops were going to arrest your ass. But now this was never going to end. I had to give it one more chance.

"I don't mind waiting a little longer so you can think it through—"

He hung up. Was he pissed off? Should I just leave? I glanced at Billy, but I couldn't read his expression.

The phone rang a minute later.

John said, "It still doesn't feel right. Let's try for tomorrow."

"I told you—that's not going to work."

"Because of Evan?" His tone made it very clear what he thought of Evan, and I realized my mistake.

"No, I've got a lot of stuff to do, work, Ally, shopping." I had to get off the phone fast. "I guess we'll just have to arrange something for another time. Take care, John. Drive safe." I hung up before he could say anything else. When I walked by Billy I shook my head—subtly, in case John was watching. As I climbed into the Cherokee a text came through on my cell. Billy: *meet us at the station.*

Great. More coffee and more talking. At least they had a bathroom. On the way there, Evan called.

"Hi, you been trying to get hold of me?"

"Oh, *Evan*. You're going to kill me."

One of his heavy sighs. "What did you do now?"

"I didn't want to tell you in a message, so I kept calling, but your stupid receptionist said you were—"

"Hey, freak show—calm down. What did you do?"

"I set up a meeting."

"Jesus Christ, Sara! When?"

"It was supposed to be today, but—"

"*Today?* And you didn't tell me?"

"I was *trying* to tell you, but you didn't answer."

"When is it?" He sounded scared. "I'll drive down and—"

"It already happened, but—"

"*What?*"

"He didn't show up. You were right, he's just manipulating me." I filled him in on everything. "But that's it. I'm done now, Evan."

"I've heard that before."

"No, this is really it. I'll change our numbers again. Maybe we can move, or go stay at the lodge like you said. I can homeschool Ally. Or maybe we should just sell the house. I don't know, but I'm going to tell the police they can't tap our phones anymore. I won't watch the TV or read the papers—"

"Slow down. I've got a big group here tonight, but I'll drive down first thing and we can talk about this."

"Are you sure?"

"We'll figure it all out, okay? Just don't make any decisions until I get home and don't change anything—*please*."

"Okay, okay."

"I mean it. I don't want to come home and find a for sale sign on the front lawn."

"*Okay.* Now I have to go meet Sandy and Billy back at the station." I groaned.

"Don't let them manipulate you either."

"Everyone's manipulating me right now."

"Come on, Sara—that's not fair."

"I'm sorry. This just sucks. I wish I didn't have to meet them—I just want to go home."

"Tell them to fuck off."

"I have to talk to them, but they're not going to like what I have to say."

Evan was right about the cops, and so was I. As soon as we closed the door of the interview room Sandy said, "Next time I think we should—"

"There's not going to be a next time."

She steamrolled right over me. "We need to entice him with a stronger reason to come to the island. I think you should tell him you'll let him meet Ally after all—"

"I'm not using my daughter as bait, Sandy."

"She's not actually going to be there, he just has to think she is."

"No, it's over. I want out. I'm changing my phone number today and I no longer authorize my landline to be tapped. And I want the tap off my cell."

"We understand if you need a break," Billy said. "This has—"

"I don't need a *break*, I need it to end. I've risked my life, my child, and my relationship for nothing. Evan was right—John's manipulating me, and you guys are just going to have to catch him on your own."

Sandy said, "And if he hurts another woman?"

"Then you should have caught him." I glared at her.

She said, "If we remove all the listening devices, we won't be able to protect you properly. What are you going to do if he comes after you or your family?"

"You told me before that you didn't think I was in any danger from him."

"I told you we can't predict what he'll do."

"It's interesting that when you wanted me to meet with him, you didn't think I was in danger, but now that I don't want to meet him, I am."

Billy said, "We're just saying we don't know how he'll handle being rejected by you. Last time it was an e-mail—"

"I'll block his e-mails."

They stared at me. I took a breath.

"Look, I thought if I agreed to a meeting it would end, but that's not happening. My life is totally screwed up—I'm barely working, I'm fighting with Evan constantly, I'm not spending enough time with my daughter. The more I help you, the more screwed up it gets. I'm just going to go home and continue with my life like he doesn't exist. That's what I should've done a long time ago."

Billy said, "It sounds like your mind's made up, and you have to do what's right for you. But I think you should—"

I stood up. "Thanks for understanding."

Sandy, who looked anything but understanding, shook her head and said, "I hope you can live with yourself when he finds his next victim."

"I hope you can live with *your*self. You've known about him for years and never stopped him. I've given you more leads than you ever got on your own." Her face flushed as she rose to her feet with her fists clenched at her side.

I took a step back as she said, "You—"

Billy said, "Sandy?"

She spun on her heels and left the room, slamming the door behind her.

Billy followed me out to the Cherokee. The adrenaline of the day was still pumping through my veins as I ranted and raved about Sandy.

"All right, killer," he said when I wound down. "You going to be okay tonight? If you want, I can bring some Chinese over later and keep an eye on you and Ally?"

"That's a really nice offer, Billy, but I think you're right—I need a break from all of this." I also knew how Evan reacted the last time Billy brought me food.

"Sure, but if you need me, you know the number."

"Nine-one-one?"

He laughed, but hurt flashed in his eyes and I felt bad.

"Stay safe, kid." He walked back to the station. Where Sandy was probably throwing darts at my photo.

So that's the end of it. And I think I'll end today's appointment there as well. I've had enough talking for one day. I know, not something you usually hear me complain about. Remember the days when my biggest concern was my temper? Never thought I'd think of those as the good old days, but then I never thought I'd have a killer for a father—especially one who changes his mind as much as I do.

You said I need to start asking myself what I want to do, not what's right or wrong, or what anybody else thinks. And figuring out what I want means taking an objective look at what I feel *and* what the consequences of my decisions are. Like I want John out of my life and I'm afraid he'll hurt someone. I want John caught and I'm terrified he'll come after my family. Then you said I have to make a decision and stick with it. So that's what I'm doing. Because I want my sanity back *and* I'm afraid it's too late.

SESSION NINETEEN

I don't know who to listen to anymore. I'm so messed up right now I'd probably walk into traffic if you thought it was a good idea—sure would make things simple in a hurry. God, this nightmare just won't end. Be careful what you wish for. All I wanted was a father who cared about me. Oh, he cares, all right. He cares so much it just might kill me, if he doesn't kill everyone I love first.

Last night John called again. Lord knows what he wanted this time, and I'll never know because I turned my cell off. He tried the cordless a couple times too, but I ignored it. Billy didn't call to tell me John's location, probably hoping the curiosity would get to me, but I didn't want to know. I couldn't wait to change our numbers—the only thing that stopped me was Evan saying hold off. But it pissed me off no end when I realized I'd left the station without the cops confirming they'd remove the tap from my cell, and they probably still had the landline tapped. When Evan called later he still had a lot to do before he left in the morning, so we just said our good nights and agreed to leave the big decisions until he was home. I could ignore John for another day.

This morning, which feels like a million years ago, I dropped Ally off at school—it's her last day before summer vacation—then rushed around like mad cleaning the house. I was surprised Evan didn't call when he left the lodge but figured he just got busy. It's not easy for him to leave at the last minute. His phone kept going to voice mail, so I was sure he was already on the road—the cell coverage sucks up there. Around ten I stopped vacuuming to throw another load of laundry in and heard tires on gravel, then Moose streaked to the door barking. Evan was home!

I raced to the front door—and saw Billy and Sandy get out of the Tahoe. My guts clenched at the sight of their grave faces and dark sunglasses.

Billy said, "Can we come in?"

"Evan's due home any second, but sure."

This time I brought them into the living room. Bad news deserves formality. After they were settled on the opposite couch I took the plunge.

"Another girl's missing, right?"

"Sara . . ." Billy removed his sunglasses. "Evan was shot at the lodge this morning and—"

"What!" I stared at them for a moment as my heart hammered in my chest. Then I jumped up. "Is he okay?" My eyes flicked back and forth between them, desperately trying to read their faces.

"He's going to be all right," Billy said. "He's been flown to the hospital in Port Alberni."

"What *happened*?"

"He went down to the dock early this morning. That's when he got shot. He managed to drag himself into one of the boats and used the first-aid kit to stop the bleeding until one of the guides found him."

"Okay. I just. I have to—" I whirled around and grabbed my purse off the hall bench, searched for my keys, my cell phone. How was I going to get Ally from school? Could Lauren pick her up? Should I get her on the way?

Sandy said, "We'll take you to the hospital."

Moose. I had to ask a neighbor to let him out. What else? A client was coming by to pick up a headboard. I flipped open my cell, but Sandy grabbed my wrist.

"Hold on."

I yanked free. "I have to call someone about Ally."

"We understand, but we need to go over a few things with you first."

"It had to be John."

Billy said, "That's why we—"

"I have to tell my family." How was I going to explain this to them?

Sandy said, "We have some ideas around what you should say."

I turned to Billy. "He didn't . . . kill him. It was just a warning, right?"

"We don't think so. One of the cooks went out for a cigarette around the time Evan was shot and heard something in the bushes. We think he spooked John before he could finish the job."

John wanted to kill Evan. Because of me. My eyes filled with tears.

"I have to get Ally from school *right now*."

Sandy said, "A couple of members are at the hospital with Evan and we have a patrol car watching the school. You can go up with Billy to see Evan and we'll send an officer to pick Ally up. Just call the school and explain they're a family friend. We don't want to scare everyone into thinking there's a killer on the loose."

Except there *was* a killer on the loose. One who was really pissed off at me and really good at making his point.

"Ally knows she's not supposed to leave with a stranger. I could call one of my sisters, but then I'll have to tell them what's going on, and—"

"Let's not do that right now," Sandy said. "Ally knows me. I'll pick her up and watch her while you visit Evan."

I shook my head. "I told John I couldn't meet him because Evan was coming home. He must've decided he should just—" My voice caught.

Billy's face was pained. "You didn't know he'd do this, Sara."

I looked at Sandy. "But *you* did. You warned me." Had I let my personal feelings for her get in the way of the truth?

Sandy said, "You can't dwell on what's done, Sara. You just have to be strong for Evan. We'll take care of the rest." For once she had said something I liked.

On the way up to the hospital with Billy, I called my parents from my cell. As soon as I heard Mom's gentle voice the dam broke and I started crying. I managed to pull it together long enough to tell her the cover story—the police believed Evan had been shot by a disgruntled employee. I didn't know how long that one would fly, since Evan had never pissed off anyone in his life. The thought made me cry harder.

Before I could stop her, Mom put Dad on the phone.

"What's going on?"

"Dad, Evan's in the hospital. He was shot at the lodge. He's okay, but they flew him to Port Alberni and—" I burst into fresh tears.

Dad said, "Your mother and I will meet you there."

It was probably the last thing the police wanted. But it was what I wanted the most.

"Thanks, Dad. Can you call his parents for me?" They live down in the States and although Evan and his family are close, he doesn't get to see them often. Mom and Dad fill a lot of the role for him.

"We'll let them know," Dad said. "Where's Ally?"

"A friend's watching her." First and last time I'd call Sandy that.

"How are you getting up there?"

"Billy, the police officer who's my client, volunteered to drive me."

Dad paused for a moment, then said, "We'll leave right now."

He hung up before I could say anything else. Billy told me he'd deal with it—he has no idea what dealing with my dad is like. But at that moment I didn't care. The only person who mattered was Evan. I wished I'd told him that yesterday.

The drive to Port Alberni is never an easy one—over an hour of a narrow highway winding through steep mountains where you're competing for space with logging trucks. But today it was unbearable. Thank God Billy was behind the wheel—if I was driving the speed my heart was going, I'd have had an accident. I have no recollection of anything we talked about, just vague snippets of reassurance from Billy: *We're going to catch him. Evan's going to be fine.*

At the hospital the doctor told me Evan had been shot clean through the fleshy part of his left shoulder. They were waiting for him to stabilize before they sent him to Nanaimo in an ambulance for surgery. He had muscle damage and a huge wound, but no permanent damage. I was just happy he was alive—especially when the doctor told me eight inches to the left and it would've gone straight through his heart. Hearing that just about made my own heart stop.

They'd given him some drugs for the pain and he was out cold, but they let me in to see him. His shoulder was wrapped in a huge white bandage and he had an IV stabbed into his arm. Tears ran down my face as I kissed his cheek and smoothed his hair. I hated how pale he was, hated all the tubes running out of him. But I hated myself even more for putting him in danger.

As I fussed over Evan, nurses monitored his signs and wrote things on his chart. One asked if I needed anything. *Yeah, a serial killer put behind bars. Can you do that?* Then an older nurse asked me to step out for a moment while they changed his bandage. I was about to argue when I heard Dad's loud voice asking for Evan's room.

When I went to meet my parents I noticed Billy talking to two policemen in a small waiting area. He straightened up when he saw my father and started toward him, but Dad walked right past him and came up to me.

"How's Evan doing?"

"He's asleep right now. He's going to be okay, but he has to have surgery. They'll wait until he's stable, then take him to Nanaimo and—" I stopped as I saw my sister hurrying down the hallway.

Mom said, "Lauren came up with us. She was just calling Greg."

Lauren and I fell into each other's arms. "I can't believe Evan was shot. You must be terrified." Her body vibrated against me, sending a fresh wave of fear through my own. *Yes, this is bad. This is really, really bad.*

We pulled apart and I said, "Thanks for coming up." My voice was thick.

"Of course. Why didn't you call me?"

"I was going to, but everything just . . ."

Billy walked over. "Hi, everyone. I'm Bill." He turned to Dad and stretched out his hand. "We met at Sara's."

Dad gave his hand a hard shake. "This your case?"

"I'll certainly check on things for Sara, but no, the local officers are handling the investigation."

Dad looked up and down the hallway. "There's a lot of police around." He stared hard at me. "What's going on, Sara?"

My face felt hot. "Ah . . . what do you mean? Evan's been shot, and . . ."

Then I saw it click in Dad's head.

"This has something to do with the Campsite Killer, doesn't it?"

Mom gasped. Lauren's hand flew to her mouth.

Dad turned to me. "Tell me what's going on right now, Sara."

I looked at Billy helplessly. He saved me again.

"Let's find somewhere private to talk."

Billy led us into an empty room and filled them in while Mom grew paler and paler. Lauren shivered during the entire conversation. After Billy finished, Dad looked at me and shook his head.

"This whole time you've been lying to us."

"Dad, I—"

Billy said, "Sara didn't want to keep it from you. She was under strict orders not to talk about this with anyone. It could have damaged the case and put her family—all of you—in danger. She's been a great help to us."

Dad said, "You didn't explain how Evan wound up shot."

"John, the Campsite Killer, he wanted to meet with me again, Dad. And I said I couldn't, because Evan was coming home."

"Where's this scumbag now?" Dad's face turned dark. "Where's Ally?"

"She's with another officer," Billy said. "She's well protected."

"What are you doing to catch this man?"

"Everything in our power, sir. Your daughter was a big part of our investigation, but we'll continue in a different direction now."

"Why's that?"

"Because I won't help anymore," I said. "Evan didn't want me to meet with him in the first place, but I was worried he'd kill another woman, but now that Evan's been shot, I'm not—"

"Evan didn't want you to meet him, but you did it anyway?"

We stared at each other. Mom said, "She thought she was doing the right thing, Patrick."

Dad walked over to the window and looked down at the parking lot. His arms were crossed in front of him, his broad back a wall I've never been able to cross.

The four of us stood in awkward silence, all staring at Dad.

"I better go talk to the other officers," Billy said. "If you have any more questions I'll be in the hall." No one said anything as he left.

After a moment Dad said, "Evan was right—you should've just stayed out of it."

"Dad, I was trying to *help*."

He turned around and looked hard at me. "Let the police handle it from now on, Sara." As he headed out of the room he said, "I'm going to find the doctor."

Mom gave me a consoling smile and touched my hand. "He's just upset."

"I know, Mom, but don't you think I am too? He has no idea how much pressure I've been under. The cops, Julia—they were all pushing me to do this. It's not like I came up with the idea on my own."

"Julia?"

"My mother." Mom recoiled like she'd been hit. *Crap, crap. Crap.* "I mean my *birth* mother. She wanted me to meet him and—"

"You've seen her again?"

"I went to her house a couple of times, but I couldn't mention it to you because we were talking about the case. She's been terrified for years—it was really important to her that he be caught. And I wanted to help because . . ."

"Because she's your mother."

"That's not it at all, Mom—I just felt bad for her."

"Of course you did, sweetie. You're a caring person."

"Yeah, well, that bit me in the butt."

"Anyone else would've just walked away, Sara. You give yourself to everything you do, and everyone you love." She smiled, but the look in her eyes broke my heart. She said, "I'd better make sure your father's being polite to the nurses," and hurried after Dad.

I turned to Lauren. "Great, now Mom's upset."

"Don't worry about that right now. Just focus on Evan."

I sighed. "You mean the other person I hurt?"

"It's not your fault, Sara."

"No, Dad's right. I screwed up. I told John that Evan was the reason I couldn't meet him. I should've known how much that would piss him off."

"You didn't know he was going to hurt him."

"Evan wanted me to stop this a long time ago. I should've listened."

"I can't believe you've been going through this all on your own."

She stepped forward and wrapped her arms around me. I leaned into her shoulder and started to cry.

We waited outside Evan's room for a couple of hours. Billy stayed near the other cops, where they talked in low voices, and Dad sat in a chair with his arms across his chest, when he wasn't pacing up and down the hallway. Mom flipped through a magazine but kept looking at Dad, Lauren, and me. Lauren went to the cafeteria and got us all something to eat, but I could only sip a coffee. So she sat beside me, talking about the boys or the house or her garden. The chatter was comforting, but I was barely able to focus on what she was saying as I watched doctors and nurses, worrying every time anyone stopped outside Evan's room.

Dad looked at his cell, then got up and walked down the hall. After a few moments he came back.

"I've got to get down to Nanaimo—a chain broke on the skidder."

Mom stood up. "Are you going to be okay if we leave you, Sara?"

"I'm fine, Mom. It will probably just be a lot of sitting around."

Lauren said, "I can stay."

"No, you've got the boys. I'll be okay."

Mom said, "We can come up later."

"Thanks, Mom. But they'll probably be sending Evan to Nanaimo tomorrow. You might as well just wait and visit him there."

"Make sure to let us know if anything changes or if you need anything, sweetie."

"Of course."

I spent another hour waiting with Billy, but now I was the one pacing up and down the hall. A nurse came by and told me Evan had woken up briefly and they'd given him more pain medication. He'd probably be sleeping for the rest of the day, if I wanted to go home and get some of his things.

Billy was on his phone when I went to find him.

I said, "Everything all right?"

"Yeah, just touching base with Sandy."

"Is Ally okay?"

"They're having a great time."

I breathed a small sigh of relief.

We were only ten minutes out of town when my cell rang.

I looked at Billy. "It's John! What do I do?"

"If you don't think you can remain calm, you shouldn't—"

NEVER KNOWING · 361

"But if he's still close by, you might be able to get his location and catch him, right?"

"It's the best chance we have, but you need to think about what you say before you—"

I answered on the next ring.

"What do *you* want?"

"Sara! I'm on the island, what time can we meet?"

"You actually think I'm going to meet you after you shot *Evan*?"

Silence.

"You screwed up big time, John. Don't ever call me again. This is over." I hung up the phone, my whole body shaking.

Billy clasped my shoulder. "You okay?"

I nodded as adrenaline pumped through my body. I realized my teeth were chattering.

"Yeah. God, no, I'm not. I'm sorry I couldn't talk to him for longer—I lost my temper. But I think—I think I'm having an anxiety attack. My chest . . . it's all tight, and . . ." I sucked at the air.

"Just take some slow deep breaths, Sara. You need—" His phone rang. "Reynolds here. . . . Okay, I'll let her know."

"What's going on?"

"John's cell pinged off a Nanaimo tower, so he's in town."

He gunned the Tahoe. Now my body was shaking even harder.

"God, he must be totally freaking out that I hung up on him."

"He's not going to be happy about it." Billy's hands gripped

362 · Chevy Stevens

the steering wheel so hard the muscles in his forearms were corded.

"You think he still wants to meet me? But I told him it was over, and—"

"This is a man who doesn't like to be told no."

My chest tightened again and my face felt hot.

"Do you think I *should* meet with him? If I don't, will he go after Evan again?"

"Emotions are high on both sides right now, so it might not be the best time to meet. But if he's acting impulsively, he's more likely to make mistakes, and—"

"I think I'm having another anxiety attack." I pressed my hand against my rocketing heart.

Billy looked worried. "Maybe we should go back to the hospital and—"

"No." I sucked in a lungful of air. "No, I have to talk to my psychiatrist."

"Right now?"

I nodded rapidly. "I have to or I'm going to lose it, Billy. I need to calm down, but I can't unless I talk to her and—"

"Call her."

I didn't expect that you'd want me to come in right away. I thought we could just do this over the phone, but I guess I did sound one panic attack away from all-out hysteria. I want to be with Evan, but every other part of my body's screaming at me to get home as fast as I can to be with Ally. Of course, you're right, I need to calm down first. Part of protecting her is making sure she doesn't see her mother go off the deep end.

Poor Billy—he's waiting out in the Tahoe. I told him he could go grab a coffee, but he said he was staying to make sure I was all right. Only way I could come here was if I called home first and talked to Sandy, then Ally, who's having a great time. When she put Sandy back on the phone she said she'd guard Ally with her life. I believed her. I may not like Sandy, but I'm pretty sure if she saw John she'd shoot him on the spot.

As for me, I'm spinning in every direction, bouncing all over the place. I just wish I knew what kind of shape John's in right now, if he's in a full-on manic state too. But he has to be—why else would he shoot Evan? He must be escalating—and I went and hung up on him. I know what I'm like when I'm losing it, how out-of-control I feel—like *right now*—but I don't have a gun. Lord knows what I'd do if I did. Actually, that's not true. I know exactly what I'd do.

SESSION TWENTY

I'm so sorry about what happened. God, I can't believe you still wanted to see me after what you went through. It doesn't matter how many times you tell me I shouldn't blame myself, I can't help thinking I should've sensed something. I was just so upset I wasn't thinking straight. I'm *still* not thinking straight. But I don't feel like I should be bothering you with any of this, so if it's too much, you have to tell me, and I'll stop. You might have to tell me a couple of times, because we both know I don't stop easily. Something else I got from my father.

After our last session Billy took me back home, where Sandy was waiting. Ally was upset about Evan—Sandy had told her he'd hurt his shoulder on the boat, as we agreed—but I convinced her he's going to be fine. Then she told me about all the fun things she and Sandy had done. I was surprised Sandy is such a kid person, didn't see that one at all, but they'd made a fort and played dress-up—even staged a singing contest. I usually look frazzled after a day with Ally, but Sandy's cheeks were flushed and her eyes glowed. Then again, maybe it was from excitement that John had called again.

Billy heated up some frozen pizzas while I fielded calls from concerned friends and workers at the lodge. I checked in with Mom and Lauren, who both offered to come over, but I said I was okay. I didn't tell them John had called or that he was still in town. I also phoned the hospital several times, but there was no change in Evan's condition. When he woke up again they gave him more medication, so he was asleep when I called. There were a couple of calls from unfamiliar numbers I didn't answer, just checked my voice mail with a racing heart. Was it John? Was he coming for me? But there was never a message. The police traced the calls to pay phones in Nanaimo.

After we ate—well, they ate and I stared at my food—Billy and Sandy cleaned up while I gave Ally her bath. Then I let her watch TV in my bed so the adults could talk downstairs.

Sandy said, "That's a great kid you have there."

"Thanks, I think she's really special."

"She is." Sandy took a sip of her iced tea. "Have you given any more thought to meeting with John?"

Didn't expect her to cut to the chase that fast.

"I still don't know what I'm going to do. Evan, my dad, my psychiatrist—*no one* thinks it's a good idea."

Sandy set her glass down hard and sat straight in her chair.

"Even though he shot your fiancé, you don't want to try to stop him?"

"Of course I want to stop him, but my psychiatrist thinks he's escalating and might kill me if—"

"That's why it's important we arrest him soon."

I glanced at Billy, waiting for him to jump in, but he was silent.

"Sandy, you can't guarantee something won't go wrong and he'll get away."

"No, and we can't guarantee your safety now—or Ally's."

"Are you seriously trying to use my daughter to scare me? I think about that every day, I don't need you to—"

"I'm not trying to scare you, but when he feels rejected he—"

"I *know*. I've been thinking about that since he called again, since he shot Evan, but if I do this I stand to lose my fiancé, my family, and possibly my life."

Billy said, "I think Sara just needs a break tonight, Sandy."

"I'm *fine*. But if one more person tells me what I should do, *I am going to lose it*."

Sandy lowered her voice. "Sara, I can understand what you must be going through, but I also know you don't want to leave a serial killer out there when you have Ally to think about."

"I'm sick of you trying to make me feel guilty. You're just pissed off because you can't catch him."

Her mouth opened like she was about to say something, but then a voice from the doorway said, "Mommy, it's time for my story."

"Okay, sweetie, I'm coming." As I took Ally's hand and led her off, I felt Sandy's gaze burning into my back. When I came downstairs later she was gone and Billy was sitting at the table, playing solitaire.

"Where'd Sandy go?"

"She needed to do some follow-up work at the station."

"She hates me." I sat down with a sigh.

"She doesn't hate you, Sara."

"Well, can't say I'm her biggest fan."

He grinned. "Couldn't tell."

"You know, Nadine—that's my psychiatrist—didn't actually say she thought John would kill me."

"No?"

"She just said it sounds like he's in a manic state and might be more dangerous. Then I think about what you said—that if he's freaking out he might be easier to catch. I want to do it, and if he hadn't shot Evan . . ."

"You don't have to decide tonight. But just remember, 'A swooping falcon breaks the back of his prey; such is the precision of his timing.' He's in striking distance, Sara."

"I know, I know." I sighed. "Well, I told Nadine I'd sleep on it, then I'm going to call her in the morning before I drive up to see Evan."

"It's great you have someone like that in your life."

"Evan thinks so too." I laughed. "Saves him a lot of grief when I work things out with her first." Then I thought of Evan alone at the hospital and a fresh wave of anxiety washed over me. "I'm going to call the hospital again." The nurse told me Evan was stable but he'd be heavily sedated for the rest of the night, so it would be better to come back in the morning.

"I should be up there with him, Billy. I hate this."

"I'd feel the exact same way, but it's getting dark and that road isn't safe at the best of times."

"But what if he takes a turn for the worse or John goes there and—"

"Then it's the last place you should be. Number one, Evan is well guarded. The members watching him are senior officers. Number two, I'm sure the doctors are keeping a close eye on him. They'll call if there are complications. If you were my fiancée and I was in the hospital, I'd want you to stay where *you* were safe."

I groaned. "Evan would probably say the same thing."

"With John in town you should have protection. We can call Sandy or I can—"

I held up my hand. "Not Sandy. I'll make up the spare room."

"I should probably stay down here on the couch—closer to the door."

"Sure." Even though it was still early evening, I brought down some blankets and started making up the couch. Billy came over to help. As he reached for the edge of the sheet our arms brushed, which made me break out in goose bumps. At the same moment I thought, *Billy smells good.*

I stepped back quickly.

Billy stopped tucking in the sheet and straightened up. "You okay?"

My face burned as I said, "Yeah, totally. But my neck's a

little sore. Think I'm just going to have a hot bath and hit the sheets." I headed for the stairs. "It's been a long day. And I told Nadine I'd call her early—she's doing some research tonight about serial killers. Not that I'll be able to sleep." *Shut up, Sara.*

"Why don't you take something? Didn't you say your psychiatrist prescribed something for anxiety?"

"Ativan." I glanced at him. "But is it safe for me to take something with John out there?"

Billy spread his arms wide and grinned. "Who's going to get through me?"

I forced a smile back. "Thanks for staying over, Billy."

"Just doing my job, little lady," he said in a John Wayne voice as he pretended to swagger. I laughed, then spun around and started up the stairs.

Billy said, "Wait, what's your alarm code—I'll set it."

I rattled the numbers off as I was still walking. At the landing I said, "Okay, good night, then," but didn't wait to hear his response before I shut the bedroom door. I stood in the middle of my room and shook my head. God, Billy must be totally wondering why I was acting weird. I was wondering that myself. As I watched Ally's pink-fleece-clad chest rise and fall—she was sound asleep on my bed with Moose—I went over the moment in my mind.

Why was I suddenly noticing how good Billy smells? The entire time I'd been with Evan I'd never found another man attractive—not once. The only reason I never felt bad about spending so much time with Billy was because it was nothing. Nothing for him and, I thought, nothing for me.

No, this was stupid, it was still nothing. I was allowed to notice something nice about a good-looking man—I wasn't dead. And it wasn't like I threw him down on the couch and jumped his bones. I'm sure there were women at the lodge Evan thought were pretty. This didn't mean anything. It was probably one of those transference things. Billy represented safety and I was distracting myself from my real fear: losing Evan.

I poured a hot bath and soaked in the lavender-scented bubbles. But I couldn't stop thinking about Evan being shot. Even though I hadn't been there, I could see his body jerk with the impact, see him fall, then drag himself to the boat. My mind tortured myself with thoughts of what might've happened if John had been successful. Then I thought of all the times I'd been short with Evan lately or ignored him completely because I was so caught up in my drama.

I gave up on the bath and popped an Ativan, then pulled on one of Evan's shirts and crawled into bed with Ally and Moose. Ally was on my side, but I left her there and whispered a good night as I kissed her cheek and smoothed her hair off her face. The book Billy had given me was still on the night table where I'd put it the day we went for a drive. Hoping it might distract me, I thumbed through the pages. One quote—"All warfare is based on deception"—jumped out. I'd tried to deceive John, but he won that battle hands down. As I scanned more pages I saw how Billy might've used some of the strategies, especially the ones about espionage and waging war.

Then I saw a quote that jarred me. "In the whole army none should be closer to the commander than his spies, none more highly awarded, none more confidentially treated." Had Billy been using some of these strategies on *me*?

Nice, Sara. You found the man attractive and you're feeling guilty, so you're looking for ways to make him a jerk. Billy was just a dedicated cop. I put the book back on the table. Then I buried my face in Evan's pillow, inhaling his clean scent, telling myself over and over, *Everything's going to be fine. Everything's going to be fine. Everything's going to be fine.*

The next morning I made breakfast while Billy entertained Ally, but it looked like it was Ally who was entertaining Billy as she tried to wrestle one of her stuffed animals away from Moose. I was glad they were having fun, since Billy was going to watch her when I went up to see Evan. Billy said Sandy could stay with Ally and he'd escort me to the hospital, but I needed a little space from him after my weird reaction the night before. Not that I told Billy that. I just said I needed the drive to clear my head and asked if a patrol car could follow.

He said, "I would've sent one whether you liked it or not. Someone's gotta keep an eye on you." Then he smiled and I tried to smile back, but my mind was spinning with worry. I'd tried to call you a couple of times that morning and was upset when you didn't answer. When I mentioned it to Billy he said you probably had an emergency with another patient, but I thought, *What could be more important than a serial killer?*

On the way to the hospital I put everything else out of my mind and focused on what I wanted to do about John. He'd just proved by shooting Evan that he wasn't going to go away quietly. I thought about stopping at Lauren's or my parents' on the way home to hash it out, but part of me didn't want to add more opinions to the mix, especially when I already knew what they'd be. My mind bounced all over the chart, but it kept going back to my original thought: meeting John was the only way out of this whole mess.

Before I went in to see Evan I sat in the parking lot of the hospital and tried to pull myself together. I was going to be upbeat and positive for him. The last things he needed right now were my fears and angst. I could do this. My resolve was rewarded as I walked into Evan's room and he flashed his best boyish grin.

"Hi, baby. I don't think your father likes me."

I burst into tears.

"Aw, Sara, don't cry. That was supposed to make you laugh."

I hurled myself into the chair beside his bed and leaned on the mattress.

"I'm so sorry, Evan. For all of this."

"You goof, you didn't shoot me. Wait, *did* you?" He smiled.

"*No.*"

"Then shut up and give your fiancé a kiss." After we shared a lingering kiss, and then another, I told him everything that had been happening. I wanted to tell him John had called again, but the nurses kept interrupting. Then the doctor came in. He'd just finished telling us Evan was going to be transported down to Nanaimo that afternoon when one of the officers stepped into the room.

"Excuse me, Sara. Constable Reynolds would like you to call him."

I looked at Evan and he said, "Go." I walked outside and called Billy's cell.

"What's up?"

"Something's happened, Sara."

My stomach dropped. "Ally—"

"Ally's fine. It's your psychiatrist—someone attacked her as she was leaving her office last night."

I felt a flash of relief that Ally was safe, then the rest of his words connected.

"Oh, my God! Is she okay?"

"She was knocked down and hit her head on the curb. She'll be fine, but she's in the Nanaimo hospital for monitoring."

I collapsed into a chair in the hall. *Knocked down* . . . I saw her head smashing into the curb, her silver hair turning crimson. What if she slipped into a coma? What if she *died*? I forced myself to take a breath. *Don't panic.* Nadine was going to be okay. Then a new thought.

"Was it John?"

"We're considering that possibility, also patients she may

have had a problem with recently. She lost consciousness briefly and was attacked from behind, so she didn't get a look at the assailant. He took off when some people exited the office next door. I know she's important to you, so Sandy's going to switch off with me here and I'll go talk to the investigating officers. That okay with you?"

"Of course. I can't believe this." My eyes filled with tears.

"I'll keep you posted. Meanwhile, Sandy will take good care of Ally until you get home."

"Thanks, Billy."

As soon as I hung up the phone I ran back to tell Evan what had happened.

"I'm really sorry to hear that. Are *you* okay, baby?"

"No! God, he shoots you and now he attacks *Nadine*?" I paced around his room.

"They don't know for sure it was him, though?"

"It has to be. I just went there last night—he probably followed me and I took him straight to her." I shook my head. "This isn't his pattern at all. He must be totally losing it."

"Have you heard from him?"

"Not since yesterday. He called when Billy was driving me home. He wanted to meet again. I hung up on him, but—"

"You can't meet him."

"But John's gone after Nadine now—who's next? This is *bullshit*. I'm sick and tired of his games. He needs to know he can't just—"

"Sara, you can't—" As he reached for my hand his upper body shifted and he dropped his arm back onto the bed with a groan. He took a couple of breaths.

"Should I call the nurse or—"

"I'll check myself out right now if you're going to meet—"

"Okay, okay. I won't go near him."

"Promise."

I put a hand over my heart. "I *promise.*"

He looked exhausted. "You going to see Nadine?"

"I'm staying with you until they're ready to take you to Nanaimo."

"I'm fine. But you have to go see her or you won't be able to focus on anything else."

"She's probably not allowed visitors."

He shrugged, then winced. "Just say you're her daughter."

"That could work. I think she does have a daughter around my age, but I'm pretty sure she doesn't live here. Nadine never talks about her, though—I just saw a picture in her office once. Nadine's a widow, you know. God, I wonder if she's all by herself. . . ."

"They're taking me to Nanaimo soon anyway. You can meet me there after you see her."

"I want to stick around until they load you up and make sure you're okay."

"Yeah, that's exactly what I need—you all stressed out about Nadine. Just go and I'll meet you at the hospital in a few hours. Besides, I want to take a quick nap and there's no way you'll be able to just sit here."

"I could too."

He gave me a look.

I sighed. "Okay. I'll bring Ally with me later if the police think it's safe."

"I miss my Ally Cat. Now let's play doctor before you go. I'll let you check my temperature. . . ." He wiggled his eyebrows and laughed as I pretended to unplug his IV.

After Evan and I kissed good-bye—a couple of times—I headed out. When I passed the nurses' station one of them held up a phone.

"There's a call for you." I stopped and stared at her. Who would call me at the hospital?

I never made it to see you that day, Nadine.

SESSION TWENTY-ONE

Since John attacked you, I've been going through hell. You should be the one who's terrified, and I'm sure you are. But I feel like I'm losing my mind—what's left of it. I wake up with a blanket of anxiety wrapped around me and I go to bed with it. Every muscle of my body aches. I massage my calves to release the tension. But it doesn't work. So I take muscle relaxants and have a hot bath. Then I stumble back to bed half buzzed and groggy. I roll into a ball, cocoon myself in safe words, telling myself it's over. But I still wake up clawing at my legs.

When the nurse handed me the phone I thought it might be Dad or Lauren unable to reach my cell, but when I said, "Hello," John answered rapid-fire.

"We have to meet today."

I stretched the cord as far as I could and moved away from the desk. "How did you know I was here?"

"We *have* to meet."

I looked over my shoulder, wondering if the nurses could hear, but one was gone and the other was writing something on a chart at the end of the hall.

"I can't just drop everything for you. I have to think about—"

"There's no *time*."

"You had time to attack my *psychiatrist*." Rage made my voice shake. "Do you think hurting people I care about is going to make me like you?"

Dead silence from the other end of the phone.

I glanced down the hall. The officer sitting outside Evan's room flipped through his magazine, oblivious to the fact that I was talking to the man he was supposed to be protecting me from.

John was still silent, so I said, "You *have* to stop this."

"You have to help me. You're the only one who can, Sara." He sounded desperate. Not as desperate as I felt. What should I do? Was it just a trick? But what if it wasn't?

It didn't matter. I knew what I was going to do. I closed my eyes.

"I'll meet you, okay? And we'll talk about it. But I can't get away for a while."

"Ally has to come too."

My body jerked like he'd hit me and I clutched the phone. "I already told you no."

"She *has* to. You and Ally have to come live with me."

"Live with—we can't *live* with you. That's not possible."

"You *have* to." His voice was frantic. "If you come I won't hurt anyone else again. I'll stop forever. But if you don't, I'm—I'm going to kill your shrink, and I'll finish off Evan too. I'm sorry it has to be like this, but it's an *emergency*."

"John, please, don't do anything to—"

"I won't do any of it if you come. They'll be safe."

My mind spun. *Think, Sara. Think.*

"We can meet, okay? We can meet and we'll talk about it."

"No, that's not good enough. You and Ally come or I finish them off."

"*Okay.* Just give me a bit to make a plan. The police, they're watching the hospital and our house because they don't know who shot Evan. It's not safe for me to meet you right now. I have to find a way to sneak off."

"If they find out about this call, I'll kill Evan, if you tell them you're meeting me, I'll kill Evan. If you bring them with you, I'll kill Evan. If—"

"Stop *threatening* me! I have to be careful how I do this. I need some time. To think. You can't just—"

"It has to be this afternoon—at the park."

This afternoon?

"Ally, she's at school. If I yank her out, people will ask questions—and there's a patrol car watching her."

He paused for a moment, then said, "Tonight at the park— six o'clock. Make sure *no one* follows you. Tell anyone, and Evan's dead."

He hung up.

———

My legs were shaking as I walked back to Evan's room. I stopped at the door and peeked in. He was sleeping. I watched him for a moment, still struggling to get a grip on everything that had just happened. No point waking him and asking what to do—I already knew his answer—so I left. The patrol officer who was supposed to be guarding him was getting a coffee from the vending machine at the end of the hall. Should I tell him about the call? But what if John was watching from somewhere in the hospital?

I had to think, had to focus. Should I meet John alone or talk to the police? But what if I talked and John made good on his threat?

No, I had to tell the police. This was too big. But if John found out, he said he'd kill Evan. *Stop, Sara, think it through.* There was no way John would know if I talked to the cops, he was just trying to scare me. But when I tried to call Billy, there was no answer. He was probably at the hospital with Nadine. I had to talk to someone *now*.

Sandy answered on the first ring. I started filling her in.

"You have to slow down, Sara. I'm not getting all of this."

"There's no way I'm taking Ally to meet him, Sandy. I told him she was in school. But I don't know what to do."

"Yesterday you were dead set against meeting John. How do you feel about it now?" Her voice was tense.

For a moment I panicked. Dad and Evan would *freak*. Then I felt all my pieces snap into place. It didn't matter what anyone else thought. There was only one way this was ever going to end.

"I want to do it. I'm ready. But I can't bring Ally. If I

show up, as bait or whatever, can you arrest him before he realizes Ally's not with me?"

"If he's watching from a distance and sees she's not there, he might follow through on his threats."

"There's got to be some way to flush him out that doesn't involve Ally."

She was quiet for a moment, then said, "Let's talk about it when you get here. Just drive home slowly and don't do anything abnormal in case John's following. Don't alert the officers at the hospital, I'll take care of it. Don't even pick up your cell while you're driving—he might panic if he thinks you're calling us. Think of him like a bomb, Sara. It won't take much to set him off."

"But what if it's him calling?"

"Do *not* engage in another conversation with him until we have a plan."

"Are you going to beef up the security for Evan and Nadine?"

"They're already under protection. If we send more and he's watching, he'll know you've alerted us."

"What about Billy, should I call him and—"

"I'll fill Billy in." Her voice was firm. "Just stay calm and we'll talk more when you get here."

The next hour was the longest drive of my life. It was already a hot day, but my body was slick with nervous sweat, my hands clammy as I gripped the wheel. I didn't have cell coverage most of the way, so I wasn't sure if John had tried

382 · Chevy Stevens

to reach me again. I checked my rearview mirror constantly, wondering if he was following or if he was down in Nanaimo. What if he was watching Ally's school and realized she wasn't there?

Still running worst-case scenarios in my mind as I neared my house, I shot through a yellow light and the patrol car following me stopped at the red. He turned on his lights, but a large tractor-trailer was going through the intersection. As I pulled in my driveway, I noticed that the patrol car normally parked on the road was gone. He must've been relieved by the one following me. I jumped out of the SUV and sprinted to the front door.

I shoved my key into the lock and called out, "It's me—Sara. I'm home." No sounds of feet running. No Moose barking.

As I turned the key I realized the door wasn't locked. Sandy would never leave the door unlocked. I hesitated—could John be inside? Adrenaline rushed through my body. My *daughter* was in there.

I pushed open the door.

The house was quiet.

"Sandy? Ally? Hello?"

I raced upstairs and checked Ally's room. She wasn't there. One of her shoes was kicked off into the middle of the room. She was wearing them this morning.

I ran down the hall to my room. Empty. Were they in the backyard? I sprinted downstairs and opened the sliding glass door. As soon as I stepped out I saw Sandy hog-tied on the ground by my feet.

For a minute my mind couldn't compute the image, then it hit. I dropped to my knees beside her.

"*Sandy!*" I wanted to shake her and scream, *Where's Ally?* But her face was turned to the side and a rivulet of blood trickled from her nose. The back of her head was matted with blood. I spotted an envelope lying near her shoulder, my name scrawled on it in bold letters. There was a cell and a folded piece of paper inside. I unfolded the note. The writing was messy, but the words leaped out: *if you ever want to see Ally again don't tell anyone.* . . . Before I could read the rest something fell out of the envelope. I picked it up. It was a lock of Ally's hair, one soft, dark ringlet. The air left my throat in a long moan.

A man shouted from inside the house, "Everything okay? The door was wide open!"

The patrolman.

I opened my mouth to scream that Ally was missing. *Stop, think.* What if John killed her? If I told the police she was gone they'd never let me out of the house.

I heard myself yell, "Sandy's hurt!"

His feet were heavy. "*Officer down. Officer down!*" He came through the sliding glass door with a radio to his mouth. I shoved the cell and note into my pocket and stood up on shaky legs.

"She's breathing, but her head's bleeding, and—"

He pushed me out of the way, checked Sandy's pulse. I stared at his back. Should I tell him about the note?

If you ever want to see Ally again . . .

I backed away unsteadily. In the living room I stopped

and read the rest of the note. The words danced before my eyes.

Drive north. Come alone. I'll call with directions. If anyone follows she's dead.

Sirens wailed in the distance. Should I wait? A voice in my head screamed, *Leave, get Ally, there's no time!* I sprinted out the front, grabbed my keys out of the door, jumped into the Cherokee, and gunned the engine. I reversed down the driveway, narrowly missing the side of the parked patrol car. At the end of the driveway, I slammed the Cherokee into drive and stomped my foot down hard on the gas.

As I barreled down the road, my mind raced to come up with a plan, but all I could think about was Ally. I had to get to her—fast. Right now the cops' priority was Sandy, but any minute they were going to notice we were gone. I had to ditch the Cherokee. Could I make it to Lauren's? No, too far. A neighbor! Gerry, the old man a few houses down, had a truck he never used and a long driveway. I pulled in, parked in a small clearing blocked from the house by trees, then ran up to his door.

He didn't answer my frantic knock. I hammered at his door again. I was about to leave when the door opened. Gerry's white hair was sticking straight up and he was wearing a robe.

"Sara, you have blood all over you!"

"Gerry—I need your truck. I was walking and Moose got hit by a car. I don't have time to run back to my house."

"How awful. Of course." He shuffled toward the kitchen with me hot on his heels, then rummaged through a basket on the counter as I fought the urge to throw him out of the way.

When he held the keys aloft I practically snatched them out of his hand, then shouted, "Thanks!" over my shoulder as I raced out the door to his old red Chevy.

John didn't say which highway to take out of Nanaimo, so I got on the parkway bypassing the city and headed north. Because the highway is inland there's just forest on either side of the road and long stretches between each exit. The cell coverage also gets spotty and I worried about missing John's call. The cell I'd found near Sandy was lying in my lap and I touched it several times.

Come on, you asshole. Tell me where my daughter is.

My head spun with terrifying images of where Ally could be and what John could be doing to her. Should I call the police? Was I costing them precious time? One minute it seemed like the right thing to do, the next minute I panicked, thinking about John finding out and killing Ally.

Thirty minutes down the highway, my body was still vibrating with adrenaline and my thoughts were all over the place. I was looking at the road but not seeing anything. I ran a red light. Tires screeched as cars swerved to avoid me. Another jolt of fear ricocheted through my body. I realized I was crying when a drop landed on my arm. Billy's voice cut through the noise in my head: *whenever you feel yourself panicking, just breathe, regroup, and focus on your strategy.*

I sucked in a deep breath through my nose and forced it

out my mouth, repeating the process until I was finally able to grab on to a thought. What was the next step? John was going to call. Then what? He was going to tell me where to meet him. What was I going to do then? All I had to do was play along, tell him whatever he wanted to hear, and wait for a chance to—

The cell phone rang.

I scrabbled for the phone and yelled, "*Where is she?*"

"Are you driving?"

"Is Ally okay?"

"Did anyone follow you?"

"If you've hurt her, I'll—"

"I wouldn't hurt her."

"You hurt that police officer—"

"She was going to shoot me. And you lied again—Ally wasn't at school."

"Because I was worried you would do something crazy, and I was *right*. You can't just take my child and threaten to—" My voice broke.

"It was the only way you'd come. I know you've been talking to the police. I'll explain everything later."

"Please don't hurt Ally. I'll do whatever you want, just don't hurt her. I'm *begging* you."

"I'm not going to hurt her—she's my granddaughter. I'm not a monster. But if you tell the cops or lead them to me, you'll never see us again."

He *was* a monster. One of the worst this world had ever seen.

"I won't—"

"Shut up and listen."

I bit my tongue. He had Ally.

"Turn left at Horne Lake Road, then park by the old concrete divider at the first clearing. In the culvert there's a box with a blindfold. Put it on and lie down in the front seat of your Jeep."

He knew I had a Jeep Cherokee. He *must* have been following me.

"I took a neighbor's truck."

"You've got your old man's smarts." He laughed, then said, "See you soon." I was just about to hang up when he said, "Knock, knock."

I clenched my jaw.

"Who's there?"

"*Sara* reason you're not laughing?"

My voice cracked as I said, "I'm too scared about Ally."

"She's safe—I tied her up so she can't go anywhere."

"What do you mean she's—"

"It'll be fine. You two will have fun with me, you'll see." He hung up.

I screamed at my windshield.

The cell was hot in my hands. My breath coming in quick, short gasps. This was bad, this was really bad. I had to call the police. They were professionals; they'd know what to do. But what if John had a police scanner? He'd disappear with Ally and we'd never get her back. I thought of the lock of hair in my pocket, the uneven edge like he'd hacked it with a knife, and a fresh wave of terror rushed through my body. I put the phone down.

Twenty minutes later I finally spotted the turnoff for Horne Lake, and as soon as I parked in the gravel clearing I located the culvert. Sure enough, there was a box in it. As I walked back to the truck I checked the cell, but there was no coverage. I was on my own.

My heart going nuts and my mouth dry, I wrapped the blindfold around my head and lay down on the front seat. The sun was beating through the windshield and I hadn't had any water for hours. Sweat trickled down the side of my face. About ten minutes later I heard a vehicle coming down the road. My body tensed. When the vehicle pulled off the road into the clearing and alongside my truck, I started to shake.

A door opened, slammed, then heavy footsteps. My truck door creaked open and a hand patted my shin. I jerked back, knocking my head on the doorframe.

"Bet that hurt." John sounded concerned. "You okay?"

"Can I take the blindfold off?"

"Not yet. Shimmy to the end of the bench seat and I'll guide you out."

When a large hand wrapped around my leg it was all I could do not to kick him. As I wriggled out, my knees bumped into something and I braced for a blow, but nothing happened. I was standing now and sensed his presence in front of me. I wondered where Ally was and tilted my chin up to peer under the fold of fabric I'd tied loosely around my eyes but couldn't make anything out. His hand lightly gripping my elbow, he led me a couple of steps forward, then paused. His hand left my arm and I jumped as he slammed Gerry's truck door behind me.

"Where's Ally?" I said.

"Back at camp."

"You left her *alone*? She's six. You can't just—"

"She doesn't believe I'm her grandfather—you have to tell her. She won't stop screaming." He sounded frustrated. My heart broke, thinking how scared she must be.

"She'll be okay once she sees me." I prayed it was true.

He led me a couple more paces, then a door opened.

"Watch your step," he said as he lifted one of my legs and placed it inside a vehicle. I flinched at the sensation of warm rough hands on my calf, but he didn't linger. The door slammed beside me. My throat tightened in panic. What if this was just a ruse to get me alone? What if Ally was really still back in the house, maybe tied up in the garage with Moose? My mind couldn't go to the other, far worse possibility. Instead I focused on what the books said about dealing with a serial killer—there's *no* dealing with them. Negotiation, pleading, or resisting generally doesn't end well. Escape is your best option. I had to keep him calm until I found Ally, then look for a chance to escape.

He started the truck and it clunked as he shifted into gear. A standard. I had no idea if the information was useful, but it made me feel better to know *something*.

"So here we are, finally together."

"I don't understand why you came to the house early. I thought we were going to meet later at the park and—"

"You weren't going to meet me, Sara."

I was silent, trying to think of a response that wouldn't sound like a lie.

Finally I said, "You didn't give me a chance to think—"

"I told you, there wasn't any time. I'm not crazy—I know what I'm doing." He sighed. "I'll explain later." Then he said, "I brought some of my guns to show you—my Browning .338 and my Ruger 10/22. I really wanted to show you my Remington .223—that's a *great* gun, but the firing pin broke on me last week and it's still at the shop." He paused. Even though I couldn't see his face, I sensed he was waiting for a response.

"Sounds great." But it would be better if I could convince him to let me hold one. My mind filled with images of shooting him and fleeing with Ally. He changed subjects, explaining how different the lush coastal forest is on the island compared to the drier scrubby terrain of the Interior. I wasn't sure if he was just excited to have an audience or nervous, but he barely stopped for breath.

When it felt like we'd been bouncing over potholes for a while, I said, "Sorry to interrupt, but is Ally okay where you left her? It's hot, does she have water and—"

"I know how to take care of a child." He was annoyed again. "She's just scared because she doesn't know me. But when she sees you she'll be fine." I was glad that he seemed to want to keep us happy. But what was going to happen if I couldn't calm Ally down? She had to be terrified.

"John, there was a female police officer at the house. Did Ally see you hurt her?"

"No." Thank God for small mercies. "I didn't want to hit that woman so many times, but she wouldn't go down."

My body started to shake.

The truck slowed for a few curves, then bumped and swayed over rough ground like we were on an old logging road. After another few minutes it came to a stop. John got out and slammed his door.

A moment later my door opened. "You can get out now."

As soon as I stepped out of the truck, he lifted my blindfold off and I was standing in front of my father. In my nightmares his face was always angry and twisted, so I was shocked to see that he was handsome in a rugged kind of way. I couldn't stop staring. It was all there—my green eyes, my bone structure, even my left eyebrow that arches higher than the right. His hair was cut short, but it was pretty much my shade of auburn. He was a lot taller and broader than I was, but we both had long limbs. Dressed in a workman's jean jacket, plaid shirt, baggy faded jeans, and hiking boots, he looked like a lumberjack. Or a hunter.

When he hitched up his pants, his eyes slid away from mine and he smiled awkwardly.

"So . . . here I am."

I said, "You look like me."

"No, you look like me." He laughed and I forced myself to laugh back, but my eyes were searching the camp. *Where is Ally?* We were in a small clearing surrounded by fir trees. On my right a camper trailer was parked a few feet from his truck—a red Tacoma. A plastic fold-out table was set up near a fire pit, which was surrounded by a couple of canvas chairs and a smaller pink plastic chair with a Barbie head stenciled on the back. John turned in the direction of my gaze.

"Do you think she'll like it?"

I glanced back at him. His eyes were anxious.

"She'll love it."

He looked relieved.

"Where is she?"

He smacked his head, like he couldn't believe he forgot, then motioned me to follow him to the camper. He took his key and opened up the back.

As soon as the door swung out I said, "Mommy's here, Ally." I peered around his broad back but couldn't see anything in the dim camper. I heard a small noise.

"Sweetie, you can come out now."

A scrambling sound, then movement under the table. I could just glimpse the top of Ally's head as she crawled out, but when she saw John she scooted back under the table.

He looked wounded. "Tell her not to be scared—I'm not going to hurt her." If only I could believe it.

I stepped into the camper. "Ally?"

When I peered under the table her big green eyes gazed up at me. Her mouth had a bandanna tied over it and so did her wrists. She threw herself into my arms with muffled whimpers.

"Oh, my God! You *gagged* her." My fingers fought with the knot at the back of her head.

"I made sure she could breathe—I told you, she wouldn't stop screaming."

I had the bandanna off, but Ally was almost hyperventilating. I forced myself to keep my voice calm.

"Ally, take deep breaths. It's okay, I'm going to undo your hands, everything's fine. Just do what Mommy says, okay?"

She was still gasping while I wrestled with the knot on her wrists. I had to calm her down. Then I remembered a game I used to play with her when she was younger and her attention span was even worse.

"Remember wiz-a-boo, sweetie?" Ally's body stilled.

John said, "What's that? What are you telling her?"

"It's just a word that means we can trust someone because they're a friend." It actually meant to pay very careful attention to Mommy because the fairies were listening. If she was a good girl, they left little presents for her around the house—glass flowers, tiny bells, little crystal shoes. She soon caught on that it was me leaving the trinkets, but I hoped she understood what I was trying to tell her now—she *had* to listen to me.

She lifted her head and looked into my face with tear-filled eyes.

"The man cut my hair and he tied my hands and put me in here and—"

John said, "I didn't want you to hurt yourself." I glanced out. He was pacing at the back of the camper. "Tell her! Tell her who I am."

I took a deep breath. "Remember when Mommy told you she was adopted? Well, this is your grandfather."

She stared at me and her voice quivered as she said, "He is *not*!"

"Yes, he is, Ally, he's my real father. Mommy has two dads, like you. But I didn't know about him until recently. He wants to get to know you, but he just did it the wrong way and he's sorry he scared you."

John said, "It's true, Ally. I'm sorry."

Ally was sobbing. "He hurt my hands." She buried her face in the crook of my neck. Her body shook against mine. I wanted to kill John.

"He didn't mean to, honey. Did you, John?"

"No, no, of course not! I tried not to tie them tight, but she was squirming."

"See? He's really sorry. He has a new chair outside just for you. Let's go see it, okay?"

John said, "It's a Barbie chair, but I didn't know which one you like—I bought the blond one. I didn't know you had dark hair."

He sounded concerned, so I said, "The blond one is Ally's favorite." Ally's head popped up and her mouth started to open. I quickly gave her a smile and a wink. *Please, please, please.*

Ally paused for just a moment. "She's the prettiest."

I gave her a big smile. "Yes, she is."

I glanced at the door to see if John was buying it. He clutched at his heart.

"*Phew.* I spent hours trying to get the right one." He motioned with his hand. "Come out so we can sit by the fire and talk."

I stood up and took Ally's hand. I glanced around the camper for any possible weapons, but there were only plastic shakers on the table. Ally let me lead her to the door. I jumped out first and spun around to lift her out, but when I tried to set her down she clung to my neck. I carried her over to the fire, where John was fussing with the chairs. He moved one closer, then put it back, then moved it closer again. I stood and waited with Ally's face buried in my neck.

Finally I said, "That's good."

He stepped back. "All right, then. But let me know if you get too hot—we can move them wherever you want."

As I sat down—Ally still wrapped around me—John threw a couple of logs on the fire. Then he sat in his chair, but his body was tense. He scratched the side of his head and gave me that awkward smile again as his eyes slid past mine.

"You want some lunch? Kids are always hungry." He stood. "I've got some moose sausages in the cooler."

Ally's voice was panicky. "I don't want to eat Moose."

"He doesn't mean our Moose, Ally."

John laughed. "I got a big yearling this spring and had most of it made into sausages and hamburger." He walked toward the camper. "Meat melts in your mouth—doesn't taste gamey at all." As Ally made a face, I shook my head and brought my finger to my lips.

"Sounds delicious," I said to John's back.

John reached for a blue cooler under the camper. While he was busy I looked around, but there was nothing I could grab. I eyed a couple of blocks of wood and wondered if I could knock him out with one, but they were big and I wouldn't be able to lift one quickly, which meant I'd lose the element of surprise. Maybe later when he was sleeping? The thought of spending the night with him sent a new wave of terror through my body.

John set a package of sausages on the table and a carton of eggs, then stepped back into the trailer. My blood surged with adrenaline as he banged around, and my muscles tensed—every cell in my body saying, *Run!* But I stopped myself. Even though I hadn't seen his guns yet, I knew he had them. And carrying a six-year-old, I needed a big head start—Ally wasn't fast enough running on her own. Biding my time and trying to talk my way out of this was still my best chance of escape.

John emerged from the trailer with a handful of condiments, set them on the table, then went back in and came out with some plastic glasses and plates.

"Aren't you going to try your chair, Ally?" He was setting the table.

She turned and glared at him. "No."

He frowned and set the last plate down, then rested his big hands on the table. Anxiety hummed in my chest and I held Ally tighter.

John said, "I thought you said you liked it."

Ally's mouth opened, and I quickly said, "She does—she's just scared of wrecking it. But you won't be mad at her if she does, right, John?"

John laughed. "For breaking a chair? Of course not!"

Ally stared at me. I smiled and said, "See, it's okay. You

can sit in it." With my chin tilted down so her head blocked my lips from John's view, I mouthed, *Go, now.*

She eased off my lap and with one eye on John pulled the chair close to me and clutched my hand. I tried to give her a reassuring smile, but she was watching John. I noticed tear tracks on her face and felt sick. She must be so confused. Here was a man who hurt her, and now I was telling her to do what he said.

John had everything out on the tables—salt, pepper, butter, syrup, bread. He moved the plates around a couple of times, lining up everything just right, then looked at me.

"I got the plates yesterday, but I didn't know what color . . ."

"The green's pretty. Thanks."

"Yeah?" His face lit up.

I nodded and prayed he'd be stupid enough to give me a knife, but he didn't lay any cutlery on the table. Instead he set a metal rack in the middle of the fire, then got a cast-iron frying pan from the camper and put it on the rack. "I can't wait to show you the ranch I bought for us to live on," he said as he arranged sausage links in the pan.

Ally said, "I don't want to live at a ranch."

I shot her a warning look. John used a plastic spatula to move the sausages around, then set a smaller frying pan down beside it and cracked some eggs into it.

"Hope scrambled is okay?" The awkward smile again. He looked at Ally. "I have chickens at the ranch, so we'll have fresh eggs every day. I'll show you how to collect them. Place came with a couple of cows, so we can have milk, and I'll teach you how to make cheese."

Ally said, "What about horses?" I held my breath.

John said, "We can get some horses. Sure." He nodded. "You can even have one of your own. Maybe a pony."

I let out my breath and said, "That's really nice of you. Isn't that nice, Ally?"

Ally said, "Can I name it?" *Come on, Ally, don't piss him off.*

John said, "Sure, whatever you want." The sausage was now sizzling and he moved a few links around.

Ally said, "Can I bring my dog?"

John shook his head. "We can't go back and get him." My body stiffened. Here we go. Ally's face flushed.

"I don't want to go to your *stupid* ranch."

My pulse sped up. John pointed the spatula at Ally.

"Now, listen here, young lady—"

Ally stood up. *"I don't want to go."*

John's face flushed as he leaned forward in his seat. His hand rose.

I stood up and kicked the underside of the metal rack as hard as I could. It flipped up into the air, sending the large frying pan flying toward John, hitting him square in the forehead with a loud *thunk* and splattering hot grease across his face. He screamed and clutched his face and started rolling on the ground. I lifted Ally into my arms and ran like hell.

SESSION TWENTY-TWO

I'm not ready to talk about what happened, but I have to. I need to find some way to deal with this or the memories are going to eat me alive. Every time I close my eyes they all come rushing back in, drowning me in panicky thoughts. I wake up in the middle of the night, my heart pounding, my body slick with sweat, my mind racing. And one thought repeating over and over: *if you stop running you will die.*

Terror propelled me into the forest and toward the sound of a river. A second later I realized I should've headed to the road where there was a chance for help, but it was too late now. As I raced through the woods, trees and branches tore at my arms. John yelled my name back at the camp. Ally screamed.

"Ally, stop—you have to be quiet!" I pumped my legs hard, leaped over logs. My arms ached from Ally's weight. John yelled my name again. I ran faster.

Go, go, go!

I raced along the bank above the river, hoping the roar of the water would muffle any sounds. My foot caught on an exposed root and I slid all the way down to the river's edge. The cell fell out of my pocket into the water and I narrowly missed landing on Ally. She screamed and I covered her mouth with my hand. "Shhhh!" Her face was white and panic-stricken. I knelt down.

"Climb on my back and wrap your legs around my waist."

Once she was up and had a good grip around my neck, I took off again. I was following the edge of the river, forcing my way through dense foliage, crawling over downed trees, slipping on moss-covered rocks, and ducking branches when I heard John yelling through the woods.

"Sara! Come back!"

My body flooded with fresh adrenaline and I ran as fast as I could, slipping and sliding on the rocks. I lost my balance as Ally shifted her weight, and fell hard on my left knee. I flung out my elbow to keep her from falling and scraped the palm of my hand bloody on a rock.

Get up! Run!

The sound of rushing water grew louder as we neared the top of some falls. Ahead of me the shore ended in a wall of dense brush and logs cast off from the winter's floods. I was trapped. My eyes searched the bank frantically. How was I going to get around this?

I glanced at the opposite side of the river, but the water was moving too fast. I looked up the bank to my left and spotted a narrow opening under the lower branches of a fir tree. I clambered up, Ally's weight working against every step. Finally I squirmed through, then followed a trail a few yards until it doubled back and came out above the edge of the falls. It looked like animals had forged a path down the side of the falls, but it was steep and rough.

As I gazed down, a wave of vertigo washed over me. I grabbed on to a branch and closed my eyes. I couldn't get down there carrying Ally. What was I going to do? There was no way I was going to be able to outrun John. I heard Julia's voice in my head. *I hid in the woods for hours. . . .*

We could hide. But then what? Eventually I'd have to come out with Ally and he'd still be in the woods—waiting. This was never going to end. A startled grouse ran out of the brush in front of us, dragging her wings and pretending to be wounded so we didn't notice her young. That's what I needed—a decoy, something that would distract him. I looked into the forest, looked down at the river. The river—

John told me he can't swim.

I turned to my left and headed into the woods. Thankfully I only had to go a few yards before I spotted a small cave cut into a rock face. I set Ally down beside it and dropped to my knees in front of her.

"Ally, I need you to really listen to me now. I want you to stay in this cave, and you can't say anything—not a peep—until I come get you."

"Nooooooo!" She started to cry. "Don't leave me, Mommy. Please. I'll be really, really quiet."

Tears came to my own eyes, but I grabbed her hands and squeezed them.

"I don't want to leave you, sweetie, but I'm going to get us out of here. I *promise*."

John's voice called out through the woods. "Saaa-rrrrraaa . . ."

He was close.

"I need you to be superbrave now, Ally Cat. I'm going to be making lots of noises and yelling your name over and over, but it's only to fool him. It will all be pretend. So you can't come out, okay?"

She nodded, her eyes huge. I kissed her cheek hard.

"Now go—quick like a bunny." As she turned to burrow into the hole, I said, "Remember, Ally. You're helping me fool him, so no matter what, don't come out." My mind filled with the horrifying image of her skeleton found years from now and I prayed I was doing the right thing. I grabbed her hand and kissed her little fingers one last time.

When she was squeezed in as far as possible, I whispered, "I'll be back soon. See you later *Ally*-gator."

She whispered back, "In a while, crocodile."

I took a breath and left my child behind.

I headed straight back down the trail and toward the river. Just before I broke out of the forest and onto the top of the path that would take me down the side of the falls, I paused to listen for John but couldn't hear anything over the roar of the water. I knew I wouldn't have much time, so I slid down the steep path on my hands and knees, grasping at ferns and branches to stop myself from tumbling over the edge. Then I was at the bottom, where the falls dropped into a jade-green pool of icy mountain water.

I pulled off my running shoes and stared down into the river.

"Sara!" John bellowed from somewhere in the forest above.

I took a deep breath and dove straight in. The frigid water sucked the air out of my chest and I came to the surface coughing and spluttering. After I sucked in a lungful of air, I dove in again, and when I popped back up to the surface, I yelled, "Ally!" as loud as I could—terrified she'd forget my warning and come running. I dove several more times. Between dives I scanned the shore for John.

Finally I spotted him picking his way down the side trail. I frantically slapped at the water, spinning my body around, then dove under again, coming to the surface screaming.

"Ally! Someone *help me*!"

I dove in again and when I popped up, John was standing on the shore holding a rifle by his side. Angry red marks from the hot grease striped his face, and his forehead was crimson and blotchy.

"John, Ally fell in and went over the falls!" I poured every ounce of my fear and terror into my voice. "She's going to *drown*!"

He ran forward and stood on the very edge of the smooth rock jutting out into the water.

"Where did she go under?"

As I treaded water, I shook my head and choked out, "I don't know. I can't find her." My teeth chattered as I said, "Help. I'm sorry, John. Help me!"

He hesitated for a moment, then said, "We should look downstream. The current may have carried her farther."

I reached for the large flat rock he was standing on like I was going to crawl up, then let my hands slip off the wet surface and splashed back into the water. He leaned over the water and reached out. I swam closer.

I only had one chance at this.

I braced both feet on a large boulder below. As I gripped one of his hands, I let my fingers slide out so that he leaned forward farther to catch me. When his entire upper body was leaning over the water, I grabbed his hand and pulled with all my strength while twisting my body to the side.

John crashed into the water behind me. He came to the surface spluttering and slapping at the water with his hands.

"Sara, I can't swim!"

I quickly paddled to the shore and tried to lift myself up onto the rock, but he grabbed the back of my leg and pulled me into the river with him. My throat filled with water.

I twisted out of his grasp and kicked back up to the surface, gasping for air. He had hold of my shirt and came up with me. I clawed at his face and rammed my knee into his groin under the water. His grip loosened and I propelled myself backward.

Our struggle had pushed us downstream and closer to the shore, where the water was shallower. John would be able to reach the bottom soon. As my feet found loose rocks under them, I started to rise. John was behind me again, but in his panic he didn't realize the water was only a few feet deep. He grabbed at my waist and pulled me down. As I came up for air, I kicked back with my feet and my heel connected with his chin.

My hands grasped at rocks under the water and I used them to pull myself away. This time he'd also found purchase on the rocks and he was beginning to rise behind me.

My hands found a large jagged rock. I twisted my body around as he reached for me.

"Sara, I was only trying to—"

I rose up and hit him in the temple as hard as I could. His fingers reached to touch the bloody gash that opened up on the side of his head. He fell to his knees. "Sara . . ." His voice was agonized. Blood poured from the wound.

I scrambled to my feet. With both hands holding the rock, I swung hard and fast, smashing it into his temple with a loud *crack*. The rock slipped out of my hand and splashed a few feet down the river.

He fell forward into the water, then pushed himself up on his hands and knees, swaying. He shook his head and reached for me as I scrambled backward. His torso landed on my legs. I squirmed to the side and got to my feet. He rose unsteadily. I kicked him in the side of the knee. He stumbled and lost his balance, falling onto his back. I leaped on him and drove all my weight down onto his chest. His head went under the water and he thrashed around, clawing at my legs. I left one knee on his chest and pressed my other down hard on his throat. He bucked again, almost dislodging me. My hands grasped at another rock in the water. I hit him in the head. He struggled harder, hands clawing at my legs. I hit him again, and again, and again. I realized I was screaming. The water around his head turned red.

He was still.

My heart pounded as I gulped at the air. I stayed kneeling far longer than he could hold his breath underwater. Finally I lifted my knee off and stood up, stumbling backward on suddenly weak legs. His body floated up slightly. His face was a shocked mask, his mouth open, red hair mixed with blood. A gash on the side of his head exposed white bone.

I scrambled over the slippery rocks to the shore, then hunched over, gagging up water and fear into the sand.

I had killed him. I had killed my father. I stared at his still body, watching it drift with the current while mine shook violently.

I staggered back up the trail. Exhausted, I slipped several times, grasping at roots and ferns to pull my bruised body back up. When I was at the top, I got disorientated and couldn't find the trail into the woods where I'd left Ally. I spent a heart-stopping few minutes retracing my steps until I recognized an old twisted cedar tree and found the cave.

"Ally, it's me, it's safe to come out now." When she didn't answer I panicked, but then I heard movement and she threw herself into my arms, almost knocking me over. We clung to each other, crying.

Finally she pulled away. "I heard you yelling, but I stayed hid like you told me."

"You did great, Ally. I'm really proud of you."

She wrinkled her nose. "You're all wet."

"I fell in the water."

She looked around, her eyes huge, then whispered, "Where's the bad man?"

"He's gone, Ally, and he's never coming back."

She hugged me tight. "I want to go home, Mommy."

"Me too."

Back at the camp the fire still smoldered and a shiver snaked down my back at the sight of the frying pans on the ground and John's chair lying on its side. I'd lost the cell in the river and was hoping he'd left his in the camper or truck. But a quick look around didn't turn up a phone or his keys.

Now that some of the adrenaline was wearing off, I couldn't stop shaking. I pulled on a jacket John had hung up in the camper, gagging at his scent mixed with wood smoke, and searched for the truck keys. When I hadn't found them after ten minutes I started to panic. Ally, terrified from her ordeal, was following close behind as I ransacked the camper and truck.

John's keys must be on his body or in the river. I debated my options—go back down to the river and see if they were still on him or head to the road with Ally and find help. I'd driven for a long time with John and never heard another vehicle. Ally would get tired fast, and I didn't know how long I could carry her.

I was still trying to figure out what to do when Ally said, "I'm *hungry*."

As I searched through John's provisions, a chill came over me every time I noticed some little detail about his life. He liked whole milk and white bread. He had junk food stored everywhere. He liked Orange Crush and Coffee Crisps. It was the last one that shook me up the most. They were my favorite. Finally I found some peanut butter and made Ally a sandwich.

Then I said, "Ally Cat, you're going to have to wait here for me for a little bit while I go down to the river, okay?"

"No!" She started to cry.

"Ally, it's *really* important. I won't be long and you can hide in the camper if you—"

She started to scream, *"No, no, no, no!"* and dropped the sandwich as she threw herself at my knees. There was no way I could leave her, but I couldn't let her see John's body either.

We'd walked for over an hour when I finally heard a vehicle coming down the road. As I turned and spotted the white forestry truck, I waved my arms. The truck came to a stop beside us and a smiling old man rolled down the window.

"You ladies lost?"

I started to cry.

After the cops pulled John's body out of the water and investigated the scene, they found his wallet under the seat of his truck. His name was Edward John McLean, and once

they ran some checks on him they found out he was a blacksmith who traveled through the Interior. The blacksmith
thing fits with the metal dolls, and Billy said the noises I'd
heard in the background on some of the calls were probably
horses. Since then they've found his trailer with all his
tools parked at a motel near Nanaimo.

Sandy's okay. She had a concussion and spent a couple of
days at the hospital for observation—Evan and she were
there at the same time. Right after I gave my statement
the day I killed John, I made the cops take me straight to
Evan. When the police told him Ally and I were missing,
he wanted to hold off on his surgery, but the doctors said
it was too risky to wait, so he had to go through with it. He
was just waking up when Ally and I got to the hospital, and
he cried at the sight of us.

Ally and I brought Sandy flowers. When Ally handed
them to her and said, "Thanks for trying to save me,"
Sandy looked like she was fighting hard not to cry. I thought
she'd quiz me about everything that had happened with
John, but she didn't say anything, even when Ally told her
about hiding in the cave. I'd gotten so used to Sandy always
being fired up about something it was weird seeing her
pale and looking depressed. She was probably unhappy she
didn't get to kill John herself.

Billy had already filled me in on how John was able to
abduct Ally in the first place. He'd started a fire down the
road in someone's woodshed so the officer parked outside
our house had to investigate. Then he hid his truck in our
next-door neighbor's driveway and doubled back through

our yards. He was in our backyard, probably planning to break in, when Sandy turned the alarm off and opened the sliding glass door to let Moose out for a pee. John jumped her and she was down, though not without drawing her gun. He'd left the back gate open and Moose fled the scene—a neighbor found him later that day.

Ally was in her bedroom when the "bad man" came in and told her Sandy wanted him to take her to her mommy up at the hospital. Ally didn't believe him at first, but he said Moose was already in the truck. That did it.

The cops weren't impressed with me for taking off after Sandy was hurt, but there's not much they can do about it now. I had to give a statement about killing John, though, and the Crown has to investigate, but Billy said there's no way it won't be ruled self-defense.

Evan also gave me hell for going after Ally myself and not waiting for the cops, but he let it go—I think he was pretty shook up by how close we all came to losing one another. He's not the only one.

Guess I'm even more like my father than we thought. I know it was self-defense, but I still *killed* a man. And not just any man, my own father. I wonder how God will feel about that one. I'm still not sure how I feel about it myself. I think what scares me the most is not that I did it, but that I didn't even hesitate.

SESSION TWENTY-THREE

I'm so frustrated right now. What pisses me off the most is that after our last session I was actually starting to feel good again. I was just so glad everything was over that life took on this euphoric cast. The media frenzy died down. Evan and I never fought, my child could do no wrong, I loved my family and every one of them loved me back. Food even tasted better. But the more normal things turn, the more things, well, turn back to normal.

This morning Melanie came over to pick up the song list Evan and I made for the wedding. I'd spent the weekend ripping apart the house trying to find the CD she gave me, to no avail, so we decided it was just easier to let Kyle do it than have a family war. Right now I'm all about easier. But then last night Evan found the CD—I'd managed to put it back in the wrong case after still not playing it. We listened to it and turns out they aren't half bad, but the real stand-out was this woman singing in the background. Her voice was amazing, sort of Sarah McLachlan meets Stevie Nicks.

When Melanie arrived I was in the backyard trying to water my pathetic attempt at a garden. We went inside and I gave her the list.

"On the CD there's a woman in the background," I said while her eyes scanned the page. "Do you know how to contact her?"

Her head jerked up. "Why?"

"I was hoping she'd sing at the wedding too."

Melanie's face flushed and she stared down at the CD.

I said, "Was that *you*?"

She looked up and her eyes flashed. "You don't have to sound so surprised."

"Well, I am. You've never sung before—that I know of."

She shrugged. "I sing at the pub sometimes."

"You should totally pursue singing, Melanie. You could really be something."

"Instead of *just* a bartender?"

"That's not what I meant." I remember the vow I made since my near-death: to be more patient and forgiving. "But I'm sorry if it came across like that. I just think you sound incredible. I'd love it if you sang at the wedding. Please?"

She looked at me, then shrugged.

"If you want. But not all the songs, because I still want to dance."

"Thanks, that would be great." We were quiet for a minute and I said, "So you want to stay for a coffee?"

She looked startled. "Sure."

We took our mugs into the living room and sat on opposite couches, glancing at each other, taking a sip, then looking away. The silence built. Something had been bothering me recently that I wanted to ask her about, but I didn't want to start a fight. Evan told me to let it go. I agreed with him at the time, but she was here now and we seemed to be getting along. I lasted another two seconds.

"Did you see the photos in the paper of my birth father?" She nodded. "You ever see him in the bar?"

She shook her head. "Why?"

"He just knew some stuff about Ally, and I was wondering—"

"*Unfuckingbelievable.* You *still* think I'm the one who told that Web site, and now you think I told a serial killer about *Ally.*" She set her coffee down with a crash and stood up.

"No! I just thought you might not have known who he was and—"

"You think I'm stupid enough to tell a stranger about my niece?"

"It has nothing to do with being *stupid.* He seemed like a nice guy and he might have been able to get stuff out of you without you even—"

"Believe it or not, Sara, when I'm working, I'm working—not chatting with freaks at the bar. But thanks for blaming me once again."

"I'm not blaming you, Melanie. I'm just trying to tie up a loose end."

She laughed as she picked up her coffee and walked to the kitchen.

I stood up and followed her. "Where are you going?"

"Somewhere people don't accuse me of getting their kid abducted." She set the mug on the counter with a thud.

"Melanie, you're totally blowing this out of proportion. I didn't—"

"You're one to talk—you're the freak-out *queen*." She picked up her purse from the counter and walked out, slamming the door behind her.

I was still fuming when Billy called a half hour later. I thought once John was dead that would be that, but they're still working backward to learn more about him—Billy said it helps them with other serial killers. They've found out quite a bit, but not what I'd expected, which was a basement full of corpses and stacks of porn tapes. His house was tidy, in a bachelor kind of way, and the only tapes he had were videos on hunting. But it doesn't look like he spent much time there. He didn't have anything personal around, no photos or keepsakes, and he slept in a sleeping bag on top of his mattress.

They tried to match some missing-women cases up to where John may have been during certain years—he lived a nomadic life—but nothing connected. People who'd hired him said he was pleasant enough and always had a joke at the ready. But he got in fights with a few customers over the years who he felt had "tricked" him out of his payments.

We were right about one thing: he was known in most of the towns he'd called me from. He was also an avid gun collector and a member of a few gun clubs.

I said, "Did you find the one he used to shoot Evan?"

"The ballistic report said the shell casing recovered at the scene was from a Remington .223. It matched up with some found at other crime scenes, so we know he was shot from the same gun, but it wasn't with John's belongings. We're checking with a few gun dealers, but I doubt we'll ever find it. By the way, did you ever finish that cherry table you were working on? I saw one just like it at an antique store the other day that needs refinishing. Think you could look at it sometime and tell me what you think?"

"Sure, how much did they want?"

The rest of the call we talked about antiques, then Evan beeped in to ask me something, so I had to go. But later, when I was trying to clean up the shop, I remembered John telling me the Remington .223 was his favorite—and that it was being repaired. How did he shoot Evan with a gun he didn't have?

The front door banged. Evan was home. While he packed his hockey bag with clothes to take to the lodge, I sat on the bed and told him about my morning, starting with the fight with Melanie.

"I can't believe she acted like that when I asked her about John."

"I told you to let it go." He rummaged through his drawers,

tossing socks into his bag with his good hand—his left arm was still in a sling.

"I just asked her a simple question."

He glanced over his shoulder with his eyebrows raised.

"Sara, your questions are never simple."

"I wish you weren't going back to the lodge."

"Me too. I have to get a ride up with Jason and he drives like an old man." He laughed, but I glowered. "Baby, come on, I haven't been up there in weeks and everything's a mess. You said you wanted to get back to work too."

"I tried after Melanie left, but then Billy called and I started obsessing again."

"About what?"

"Billy said the shell casing they found at your lodge was from John's Remington .223, but they can't find the gun. Then I was thinking about it later and John said that gun was getting repaired. Don't you think that's weird?"

"He probably had a couple of them and ditched one right after he shot me."

"Maybe . . . but I got the feeling he really loved *that* gun. Why would anybody have two?"

"Well, no one else would've shot me."

I paused for a moment. "You know, it's weird that John only injured you. I got the impression he was a good shot—he never missed a victim before."

"Baby, it was him." Evan went into the walk-in closet, came out with a few pairs of jeans, shoved them in his bag.

"I know. Just saying the gun thing's weird. . . . We still don't know for sure he attacked Nadine—she wasn't shot, which was totally John's style, just hit in the back of the head. And she never saw who did it. I wonder if they ever followed up on any of her patients. Maybe I should talk to Billy and see what he thinks."

"Sara, leave the guy alone."

"What does *that* mean?"

"You must be driving the police nuts. The case is over but you're still pestering them." He went back into the closet and came out with another pair of jeans. "Where's my Nike baseball cap—you were wearing it yesterday?"

"I don't know, but I can't believe you just said that. I'm not pestering them, I'm *helping* them. I have to tell Billy about the gun. They could match it up with an old case or something. What if John killed a woman they didn't know about and her family's been searching for her for years and—"

"Sara, you're driving *me* nuts. I just packed six pairs of jeans and no shirts."

"Fine. I'll get out of your way, then." I stood up.

"You don't have to leave, just talk about something else." But I was already walking out of the room.

I was staring at a table in my shop, thinking about everything Evan had said and working myself into a complete lather, when he came to find me.

He said, "I'm going."

I studied the grains in the wood, traced them with my fingers.

"Come on," he said.

He came over and wrapped his arms around me.

I was stiff in his arms. "I'm pissed at you."

"I know, but give me a hug anyway."

"I hate that you don't take anything I say seriously."

"That's not true, Sara. I just wish you didn't read so much into everything."

"So you think I'm just overreacting?"

"Let's see, you accused your sister of chatting up a serial killer and now you think someone else shot me for no reason? Hey, maybe it was *Melanie* who shot me."

Tears of frustration stung my eyes. "I'm just saying we don't know—"

"Baby, Jason's waiting outside. I'll call you tonight, okay?"

"Fine, go."

He left a couple of hours ago, and I was so riled up I spent the entire time until our appointment going over the case in my mind again. I even went back over all my notes, the time line, everything. This gun thing is making me insane.

So maybe I'm just grasping at straws, mostly because Evan didn't take me seriously, and maybe the gun thing isn't important, but I called Billy and told him something was bugging me about the case. He was in the middle of a meeting but said he'd stop by later. Why can't Evan be like that? Billy never makes me feel like I'm some drama addict.

SESSION TWENTY-FOUR

Now you're going to make me cry. I understand you need some time off before you decide whether to move your practice to Victoria—you've been through a lot yourself in the last while. God, I don't know how you kept seeing clients during everything. And thanks for the referral to your friend. I'll probably give him a try, at least until you decide what you're doing. But I can't believe this might be the last time I sit on your couch, the last time I'm in this office. I hope it's not. But I guess time will tell. Time tells a lot of things. My whole life I've bucked against time—usually because it wasn't going fast enough for me. But then there are moments when it's hurtling toward you and you'd give anything to stop the clock.

Billy came over after Ally was in bed. As I let him in I told him to sit at the table while I finished up some dishes, but he grabbed a tea towel.

We worked in companionable silence for a minute or two, then he said, "So where's Evan tonight?"

"He had to go back to the lodge." I snorted. "He couldn't wait to get out of here."

"Uh-oh. You guys fighting?"

"It's just the usual stuff." I sighed. "He wants me to move on and forget about the case, but it's not that easy for me. The loose ends are driving me nuts."

"So what's bugging you?"

"Remember when you said Evan was shot with John's Remington .223? Well, I remembered later that John told me his gun was in the shop—the firing pin was broken."

"Huh. Interesting, but he probably had another one."

"Evan said the same thing, but John always talked about that one being his *favorite*, like it was the only one for him. I mean, you heard the tapes. He talked about guns like they were girlfriends. Then I started thinking . . . look, I know this sounds crazy, but how do we know for sure he shot Evan?"

His eyebrows shot up. "Who else did you have in mind?"

"Yeah, that's the hole in my theory." I made a face and grinned. "The only other person who'd want Evan out of the way is Sandy."

"Wow, Sara. I know you don't like her, but that's harsh."

"It's not that I don't like her—she doesn't like *me*. I hate that! Anyway, I know it wasn't her, I'm just saying it's weird about the gun. He probably had two, like you said, but can you look into it so I can stop obsessing? If he was part of those collector groups maybe he had to list all his guns for them?"

"Sure, I'll look into it. But just for argument's sake, if it wasn't John, who else had a motive to shoot Evan? Don't forget a shell from John's gun was found at the scene."

"I know John's the only possible suspect, but the gun thing doesn't fit." I laughed. "It's like OJ's gloves."

As Billy finished drying the last dish, I took the tea towel from him.

"I'll put the dishes away. Sit."

He turned and pulled out a chair at the table.

"Just out of curiosity, why did you think Sandy wanted Evan out of the way?"

I shrugged. "She was obsessed with catching John and she knew Evan was the reason I wouldn't meet with him—she also thought my therapist was advising me against meeting him. It would've been easy for her to plant a shell at the scene and frame John. Three for three."

"That's it?"

I reached to put away the last plate. "Well, it was after my last fight with Sandy that Nadine was attacked. John always shot people—he didn't jump them in parking lots. When John called me at the hospital he was really keyed up and kept saying he had to meet me. Not like he was anxious, like he was scared."

I hung up the tea towel. Billy was watching me intently, his head tilted to the side. God, it was nice to talk to a man who actually listened and didn't just tell me to *let it go.*

I said, "And I was thinking tonight that it's weird he went straight to my house that day after he called me at the hospital. How did he know Ally was here and only one officer was watching her? Plus he knew I'd been talking to the police—he said he was going to explain later but he never got the chance. Maybe he'd been doing countersurveillance like you said and he saw something." Moose came downstairs from Ally's room and I let him out the sliding door. "Don't you think some of that stuff is weird?"

I sat down at the table in front of Billy. He heaved a sigh.

"In cases where the suspect dies it's hard to fit every piece together, Sara. But that doesn't mean there's more to it—it just means we don't have all the answers. I'll check into the gun, but I wonder if you're having a hard time letting go for another reason."

"What do you mean?"

His voice was cautious. "You might still be trying to deal with John's death. Or maybe you're having a hard time facing some other things in your life. Your wedding is coming up, and—"

"It's not that. It's just all these little mysteries really bug me. They make me feel like it's not completely over yet. I'm going to go online later and look at some gun forums. John spent a lot of time on the computer—bet I can find something."

"It's pretty unlikely John would list unregistered guns, or use his real name on a forum. Even if we did find a list somewhere, we'll never know if it's accurate. There's no way to verify how many guns he owned."

"Good point." I took a deep breath and let it out in a long exhale as I turned everything over in my mind. "Maybe

I'm looking at this the wrong way. If we can't prove he *didn't* shoot Evan, let's see if there's any evidence other than the shell casing that proves he did. Tofino's almost three hours from here. John would've had to fill up with gas somewhere along the way. Did you find any receipts in his belongings?"

"I don't believe so, but that—"

"Guess he could've just paid with cash. Oh! We should hit all the gas stations on the way with a photo of him. It wouldn't be hard—there's only one main route. Don't most stations have cameras now? People usually fill up in Port Alberni because it's the last stop. We should start there. After I drop Ally off at school in the morning we can—"

Billy held up a hand. "Whoa. I don't have time to canvass gas stations."

"Okay. But I'm not going to be able to relax until I figure some of this out. I'll go to every gas station myself if I have to." I smiled. "I'm relentless."

"That you are." He smiled back. "Let me think about it. Got some coffee?"

"Sure."

I poured a cup, then turned around.

Billy's gun was pointed at me.

I laughed. "What are you . . ." Then I saw the expression in his eyes.

He said, "Put the cup down on the counter."

I didn't move a muscle. "What's going on, Billy?"

"You never leave anything alone."

"I don't understand—"

"It was *over*, Sara. No one would ever have found out." He shook his head.

I stepped back until the edge of the counter pressed into my spine. What the hell was going on?

"Billy, you're scaring me." I scanned his face for any sign that this was a horrible joke, but he looked serious. "What did I—"

"Put the cup down."

As I turned to set it on the counter my mind scrambled. *Is this for real? Do I need a weapon? Should I try to throw the cup at him? Can I grab a knife?* I glanced at the end of the counter.

"Don't even think about it. I'm three times your size and three times as fast." He stood up and walked toward me.

"Why are you doing this? Did Sandy—"

"Sandy didn't do anything." He stopped in front of me

I searched his face. "Then why are you—"

"Because you're right—I did fill up in Port Alberni. But I'm not going to wait to find out if there was a camera."

"It was *you*? You shot Evan?"

"'The warrior skilled at stirring the enemy provides a visible form and the enemy is sure to come.'" Billy stared at me, his eyes slits. "Evan was in the way and you needed some incentive. I also knew it would flush John out—he'd want to protect you."

I couldn't believe what I was hearing.

"You tried to kill Evan so John would think someone was after *me*?"

" 'I attack that which he is obliged to rescue.' "

Everything started to fall into place.

"He knew something was wrong," I said. "That's why he was so panicky when he called me at the hospital and was making all those threats—*that's* why he didn't call my cell. He was *rescuing* Ally." I sucked in my breath. "Did you attack Nadine, too?"

"I didn't touch her. And if I tried to kill Evan, he'd be dead. I just needed to injure him for my plan to work. And I was right. You reacted, John reacted, and now he'll never hurt another woman." He stepped closer. "But now we have a problem."

My legs turned to liquid. "I won't say anything, Billy. I swear."

"Unfortunately, I can't take that risk."

The words poured out. "There's no risk. I'm not going to tell anyone. You made a mistake—but you were just trying to catch John. Even if someone did find out, you wouldn't be in that much trouble—"

"I didn't make a mistake." He looked as calm as ever. "I shot someone, Sara—that's attempted murder. I'd go to jail for a very long time. But that's not going to happen."

The way he said it terrified me. He wasn't scared or panicked, much less desperate. He sounded confident.

My body started to shake. "What—what are you going to do, Billy? You can't shoot me. Ally's upstairs and—"

He held his fingers up to his lips. "I have to think."

I shut up. He stared at me. His eyes were dark. The kitchen clock ticked.

I started to cry. "Billy, please, you're my friend. How can—"

"I like you, Sara, but 'the wise leader always blends consideration of gain and harm.' There's no gain in letting you live. But there's great harm."

"No, I *swear*. There isn't any—"

He held up a hand. "I've got it. I'm not going to do anything." My heart lifted for a moment, but then his eyes met mine and he said, "You are."

My vision blurred as my blood roared in my ears. For a moment the room spun and I gripped the counter behind me. My head pulsed, but I couldn't focus on anything, couldn't think.

He said, "We're going upstairs to get those pills your shrink prescribed, then you're going to take all of them and write a suicide note."

"Billy, this is crazy! How can you do this? What about Ally?"

"She'll be fine if you do everything I tell you."

"You can't make me write—"

"Do you love your daughter, Sara?" His eyes were resolute. I didn't know if he'd actually hurt Ally, but I didn't want to find out.

"I'll do it, I just—"

He motioned with the gun. "Let's go."

"Can we just talk about this for a—"

He gripped my arm hard and pulled me away from the counter. Then, with the gun pressed against my lower back, he urged me upstairs. With each step my mind tried to formulate a plan, but all I could think was, *Please, Ally, don't wake up.* At the top of the stairs we turned and walked down the hall past her room, my heart hammering so hard it hurt. As we entered my bedroom tears started to slide down my face.

"Where are your pills, Sara?"

"In the—in the bathroom." This was really happening, I was going to die.

"Open the medicine cabinet and take out the pills, but nothing else." I stared at myself in the mirror. My eyes were huge, my face pale. I opened the cabinet and took out the bottle.

"Fill up that glass with water." Billy motioned to the glass I'd left on the counter earlier. "Hurry up."

I turned on the tap.

"Billy, *please*, you don't have to do this."

His voice deepened. "Take them."

I emptied the bottle into my shaking hand and stared at the small white tablets. The glass was cold in my other hand.

Billy said, "If you don't swallow them, I'll have to shoot you. Ally will hear, then she'll come to—"

I pushed the pills into my mouth, choking on the chalky, bitter taste. I held the cold glass to my lips and took a swallow of water, then another as pills lodged in my throat, the bitter taste traveling up the back of my nose.

"Those ones too." He pointed the gun at a small bottle of Percocet I keep for migraines.

When I was done he nodded and said, "Now we have to mess up your bed."

"But I don't—"

"You were trying to go to sleep, but you were so depressed you decided to end everything once and for all."

With the gun still pointed at my back, I tugged the blanket free.

"Now strip."

"Billy, you don't want to do this."

He raised the gun and pointed it at me. "Right, I don't. But no way in hell I'm going to jail."

The books said to fight. But they didn't say what to do if the threat was a cop. And they didn't say what to do if your daughter was in the other room. I pictured Ally skipping in to wake me in the morning, climbing into bed next to my cold body.

I pulled my sweater over my head. He motioned with the gun to my pants. I unzipped them and tugged them off, leaving them on the floor.

I stood before him in my panties and bra. He was looking around the room, at the bed, at the door. Like he was making sure the scene was right.

He stepped closer until his huge body was directly in front of me.

"Take off your bra." After my bra fell to the ground, I crossed my arms over my breasts. My whole upper body was shaking.

"Drop your arms."

"Billy, *please*, I don't—"

"If you don't, I'll have to do it myself."

I dropped my arms.

"Now take off your panties."

Tears streaked my face as I peeled them off. I choked back a sob.

"Are you going to rape me?" I thought of Ally in the next room. I couldn't scream, no matter what he did to me I couldn't scream. "It doesn't have to be this way. I'll sleep with you and—"

"I'm not going to *rape* you." He looked insulted. "I'm not like your father. I don't have to force myself on women."

My temper reared but I held it in. *Shut up for Ally. Do it for Ally.*

He motioned to the dresser. "Put on your pajamas."

I took out one of Evan's T-shirts—one he knows I hate—and a pair of his boxers, which I never wear, hoping he would notice these details after I was dead. I put them on.

"Now we're going to get some paper for your suicide note."

After I found a pen and a pad of paper in my office, we headed downstairs. Once we were in the kitchen, he gestured to a half-empty bottle of Shiraz on the counter.

"Take that and sit at the table."

I sat and stared at him.

"Drink some straight from the bottle."

I took a swill.

He said, "Again."

I did it, gagging on the last mouthful. Some spilled on my T-shirt. I thought about the lethal concoction already spreading through my veins, wondered how long it would take to stop my heart. Billy looked around the kitchen and back to me, assessing the scene again.

"Good. Now start writing. When the pills kick in you're going to go lie on the couch."

"Ally, she'll find me in the morning and—"

"I'll stop by first thing and find your body before she wakes up. And I'll make sure she's out of the house when the police show up."

"Promise you won't let her see me."

"Sure."

When I picked up the pen my hand was shaking violently. I had to think of something that would stall him so I could come up with a plan. But even if I could get to the alarm—then what?

"Write the letter, Sara."

It wasn't hard to write a sad good-bye letter. I told them how much I loved them, how sorry I was, how much I was going to miss them, but this was the only thing I could do. I cried the whole time I was writing. I wanted to stab Billy in the eye with the pen, but you couldn't stab a man with anything when he was pointing a gun at you. Ally would be okay. Evan would take care of her. She'd grow up hating me, thinking I'd abandoned her. But at least she'd get to grow up.

When I was done Billy said, "Now we wait."

Fear tight in my throat, I said, "You're never going to get away with this."

"No one will ever suspect me—and you know it."

The phone rang and we both jumped. I looked upstairs, praying Ally didn't wake.

"Let's hope she's a deep sleeper," Billy said as it rang for the second time. She is once she gets going, but she hadn't been asleep for long. I held my breath as I waited for her to call out for me. Thankfully she was silent and the phone didn't ring again—it must have gone to voice mail. I remember Melanie's number was on the call display when I first got home. Thinking she'd called to tell me off, I'd ignored it, but now I wished I could call her and tell her I was sorry a million times over. My chest heaved with the effort to hold in panicky sobs.

It had been at least fifteen minutes since I'd taken the pills. I couldn't stop the tears streaming down my face now. I was going to die and I didn't get to kiss my daughter. I'd barely hugged Evan good-bye. We never got a chance to be married. *Stop it, Sara. Calm down so you can think of a way out of this.* If I kept talking, I might be able to stay alert enough to at least buy myself some time to come up with a plan.

"They might not suspect you right away, but they're not going to believe I killed myself. My family, Evan, my therapist, everyone knows I wouldn't do this to Ally—and I'm getting *married*. I was just talking to one of my sisters about my bachelorette party. Why would I—"

"There's a suicide note in your handwriting. They'll believe it." But something flickered in his eyes.

"My phone records show we talked tonight—you were the last person to see me alive. Your fingerprints are all over the dishes."

"I came over to talk to you because you were upset." He shrugged. "I didn't realize you were suicidal."

"But you're a trained professional, you should've known. There'll be an investigation, Billy."

"I'll deal with it. This will work."

He was too calm. Nothing was shaking him. Panic came crashing back in on me, paralyzing my every thought except that time was running out. I was going to die.

I stared at Billy. Everything started to feel distant and slow, like I was moving underwater. I heard a roaring in my ears and wondered if I was going to pass out. Then Billy shifted his stance and my eyes landed on his tattoos.

Weakness stems from preparing against attack. Strength stems from obliging the enemy to prepare against an attack.

That was it. I'd found my strategy. I had to go on the attack. The fear left my body as my mind cleared.

"Like how your plan to catch John worked?"

His eyes narrowed. "It did work."

"You never caught him—I killed him. I had to do your job for you."

His hand tightened on the gun. I flashed to the conversation we'd had about how he used to have a temper. He'd trained himself to channel it and to hold it in, but that didn't mean it wasn't still there. What had he said about kickboxing? The opponent who loses his cool loses his coordination. Maybe if I provoked him, he'd let down his guard and I could make a break for the phone or the alarm.

"*The Art of War* didn't help. It's all just a bunch of crap."

"This case *proves* it works."

He said the words with conviction, but there was a slight flush to his neck. I'd touched a nerve.

"Nobody will take that stupid book you're writing

seriously—definitely not the RCMP. Even Sandy doesn't listen to you."

The flush crawling up his neck darkened. "She will. When she reads it and sees how it helped the case."

"But you're leaving out the part where you shot Evan, aren't you? That's why you're killing me. Because if the truth comes out, then everyone knows you're a liar—all your strategies and plans are bullshit. You broke the *law*."

"It works. I just needed one big case to prove it. And I did."

"No, Billy, you screwed up. You told me I had to be patient but you took matters into your own hands. Then an officer—your *partner*—got hurt. You rushed things and it escalated John."

"John had to be stopped. Because of my actions he'll never kill another woman."

"But if you kill *me* you're a murderer too, and—"

"I told you, I'm not going to jail—not for saving lives."

"You didn't care about stopping a killer *or* saving lives. Everything you've done all along has been for yourself." His eyes were still dark, but he'd managed to calm himself down. I was starting to feel drowsy and light-headed. I had to take another shot. "You don't care about any of the people he murdered."

"You don't know the first thing about me."

"I know the RCMP are going to laugh when they find out what you did. This isn't the first time you screwed up. Remember the old lady who got shot because you broke into that rapist's house?"

He stood up. "You stupid bitch. You don't—"

"You couldn't control the case and you couldn't control me. You broke the law to make the case fit the strategies, not the other way around."

"If I was you, I'd shut up now." A vein started to pulse in Billy's forehead and he took a step toward me.

We both heard the crunch of tires on the gravel outside at the same time.

"Don't move," Billy said. "Shit, it's your sister. You say one word and I'll blow her head off." Oh, God, Lauren.

I wanted to scream and warn her, but Ally was in the house and it was too late. Billy was already opening the door.

"Hi, Melanie. Your sister's in the kitchen." Melanie? Why was she here?

She walked in, spotted me sitting at the table.

"Hey, I forgot my cell. I tried to call—" She saw my face, turned to look at Billy. He had the gun pointed at her head. As she gasped and took a step backward, the sob I was holding in my throat broke free.

Billy walked forward with the gun still aimed at her.

"Sit down at the table with your sister." She turned and looked at me, then glanced at the sliding glass door. "Don't even think about it. Sara's already realized what will happen to Ally if anyone does something stupid."

Melanie's eyes met mine. I nodded.

Billy said, "Sit *down*, Melanie."

She pulled the chair out beside me.

"Put your hands on the table where I can see them."

She did, slowly.

"Sara was just in the middle of killing herself. She's already taken the pills." Melanie's gaze flew to my face. My eyes told her it was true.

She turned to Billy. "You can't make both of us kill—"

"Shut up. I just have to adjust my plan." He started to pace.

Melanie tried to stand up. Billy smacked her in the face with the back of his hand. She fell back into her chair with a yelp.

"Do you want to wake up Ally?" he said.

I said, "She's right, Billy. How are you going to explain two deaths?"

He pointed the gun at me. "I told you to *shut up*." He continued pacing. Then stopped and spun around. "John had a large fan base, all murder groupies—they're angry you killed him. One of them decided to seek revenge." He nodded. "I can make that work."

Billy walked over to the knife block, picked up the biggest one, and hefted it in his hand, like he was testing its weight. He sliced it through the air, once, twice.

Melanie said, "Or I can help you." I gasped. But she didn't look at me. She said, "Suicide is way more believable— there's already drugs in Sara's system. We don't have to hurt the kid. But it would look better for you if I'm the one to find Sara's body. I could try to revive her, but . . ." She shrugged.

"You think I'm going to fall for that?" But he sounded tense. He knew she was right.

"I hate Sara." Melanie spit the words out. "I've *always*

hated her. She's not even my real sister. If she dies, I'll owe you for the rest of my life." She dropped to her knees off the chair. Startled, Billy stepped back, the gun pointed at her face, but she crawled forward on her knees. "I'll even tell the cops I saw her today and she was really depressed."

From the side, I saw a gleam in Melanie's eye. I wanted to say something, anything, but my tongue felt thick and my vision was a little blurry. The pills were definitely kicking in.

Melanie was in front of Billy now. He didn't move.

"I'm your best chance to get out of this," she said. Billy's face was intense, his forehead covered in a fine sheen of sweat.

Her hands at her sides, Melanie rose, still on her knees, so her mouth was right in front of Billy's crotch. He stared down, transfixed.

"I'll do *anything* you want, Billy."

I finally found my voice. "Doesn't matter what she says—you'll never get away with this. And when your *father* finds out, he'll—"

Billy looked up. "You bitch—"

Melanie rammed her forehead into his crotch. He let out a huge bellow and stumbled backward. The knife fell out of his hands and skidded to my left. I lunged for it, but my body was slow to respond and I hit the floor with a thud.

Melanie and Billy were struggling for the gun. He grabbed her by the hair and slammed her head into the fridge. I reached for the knife but my fingers closed around air. I looked to my left and saw Billy dive for the gun on the floor—Melanie kicked it away in time.

He punched her. She went down and stayed down. Now he was coming for me. My vision was blurry, but I could see the gun in his hand. I searched the floor in frantic swoops. Just as my fingers closed around the knife, his hands grasped my feet and he hauled me out from under the table. I tried to grip the table leg with one hand, but he pulled harder. Then I heard a small voice.

"Mommy?"

Billy let go of my leg and straightened up. I thrust the knife into his thigh. He screamed and clutched at it. I was still gripping the handle as he wrenched his body backward until I was left holding the knife.

"*Mommy!*"

Blood from Billy's leg was turning the front of his jeans dark. He dropped to his knees. My vision was getting worse.

Ally was still screaming. Billy crawled toward the gun, which had ended up near the sliding glass door. Moose was going nuts through the glass.

With the knife in my hands I crawled after Billy, but my body swayed. I focused my blurred eyes on his back as he stretched for the gun. When I was right behind him, I raised my hand with the knife. He saw me in the door's reflection and kicked backward, catching me under the chin and knocking me into the cupboards. Ally screamed and ran toward me.

I yelled, "*Stay there!*"

Billy spun around, his face a mask of red rage, and pointed the gun at me. I used my last bit of strength to brace on my elbows and kicked my heel hard into the wound in his thigh. He screamed and I kicked out again, managing to connect with his hand and knocking the gun across the kitchen.

It landed at Ally's feet. She had her hands over her ears as she screamed and screamed. Billy and I scrambled after the gun. I pulled myself onto his back and tried to wrap my arms under his neck. He got to his feet with me clinging to him and roared as he stumbled backward.

We hit the sliding glass door with a thud that knocked the breath out of me. As he stepped forward I slid off his back and landed on the floor hard, gasping for air. My mouth filled with the metallic taste of blood. He spun around and started to kick me. In my chest, my legs, my head. Pinned against the glass, I had nowhere to go. Behind me Moose barked frantically.

Melanie's voice rang out. "Leave my sister alone, you *fucker*."

The loud crack of a gun. The images were blurry, but I could make out the stunned expression on Billy's face and a circle of blood opening up on the front of his shirt. Another shot rang out and he collapsed on top of me.

Everything turned dark. Hands were on my arm and someone was pulling me hard, and then there was a finger down my throat.

"Sara, throw up!"

I fought the finger, but it jammed in deeper.

Melanie's voice said, "Ally, call 911!"

I hope to God you never have to have your stomach pumped, Nadine. Not a lot of fun—nor is hanging out in the hospital for two days. You wouldn't believe how loud it gets in there sometimes, especially at night. But I never slept anyway. The fact that John took the blame for attacking you and shooting Evan still haunts me. He must have suspected it was someone on the force. But it's hard to know what was going on in his head. I wonder sometimes why he didn't just tell me it wasn't him, but I wouldn't have believed him. And he probably knew it.

He must have also known all along I was working with the cops and set up the meetings to test me. But I don't understand why he kept phoning. He had to have realized he was taking a chance with each call. Was he that confident they wouldn't catch him, or did he want a connection with me so badly he was willing to take the risk? I'd betrayed him, again and again, but he still tried to protect me. If I was carrying guilt for killing him before, I'm dragging heaps of it now. I understand your theory that I might be focusing on my father's rescuing me as a way of reconciling myself with his being a serial killer. But it's the opposite. Knowing he wasn't all bad is a whole lot harder than believing he was pure evil.

I keep thinking about that last day with John—my only day with him—how hard he was trying to please me. And when I attacked him in the river . . . I wonder what he'd been trying to tell me. I'll never know. There's a lot we'll never know about this case, which is what I'm having the hardest time with. Acceptance and letting go isn't really my thing. But I need to if I'm ever going to find some sort of peace.

The cops were hard on us when they first took our statements, but as soon as they found the Remington .223 in Billy's attic and discovered a shell casing missing from an evidence box, they changed their tune. Sandy came to see me in the hospital. Turns out it was Billy who convinced Julia to speak to me about meeting John. He'd been filling her in on the case all along, part of his strategy to scare the crap out of her so she'd turn around and pressure me. Sandy only spoke to her a couple of times. Julia wasn't lying after all.

Sandy apologized for being so obsessed by the case and admitted she was hard on me. But it was part of a plan. After it became clear Sandy and I didn't connect, Billy suggested she act as the aggressor and he be the nice guy. She still feels bad that John got Ally, and she's mortified that she didn't know what her partner was up to. When I told her I knew she'd done the best she could, I swear I saw tears in her eyes. I look at her differently now—or maybe I'm just finally seeing her.

When they searched Billy's house they also found a few books about *The Art of War* and some other Chinese classics. On his hard drive they found a draft of his own book, titled *The Art of Police Work*. He'd used several famous cases for examples, but most of the strategies were applied to his "one big case," the hunt for the Campsite Killer. He also had notebooks on John and copies of every file.

Another mystery was solved when they searched Billy's browser history and found all the Web sites where he'd posted a link to the original article about the Campsite Killer being my father. He made sure it spread across the Internet—obviously in hopes of flushing out John. When the police looked into it they discovered he'd even posted the article on some where-to-camp-in-BC forums, using the screen name The Dark Knight. The worst part is that he linked to my business directory, which is probably how John got my cell number.

When I got home from the hospital I read *The Art of War* front to back, still trying to make sense of Billy's actions. But in the end I was just left with the feeling he'd interpreted each quote for his own purposes. There was one line in there that basically summed up his entire friendship with me: "Command them with civility, rally them with martial discipline, and you will win their confidence." Now I realize just how much Billy was manipulating me all along—keeping my spirits high, bringing me food, getting me ready for the next "battle," even stealing Moose so he could help me find him.

First thing Dad said was, "I knew there was something off about him. He didn't dress like a cop." I started to argue that Billy's dressing nice didn't mean squat, then realized I was feeling defensive for liking Billy. That's the hardest part, that I liked him. But maybe you're right and it wasn't

Billy I liked so much as what he was teaching me. I know he just needed me to be calm so he could use me. But he did help. Even now when I get stressed out or start to panic I think, *Breath, regroup, just focus on your strategy.*

If this whole situation taught me anything, it's that even though I was terrified 95 percent of the time, I did handle everything that was thrown at me. Now I just have to remember to keep moving forward when everything is going sideways. I doubt I'll ever be cool in a crisis—I'm just not wired that way. But maybe I'll stop freaking out about the fact that I freak out.

The police still don't know who attacked you. Billy could've snuck out that night—I even told him the alarm code after he encouraged me to take an Ativan. But he would've bragged about it. Sandy still believes it was John, but I don't think it was him either. Don't worry—I'm staying out of this one. When I told Evan the same thing, he just laughed and said, "Riiiight." But I swear this time I'm leaving it to the police.

Evan feels like a total jerk for blowing off my concerns about the gun, but he's also pretty proud of himself for never trusting Billy. He's been getting way too much mileage out of that one, but overall he's being really sweet. All the fighting we went through scared me, but in the end it made me realize we can have differences and still be right for each other. If we can make it through two killers, marriage is going to be a piece of cake.

He brought Ally to see me in the hospital. She got super-upset the first time—nothing like seeing your mommy with tubes coming out of her—but one of the doctors explained everything and she calmed down. She loved coming after that because I gave her my puddings.

She slept in our bed both nights I was in the hospital—Evan said she kept waking up screaming. We've been taking her to see that therapist and she's getting better, but she's still a little clingy. She's also been throwing some *major* temper tantrums, so we have to work on that. But in the last month she's been abducted, watched her mom and aunt get beat up, and seen a man get shot to death. She has to let it out somehow.

Melanie came to see me the first day I was in the hospital. I was sleeping, but when I opened my eyes she was sitting in the chair beside me, flipping through a *People* magazine. Evan told me she had a minor concussion, so I wasn't surprised to see the bandage on her forehead, but the black eye was a shock.

I cleared my throat, which was still swollen from the tube the doctors had jammed down it.

"Nice shiner."

She smiled at me. "Beats yours."

I smiled back. "I like purple, makes my eyes look greener."

We laughed, but then I groaned.

"Stop, that hurts." Our eyes met and our last moment with Billy surrounded us. She shifted her weight in the chair.

"The stuff I said . . ." She cleared her throat. "I didn't mean it."

"Yeah, I know. But our relationship does kind of suck."

Anger flashed in her eyes, but I held up a hand.

"I overreact and I have a temper." I took a deep breath, which made me cough, which hurt like hell. Melanie handed me my water. After I took a sip I said, "And you're right, sometimes I judge you. But I'm just jealous because of how Dad treats you."

"Well, don't be, because he's embarrassed I turned out to be such a disappointment. He's always going on about how well you've done for yourself. And he *hates* my boyfriend." I'd never looked at it from her perspective before, never realized how much she also wanted Dad's approval.

"You're not a disappointment. But he does hate Kyle."

She laughed. "It doesn't help that he thinks Evan's perfect. I know Kyle is different, but he's fun and he makes me feel good. You've never tried to get to know him."

"You're right. But I will, okay?"

"Okay." She smiled. "I don't see us going on double dates, though."

I laughed, then held my side and gritted my teeth. Once the pain had passed, I said, "You're probably right, but you never know." I touched her hand. "Hey, you know what? When you were really little I snuck into your room one night. I thought if I gave you away, Dad would love me. But I stayed in your room for hours watching you sleep."

"You were going to give me *away*?"

NEVER KNOWING • 445

I smiled at the expression on her face.

"The point is I decided to keep you. Thank God—or I'd be dead right now."

She laughed. Then she rested her forehead on my hospital bed and started to cry.

"Oh, Sara, I thought you *were* dead. You passed out and I couldn't get you to wake up. All I could think was that you were going to die believing I hated you."

I patted the back of her soft hair. "I know you don't hate me. And I don't hate you either—even when you piss me off. Lauren says you and I are a lot alike and that's why we fight so much."

Melanie's head popped up. "We're not alike at all."

"That's what I said." We eyed each other.

She said, "Oh, fuck."

When Lauren brought me some clothes from the house, I filled her in about my visit with Melanie.

"I think we might be okay. I'm sure we're still going to fight, but at least we're talking about it now. I still wonder how John knew all that stuff about Ally, but I never really thought Melanie had anything to do with it and now I'm positive."

Lauren turned away and started unpacking my bag.

"Evan should get you some herbal teas for when you get home."

"Lauren?"

She continued unpacking. "Peppermint will help your stomach. And get some herbal cleansers from the health food store—they'll help with the toxins."

"Lauren, can you look at me for a minute?"

She turned around with a pair of my pants in her hands. I scanned her smiling face and her too-bright eyes. My stomach fluttered.

"Do you know something?" My voice was still raspy from the tube.

"About what?" Lauren's wholesome face isn't built for lies.

"What did you do, Lauren?"

She stood there a moment, then dropped into the chair beside my bed.

"I didn't know it was him."

"What *happened*?"

Her mouth turned down. "A man called and said he was from the newspaper and he was researching what children are interested in these days for an article. He said he got my name from a parent I know—Sheila Watson, she's a neighbor—so I told him about the boys. Then he asked if they had any relatives, and when I said they had a cousin, he wanted to know what she liked. I told him, but when he kept on with more questions about Ally I asked his name again and he hung up. I told Greg about it and he said we shouldn't say anything—it would just scare you."

For the first time in my life, I wanted to hit Lauren.

"I can't believe you didn't tell me—especially after Evan was shot!"

"I didn't know for sure if it was the Campsite—"

"Oh, right." My face was hot. "You just didn't want to say anything because you knew I'd be pissed off. He knew how to get to Ally!"

Lauren gnawed on her lip. "Greg said he would've done it no matter what. I feel horrible for telling him about Ally—he just sounded so *nice*."

We were both quiet as I looked at her flushed face. Then something else clicked into place.

"Did you tell someone the Campsite Killer was my father? Is that how it got leaked?"

Her face was now scarlet. "Greg . . . sometimes he talks too much when he's been drinking. He didn't know one of the guys in camp was dating a reporter from that site, or he—"

"You told him, even though I asked you not to tell *any-one*, not even Greg? *You* started all of this?" I was gripping a magazine so hard the edge was cutting into my hand. Then I realized something else. "Wait a minute. Greg tells stupid jokes when he's drunk, but he doesn't gossip. He knew this could really mess up my life. Why would he let it slip?"

Lauren's cheeks flushed again.

I stared hard at her. She looked away.

"Did he do this on *purpose*?"

Lauren still wasn't looking at me and her face was desperate, like she wanted to say something but couldn't. I didn't believe this was a drunken blunder. Was Greg mad at me because he thought Lauren had talked to me about his drinking? No, that wasn't it, she was too loyal and he knew it. There had to be some other reason—or person.

I felt my way slowly. "Was he trying to embarrass Dad?"

Now Lauren met my eyes and I had my answer.

"*That's* it?" I wasn't sure what hurt more: that Greg threw me under the bus to get at Dad or that he knew I was the way to do it.

"I think so." Her voice was resigned. "He swears he didn't know about the reporter. But he was so mad when Dad promoted the other foreman. . . ."

"You sat there listening to Dad give me a hard time and your *husband* leaked it?"

Lauren's eyes filled with tears. "I'm so sorry—"

"Damn right you should be sorry." I was breathing fast, which was sending stabbing pains through my ribs, but I was too pissed off to care.

She said, "I tried to tell you a couple of times, but I was worried Greg would lose his job and Dad would be mad and—"

"Treat you like crap?"

"He's the only father I have."

"He's the only one I have too, Lauren."

Lauren stared at the blanket on my bed and her face turned sad.

"I know things were different for you," she said. "It's not right how he treats you."

I was silent, all my angry words dying in my throat.

"I'm sorry. I never stuck up for you when we were growing up. None of us did."

Now I was the one crying. "You were just a kid."

"But I'm not now." She took a deep breath. "I'll tell Dad."

"He'll fire Greg."

"I'm tired of hiding. I have to make some changes in my life. You're more important—you're my sister." Her eyes met mine. "I just want you to be happy."

"I *am* happy." And then I realized I was. I had everything I needed.

My last visitor in the hospital was the last person I expected to see. As I flipped through channels on the TV, there was a light rap on the door. I glanced over, thinking it was one of the nurses, and saw Julia standing there. She looked elegant in a white linen pantsuit. She also looked *really* uncomfortable.

"May I come in?"

It took me a moment to find my voice.

"Sure, of course." I clicked off the TV. "Have a seat." I nodded to the chair beside the bed, but she moved to stand near the window. She fiddled with one of the flowers in the vase, plucking a petal off and rolling it in her fingers. Finally she turned and said, "I haven't spoken to you since you killed him. . . ." Her voice drifted off and I fought the urge to fill in the silence. *Why are you here? Are you happy he's dead? Do you still hate me?*

"I wanted to thank you," she said. "I can sleep now." Before I could respond she met my eyes. "Katharine's moved out."

Not sure why she was sharing this, I said, "I'm sorry."

Her face turned reflective. "It was easy to blame everything wrong in my life on him."

"What he did was—"

"He's gone now. And I see now, things I've done—what it did to people around me. How I pushed them away. . . ." Her eyes fixated on the photo on my side table. "Is this your daughter?"

"That's Ally, yes."

"She's very pretty."

"Thanks." She was still staring at the photo when my mom came into the room with the coffee I'd asked for a few minutes ago. When she saw Julia she startled.

"Oh, I'm sorry. I'll come back."

"It's fine, Mom. Please stay."

Julia's face flushed and she gripped her purse. "I should go."

I said, "Wait a second. Please." She stiffened. "Julia, I'd like you to meet my mother, Carolyn."

Mom looked from Julia to me and her face lit up. I gave her a smile, my eyes telling her everything I wanted to say. She smiled back.

She turned to Julia and reached out her hand. I held my breath. Julia extended hers. Mom held it for a moment with both of her hands and said, "Thank you for giving her to us."

Julia blinked a couple of times, but she said, "You must be proud. She's a brave young woman."

"We're *very* proud of Sara." Mom smiled and my throat tightened.

Julia said again, "I should go." She turned to me. "I still have my father's woodworking tools. When you're better you can come have a look if you like. There might be something you want."

"Sure. That would be great." I was as surprised by the offer as I was by the fact that my creative side might not have come from John after all.

She nodded briskly and strode out of the room.

Mom looked at me and said, "She seems nice."

I raised an eyebrow. "Really?"

"She comes across a little angry. But she reminds me of your father."

"How are you seeing *that*?"

"They act angry when they're scared." She settled into the chair by my bed. "Do you know your father stayed by your side all last night while you slept?" She smiled, then looked back at the door Julia had just exited. "You have her hands."

Yesterday I was making Ally breakfast and just as I served her pancakes with extra blueberries and whipped cream— I've been spoiling the heck out of her—I moved too fast. Ally saw me wince.

"Poor Mommy. What cheers you up when you're sick?"

"You cheer me up."

She rolled her eyes. "It's a *joke*."

My heart started to flutter.

She said in a singsong voice, "What cheers you up when you're sick?"

I played along.

"Pickles?"

"A get wellephant card!" She dissolved into giggles.

"Where did you hear that joke?"

"I don't know." She shrugged her little shoulders. "I like jokes." She grinned with her gap-toothed smile, and I wanted to tell her those jokes were silly. I wanted to take any part of John that's in her and pull it out. But as I watched her take a big bite of her pancake, her face still in smiles, I thought about a father who didn't let his little boy tell jokes.

"I like them too, Ally."

ACKNOWLEDGMENTS

This book would not have been possible without the help of some amazing people who shared their time and knowledge. Without them, and the countless cups of tea and bowls of popcorn that were consumed during the writing of this novel, I wouldn't have made it through. First, I'd like to thank my aunt, Dorothy Hartshorne, for brainstorming sessions and "this-or-that?" e-mails, and my uncle, Dan Hartshorne, for teaching me about firearms. Once again, a big thank-you to Renni Browne and Shannon Roberts, whose valuable feedback always takes my writing to the next level. I'm also deeply grateful to my critique partner, Carla Buckley, a true friend and a brilliant writer who keeps me cyber-company on those long, lonely days at the keyboard.

For sharing their professional expertise, I'd like to thank Constable J. Moffat, Staff Sergeant J. D. MacNeill, Doug Townsend, Dr. E. Weisenberger, Nina Evans-Locke, and Garry Rodgers, who all generously shared their time. You can be sure any mistakes are mine. Special thanks to Tamara Poppitt, who taught me about six-year-old girls; Sandy Jack, who read my first draft and let me use Eddie, her French bulldog, for inspiration; and Stephanie Paddle, who didn't laugh when I asked strange medical questions—and trust me, they were usually strange.

A writer needs a strong support system and I'm blessed to have that in my agent, Mel Berger, who always answers my questions and epic e-mails with wit and wisdom. Graham Jaenicke also provided much-needed support and e-mail entertainment. I feel very lucky to be working with St. Martin's Press and my editor, Jen Enderlin, whose insights are always bang on, even if I'm sometimes slow to see the light. My gratitude also to Sally Richardson, Matthew Shear, Lisa Senz, Sarah Goldstein, Ann Day, and Loren Jaggers. Thanks to my Canadian publicist, Lisa Winstanley, who deserves all the hamburgers in the world for her color-coded schedules.

I'd like to thank Lisa Gardner and Karin Slaughter for going above and beyond to help out a new author. Don Taylor, you're a true gentleman. I'd also like to thank my foreign publishers, who take my vision and share it with the rest of the world. A special thanks to Cargo, who brought me to Amsterdam. I came home inspired and ready to write.

As well, I'm grateful to my friends and family who make this all worth it and who understand when I drop off the face of the earth for months. Last, but never least, my husband, Connel, my rock when the rest of the world is spinning.

Turn the page for a preview of Chevy Stevens's upcoming novel

Always Watching

Coming in 2013

CHAPTER ONE

The first time I saw Heather Simeon she was curled into a ball in the seclusion room at the hospital, the thin blue blanket tight around her, the bandages a sharp white line circling her wrists. Her blond hair obscured most of her face. Even then she still gave off a sense of refinement, something in her jawline, the high cheekbone, barely visible through the veil of her hair. The arched eyebrow, slightly darker than her hair, and well-shaped; the patrician nose, the delicate outline of pale pink lips. Only her hands were a mess: the cuticles raw and bleeding, the nails jagged. They didn't look bitten, they looked broken. Like her.

I'd already read her file and talked with the emergency psychiatrist who'd admitted her the night before, then gone over everything with the nurses, most of whom had worked in PIC—the Psychiatric Intensive Care unit—for years, and who were also my best source of information. I might spend fifteen minutes to an hour with each patient during my morning rounds, but the rest of the time I was at my office in the mental health building, treating patients who're out in the community. That's why I like to bring a nurse with me when I first meet a patient, so we're on the same page with the care plan. One of the nurses, Michelle, a cheerful woman, with curly blond hair and a wide smile, was with me now.

Heather's husband had come home the night before to find her sprawled on the kitchen floor, blood dripping from deep lacerations on her wrists, the butcher knife still lying nearby. When she was admitted to the hospital she had become agitated, crying and fighting the nurses. The emergency room doctor had run a drug screen and it came back clear, so she'd been given Ativan and placed in the seclusion room, where she would be under close observation on the monitor—a nurse would also check her every fifteen minutes.

She'd been sleeping all night.

I shifted my weight. Heather opened her eyes, blinked a couple of times, then rolled over in the bed. She gazed up at me, licked her lips—which were dry and chapped—then swallowed. Her mouth parted like she was going to say something, but only her breath escaped in a long sigh. Her eyes were dark blue.

My voice gentle, I said, "Good morning, Heather. I'm Dr. Lavoie, the attending psychiatrist." When I had my private practice up-island, my patients had called me Nadine. But since I'd moved to Victoria to work at the hospital, I'd started using my formal address, had come to like it, the emotional distance—the reason for my move in the first place. "Would you like some water?"

She blinked again, stared somewhere over my shoulder. Her expression was blank, devoid of sorrow or anger. She may not have been able to check out physically, but she had definitely disappeared emotionally.

"I'd like to talk with you for a little bit if that's okay."

She glanced at me, her eyes skimming past, landing on Michelle. She pulled the blue blanket tight around her.

"Why . . . why is she here?" Her voice was a whisper.

"Michelle? She's one of our nurses."

On the psychiatry floor the doctors are generally in business casual, the nurses dressing more for comfort. Michelle tended to favor fun clothes, today a funky striped shirt with dark denim dress jeans. Unless you noticed her ID badge around her neck, you might not realize she was a nurse.

Heather's body language was defensive, almost cringing under the blanket, her gaze flicking back and forth between us, like a cornered animal. Michelle, picking up on Heather's energy, stepped back, but Heather still looked overwhelmed. Some patients didn't bat an eye when we brought a nurse in with us, but others turned hostile, feeling ganged up on.

I said, "Would you be more comfortable just talking to me?"

She gave a small nod as she worried a corner of her bandage with her teeth. Again I was struck with the image of a wild animal trying to escape from its bindings. I glanced at Michelle, signaling that was okay for her to leave.

Michelle smiled at Heather. "I'll check on you later, honey. See if you need anything."

I liked Michelle's warmth with the patients, had noticed it before. She'd often sit and talk with them, even on her breaks. When the door had closed behind her, I turned back to Heather.

"I'm just going to ask some basic questions, so we can get to know each other, all right?" I paused but she was staring at the ceiling, her face blank. I said, "Can you tell me how old you are?"

She slowly said, "Thirty-five," as she looked around, starting to become more aware of where she was. Everything about the room was like something out of a horror film: the small plastic window in the heavy metal door. The clear plastic cover on the window, scratch marks down it like someone had tried to claw their way out—and they had. The room had always disturbed me. But Heather's face was still blank.

"And your name?"

"Heather Duncan . . ." She shook her head, catching herself, but the movement was sleepy, delayed. "Simeon. My name now, it's Simeon."

I smiled. "Did you get married recently?"

"Yes." Not *yeah*, or *uh-huh*, but *yes*. She was educated, brought up to speak clearly. Her gaze focused on the heavy metal door. "Daniel . . . is he here?"

"He's here, but I'd like to talk with you first." I was late coming in that day—one of my patients at Mental Health had gone off his meds and his case worker was worried—so it was almost lunch time. The nurses had told me that Heather's husband, Daniel Simeon, was in the waiting area, and had been there for hours. "How long have you and Daniel been married?"

"Six months."

"What do you do for a living?"

"I don't do anything—I'm unemployed."

Maybe a recent job loss triggered her suicide attempt.

"What did you do before?"

"I worked in the store. We take care of the earth."

I noticed that she'd used present tense for the latter part of the sentence. Wondering if she had a business with her husband I said, "Are you a landscaper?"

"It's our job to tend and keep the land." I was confused. Did she mean something with agriculture? But underneath my confusion there was something else, an uncomfortable flutter in my stomach about the phrase. I tuned into the sensation, traced my thoughts back. She'd said it like she was reciting an expression she'd heard many times. She was repeating it, not speaking for herself.

"I heard you had a bad night. Would you like to tell me what happened?"

"I don't want to be here."

"You're in the hospital because you've been certified under the Mental Health Act." Because she was actively suicidal, Heather had been involuntarily admitted. Two doctors had signed the documents and she wouldn't be able to leave until one of us signed off. "You tried to hurt yourself, and we don't want that to happen again, so we're going help you get better."

She pulled herself up into a sitting position, and I noticed how thin her arms were as she braced herself on the mattress, the veins popping. They shook like the effort of holding up her body was exhausting. She tilted forward for a second, before she righted herself, the small movement throwing her off balance.

She said, "I just wanted it all to stop." Her eyes filled with tears, which weaved down her face, dripped off her nose. One landed on her arm. She stared at it as though she didn't know how it got there.

"What did you want to stop?"

"The bad thoughts."

"So you're having troubling thoughts?"

She nodded. "My baby—" Her voice caught and she flinched, gritting her teeth as though something had stabbed her deep inside.

"Do you have a child?" The file hadn't said anything about children.

Another tear slid down and dropped onto her arm. "I was three months pregnant. I started bleeding . . ." She took a breath and let it out, slowly through still clenched teeth.

I paused, a beat of silence in honor of what she'd just told me, and then gently said, "How long ago did you miscarry?"

"A week."

"I'm very sorry to hear that. That must've been painful for you. It's normal to have feelings of depression after losing a child, but we can help you manage your emotions, so they aren't so overwhelming. Your file said that your doctor had prescribed Effexor last year. Are you still taking it?"

"No."

"When did you stop?"

She stared at my shoes. There was a slight tone of sleepy-defensiveness in her words as she said, "When I met Daniel," and I knew she felt guilty that she'd stopped taking them, felt ashamed that she needed them. People suffering depression often stop their medication when they fall in love, the endorphins creating their own natural antidepressant. But then real life kicks in.

"Well, the first thing I'd like to do is put you back on the antidepressant." My voice was casual, conveying, *This isn't a big deal. You're okay.* "We'll start you off on a low dose and see how you do. Your file mentioned that you also went through a hard time a few years ago." Her previous two suicide attempts had been with pills. She'd been found at the last second in each case, but now that Heather progressed to more violent means, she might not be so lucky next time. "You were referred to a psychologist. Are you still seeing him?"

She shook her head. "He didn't help. But when I met Daniel, I was getting better. He's a good man . . ." She looked sad, almost regretful.

"The nurses said he stayed here all night, and just went home this morning to get some of your things."

Her face was creased in worry. "He must be so tired."

"I'm sure Daniel just wants you to get well, and we're here to help with that."

Her eyelashes glimmered with fresh tears, making her eyes seem even bluer, like sapphires set in diamonds. She was so pale you could see every vein in her neck, but she was still hauntingly pretty. People always assume that beautiful people have no reason to be unhappy. It's usually the complete opposite.

She said, "I want Daniel." Her eyelids had begun to droop, the effort of talking draining what little energy she'd had left.

"I'm going to speak to him first, and then we'll see if we can arrange a little visit." I wanted to get a sense of what kind of emotional shape he was in, so he didn't make the situation worse.

She swallowed like her mouth was still dry from the drugs and slurred slightly when she spoke. "They can't find me in here." She said the words to the room as though she'd forgotten I was there and was just reassuring herself.

I said, "Who are you afraid's going to find you?"

I had expected her to say something about her bad thoughts, so I was surprised when, answering more on reflex than any real awareness of my presence, she said, "I want them to leave us alone, but they just keep calling and calling." She picked at her cuticles as she spoke, tearing at a small piece of flesh.

I said, "Is someone bothering you?" Her file hadn't said anything about paranoia, or hallucinations, but sometimes in a severe depression, which Heather was clearly suffering from, psychosis is possible. She might also be having difficulties with some people in her life, which we needed to know about.

She started to worry the bandage with her teeth again,

rocking herself slightly, the expression in her eyes vague and disconnected. I began to consider that she might also be suffering from some post-traumatic stress syndrome.

I said, "This is a safe environment—it's a place for you to get better. We can bar anyone you don't want to visit and there is a security guard on the floor at all times. No one can get to you." One of the first steps when dealing with a possible post-traumatic stress disorder is to establish safety, which isn't always easy if they still have contact with the abuser. If there was a real threat, I wanted to make sure Heather felt secure enough to tell me what was going on, and if it was just paranoia, she also needed to feel protected so we could begin to treat her.

"I'm not going back." The last part was said as though she was warning herself. "They can't make me." She slurred the words again. The combination of medication and emotional exhaustion made her sound like a drunken teenager reminding herself not to make any noise when she snuck back into her house.

"Who are 'they'?" I still couldn't ascertain whether there was any truth to her fears, or even what they were exactly.

She didn't answer, just closed her eyes, almost dozing off.

"Heather? Do you want to lie down?"

Her eyelids fluttered. When she didn't respond I repeated, "Heather?"

She forced her eyes open, met mine with a flash of confused alarm. As we held gazes I could feel her sluggish thought process, her wondering what she had told me. Fear, and something else, something I couldn't name yet, rolled off her body in thick waves, pressing into me. I fought the sudden urge to step back.

She said, "I need to see Daniel," then her head lolled forward and her chin dropped onto her chest. "I'm so tired."

"Why don't you get some rest while I talk to your husband."

She curled up under the blue blanket in the fetal position, her face to the wall, shaking even though the room was warm.

Her voice now barely a whisper, she said, "He sees *everything.*"

I paused at the door. "Who sees everything, Heather?"

She just pulled the blanket over her face.

1. *Never Knowing* is a novel about discovering who you are, where you come from, and what influences have shaped you. Sara worries that she inherited her anger management problems from her biological father and that her daughter may be affected as well. This fear implicitly raises the old question of nature vs. nurture. Which do you think exercises the greater influence over an individual's behavior? Or is it a combination of both? Or something else entirely?

2. This novel deals with the issue of adoption rights, specifically the right of the birth parent to anonymity versus the right—and occasionally the need—of the adopted child to have the knowledge of who they have come from and how. Do you have any thoughts on how those frequently competing interests can be balanced?

3. If you were Sara Gallagher, would you want to find out who your birth parents were? Do you think this question would change for her if she'd had a happier upbringing?

4. When confronted with her birth mother's reaction, Sara does not give up. Would you have given up? How would you feel in her shoes?

5. Do you believe in pure evil? Do you believe Sara's father was pure evil or was there any sense of humanity in him? Why or why not?

6. Describe the dynamics of the three sisters. Did anything feel familiar to you? Do you believe one sister was more damaging than the other? Why or why not?

7. Even though the police use Sara as bait to lure her father, do you think there was something else at play, with regards to the dynamics between Sara and John?

St. Martin's
Griffin

8. Do you believe police always act in the best interest of justice? In this case, when did you suspect that something might be amiss?

9. Do you agree or disagree with Shakespeare's famous statement: "What is past, is prologue"?

10. Under what circumstances could you take someone's life? Under what circumstances is it ever justified?

11. Was there any twist in this book that you did not see coming? What surprised you the most?

12. In the end, who lost the most from these events? Who gained the most? Who will be able to move on from here? Who will not?